"We won't let you down, Commander," Konya said.

Cruzen added, "Or Doctor Crusher or the captain, for that matter."

Nodding in approval, Worf replied, "I know you won't. I would accompany you myself, but the success of this mission requires stealth, not just in your own actions but also those of us who will be covering for your activities. It is the captain's and Doctor Crusher's hope that your departure from the *Enterprise,* and your apparent travel to Deep Space Nine, will provide sufficient misdirection to allow you to get to Jevalan and carry out the doctor's mission."

"I can't say this is the weirdest assignment I've ever been given," Konya remarked, "but I think it might make my top ten."

"Tell us where it ranks when you get back," La Forge replied.

"Will you be buying the drinks for that, Commander?" Cruzen asked, smiling.

The engineer chuckled. "Tell you what: The two of you get yourselves and Doctor Crusher back here in one piece, and I'll fly the runabout to Syrinx III myself."

"Deal."

La Forge and the two security officers shared a brief laugh over the quick, easy exchange, during which Worf remained silent. Once the moment passed, the first officer put his hands behind his back again.

"Captain Picard has one item he asked me to pass on to you. In his words, it goes without saying, but he wanted to say them, anyway." For the first time, he allowed himself a small smile. "You safely to the *Enterprise.*"

Don't miss these other exciting novels in

THE FALL

STAR TREK®
THE FALL

PEACEABLE KINGDOMS

DAYTON WARD

Based upon *Star Trek* and
Star Trek: The Next Generation®
created by Gene Roddenberry
and
Star Trek: Deep Space Nine®
created by Rick Berman & Michael Piller

POCKET BOOKS
New York   London   Toronto   Sydney   New Delhi

Pocket Books
A Division of Simon & Schuster, Inc.
1230 Avenue of the Americas
New York, NY 10020

This book is a work of fiction. Any references to historical events, real people, or real places are used fictitiously. Other names, characters, places, and events are products of the author's imagination, and any resemblance to actual events or places or persons, living or dead, is entirely coincidental.

First Pocket Books paperback edition January 2014

POCKET and colophon are registered trademarks of Simon & Schuster, Inc.

For information about special discounts for bulk purchases, please contact Simon & Schuster Special Sales at 1-866-506-1949 or business@simonandschuster.com

The Simon & Schuster Speakers Bureau can bring authors to your live event. For more information or to book an event, contact the Simon & Schuster Speakers Bureau at 1-866-248-3049 or visit our website at www.simonspeakers.com.

Cover design by Alan Dingman; cover art by Doug Drexler

Manufactured in the United States of America

10   9   8   7   6   5   4   3   2   1

ISBN 978-1-4767-1899-6
ISBN 978-1-4767-1902-3 (ebook)

For Michi, Addison, and Erin

Historian's Note

On August 27, 2385, during the dedication of the new Deep Space 9, the president of the Federation was assassinated (*Star Trek: The Fall: Revelation and Dust*). Nanietta Bacco's death aided in the fall of the Cardassian government (*Star Trek: The Fall: The Crimson Shadow*) and drove Doctor Julian Bashir to break his Starfleet oath and commit treason (*Star Trek: The Fall: A Ceremony of Losses*).

Citing the assassination, officials from within the Federation president's administration began putting into motion a wide range of unorthodox schemes: ignoring the chain of command and giving secret orders to Starfleet as well as creating and dispatching special operations teams tasked with finding the assassin. Troubled by President Pro Tempore Ishan Anjar's actions, Admiral Akaar ordered home the *U.S.S. Titan*, promoted Will Riker to rear admiral, and tasked him with finding out what Ishan was up to (*Star Trek: The Fall: The Poisoned Chalice*).

Just weeks before the special election for the remainder of Bacco's term, Andor was readmitted to the Federation, allowing Kellessar zh'Tarash, the presider of Andor, to run for Federation president.

The main narrative of this story takes place between October 13 and October 27, 2385.

Prologue

Gil Cetal Lagrar ran onto the balcony of his office and stared across the courtyard in time to see the front of the three-story barracks building coming apart. Echoes of the explosion still lingering in the air now were drowned out by the low roar of crumbling metal and thermocrete. A cloud of dust billowed outward from the base of the collapse, expanding to obscure the light poles situated at regular intervals around the encampment.

"What happened?" Lagrar called out as he caught sight of four soldiers emerging from cover near an adjacent building. No sooner did he ask the question than alarms began wailing across the compound.

One of the soldiers, his sidearm in his hand, gestured with the weapon toward the damaged barracks. "We don't know, sir!" he shouted, just barely audible over the sirens.

Looking around the compound, Lagrar saw more soldiers—most of them armed—exiting the other buildings. The officers in charge already were organizing the soldiers into groups or sending them to different areas of the camp. That was good, Lagrar decided, for as the officer on duty and in charge of the guard detail this evening, he had his own responsibilities to oversee.

After checking with the sentries who were manning posts around the compound's perimeter and the buildings that housed the Olanda labor camp workers and ordering the soldiers at those locations to maintain their positions, Lagrar made his way outside, getting his first real look at the destroyed barracks. Emergency teams already were moving about the edges of the destruction, working to extinguish the few small fires that had broken out amid the rubble. Lagrar heard the faint, high-pitched warbling of scanners and calls for assistance as soldiers and other support personnel scrambled over the wreckage in search of survivors. Searchlights were being moved or repositioned to focus on the scene and to provide illumination for workers. Over it all, the alarms continued to echo in the night air.

Just hours before daybreak, how many soldiers and others had been inside the building? Too many, Lagrar knew, just as he was certain that the explosion that had caused this damage could not be a simple accident.

Sabotage.

His communications device chirped for his attention. Activating the unit, he snapped, "Lagrar."

"This is Glinn Virat," said the voice of the officer responsible for the guard detail overseeing the workers' compound. *"I am already receiving requests from emergency teams for labor parties to help with moving debris."*

"Absolutely not," Lagrar snapped. "Someone from over there may well have planted the bomb. No one leaves or enters that camp until further notice. Anyone who violates that order, whether Cardassian or Bajoran, is to be shot. Is that understood?"

Virat replied, *"Understood, and I approve. However, I imagine the commander will take issue with such a directive."*

"Perhaps," Lagrar said, "but as I am the officer in overall authority of the entire guard detachment, such decisions fall to me during alert situations. I will answer to Pavok once we restore order." He knew that his decree would be called into question by the camp's commander, Gul Pavok, but Lagrar had no time now to worry about things such as his superior's ego and whining about having his authority circumvented or ignored. At the moment, containment of the current situation—along with identifying those responsible—and seeing to the rescue of any survivors was of paramount importance. If a few impudent Bajorans and even some of his own stubborn or stupid subordinates had to be sacrificed to meet those goals, then it was a price Lagrar was willing to pay. Worrying about Pavok's reaction and accompanying temper tantrum could wait.

Another tone sounded from his communicator, and Lagrar tapped the device to change the frequency. "Lagrar."

"Checkpoint Three, sir," replied the voice of Gorr Foral, one of his subordinates on the evening's guard detail. *"Intruders detected near our position!"*

Lagrar began running across the compound, bypassing the scene of destruction before him as he headed for the perimeter fence and the watchtowers positioned along its length on the encampment's far side. "Don't let them escape, but I want them alive!"

Another voice, this one belonging to Garresh Bilek, barked, *"I am moving additional sentries to that area, sir!"*

For the moment, Lagrar set aside the question of how any such intruders might not have been detected before the barracks explosion. Foral was but a low-ranking soldier, assigned the most menial of tasks for the night's guard detail, and was one of two sentries manning a watchtower along the perimeter. Any questions pertaining to possible lapses in duty would be directed to Bilek, the garresh assigned to oversee all the guards on post this evening.

Later, he reminded himself.

Checkpoint Three was the most distant of the towers along this expanse of perimeter fence, and Lagrar recalled that it was one of the few areas of the compound that was not covered by visual sensor feeds transmitted to the camp's command post. If he were considering a covert infiltration, he might well have selected a point along that section. The barriers themselves consisted of a metal framework within which ran a series of force-field generators. They did have certain limitations, such as the support stanchions that powered different segments of the field. The same type of barricades were used to contain the Bajoran workers in their own separate compound, which was guarded in similar fashion with sentries positioned in towers around its boundary. In theory, someone with the proper knowledge, training, and opportunity could thwart the field and enter the camp undetected.

Then there was the troubling possibility that the saboteurs may even have had assistance from someone on the inside. Worse, the party or parties responsible for the attack may already have been in the camp. Any number of Bajorans—personal assistants, kitchen and sanitation workers, house servants, comfort women and men—would have time and opportunity to enact such a bold attack, particularly if the assault had been planned and coordinated well in advance.

If that was the case, Lagrar would urge Gul Pavok to execute every Bajoran who had been inside the compound at the time of the explosion. Though resistance efforts on the part of the laborers was nothing new, either here or at one of the other camps scattered across the face of the planet, this incident by far was the worst manifestation of that defiance. It now was past time to make a powerful statement that such wanton destruction and any further acts of rebellion would not be tolerated. Putting to death a few dozen Bajoran laborers, regardless of their involvement in this attack, would send just the right message.

Sounds of weapons fire from somewhere ahead made Lagrar draw his disruptor pistol and quicken his pace. He rounded the corner of a smaller building near the perimeter barrier in time to see a figure—Cardassian—falling from the watchtower. The soldier's body landed with a heavy thud on the grass and remained still while his companion in the tower was leaning over a parapet and aiming his disruptor rifle at a target Lagrar could not see. Pale yellow-white bursts of energy rained down from the tower as the guard fired, and Lagrar caught sight of two dark figures also falling to the ground. A third one dropped to a knee and raised his arm, the silhouette of a weapon in his hand. He fired at the tower, and the remaining guard fell back, out of sight.

Sprinting toward the assailant, Lagrar covered open ground in immense strides. He raised his own disruptor as the intruder turned to run. Drawing abreast of the unknown attacker's dead companions, Lagrar recognized them both as Bajoran, one male and one female. The remaining interloper was heading for a section of the barricade between two sets of force-field generators, and even from this distance Lagrar could see that the indicators and other gauges on the control panel for these units were dark. The power for that section had been disabled.

"Halt!" Lagrar shouted, firing his disruptor so that its beam just missed the intruder and struck the barricade's metal framework. The Bajoran, a male, ceased his running and held his hands out away from his body. "Drop the weapon!" Lagrar ordered, continuing to close the gap between them. Without turning to face him, the Bajoran allowed the disruptor pistol to fall from his hand, and it landed in the grass next to his feet. "Kick it away from you!"

Once the Bajoran complied, Lagrar reached for the restraints that should have been in a pouch on his belt, only to realize that with the exception of his sidearm, he had neglected to bring with him his other uniform accessories. The restraints, along with his baton and the badge he was supposed to wear to indicate his authority—all were lying on the desk in the duty office. He grunted in irritation, but it was only one Bajoran.

"You will turn toward me, slowly," he ordered, training the muzzle of the disruptor on the center of the Bajoran's back. "Do not attempt escape or resistance, or I will kill you where you stand."

The Bajoran did not move. "You won't kill me. My friends are already dead, and you need me to find out what happened back there."

Was it Lagrar's imagination, or was the worker's tone one of self-confidence? Even arrogance? Lagrar almost fired his weapon just to alleviate his growing annoyance.

"Turn around," Lagrar hissed. "I won't tell you again." After a few moments, the intruder began slowly to turn toward him, and Lagrar saw that he was young, little more than a child. "What is your name, Bajoran?"

Cloaked in shadow, the man's left arm was invisible just for an instant as he turned, but it was enough for him to reach to his waist. Lagrar saw the movement too late, and by then, the Bajoran's hand and the other disruptor it held was aiming at him. The last thing Lagrar saw before the weapon fired was the Bajoran's face.

"My name is Ishan Anjar."

One

"*And just as we did more than two centuries ago, the people of Andor stand once again with the United Federation of Planets, and we are humbled that you have welcomed us now as you did then: as friends and allies. As such, we Andorians rededicate ourselves to the principles that have guided this unrivaled coalition from its first days, speaking as one voice for freedom, for security, for the right of self-determination. We renew our pledge to join with our fellow beings from worlds across the Federation, serving and protecting each of its citizens as though they were born of our own world.*"

Thunderous applause stopped Kellessar zh'Tarash as she stood before an open session of the Parliament Andoria. Propping himself against the edge of his desk, Admiral William Riker watched the speech as it had been recorded for later broadcast across the quadrant via the Federation News Service. The current leader of the Andorian government's Progressive Caucus seemed almost regal on the large viewscreen that dominated the far wall of Riker's new office at Starfleet Command Headquarters.

"She certainly knows how to blow the doors off the joint, doesn't she?" Riker asked, gesturing toward the screen.

Seated in an overstuffed chair in one corner of the office that afforded her an unfettered view of the broadcast, Deanna Troi turned from the screen to regard her husband.

"She's quite something. The people of Andor seem to have a great deal of faith in her, and her support looks to be growing across the Federation."

On the viewscreen, zh'Tarash continued. *"Though we may have lost our way for a time, we are reminded that the Federation's compassion and sense of unity made us a stronger world than if we had continued to stand alone. Indeed, those very ideals were exhibited yet again during a time of dire need, and it is our hope that we will have the opportunity to express our eternal gratitude for the service the Federation has provided to our world and our people. It is this cooperative spirit that has compelled me to seek the office of President of the United Federation of Planets.*

"If it is the will of the people that I am allowed to serve you in this manner, I will commit myself to demonstrating that the Federation is deserving of its place of prominence in the cosmos, not through threat of force but by continuing to extend the hand of friendship. It was Nanietta Bacco's firm belief that no sentient species in this galaxy could have a greater friend or ally, and I promise you that I will spend each day proving that she was right. This I pledge, to every citizen of this Federation, which we Andorians are honored once again to call our family."

"Computer, pause playback," Riker said, and the image on the screen froze as members of the Parliament Andoria were rising to their feet to once more applaud zh'Tarash. Folding his arms, the admiral blew out his breath, shaking his head. "I'll bet Ishan is climbing the walls right about now."

"Polls indicate an overwhelming approval of Andor's readmission," Troi said. "It's an interesting change from surveys taken after their secession."

"I remember." Public reaction had been intense following the explosive announcement three years earlier that Andor, one of the Federation's founding members, had decided to withdraw its membership following a close, tumultuous vote by the Andorian government. Common sentiments had included feelings of anger and betrayal, owing in large part to a lack of knowledge of the events leading up to the unprecedented decision. It had been reported that Andor's secession was triggered by knowledge given to them by the Typhon Pact that Starfleet had examples of alien technology and information that might have led to a cure for an escalating reproductive predicament that was threatening the eventual extinction of the Andorian people.

While that was true in and of itself, what was only now being told to the public's satisfaction were bits and pieces of the larger story surrounding the still-classified nature of Operation Vanguard and the data and materials it had collected, which were all that remained of the ancient race known as the Shedai. Chief among the discoveries made more than a century ago was the so-called "Shedai Meta-Genome," which Starfleet had found to carry enormous potential to expand or even redefine any number of scientific and medical principles. After everything that had transpired during Starfleet's all-but-disastrous attempts to understand the Shedai and the awesome power they once had commanded, someone within the Federation hierarchy had decided that the entire project should be buried and forgotten, citing the potential for unchecked abuse should such knowledge fall into the wrong hands.

Though Starfleet had shoved the collected data and materials into the depths of a classified archive facility and consigned almost everyone who had survived the operation to relative obscurity, other parties who had acquired information and understanding into the Shedai continued to perform their own research. One such group was the Tholian Assembly, who, after emerging from their normal seclusion to join the Typhon Pact, had approached Andor with the knowledge they now possessed, having discovered that the Meta-Genome held the potential to end forever the planet's fertility crisis. The Tholians also had managed to spin the truth about Starfleet's involvement just far enough to paint it and the Federation as having somehow betrayed the Andorian people by not sharing with them their own cache of information about the Shedai and the Meta-Genome.

And the rest, Riker mused, *as they say, is history.*

"Even though the full story behind Operation Vanguard remains classified," he said, pushing away from his desk and moving to the window set into his office's rear wall, "the parts Starfleet's been releasing seem to be appeasing the public." His own knowledge of the top-secret project did not extend much beyond the official information releases distributed by Starfleet Command to the press, and Riker knew that the bulk of the operation's history likely would remained cloaked in shadow for years if not decades to come. "They're being smart about it, focusing on the good it's done for Andor, even though the whole thing would never have happened if not for Julian Bashir." The former chief medical officer of Deep Space 9 had accessed the classified Shedai data and used it to develop a cure for Andor's dilemma, and while the Andorians considered him a hero, Starfleet had no choice but to charge him with espionage and possibly even treason. At this moment, arrangements were being finalized for Bashir's return to Earth for trial. If there was a way to save the doctor from permanent disgrace and incarceration, Riker had yet to conceive of it.

One problem at a time, Admiral.

"It doesn't hurt that zh'Tarash is advocating using the entire affair as the catalyst for reaffirming Andor's bond with the Federation," Troi said. "Polls indicate her popularity is growing every day. At the rate she's gaining on Ishan, this could end up being a very close election."

"Don't count Ishan out yet. There's still plenty of time for him to pull a rabbit out of his hat."

The upcoming special election to select a successor to

the late President Nanietta Bacco now was mere weeks away, in keeping with Federation law that such proceedings were required within sixty days after a sitting president's death or permanent removal from office. It now had been more than a month since Bacco's assassination during the dedication of the new Deep Space 9 and the nomination of a president pro tempore to hold the office for the period leading up to the election. For this, the Federation Council had selected Ishan Anjar, a relatively junior council member representing the planet Bajor. Ishan had been serving in this capacity for less than a year at the time of his appointment, which many within the Federation government and Starfleet had viewed as a questionable choice, made as it was while preliminary evidence had implicated a Bajoran as Bacco's assassin. There were those who believed Ishan's selection was intended as a symbolic gesture to the people of Bajor, to demonstrate that the Federation would not allow the heinous actions of one individual to undermine its relationship with an entire civilization.

With the special election drawing ever nearer, the two front runners had staked out their platforms, each opting to place themselves on the opposite sides of what had become the hasty campaign's key issue: security. Ishan Anjar was advocating a much more proactive stance with respect to the Federation's role in interstellar politics, wanting to prevent future threats from enemies like the Borg or even more "conventional" adversaries like the Typhon Pact. Though Kellessar zh'Tarash was expressing similar sentiments, her vision was more in line with what many—Riker included—considered to be bedrock Federation principles, with peaceful coexistence being the ideal goal even while standing ready to meet whatever threat might present itself. Many had noted that there existed only a fine distinction between the two philosophies, but the relevant differences in attitude all were to be found within that narrow rift. Ishan was encouraging a more aggressive stance with respect to potential conflicts, even putting forth the notion that preemptive action was justified against verified targets presenting clear and imminent danger to Federation interests. Amity could be maintained, he reasoned, but any threat, no matter how benign it might appear on the surface, had to be met with overwhelming force.

Peace through superior firepower. Riker released an irritated grunt at his own dour joke. Despite a lifetime devoted to Starfleet service even after all the threats he had faced, such an attitude still sounded alien to him. It certainly was not in keeping the oath he had sworn, and while many railed against such a fundamental shift in thinking, Ishan Anjar seemed to be enjoying the growing support from a vocal segment of the population still reeling from the loss of a beloved leader.

"If Ishan wins the election," Troi said, rising from her seat to join Riker at the window, "there's no telling how far he'll go to get what he wants. Just based on what we believe he's done to this point, the possibilities are frightening."

In light of recent revelations, Riker had been forced to consider the very distinct possibility that Bacco's assassination and everything that had followed was part of some larger plan with the ultimate goal of elevating Ishan to the presidency in order to push antagonistic policies that, though motivated by the legitimate cause of securing the Federation against possible enemies, ultimately would lead to war with the Typhon Pact. On this matter, Ishan Anjar had spoken at length, citing his own experience as a Bajoran living under the oppressive rule of Cardassian Occupation. Never again, the interim president had vowed, should anyone be forced into such a hellish existence.

As for Ishan's extraordinary career trajectory, it had become obvious to Riker and others that it all had been orchestrated by Ishan's close confidant and former chief of staff, Galif jav Velk. Having served as a member of the Federation Council's support staff since before Ishan's arrival, Velk had a deserved reputation as someone who suffered no fools while knowing how to get things done, even if it meant ruffled feathers, bruised egos, or bloody noses. The Tellarite's stance with respect to the issue of Federation security, like Ishan's, was well-known and widely regarded, particularly in the wake of the Borg invasion that had taken place four years earlier and driven the Federation to within a hairsbreadth of annihilation.

"The question I've been asking myself," Riker said, "is how much can Ishan do without his biggest cheerleader? If Velk was really propping him up behind the scenes, how far can Ishan go without him? Was Velk the one with the contacts—and the guts—to pull off all of this?"

Troi shrugged. "It's too bad you can't ask him."

Insight into the true extent of Velk's involvement in pushing Ishan's plans had become apparent after intelligence data revealed the location of the assassins responsible for President Bacco's murder. Tzenkethi agents had been implicated in the conspiracy and supposedly could be found on a remote, unimportant planet on the fringes of Federation space. Velk had dispatched to the planet a special-operations team that had included Commander Tuvok, Lieutenant Commander Nog, and Riker's "brother," Thomas. Upon arriving at the planet, the team had discovered that the assassins were not Tzenkethi, but Cardassians: members of an extremist sect known as the "True Way." After a fierce skirmish that saw the Cardassians taken into custody, they were not returned to Earth but instead taken to what was revealed to be a secret "black site" prison facility on the Klingon world Nydak II.

Upon realizing that the strike team's leader, Lieutenant Colonel Jan Kincade, was working for Velk with orders to make sure the Cardassians—and anyone else who knew the truth—never left the planet alive, Tuvok and Nog attempted to mutiny against the colonel in order to escort the Cardassians to Earth for proper trial. In the resulting chaos, which ultimately had resulted in the deaths of the Cardassian prisoners, Tuvok confronted their leader, Onar Throk, who confessed to being the one responsible for killing Bacco. Throk also revealed that Velk had given him all the information and support required to carry out the assassination. Despite the Tellarite's best efforts to cover his tracks by ordering the elimination of Tuvok and Nog, the officers had been rescued by Riker and the *U.S.S. Titan*.

Perhaps to avoid being exposed as the mastermind behind Bacco's assassination and implicating Ishan as a co-conspirator, Velk had been arrested by the Federation Security Agency and remanded to a classified detention center, though the charges against him had been limited to his unauthorized use of Starfleet resources and the illegal orders sending the team to Nydak II. Riker knew it was an end-run maneuver, designed to insulate both Velk and Ishan from being implicated in the murder plot. With Onar Throk's claims being at best dubious and with no physical evidence to corroborate the story he had given Tuvok, there was no way to level such accusations and have them stick. What was needed was a confession or some other evidence that might still be out there, waiting to be discovered. To that end, Riker had dispatched a small cabal of trusted officers consisting of *Titan* senior staff members as well as his oldest and closest friend, Captain Jean-Luc Picard, to seek out and find that evidence, in whatever form it might take. Meanwhile, it went without question that no confession would be coming from Ishan, so that left Velk, wherever he might have been taken to await his trial.

Velk will never live to see any trial. Of this, Riker was certain, which was why tracking down the Tellarite—assuming he still was alive—in order to get from him the confession needed to expose Ishan once and for all was of paramount importance.

"What makes you think Velk's not dead already?" Riker asked.

"As you say, Ishan probably needs him, at least in some capacity. He'll want to stop Velk from going to trial and perhaps exposing him, but it's almost certain that he has information that could cripple Ishan if it got out or access to people who somehow are a threat to him." Troi leaned against the window, pausing to look out at the cityscape of San Francisco far below them. "For all his talk about strength, I think it's obvious Velk is the one with most of the power. Without him, Ishan may well be in over his head."

Nodding in agreement, Riker allowed his own gaze to wander over the breathtaking sight that was San Francisco at night. Though he had not yet settled into his role as a desk-bound admiral rather than the captain of a starship, he had conceded that one of the job's perks was the view outside his office. Still, even on its best night, any city on Earth could not compare to staring out a viewport at open space and distant stars.

You'll get back there. One day.

"We definitely need to find Velk," Riker said after a moment, "along with anyone else Ishan may have contacted or corrupted to get this far."

"And what if we don't find him?" Troi asked. "He's the only link connecting Ishan to President Bacco's murder."

Riker sighed. "Then we're going to need to find something else."

Two

As the doors leading to the observation lounge parted and she got her first sense of what awaited her inside the room, Lieutenant T'Ryssa Chen wanted at that moment to be somewhere else.

Anywhere else. Rura Penthe. The Delta Quadrant. Remus. Wherever.

There was no mistaking the palpable tension permeating the room. Sitting in his customary place at the head of the curved conference table and facing away from the door was Captain Picard, his head visible over the top of his high-backed chair. Standing next to the row of viewing ports that formed the room's rear wall, Doctor Beverly Crusher stopped in mid-sentence, her right arm extended and pointing an accusatory finger at Picard as she looked up in reaction to the doors opening. Her features were clouded in an unmistakable expression of anger, though she did an admirable job of composing herself upon seeing Chen.

"I'm sorry." Chen managed to force out the words. "I was told the captain wanted to see me. I can come back."

Please let me come back later please let me come back later please . . .

Without turning his chair, Picard said, "Come in, Lieutenant. Take a seat."

Fabulous.

If there ever was a situation where an ability to suppress her emotions might be useful, Chen decided this was it. Despite her half-Vulcan birthright, a childhood spent with her human mother following her parents' divorce had seen to it that she had embraced the human aspects of personality. To this day, Chen still wore her long dark hair in a style that covered the pointed ears that were the obvious outward clue as to her split heritage. Her life choices had seen to it that she was woefully deficient when it came to many facets of Vulcan customs and cultures. That especially was true with respect to the broad spectrum of physical and mental disciplines to which Vulcans subjected themselves.

I really should look into doing something about that, one of these days.

Chen cleared her throat as she stepped into the room and allowed the doors to close behind her. She was unable to shake the notion that she just had cut off her avenue of escape. For her part, Crusher moved to the table, took a seat, and crossed her arms, and Chen could not help noticing that the doctor had chosen to keep two empty chairs between herself and the captain. Saying nothing, Chen focused her gaze on the conference table and selected the seat to Picard's left. The captain spun his chair to face the table, his expression unreadable as he looked to the ceiling and called out, "Picard to Commander Worf."

A single tone sounded in the room as the intraship communications system activated, followed by the voice of the *Enterprise*'s first officer. *"Worf here."*

"Number One, a runabout will be required for departure no later than tomorrow morning. Please assign Lieutenants Konya and Cruzen as pilots. It will be traveling to Deep Space Nine with one passenger. Doctor Crusher will provide the relevant details."

Though she said nothing, the doctor did release a small, annoyed sigh.

"Understood, sir," Worf replied. *"May I ask . . . ?"*

"Doctor Crusher will provide the details, Mister Worf," the captain repeated, his tone hardening. "Make it so. Picard out." Leaning forward in his chair, he seemed to forget about the conversation that had just ended as he turned to Chen. "Lieutenant, we'll be heading back down to the surface later this morning. Another meeting is scheduled with the Grand Nagus, though I expect it will follow the same path as our previous conversations as we wait for the conference's other participants to arrive."

Crusher snorted, and though Picard said nothing, he did direct a scathing glance at her that Chen tried not to notice. It was obvious that Chen's arrival had interrupted whatever the couple had been discussing, or arguing, and that the matter was anything but resolved.

As though sensing her discomfort, Picard said, "Doctor Crusher and I were reviewing the meeting from yesterday. She seems to think that we're wasting our time at Ferenginar. Since you've been acting as my aid during these meetings, I thought it would be helpful to hear your opinion."

"Sir?" Chen could help neither the simple response nor the look of confusion she now knew was evident on her face. "Well, that is . . . I'm sure Admiral Akaar wouldn't have sent the *Enterprise* here if he didn't think it was important." When Picard said nothing in reply, she swallowed a sudden lump in her throat and added, "Right?"

"It's a total waste of time," Crusher said. "The Federation Council doesn't really think the Ferengi will join the Typhon Pact, do they? Especially now, after everything that's happened?"

Feeling her anxiety heightening, Chen forced herself not to squirm in her chair. "My understanding is that Ferengi Alliance isn't looking to join the Pact *per se,* Doctor, but that the Pact will be hoping to secure trade agreements."

"And how likely is that?" Crusher asked. "I could see it

maybe ten years ago, but now? After everything we've been through?"

Picard said, "There were those who wouldn't have believed a founding member of the Federation might secede, either. If memory serves, we all were counted among that number."

"But Andor's coming back," Crusher said. "It's all over but the parades and speeches by this point, right? Opening any sort of trade agreement with the Typhon Pact would jeopardize the Ferengi standing in the Khitomer Accords."

Chen said, "The Ferengi might see it as a profitable venture worth some risk, which they in turn could mitigate."

"After all the reforms he's enacted in order to strengthen the alliance with the Federation, Grand Nagus Rom isn't about to undermine all of that." Crusher looked to Picard. "You know that."

"Oh, yes," the captain replied, "I'm well aware of the situation, Doctor. As it happens, it's been the focal point of the discussions held during the past several days." Chen knew that Picard already had been invited to private meetings with the Grand Nagus in which the Ferengi leader had given reassurances that maintaining ties with the Federation was of paramount importance. "However, President Ishan and the Federation Council have expressed great concern over this issue, which is why the *Enterprise* and a full diplomatic team have been sent here."

Chen was not sure, but to her ears it sounded as though Picard was being less than sincere with his remarks. Was he not convinced that the *Enterprise*'s current mission was necessary? If so, he was doing his usual remarkable job of keeping his true feelings and emotions under control.

In contrast, Doctor Crusher was another matter.

"The *Enterprise* only needs to be here if someone decides to start shooting," she said. "The Pact isn't going to try anything like that, at least not out in the open, and even if they did? We're talking about the Ferengi, Captain." She paused, shaking her head before drawing what Chen decided might be a calming breath. "This isn't the job I signed up for. That's why I asked for the transfer. Deep Space Nine needs a chief medical officer, at least until they can get a permanent replacement for Doctor Bashir, and the change of view will be good for me, I think."

Transfer? That's why she was set to leave the next day in a runabout? Chen froze in her seat, not daring even to blink. Rumors had been floating about the ship for the past several days, intimating that Picard and Doctor Crusher had been "disagreeing" on a number of topics. Though both senior officers had taken great pains to keep their differences of opinion a private affair, it was inevitable that someone— a nurse, a yeoman, a bridge officer—would witness a testy exchange, generating gossip which in turn wound its way at warp speed through the crew. Chen herself had overheard whispered conversations in the officer's mess or the ship's library or even engineering. Lieutenant Dina Elfiki, one of her closest friends, had attempted to broach the subject more than once after seeing the captain and Crusher speaking in hushed tones on the bridge. Chen so far had managed to evade such discussions. Given her duties and the extended periods of time she spent in Captain Picard's presence—in particular since their arrival at Ferenginar—she had elected not to involve herself in the "scuttlebutt," as Elfiki and some of the other junior officers called it.

How's that working out for you, Lieutenant?

"A change for the entire crew wouldn't be such a bad thing, either," Crusher continued, "and that includes you, Captain. I'm not a diplomat, and neither are you, even if Starfleet keeps leaning on you for those sorts of things. There are better things this ship and crew could be doing." She turned to Chen. "Don't you think so, Lieutenant?"

Picard answered first. "We carry out the orders we're

given, Doctor." Chen heard the slight edge in his voice, which only confirmed for her that she had interrupted a heated discussion between the captain and the ship's chief medical officer. The fact that they also were married could only have added to the tension, and while it was obvious that Picard was doing his level best to maintain a strict separation between those two facets of their relationship, Doctor Crusher was being far less forgiving, even with Chen sitting right here in the same room.

Please let there be a warp core breach. Now would be a good time for that.

Turning to Chen, Picard said, "Lieutenant, I called you here so that we might prepare for tomorrow's sessions, after the Typhon Pact's representatives finally arrive." The *Enterprise* had been holding station for the better part of two weeks, waiting for the diplomatic cadre to arrive. Chen thought the entire notion of having the Federation flagship parked in orbit for no reason was ridiculous, but the captain had taken advantage of the opportunity to order shore leave for all off-duty personnel.

"Grand Nagus Rom will be sitting in on the first of the day's discussions," Picard continued, "and I expect the Pact's diplomatic cadre has been waiting for this opportunity to make their case with particular zeal. They no doubt will bring to the forefront the uncertainty in our own government with respect to President Bacco's assassination, as well as any lingering doubts regarding our resolve even with Andor's imminent return to the Federation."

He paused, glancing to Crusher before adding, "I plan to let our own diplomatic team address those issues, but I'm anticipating the subject turning to matters of security. To that end, I would like you to gather relevant facts and figures regarding Starfleet's unclassified operations during the past thirty-six months, with an emphasis on relief efforts in the wake of the Borg invasion, as well as any joint missions or exercises conducted between Starfleet and the Ferengi militia." A small grin teased the corners of his mouth. "I seem to recall at least one or two reports of Ferengi freighters or other merchant shipping traffic encountering issues while traversing space supposedly under Pact control. That might make for some interesting conversation."

Feeling at ease for the first time since entering the lounge, Chen returned the smile. "I'll get started collecting the relevant data, sir." She had read a few scattered reports regarding civilian merchant ships experiencing difficulties such as Picard described, though she did not recall any mention of Ferengi vessels. It would be interesting to see if the captain's hunch paid off and how he might use such information in the next day's round-table discussions with the Grand Nagus. "Is there anything else I can do for you, Captain?"

"No, Lieutenant. That will be all." As Chen rose from her seat, he held up one hand. "I trust you will treat this conversation as privileged?"

"Absolutely, sir," Chen replied. It was the first time in a while he had asked her anything along those lines. While their relationship had gotten off to anything but a smooth start upon her arriving aboard the *Enterprise* for duty—owing in large part to her own unorthodox attitude and methods— Picard had come to trust her, even to confide in her during missions requiring her particular expertise. She also had made great strides during her time aboard ship, thanks to the captain's standing order and philosophy that junior officers not be content with their own assigned positions. Instead, they were expected to cross train with departments and personnel outside their regular duties. Commander Worf had said as much during her first meeting with him. Speaking as though recalling a distant, fond memory of his own days as a young lieutenant under Picard's command, the first officer had informed her, "Lieutenant, our captain wants his junior officers to learn, learn, *learn*."

Despite all of this, Chen and Picard were not friends, of course, but neither were they enemies. The captain was a private man, and his relationships with officers like Worf, Commander La Forge, and even Doctor Crusher were the product of decades of shared service and sacrifice. Chen knew she had a long way to go before she earned a place within Picard's inner circle, if that even was possible. Should such a milestone never come to pass, it would not be due to her failure to live up to the confidence he placed in her.

Not a chance.

Three

Jean-Luc Picard said nothing, nor did he even move until after the lounge's doors slid shut in the wake of Lieutenant Chen's departure. Only when he and Beverly once again were alone did he look across the conference table to his wife, who now regarded him with a look of skepticism.

"Do you think she bought it?" the doctor asked.

"I believe so. For the moment, anyway." Picard offered a sly grin. "You may have come on a bit strong there at one point."

Beverly made a show of rolling her eyes. "Everybody's a critic." Leaving her chair, she moved to the corner of the table to Picard's right and leaned against it, resting her hands in her lap. "At least the hard part's over. I was getting tired of playing the game."

"It's necessary," Picard replied, reaching over to place his hand atop hers. "The fight had to seem like a natural outgrowth from a string of disagreements you and I allegedly have been having." They had been promoting their ruse for the past four days, sowing the seeds of disinformation that had led them to this meeting. "I must admit that it hasn't been easy, fighting in front of the crew."

Beverly smiled. "You prefer that we fight in private?"

"You know what I mean," Picard countered. Sighing, he let his gaze drift to the stars visible beyond the lounge's viewing ports. "I've had to keep information from the crew for security reasons before, of course, and I've even lied to them on occasion for the same purpose. I don't know why, but this deception feels different, somehow." Shaking his head, he returned his attention to Beverly. "You've not heard anything further from your friend?"

"No," the doctor replied. "Considering all the trouble Ilona went through just to get the first message to me, I'm not expecting him to risk contacting me again. It'll be up to me to reach out to him, once I'm clear of the *Enterprise*."

The odd sequence of events that had put Picard and Crusher on this course began soon after the *Enterprise*'s arrival at Ferenginar, with the ship in orbit for nearly two weeks while it and the Ferengi Alliance awaited the "pending" arrival of the ship carrying a diplomatic envoy from the Typhon Pact. Picard, making a courtesy visit to the Federation embassy, was given a message delivered to him from one of the planet's leading private financial institutions. According to the courier, the communication, stored on an encrypted data chip, was intended for Beverly and it should not be accessed using the *Enterprise*'s computer or communications system.

Curious and wary of what it might mean, Picard had crafted a ruse that allowed Beverly to beam down to the planet's surface for the ostensible purpose of joining him for dinner at the embassy. Once there, she had accessed the encrypted data chip and shared with Picard the message recorded for her by Ilona Daret, a Cardassian physician whom Beverly—so far as Picard knew—had not seen in years. After the usual pleasantries came Daret's wish for him and Beverly to talk in person at the earliest opportunity and that Beverly should travel to see him.

"It just seems odd that he would seek you out now, after all these years," Picard said. "And the message he sent you isn't exactly something that puts me at ease." The end of

Daret's recorded communication was troubling, couched as it was in the Cardassian's final, vague statement: *Ishan Anjar is not who he purports to be.*

"I have no idea what it might mean," Beverly replied. "I've checked and rechecked, and there's nothing else on the chip. I'm even having Geordi give it the once-over, but so far he hasn't found anything, either."

Picard sighed. If the *Enterprise*'s chief engineer had come away from his investigative efforts with no results, then there almost certainly was nothing to be found. Rising from his seat, Picard moved to stand at the viewing ports. "The last time I saw Daret was during that mission to the Cardassian labor planet, toward the end of the Bajoran Occupation."

Nodding, Crusher said, "Jevalan. I remember."

The aftermath of the Cardassian evacuation of that world, home to a massive mining camp operation with several thousand Bajoran nationals serving as forced labor, remained one of the more haunting experiences Picard had endured over the course of his Starfleet career. He recalled the horrific scenes that had greeted him and the rest of an *Enterprise*-D away team following the starship's arrival at Jevalan. Massive swaths of the planet had been ravaged by the mining operation, with the Bajoran slaves enduring squalid living conditions. After the closest thing to an organized revolt by the oppressed workers threatened to overwhelm the far smaller numbers of their overseers, the Cardassians evacuated the planet, but not before inflicting upon those who would rebel against them one last wave of misery, death, and destruction. The *Enterprise* was among the first vessels to bring assistance to the stricken world and those fortunate to survive the final assault, which the Cardassians had claimed to be necessary for reasons of "self-defense."

Among the few bright spots amid all the suffering and devastation was Ilona Daret, one of a handful of Cardassians—mostly physicians and support personnel abandoned by their military counterparts. Despite facing their own punishment and possible execution at the hands of the Bajorans, Daret and his colleagues had done their best to treat the scores of wounded, whether slave or former oppressor. He had been working for his fifth-consecutive day without rest at the time of the *Enterprise*'s arrival.

"Your friend Daret impressed me for a second time that day," Picard said. "The first was during that prisoner exchange you and he orchestrated." The transfer of three Starfleet Intelligence officers, injured while on a covert mission in Cardassian space and later captured by a Cardassian cruiser, had come during Picard's first year as captain of the *Enterprise*-D. Beverly and his former chief of security, the late Lieutenant Natasha Yar, had traveled into Cardassian territory in order to rendezvous with the vessel and retrieve the officers, in the interests of maintaining the fragile peace between the Federation and the Cardassian Union after a lengthy conflict.

It was during that mission that Picard had learned how Beverly had come to know the physician during the war. Their relationship began with him as a wounded prisoner following a Cardassian attack on a Federation supply depot while Beverly was serving aboard a Starfleet medical ship. After she treated his injuries, Daret assisted her and the other doctors to treat both Cardassian and Federation wounded. Picard would not see him again until the mission at Jevalan, but according to Beverly, they had continued to correspond in sporadic fashion over the years. "Where is he now?"

"I have no idea," Beverly said. "I lost touch with him after the Dominion War."

"Given the current political climate, if he's gone to such lengths to contact you, then one has to wonder just what information he's holding." Picard crossed his arms, reaching up to rub his chin as he studied the curve of Ferenginar that just was visible beyond the aft port edge of the *Enterprise*'s expansive primary hull. What he could see of the planet was concealed by heavy cloud cover, indicating yet another in the series of perpetual rain storms that tended to drench the planet. Was the foul weather supposed to somehow be symbolic?

Without turning from the windows, Picard said, "In view of how cautious he's being with whatever it is he wants to tell you, I think your idea of meeting Daret far from the *Enterprise* is prudent." Beverly had been the one to suggest the ruse of her requesting a transfer from the ship for the supposed purpose of "making a change." With the *Enterprise*'s movements likely being monitored by President Ishan, Picard knew that the Cardassian physician's odd request that she join him in person necessitated a scheme which would permit Beverly the appearance of traveling away from the ship while under official orders. The transfer to Deep Space 9, which currently lacked a chief medical officer, as Doctor Julian Bashir remained on Andor—a fugitive from Starfleet and Federation justice—offered the perfect opportunity, and Picard and Crusher's alleged relationship troubles provided a reason for her to go.

"Did I tell you that Doctor Tropp came to my office this morning?" she asked. "He'd heard the rumors about me resigning my commission and came to talk me out of it." She chuckled. "You'd think he was trying to keep me from walking out an airlock."

Picard smiled at the image of the *Enterprise*'s assistant chief medical officer doing his best to advise Beverly against undertaking any rash action. "It's that Denobulan disposition of his. It makes him perfectly suited to being a doctor. I assume you're comfortable with him working in your stead? I'll have to put in a request to Starfleet for a permanent replacement, just to keep up appearances, but I plan to recommend Tropp for promotion to CMO."

"Just so long as it's temporary," Beverly replied. "But, like you said, it's necessary. The only way we're going to pull this off is if the rest of the crew thinks I want a transfer from the *Enterprise*."

The reality of life aboard a starship was that, sooner or later, rumors seemed to find their way to every crewmember. Secrets remained private only on rare occasions, and it seemed that the more embarrassing or scintillating the gossip the faster it traveled. Such was the case with the alleged strife between Picard and Crusher, who had taken careful, deliberate steps to show only slight hints of such marital discord for the benefit of selected witnesses. Though Picard, for the most part, maintained his usual composed demeanor in front of the crew—this incident with T'Ryssa Chen notwithstanding—Beverly had decided to play up the illusion of discontent in front of her own staff.

Turning from the viewing ports, Picard said, "I know, but it doesn't mean I enjoy putting on the charade, or the fact that you'll soon be leaving me and René behind." As much as he disliked the deception he and Beverly had engineered, the separation from his wife—and hers from her son—though necessary, was not something to which he looked forward. As for René, his role in the cover story was being explained as a decision by his parents to avoid undue disruption of his normal routines while Beverly went to Deep Space 9 for what was expected to be a short-term assignment. For his part, Picard could not shake the awkward feeling at his wife leaving on a dangerous mission while he remained here, safe aboard the *Enterprise*, with their son.

Is this how she felt every time Jack left her and Wesley? There were very few days that passed without Picard thinking of his late friend and Beverly's first husband, Jack Crusher. After he was killed in the line of duty while assigned to the *Stargazer*, it had been Picard's unpleasant duty to escort Jack's body home and deliver the tragic news to Beverly.

And then fate took over, and here we are, all these years later.

"Is there any indication that anybody knows what we're up to?" Beverly asked. "I worry about all the sneaking around we've had to do. Ishan or one of his minions is still going to be suspicious, no matter how careful we are."

"Of that I have no doubt." There was no way to know if Ishan had succeeded in recruiting a spy from the *Enterprise* crew, but Picard was unwilling to risk overlooking that possibility. Hence, the elaborate deception designed to remove Beverly from the ship. How long could the ruse continue before it was exposed by Ishan or someone else?

If the last, cryptic message he had received from Will Riker was any indication, Picard knew that Ishan or someone from his circle of supporters was doing their level best to monitor any interaction between him and the admiral. Riker's communique had been a simple message, intended to warn Picard that his early suspicions about the perpetrators of President Nanietta Bacco's assassination might well be correct.

Sometimes the enemy hides in plain sight.

President Ishan, suspected by Riker and now Picard of having at least some involvement in Nanietta Bacco's assassination, seemed to be growing more paranoid with each passing day. The president pro tempore had done his level best to contain the movements and communications of numerous members of the Federation government as well as the high echelons of Starfleet's command hierarchy. Admirals Riker and Leonard James Akaar in particular appeared to be operating on a very tight leash. Then there were missions like the one given to the *Enterprise*, which Picard knew had been done simply to contain the Federation flagship and isolate him. The admiral already had set into motion a covert investigation into Ishan with the aim of finding incontrovertible truth of the interim president's culpability in Bacco's death. If such evidence existed, it needed to be found as soon as possible, preferably before the upcoming elections that might solidify Ishan's position of power. With so much at stake, Ishan and his people would not leave anything to chance.

Caution must be our watchword.

His thoughts were interrupted by the sound of the ship's intercom beeping for attention, followed by the voice of the *Enterprise*'s chief engineer.

"La Forge to Doctor Crusher."

Her eyebrows rising in surprise, Beverly reached up to tap her communicator badge. "Crusher here, Geordi. The captain's here, too."

"Sorry to disturb you both," La Forge replied, *"but you asked me to contact you if I found something on that data chip."*

Picard watched his wife's expression change at this news. Her eyes widened, and her jaw clenched. Her entire body seemed to be tensing in anticipation. Leaning forward in his chair, he asked, "What have you found, Commander?"

"Another message, sir. It's short and encrypted, text only, and was buried within the chip's data storage matrix. From what I can tell, Doctor Crusher's friend wanted her to find it, but no one else. The only thing it says is 'Remember' and two series of numbers. One group is a communications frequency and the other is a set of spatial coordinates, which the computer has identified as the planet Jevalan, in the Doltiri system."

"I'll be damned," Beverly said. "That's where he is?"

"I don't know, Doctor," La Forge replied. *"There was nothing else in the message, and I checked for other encrypted data, but that's all there is. I'm sorry."*

Picard said, "No apologies necessary, Mister La Forge. Excellent work." He waited for Beverly to terminate the communication before clasping his hands atop the conference table. "Jevalan."

"Looks that way. You should probably let Will know about this."

"Agreed." Picard needed to communicate this information to Will Riker, somehow, if for no other reason than his friend could attempt to verify that no one else at Starfleet Command or within Ishan's administration possessed this information. Once notified, the admiral also could act to protect Beverly's movements as she allegedly set out from the *Enterprise* for Deep Space 9. "Hopefully, Riker will be able to craft a scheme that will allow us to get you on your way without attracting too much attention. However, considering the short leash he's on, this sort of skulking about will carry significant risk."

Crusher sighed. "Doesn't everything, these days?"

Four

"That's the last one," La Forge said, watching as Lieutenant Rennan Konya—or, more accurately, the dark hair on top of the security officer's head, which was all that was visible at the moment—used a handheld anti-gravity lifter to maneuver a rectangular container through the aft cargo hatch of the runabout *Dordogne*. Consulting the inventory checklist on the padd he held, La Forge tapped the device's display screen, highlighting the container's serial number on his list and marking it as having been loaded aboard the ship. "With everything you've crammed in there, you're almost ready to run off and build your own starbase somewhere."

"I vote for Syrinx III," said Lieutenant Kirsten Cruzen as she stepped down from the cargo hatch and onto the deck of the *Enterprise*'s main shuttlebay. She reached up to cover her mouth, only just able to stifle a yawn. "By the way, I have to say that everyone who says gamma shift is the best shift is a stone-cold liar."

La Forge smiled at that. "Even Commander Taurik?"

"Okay, he gets a pass," Cruzen countered, "along with any vampires I may have missed." Leaning against the side of the runabout, she rapped its hull with her knuckles. "I guess I can sleep on the flight. It's something like a million hours from here to Deep Space Nine, right?"

Emerging from the cargo hatch with the anti-grav lifter,

Konya replied, "Now's probably a bad time to tell you that you've got first shift when we leave tomorrow."

"Cruel is what you are, Mister Deputy Chief of Security, sir." Another yawn escaped her lips as she ran a hand through her shoulder-length brunette hair.

La Forge listened to the banter as he made a final review of the checklist of items that had been requisitioned from ship's stores, along with the equipment requested by Doctor Crusher. So far as he could tell, everything now was aboard the *Dordogne*. The only thing left to do was put Crusher, Konya, and Cruzen aboard the runabout and send them on their way.

"I apologize for the crazy schedule," La Forge said, "but the maintenance crews only just finished prepping the ship a few hours ago. Something about a problem in one of the plasma injectors." In actuality, there was nothing at all wrong with any part of the *Dordogne*'s propulsion system— or any other onboard components, for that matter—but the fabricated explanation fed into the larger cover story Worf had instructed him to use as justification for the admittedly unusual timing of the runabout's preparations to leave the *Enterprise*. He did not enjoy lying or withholding information from his crewmates, even when security and other considerations demanded such subterfuge. La Forge took solace in the fact that the ruse would be short-lived, with Konya and Cruzen being given a full briefing by Doctor Crusher once the *Dordogne* was on its way.

"What I don't understand," Cruzen said, "is why DS Nine needs all this stuff, anyway. Aren't they supposed to be a state-of-the-art space station now?"

"We've been requested to drop off those supplies at the archeological settlement on Jevalan, in the Doltiri system," La Forge replied. "They've been having some problems with all of the civilians making port there on supply runs and whatever else gets shipped to and from that planet, and the security contingent there wants to beef things up a bit." It was a weak cover story, he knew, but it was the one Worf and Crusher had given him to use when dealing with conversations like this. "I know it's a bit of a detour, but we're the closest ship to them." Smiling, he added, "Think of it as an extended holiday."

Cruzen's eyes narrowed. "Any chance we can add a side trip to Syrinx III?"

"You've really got a thing for that planet, don't you?" Konya asked, grinning like a wolf allowed free reign in a sheep's pen.

Without missing a beat Cruzen replied, "Indeed I do. I took leave from the Academy there, and I've tried to get back at least once a year ever since."

"Anything you'd care to share with the group?" Konya asked, his smile widening.

"Maybe," Cruzen replied, bobbing her eyebrows. "If you take first shift on the flight out tomorrow."

Konya chuckled. "Done. I was always more of a Risa fan, myself." His expression grew somber. He exchanged knowing glances first with her and then La Forge. "You know, before."

"Yeah," La Forge said, offering a knowing nod. Risa was but one planet that had suffered near total devastation at the hands of the Borg during the Collective's final invasion of the Federation four years earlier. Though many of the resort world's indigenous and tourist populations had evacuated ahead of the attack, the Borg had been quite thorough in rendering the planet itself all but uninhabitable. Like so many others who had suffered similar fates, the surviving Risians had been relocated to other worlds throughout the Federation, and La Forge had heard more than one rumor regarding the possibility of the original planet's core population eventually being moved to a new star system and a world to call its own.

"Commander La Forge?"

Looking up from his padd, the chief engineer saw Konya regarding him from where he leaned against the *Dordogne,* his arms folded and his expression one La Forge had come to know all too well. Something was bothering the security officer, and he had decided that now was the time to give voice to whatever concerns might be plaguing him.

"What is it, Rennan?"

Nodding his head to indicate the runabout behind him, Konya said, "Sir, you know I don't mean any disrespect, but I have to ask: What's all this about? The Doltiri system isn't anywhere along the course to Deep Space Nine." He glanced to Cruzen. "With or without sneaking off to Syrinx. Besides, some of the stuff we just loaded aboard isn't the sort of equipment an archeological dig site needs, even if they've been having trouble with the local drunks or whoever else is supposedly stirring up trouble there. Then there's this whole business of loading out the runabout in the middle of the night, as though we're trying to avoid attracting attention." He paused, regarding La Forge for an extra moment, then said, "I couldn't help noticing that you put a security lockout on all the entrances to the shuttlebay, sir, so I guess what I'm asking is: What's the real story?"

"Commander La Forge was not authorized to give you the true details of your mission," said a deep, rumbling voice, and all three officers turned to see Commander Worf standing near the *Dordogne's* bow, his hands clasped behind his back and the metal weave of the ceremonial baldric he wore slung across his chest reflecting the overhead illumination. The Klingon had appeared as if from nowhere, and La Forge was tempted to ask if the *Enterprise's* first officer had employed the transporter in order to make his stealthy entrance into the shuttlebay. Seeing him, Konya and Cruzen both pushed themselves from their reclining positions against the runabout.

"Good evening, Commander," Konya said.

Stepping toward the trio, Worf's eyes narrowed. "I believe that you mean 'Good morning,' Lieutenant. It is, after all, zero three thirty hours."

"Is that what time it is?" La Forge asked. "I hadn't noticed. Time flies when you're having . . . well . . . whatever this is."

One corner of Worf's mouth turned upward, just the slightest bit, but that was his only emotional reaction to the engineer's words. Instead, he turned to Konya and Cruzen. "I apologize for not briefing you earlier on the details of your mission. It's a security matter requiring the utmost discretion, and Doctor Crusher is going to give you a complete briefing after you've departed."

Konya replied, "Understood, sir."

"However," the Klingon said, "I am not accustomed to sending my officers into a tactical situation without the proper information. I'm not able to tell you everything, because in all honesty even Captain Picard and I do not know all of the details. For that, you will have to rely on Doctor Crusher, and even she has not yet received all of the necessary information. I tell you this to impress upon you just how sensitive this mission will be. You are not to discuss this with anyone, including each other, until you have left the *Enterprise*. Is that understood?"

"Absolutely," Konya replied. "Whatever it is, you can count on us, sir."

Looking to La Forge, Cruzen asked, "So, I guess this means we're not going to Deep Space Nine?"

"No, but you *are* going to Jevalan, in the Doltiri system." Using his padd, the chief engineer gestured over Konya's shoulder toward the *Dordogne*. Some of the equipment and supplies are for the settlement there. That's part of your cover story. The rest of it—particularly the weapons—are for you."

"Okay," Konya said, nodding as he cast his gaze toward the shuttlebay deck. "This just got a lot more interesting."

Worf continued, "What I know is that Doctor Crusher

is traveling to Jevalan to make contact with an associate: a Cardassian physician she has known since the Federation-Cardassian War. She trusts this individual, who in turn is holding some kind of sensitive data and other materials, about which I currently know nothing."

"But Doctor Crusher knows?" Cruzen asked.

La Forge noted the fleeting look of concern that appeared on his friend's face before the Klingon shook his head.

"I do not yet believe she has specific details regarding the nature of the materials her friend will give her. According to Captain Picard, this Cardassian is attempting to protect her—and by extension, you—by safeguarding the information until you meet him on Jevalan.

"Regardless of the details Doctor Crusher will be sharing with you," Worf said, "*your* mission will remain the same: support and protect her. It's because so much else remains unknown that Captain Picard and I specifically chose you. In addition to your obvious skills and experience, you've both conducted covert assignments, both individually and as part of a team. You'll be on your own, but you both know how to adapt to rapidly changing situations and to work on your own without support. Most importantly, Doctor Crusher knows and trusts you both, as does the captain. As do I."

"We won't let you down, Commander," Konya said.

Cruzen added, "Or Doctor Crusher or the captain, for that matter."

Nodding in approval, Worf replied, "I know you won't. I would accompany you myself, but the success of this mission requires stealth, not just in your own actions but also those of us who will be covering for your activities. It is the captain's and Doctor Crusher's hope that your departure from the *Enterprise,* and your apparent travel to Deep Space Nine, will provide sufficient misdirection to allow you to get to Jevalan and carry out the doctor's mission."

"I can't say this is the weirdest assignment I've ever been

given," Konya remarked, "but I think it might make my top ten."

"Tell us where it ranks when you get back," La Forge replied.

"Will you be buying the drinks for that, Commander?" Cruzen asked, smiling.

The engineer chuckled. "Tell you what: The two of you get yourselves and Doctor Crusher back here in one piece, and I'll fly the runabout to Syrinx III myself."

"Deal."

La Forge and the two security officers shared a brief laugh over the quick, easy exchange, during which Worf remained silent. Once the moment passed, the first officer put his hands behind his back again.

"Captain Picard has one item he asked me to pass on to you. In his words, it goes without saying, but he wanted to say them, anyway." For the first time, he allowed himself a small smile. "You are ordered to return safely to the *Enterprise*."

The unexpected change in his demeanor was enough to evoke another laugh from Cruzen, who held her hand to her mouth in a futile attempt to contain it. Konya only shook his head.

"Aye, aye, sir," replied the deputy security chief.

"I think you're getting soft in your old age, Worf," La Forge said. Though Worf said nothing, the engineer was certain he saw a mischievous twinkle in his friend's eyes. Then it was gone, and the first officer's composed demeanor returned.

"I will be here to see you off," he said. "Good luck." Nodding his farewell to the trio, Worf turned and walked across the shuttlebay.

Konya said, "You just know he wants to go with us. He hates being left behind for something like this."

"You can say that again," La Forge said, offering his padd

to Konya. "He put together the list of equipment you're taking with you. Check it if you want, but I think he pretty much covered the bases."

Taking the padd, Konya examined the inventory list La Forge had been referencing during the loading of the runabout, and the chief engineer saw his eyes widen. "Portable scanner array. Motion sensors." He looked up from the list. "He's not kidding around, is he?"

"Nope," La Forge said.

"Whatever it is we're supposed to be doing," Cruzen replied, "it must really be something that will upset somebody important for the captain and Worf to go to this much trouble." She looked to La Forge. "Sir? Do you have *any* idea what this could be about?"

Sighing, La Forge said, "I wish I knew. It's all been one big mystery for me, too, at least to this point." The time he had spent decrypting the mysterious message left for Doctor Crusher by her friend Ilona Daret had piqued his curiosity, but even the *Enterprise*'s chief medical officer seemed at a loss to explain her colleague's odd behavior, let alone his request to have her join him on Jevalan.

Whatever the reasons for Doctor Crusher's mission to that distant world, the captain and Worf were pulling out all the stops to conceal for as long as possible her movements from unwanted attention. La Forge suspected it had at least something to do with Ishan Anjar and those closest to him, given the president pro tem's unusual interest in the *Enterprise* and Picard in particular. This made sense, given the captain's own alarming briefing of La Forge and the rest of the ship's senior officers regarding the ominous possibility that Ishan somehow may have been involved in President Nanietta Bacco's assassination. This bombshell revelation had been shared only with Picard's own inner circle, along with the news that agents working on behalf of the interim president might well be monitoring the *Enterprise*'s communications or perhaps even have spies aboard the ship. La Forge doubted the latter possibility, but prudence demanded extreme caution, especially now.

Just what we need; another presidential scandal.

It had not even been a decade since the *Enterprise*'s mission to Tezwa, a remote, independent world near the Klingon Border, and the revelation that President Bacco's predecessor, Min Zife, had given nadion-pulse cannons to the Tezwan government in direct violation of the Khitomer Accords. The illegal action, put into motion by Zife's chief of staff, Koll Azernal, and taken during the run-up to the Dominion War, had been intended as a fallback strategy in the event the Dominion succeeded in overpowering Starfleet forces in that region. The plan was never needed, but the weapons remained on Tezwa following the end of the war. It was a decision that eventually would take the Federation to within a hair's breadth of war with the Klingon Empire and see to Zife tendering his resignation as Federation president before all but disappearing into voluntary exile.

At least all of that was due to unforeseen circumstances, La Forge mused. *Zife wasn't sniffing around for a war, but can the same be said for President Ishan?*

Satisfied that their work here was done, La Forge keyed a command to his padd to lock out access to the *Dordogne* for everyone except himself, Doctor Crusher, Konya, and Cruzen. "Okay, you two are all set. Departure time's at zero nine hundred, so I'd suggest grabbing a few hours' sleep." He nodded toward the runabout. "You're going to be stuck inside that thing for a few days, and the bunks aren't the most comfortable."

"Anything better than a hole in the ground during a rain storm and I'm happy," Konya said, stepping away from the runabout and gesturing for Cruzen to follow. "Be sure to pack your swimsuit, just in case we make it to Syrinx III."

"Who needs a swimsuit?"

Opting not to partake in that conversation, La Forge watched the security officers make their way from the shuttle-bay before turning his attention to his padd. A quick review told him that the security lockouts on the bay's access points had been removed. He was heading to one of the exits when the reinforced hatch slide aside, revealing Tamala Harstad.

"Well, there you are," Harstad said, by way of greeting. Like him, she was dressed in a standard Starfleet duty uniform, though she also sported a blue smock of the type worn by members of the medical staff. The smock was rumpled and her dark hair, cut in a short style that left her neck exposed, seemed mussed, as though she had been running her fingers through it.

Surprised by her abrupt appearance, La Forge smiled. "What are you doing down here?" Noting again her somewhat disheveled appearance, he asked, "Did you pull an all-nighter or something?"

Harstad shrugged. "Yep. I was conducting some tests in the lab and needed peace and quiet, so I opted to work over-night to get it all done. I'm taking a break before alpha shift starts and was going to get some breakfast." She reached out to put a hand on his arm. "Then I started thinking of you and went by your quarters, but imagine my surprise when I saw you weren't there." She pursed her lips and made a mocking "tsk-tsk" sound. "Just my luck, though, that the computer knew exactly where you were hiding."

Trying not to react too much to the "hiding" remark, La Forge smiled. "Yeah. We've got a runabout scheduled for early departure in the morning, and I wanted to make sure it was ready to go."

"Don't you have other people to do that sort of thing for you?" Harstad asked, stepping closer. "Underlings, minions, serfs, or whatever the official designation is?"

La Forge chuckled. "The preferred Starfleet term is 'toad-ies,' but I couldn't sleep, and I've already got the rest of the gamma shift crew running diagnostics and doing other maintenance projects we've been putting off for a while, none of which should be confused with anything a normal person might call fun." While the gamma shift team in engineering was ensconced in just such an array of tasks, all of which were necessary if not glamorous, his main goal with assigning those duties was to keep his team occupied and away from the shuttlebay long enough for the covert launch preparations to be completed without an audience.

"Couldn't sleep, huh?" Now standing directly before him, Harstad lifted her chin and stretched to kiss him. He returned the kiss, catching the scent of whatever product she used in her hair. Vanilla. He always liked that smell. "What time are you back on duty?"

Gazing into her wide, brown eyes, La Forge replied, "I'm due back here at zero nine hundred." Like Worf, he wanted to be on hand when the *Dordogne* departed on its odd, classified mission. "I thought I might try to catch a nap before that, but I doubt I'll have much luck."

"Come on," Harstad said, taking his hand in hers and guiding him to follow her from the shuttlebay. Offering him an impish grin, she squeezed his hand. "I may be able to help with that."

Five

Kellessar zh'Tarash had long ago come to believe that there was nothing quite so relaxing as a hot bath in the open air after the end of a long workday.

It was for this reason that she had seen to the construction of an outdoor bathing area situated in the midst of the high-walled garden connected to her home. The garden itself, designed and crafted by one of the capital city's leading horticulturists, was an overflowing collection of flora from different regions across Andor, accented by a waterfall flowing from a rock formation dominating the corner farthest from the house. Soft lighting, recessed so as not to be obtrusive, highlighted the entire scene after sunset. All of the water used in the decorative display, as well as that used to care for the garden's array of plants and other foliage, was drawn from a recycling system that ensured limited waste.

Aside from an admiration for the craftsmanship that had willed into reality her tranquil refuge, zh'Tarash concerned herself with little of the garden's mechanics, choosing instead to focus on the peace and serenity it brought to her. The bathing area consisted of a large curved tub set into the ground and encircled with stone tiles leading to a walkway that connected the garden to the house. Lavatory and shower facilities sat to one side, inconspicuously nestled within a circle of overgrown shrubbery. The tub was uncovered, warmed by an internal heating unit and the unfettered rays of the Andorian sun, which at this hour was beginning to slip behind the Lor'Vela skyline.

Resting at one end of the tub and with her neck supported by a neck rest, zh'Tarash closed her eyes and relished the feel of the setting sun on her bare skin as she allowed the water—accented as it was with a special blend of fragranced, therapeutic bath salts—to soothe her muscles. Not for the first time, she considered the possibility of having a similar sanctuary installed in her office.

You should simply move your office here.

"Leader zh'Tarash?"

She opened her eyes and turned toward the sound of the familiar voice, her quizzical gaze coming to rest upon Rasanis th'Priil, her trusted aide and confidant. As was his habit, the *thaan* was dressed in a robe of muted colors, an ensemble he preferred when not working in his office, and carried a padd tucked beneath his left arm. The robe's highlights provided a pleasing contrast to his rich blue skin and stark white hair, which he chose to keep cropped close to his skull. Despite his being several years older than zh'Tarash, his fitness and dietary regimen saw to it that he looked and indeed was far more vital than Andorian males half his age. Though he never discussed the matter, zh'Tarash suspected that th'Priil's dedication to his healthy lifestyle was a holdover from his earlier career as a member of Andor's Homeworld Security forces.

"Good evening, Rasanis," she said, smiling in greeting. "What brings you out into the sun and fresh air?" She often teased her friend about his preference for indoor pursuits and had made more than one facetious promise that she would remove the roof and at least two walls from his office.

"I am able to tolerate it for brief periods, Leader," replied th'Priil without hesitation, having long ago learned to play his part in their spirited banter. He made a show of examining the tub. "I see I've arrived before you started playing with your bath toys. Were you able to get your replica submersible repaired after its disastrous encounter with the dreadful sea monster?"

Zh'Tarash laughed. "It's still in drydock, but thank you for your concern."

Holding up the padd, he tapped its screen for a moment. "I have just received updated polling information. You'll be happy to know that your popularity numbers rose again after your speech yesterday. Not just here on Andor, but across the Federation. A new projection shows you trailing President Ishan by nine percent, down from twelve before the speech. The other candidates' numbers are declining; some of their supporters look to be turning to you."

"Well, that's a nice development," zh'Tarash said, propping her head once more on the tub's neck rest. "Of course, it's easy to say the right thing when you have smart people feeding you the correct words. Please thank Leressi again for her exceptional work on the speech."

Leressi sh'Daran was a newcomer to zh'Tarash's staff, but she had wasted no time making substantive contributions to the campaign as its lead speechwriter. The passionate, unwavering message she had crafted as the cornerstone of zh'Tarash's platform in her bid for the Federation presidency already had attracted the attention of media outlets across the planet and throughout the quadrant. Sh'Daran's ability to shape articulate, energetic prose was matched only by her unbridled enthusiasm, and zh'Tarash and th'Priil had been required more than once to restrain her zeal in order to keep the young writer from losing her focus. This was becoming less of a problem with each passing day, as the election now was just weeks away and both zh'Tarash and President Ishan were narrowing their attention to the key issues that likely would have the greatest influence on voters readying to make their final decision. Now faced with these precious few targets, sh'Daran's energy was peaking as she honed every syllable zh'Tarash uttered for public consumption.

Th'Priil nodded. "I'll tell her when I see her later this evening. She wants to show me her draft of the remarks you'll be giving at your press conference tomorrow."

"Remember what we discussed, Rasanis," zh'Tarash said, shifting herself to a sitting position before moving to stand in the tub. "No grandstanding with respect to our poll improvements or closing the gap on Ishan. We remain focused on our message and the key issues, and let the media worry about the other things." She stepped up and out of the tub, relishing the sensation of the slight breeze cooling her wet, bare skin. Reaching for a robe, she wrapped it around her body and knotted the sash at her waist. "If there's one thing for which I have no tolerance, it's the constant dangling before us of ephemera in desperate attempts to distract us from the important questions."

Tapping controls on his padd, th'Priil replied, "You can expect at least a few questions tomorrow about Doctor Bashir. You will want to be prepared for that."

"Of course," zh'Tarash said, moving to the small table and chairs positioned near one edge of the tiled deck; a pot of tea set atop the table. Still warm thanks to the embedded heating unit, the tea smelled divine as she poured it into a waiting cup. "That's the very sort of distraction to which I refer. *Treishya* and True Heirs loyalists in the conservative media have not stopped talking about the egregious sin Doctor Bashir committed by saving us from extinction. I simply cannot imagine how any dialogue with them on that topic will end up being anything *but* constructive."

Looking up from his padd, th'Priil cocked an eyebrow as he regarded her, his left antenna twisting in her direction. A small smile graced his lips. "Why, Leader zh'Tarash, I do believe your facility for sarcasm is improving with each passing day."

"Call it a defense mechanism," zh'Tarash replied, settling into one of the deck chairs and sliding the teacup and its saucer toward her. "I have grown weary of those rigid, close-minded, would-be tyrants." Following Andor's secession from the Federation three years earlier, the Visionist party, spurred on by extremist sects like the *Treishya* and the True Heirs of Andor, had managed to take control within the halls of government, pushing aside their moderate and liberalist counterparts from the Progressive party. Since then, the Visionists had done their level best to resist all efforts at reconciliation with the Federation as well as utilizing the Shedai Meta-Genome data to resolve the ongoing fertility issues plaguing the Andorian people.

"They stand in the way of science that can save our species while clinging to outdated fallacies that have done more harm than good throughout our existence." Zh'Tarash sipped her tea. "It's madness to think that a deity as wise as Uzaveh would imbue us with intellect, free will, and the drive to learn and survive, yet judge and punish us for doing exactly what he created us to do. How petty must a god be to do something like that?"

Th'Priil released a small grunt. "My advice would be to refrain from making such comments at the press conference. You *do* recall what happened the last time this topic was broached? A melee broadcast Federation-wide is not what you want heading into the election." He paused, shrugging. "On the other hand, it might end up boosting your numbers. However, my concern about Doctor Bashir has less to do with his role in providing the cure for reproductive ills as it does the matter of his return to Starfleet authorities. According to my sources, the transfer may occur very soon; perhaps before the election. The details are still being finalized, but you will be asked your opinion on this, Leader."

"It's a Starfleet matter, Rasanis," zh'Tarash said. "Despite everything the good doctor did for us, and even though I consider him a hero to our people, there is no denying that he defied Starfleet regulations. He did so of his own free will, and he will have to answer to the charges against him." She shook her head. "I don't agree with it, of course, but to insert myself into that discussion at this point would be a mistake, as it would serve only to reopen wounds that we and the Federation are working to heal. Like it or not, Bashir's disposition is a part of that process." The doctor's actions still were being celebrated across the planet, and even the most tenacious detractors of utilizing Bashir's genetic therapy breakthroughs to resolve the fertility crisis were beginning to soften their stance on the issue. Being saved from eventual extinction as a species tended to alter one's views, it seemed.

Tucking his padd once more beneath his left arm, th'Priil said, "It's worth noting that should you win the election, you would have it in your power to pardon him."

Setting her teacup back on its saucer, zh'Tarash waved away the suggestion. "Don't mention that to anyone. Don't say it aloud, or even think it, until after the election. Even the idea that I might do something like that would undermine the discussions currently taking place. For now, we stay out of this. We have enough to worry about between now and the election, and if we win?" She sighed. "Imagine how much work we'll have to do then."

"But it will be good work."

"That it will. Whichever one of us ends up occupying that office will have a formidable standard by which we'll be measured." An unabashed admirer of Nanietta Bacco, zh'Tarash had collapsed into the arms of her lover, Rane, and wept upon hearing the news of the Federation president's assassination. Despite all the challenges she had faced during her savagely curtailed term of office, Bacco had acquired a deserved reputation as a confident, compassionate leader whose sole concern was seeing to the welfare of every Federation citizen. It was zh'Tarash's considered opinion that

Ishan Anjar was not the proper choice for continuing the work Bacco had begun. In truth, zh'Tarash was not even certain she was up to such a daunting task, but she was committed to pick up the standard that had been ripped from Nanietta Bacco's hands and carry it forward. Could Ishan say the same?

Zh'Tarash thought that unlikely.

"I am due at Leressi's office in short order, Leader," th'Priil said. "Is there anything else I can do for you before I take my leave?"

Shaking her head, zh'Tarash smiled. "No, Rasanis. Try not to work too hard, my friend. We still have a long journey ahead of us, and if the people of the Federation are willing, that journey will be longer still."

"I believe I am up to the challenge, Leader." Bowing his head, th'Priil said, "Good evening."

Once her aide was gone and she was alone in the comforting haven of her garden, zh'Tarash allowed herself a small sigh. Little time remained to her for curative respites such as this. There indeed was much work to do, now and in the future, should voters see fit to place her in that position, but th'Priil was right; it would be good work, worthy of Nanietta Bacco and the legacy she left behind. In truth, zh'Tarash relished the opportunity—and the challenge—that came with holding the Federation's highest elected office.

She was eager to begin.

Six

Looking at the table, Picard's first thought as he regarded the carnage before him was that something—or *someone*—had exploded.

"What in the world happened?" he asked, stepping closer to the table and eyeing its lone denizen. Seated in his customary place between the two chairs normally occupied during meals by his parents, was René Jacques Robert François Picard. The boy's face, hands, clothing, and the area of table before him was coated in what the captain recognized as the chocolate pudding he had given René as a dessert following his evening meal. The epicenter of the devastation was the bowl positioned before René, which appeared to have been the victim of some kind of subspace rupture. No eating utensils of any kind were visible.

"Sorry, Papa," said René, though the smile gracing his smeared face and his wide eyes seemed to indicate that he was rather pleased with himself. How much pudding had been *in* that bowl, anyway?

Despite his initial shock and disapproval at the mess before him, Picard could not resist the small chuckle that escaped his lips. "I may have to call a decontamination team," he said in the exaggerated, melodramatic manner he often used to elicit a laugh from the child. His words had the desired effect, and René released a cackle of delight.

As Picard set to the task of washing the table before turning his attention to the boy, René watched him work, giggling from time to time as his father moved pudding back to the bowl from whence it had erupted. With the table now cleaned, Picard returned the bowl and the cloth he had used to the replicator set into the room's rear bulkhead, and it was while his back was turned to René that his son spoke again.

"Papa? Where's Mama?"

"She's gone off on a trip," Picard replied, turning from the replicator and moving to take a seat next to the boy's chair. "Sometimes, the work your mother and I do calls for us to leave home for a short while." He always felt as though he might be talking in such a way that he only served to confuse René. Despite this uncertainty, the child had been demonstrating for some time a remarkable aptitude with respect to understanding and correctly employing words and phrases Picard at first thought might be beyond his comprehension. It often was difficult to remember that René had only recently celebrated his fourth birthday.

"Will she be coming back?"

Picard smiled. "Of course she's coming back. Do you really think she'd leave you here, all alone, with just me to take care of you?" Of course he was concerned by the risky nature of the mission undertaken by Beverly and Lieutenants Konya and Cruzen, but he forced away those troubling thoughts for the sake of his son. Children of such a young age, he believed, were to be spared the burden of seeing their parents worry over matters beyond their ability to understand. But what if the unthinkable happened and Picard found himself facing the prospect of explaining to René that his mother would not be returning to him?

She will return. He made himself repeat the statement in his mind as he reached across the table to sweep back a lock of René's auburn hair.

"I think she won't like that I spilled my pudding."

Leaning close so that he stared into the boy's eyes, Picard lowered his voice. "Well, we'll just have to keep that our little secret, won't we?"

"Okay," René said, offering a small shrug as he gripped his father's hand and began trying to bend his fingers. "Do you think she misses us?"

"I have no doubt she misses us and that she loves you very much. In fact, she made me promise to give you a present from her." Picard rose from his seat and kissed the boy's forehead.

"Did she say I could have more chocolate?"

Moving from the table back to the replicator, Picard replied, "I think we've had more than enough chocolate for one evening. It's time to get ready for bed."

"Will you read me a story?" René asked as he climbed down from his chair.

"Indeed I will," Picard said. Retrieving the cup of Earl Grey tea he had ordered from the replicator, he turned to see his son staring expectantly at him. "However, shouldn't you be reading to me now?"

"No!" the boy replied, smiling again. "Will you read the spaceship story?" Picard considered the book he had left in René's room the previous evening, a fictionalized account of humanity's first manned flight to Saturn in the early twenty-first century. While the historical record of the mission made for fascinating reading in its own right and was one of Picard's favorite eras of human space exploration, the stylized version created for leisure reading had become a guilty pleasure. René seemed to enjoy it as well, though Picard wondered if his son was more enamored by the story itself or the time spent with his father and listening to the words read aloud. René was reading in a rudimentary manner, but he still struggled with larger words and phrases. His enthusiasm was undaunted, and Picard had watched him spend hours on the floor of his room, storybooks and padds scattered about him as he pored over their pages, working without assistance to sound out the words from a favorite passage. Picard eagerly awaited the day when his son read aloud with a verve and passion for the written word he himself had possessed for as long as he could remember.

"Yes, we'll read the spaceship story," Picard said, glancing to the chronometer set into the replicator's control panel. "But there's something Papa has to do first. Can you wait for me?"

"Okay," the boy replied.

As he sent René to brush his teeth before bed, Picard heard the door chime sounding for attention. "Come." The doors parted to reveal Lieutenant T'Ryssa Chen standing at the threshold and carrying a padd, her expression one of uncertainty.

"Good evening, Captain," Chen said. "You asked me to report to you at nineteen hundred hours."

Picard gestured for her to enter the quarters. "Thank you for coming, Lieutenant. I know this is somewhat unusual, and I'm also aware that you went off duty an hour ago, but I hope you'll understand my need to be somewhat adaptable while Doctor Crusher is off the ship." Though he preferred to conduct ship's business or any other official matters in his ready room or the observation lounge off the bridge, he had little desire to leave René with a sitter or in the *Enterprise*'s child-care facility any longer than necessary. Duty often could leave little in the way of flexibility so far as personal pursuits and family was concerned, and Picard had come to appreciate those times when he could set aside the numerous demands on his time and concentrate on being a father. He even had made a point to encourage those among his crew with children aboard to seek a greater balance between their responsibilities as Starfleet officers and parents. Beverly still teased him about this, describing it as a monumental shift in his character from that of the man she had known for decades even prior to their joint assignment aboard the *Enterprise*'s

Galaxy-class predecessor. She was right, of course, just as she was about a great many things.

"Not a problem at all, sir," Chen said as she entered the room and allowed the doors to slide closed behind her. Pausing, she sniffed the air, and her right eyebrow rose. "Does it smell like chocolate pudding in here?"

"Courtesy of my son," Picard replied, indicating for her to follow him to his work area and to the seat positioned in front of his desk.

Chen asked, "Have you heard from Doctor Crusher, sir?"

"A few hours ago," Picard replied. "She's still en route to Deep Space Nine, of course." He did not like lying to any member of his crew, and even though he was certain he could trust Chen herself to handle such sensitive matters with the proper discretion, there simply was too much at stake with respect to the mission Beverly had undertaken. Therefore, in addition to Worf and La Forge, the *Enterprise*'s chief of security, Lieutenant Aneta Šmrhová, was the only other person besides himself, his wife, and Lieutenants Konya and Cruzen who knew the truth.

After first asking if Chen wanted something to drink, Picard then settled into the chair behind his desk and nodded to the padd she cradled in her hands. "Is that the draft of our final report to Starfleet Command?"

"Yes, sir. I know you told me to use my best judgment, but I can't help thinking it doesn't sound . . . *official* enough . . . if you understand my meaning." Chen's eyebrow arched again. "I don't think I used enough words to make all those diplomats happy."

Picard could not help the small smile her remark provoked. Chen's knack for inserting a casual comment into almost any conversation was a trait with which Picard had first disapproved of in the young officer, in particular during her earliest days aboard the *Enterprise*. However, he had come to see that when circumstances required it, T'Ryssa Chen could be as professional as any other officer under his command, and there even had been occasions where her unorthodox demeanor had come in handy. In some ways, she reminded him of himself as a younger officer, far too many years ago.

"I suspect those diplomats will never be happy, regardless of your effort." Setting down his cup and saucer, he took the padd from her and perused the report she had prepared. As they had discussed, his recommendation to Starfleet Command and—ultimately—the Federation Council was that the Ferengi Alliance was in no immediate danger of allying itself in even the slightest way with the Typhon Pact. The problem he had faced since the *Enterprise*'s arrival at Ferenginar was that such a simple, blunt statement felt inadequate in the face of the undue attention the Council seemed to be paying the matter. "So long as the Pact insists on having representatives here, President Ishan and the Council will want us here to stave off anything unexpected."

Picard shook his head, considering the absurdity of the situation. Grand Nagus Rom—in a private meeting held soon after the *Enterprise*'s arrival—had assured him that the Ferengi had no interests in doing anything to undermine their relationship with the Federation, and even Rom had expressed confusion and dissatisfaction with how his own diplomatic representatives were handling the so-called "negotiations" via subspace in the lead-up to the formal discussions now taking place on Ferenginar.

"I've reviewed transcripts from the previous two days' worth of talks, sir," Chen said. "The Ferengi diplomatic cadre, though they've been very good at not conceding anything, look to be working some angles during these discussions. I don't know that I'd call it outright defiance of Grand Nagus Rom's wishes, but they're definitely looking for an upside to all of this." She shrugged. "I guess they wouldn't be Ferengi if they didn't at least try to find a way to profit from any sort of agreement, with anyone."

Picard replied, "Many of those diplomats are holdovers from the previous Nagus, before the reforms Rom enacted. It's hard to undo generations of cultural and societal inertia. The Nagus is fully aware of what his representatives are up to, and to a point, I can even agree with what they're trying to do. What I don't understand is why we're needed to baby-sit the situation. All sides know each other's positions. No one will be shifting their stance to any appreciable degree. It's all such a waste of time."

A very deliberate waste of time, he knew, but this was something he could not share with Chen, at least for the moment. So long as the *Enterprise* was here at Ferenginar, acting on orders handed down by Ishan Anjar himself, there was little he could do that might earn him the interim president's ire. In truth, he was unconcerned about such things, but he also knew that the longer he played his role in Ishan's game—whatever that might be—the longer Beverly and her team could operate in relative obscurity as she traveled to learn whatever secrets her friend had discovered. He had not heard from her since her departure, and while that was by design as part of their plan to keep hidden her activities, it still concerned him that he did not know into what situation his wife might be venturing.

The chirp of the ship's intercom system caught Picard before he could continue his conversation with Chen.

"Bridge to Captain Picard."

"Picard here."

"Commander Havers, sir," replied the voice of the *Enterprise*'s Beta Shift watch officer. *"Sorry to disturb you, but we've received a hail from the planet's surface. Ambassador Sherwood wishes to speak with you."*

Releasing a sigh that made Chen cover her mouth to stifle a giggle, Picard first took a sip of his tea before answering. "Patch it through down here, Commander."

"Aye, sir," Havers replied.

To Chen, Picard said, "If you'll excuse me a moment, Lieutenant." Given his previous exchanges with the ambassador, he had no desire to subject the junior officer to whatever verbal skirmish might be forthcoming.

"No problem whatsoever, sir," Chen said, rising from her seat. "Is there anything I can do for you while I wait? Maybe get you transport to Deep Space Nine?"

Chen left the room, not even bothering to rein in her chuckling, and Picard turned his attention to his desktop computer interface terminal as it activated, its momentary display of the Federation seal and a current date-time stamp quickly replaced by the image of a displeased human, Anthony Sherwood.

"Ambassador," Picard said, schooling his features to remain impassive. "To what do I owe the pleasure?" Despite his best effort, Picard still heard the hint of sarcasm lacing his words, which was not lost on the diplomat.

"Captain Picard," Sherwood snapped, *"I've just been informed that you will not be present tomorrow during our session with the Typhon Pact delegation."* The ambassador was a slender man with pale skin and receding brown hair. His blue eyes were set beneath dark eyebrows that were in dire need of grooming. He looked gaunt, no doubt the result of a career spent sitting behind a desk and exuding stress over all manner of crises both real and imagined. His default expression seemed to be one of annoyance, in keeping with his typical behavior when interacting with anyone he felt was beneath him, which seemed to be everyone. Picard had disliked him from their first meeting, and that was before the other man even had opened his mouth.

Leaning back in his chair, Picard replied, "That's correct, sir. I have several shipboard matters requiring my attention before I can return to the conference." In truth, his morning schedule was free, and he had planned to spend it with René before delivering the boy to the ship's child-care center and beaming down to the planet's surface. He saw no reason to provide this portion of his itinerary to the ambassador.

"*It's been my experience that starships are stuffed to over-flowing with officers capable of carrying on in their captain's stead while he's away,*" Sherwood remarked. "*Is this not the case on the* Enterprise?"

Allowing the man a few seconds to be pleased with himself and his deftly worded and doubtless well-practiced accusation, Picard replied, "And I'm given to understand that a Starfleet presence at a diplomatic negotiation is often a sign that discourse has come to an end, usually as a product of unsatisfactory effort on the part of all participants and that direct measures now are required in order to further a given agenda. Since you're calling me at this hour, I can only presume that you've assembled a list of targets for our forthcoming orbital bombardment. Should this take place immediately, or might I first be allowed to finish my dinner?"

In his brief encounters with Sherwood, Picard had found him to be a competent if unimaginative diplomat. Though he prided himself on his ability to maintain a composed demeanor when faced even with the most insufferable individuals, the captain found his normal steadfast poise reaching its limits with the ambassador. For his part, Sherwood seemed to take delight in the effect his deportment had on those around him, which only served to further irritate Picard, resulting in his part in the current exchange.

Be the better man, Jean-Luc.

He knew it was a petty exercise to respond to Sherwood as he had, but it still offered him a small morsel of satisfaction, which heightened a bit as he watched the ambassador's face redden and his jaw clench. Still, he managed to keep his tone level as he leaned closer to his own terminal's visual pickup.

"*These negotiations are important, Captain. President Ishan is very concerned about them, and it's my job to see to it that Federation interests are protected.*"

"And a fine job you're doing, Ambassador, if I do say so myself. However, it's my contention that the *Enterprise*'s presence here does not bring anything to the Federation's side of the table, and in fact may even prove a hindrance to any continued negotiation. I do not wish to undermine the diplomatic effort with any undue show of force, even if such a display is implied and seemingly benign."

Sherwood seemed to mull this over for a moment, as though unsure whether Picard might be setting another verbal trap, but—predictably—he forged ahead. *"Your concern is noted and commendable, Captain, but your place is where your president says it is. The* Enterprise *will remain on station until ordered otherwise, and you will continue to attend the conference sessions."*

Picard said nothing, though he did count off to himself the seconds that passed before the ambassador spoke again.

"Once you've concluded whatever ship's business demands your immediate attention, of course."

"Understood, Ambassador." Picard knew that whatever authority Sherwood had been granted so far as the *Enterprise* was concerned, it did not extend toward any overt interference in the starship's operation, which included those matters Picard felt took precedence over anything currently taking place on the planet's surface. He knew also that the diplomat was aware of this but chose not to push the point any further than necessary. Ship captains in general were given wide latitude with respect to such decisions and employing sound judgment, and Picard's position as one of Starfleet's senior starship commanders gave him an even greater level of flexibility and autonomy. This had served him well in the years since the final Borg invasion as well as the vital role he and the *Enterprise* had played in the aftermath of that conflict and the rebuilding that been done across the Federation. President Bacco and Admiral Akaar had given him that authority and he had wielded it with discretion to great effect, and Picard believed that President Ishan was displeased with the status quo while having no justifiable reason to do anything about it without attracting undue attention. The captain further suspected that Sherwood's haranguing of him was a product of Ishan wanting constant updates about his and the *Enterprise*'s activities.

"I must say that I find your attitude most concerning, Captain," Sherwood said, *"particularly given the Typhon Pact's continuing attempts to undermine Federation alliances and interests. Several of your peers seem to grasp this, while you, one of Starfleet's most celebrated officers, appear ambivalent."*

Knowing he was being baited, Picard folded his hands in his lap and willed himself to remain still in his chair. "Ambivalent? I respectfully disagree with that assessment, sir. Yes, the Pact has demonstrated the ability to be disruptive, but it seems obvious that its own internal squabbles will be its ultimate undoing. The direct attacks on Federation targets have been the result of rogue factions within the Pact, not a cohesive strategy agreed upon by the member states and their governments." It sometimes was hard to make that distinction, Picard knew, but it was this odd, uncertain reality that likely had kept the Federation and the Typhon Pact from descending into an all-out shooting war. "This negotiation between the Pact and Ferenginar is but the latest example of a crude tactic designed to gauge our reactions. The Ferengi have no intention of jeopardizing in any way their alliance with us."

Sherwood's features, already darkened by the irritation that had greeted Picard at the beginning of the conversation, now seemed to harden even further. *"It's important for us to show a united front, Captain, particularly now, with the Typhon Pact looking for any weakness in our resolve that they can exploit. You of all people should understand the perils of not respecting the threat they represent. Or have you forgotten what you allowed to happen at Andor?"*

Now it was Picard's turn to be annoyed. "I beg your pardon, Ambassador, but the situation at Andor was not at all similar to this one. That was an internal matter in which the Typhon Pact covertly interfered, and the Andorian government made its own decision, for better or worse. As for your implication that I am responsible for their secession, either through action or failure of action, given that you were not even holding an elected or appointed political office at the time of the affair in question, you'll forgive me if I place little value in your take on the situation."

At last, Sherwood's emotions seized hold of whatever control he may have been exerting over them. *"How dare you talk to me in this manner? Rest assured your conduct will factor prominently in my next report to the council."*

"I trust you'll do me the courtesy of correctly spelling my name this time. Please contact Starfleet Command and ask Admiral Akaar for assistance, if you feel you require it. Picard out." Reaching for the terminal, Picard pressed the control to sever the communication with far more force than was necessary, and Sherwood's face was replaced by the Federation seal and the caption COMMUNICATION ENDED. Closing his eyes, he took several deep breaths in a bid to calm himself and push away the irritation he had allowed the ambassador to stir within him.

"Lieutenant Chen," he called out after a moment, and the young officer appeared from the other room where she had been maintaining a discreet distance during the conversation. "I apologize for you having to listen to that. I'm afraid Ambassador Sherwood does not bring out my best behavior." Was he getting too old for this sort of thing, or was his tolerance for such people simply waning?

As always, Chen could be counted upon to provide relief from the stresses of the moment.

"Not a problem, sir. I'll see to it that he's removed from the ship's holiday correspondence list."

Seven

No matter how much effort and detail might be instilled into them, holographic enemies never seemed to die in a manner Worf found satisfying. Still, he was content to continue experimenting until he achieved the desired results.

Standing amidst the crumbling remnants of the ancient, unnamed city he had chosen as the backdrop for this exercise, Worf studied his latest enemy. Separated by ten meters of dry, barren soil, the Jem'Hadar soldier returned his critical glare. The simulated Dominion warrior was the fifth opponent conjured at random by the computer from the database of potential rivals Worf had programmed into the training scenario. Behind him, four previous opponents lay unmoving among the ruins, dispatched over the course of the past hour in different iterations of the program. His muscles flexing beneath heavy clothing and armor, the Jem'Hadar fighter held a double-bladed ax in one hand, twirling the weapon as though it were a toy. His eyes, products of the training program Worf had created, glared at him with utter defiance and contempt. Though he said nothing, the challenge was clear.

Fight me, Klingon, if you have the courage.

Armed with nothing save his own two hands and the warrior's heart beating in his chest, Worf lunged at his adversary. The Jem'Hadar soldier did not retreat from the attack, but instead held his ground as Worf closed the gap. Raising his ax, the Jem'Hadar began to swing the weapon. Worf was faster, grasping the ax's handle before pivoting and pulling his foe with him, using the energy channeled into the downward strike to yank the enemy soldier off his feet. Twisting the ax, Worf felt it loosen from the Jem'Hadar's grip before his adversary dropped to the dusty soil.

At first considering turning the axe on his opponent, Worf instead discarded the weapon as the Jem'Hadar regained his feet. Lowering his shoulder, the Klingon slammed into his opponent with all the strength he could muster, hearing the agreeable sound of air being forced from the enemy soldier's holographic lungs. The Jem'Hadar brought down an elbow between Worf's shoulder blades, and the first officer growled in anger against the momentary pain as he pushed through his own assault. Lifting the Jem'Hadar off his feet, Worf slammed him down to the dirt.

As he rolled to one side and regained his footing, Worf saw his adversary doing the same, and now light glinted off something in the soldier's hand. The polished blade, long and curved, came at him and Worf's instincts took control. He sidestepped the knife's thrust and grabbed hold of the Jem'Hadar's arm. Seeing his rival's other hand reaching for him, Worf rammed his elbow into the soldier's face. The Jem'Hadar grunted, more irritated than injured, but Worf followed the strike with another elbow that found his opponent's throat. This had the intended effect, with the soldier coughing and gurgling as he stumbled backward, his knife falling to the dirt. Worf pressed his advantage, pouncing on the Jem'Hadar and driving the heel of his hand into his enemy's nose. He felt bone, cartilage, or something else crack beneath his hand, and the soldier's entire body went rigid. Worf saw the life already fading from the Jem'Hadar's eyes as he delivered a final, decisive blow, lashing out to chop at his opponent's neck. The soldier collapsed to the ground and lay there, unmoving.

"Exercise complete," reported the voice of the *Enterprise*'s main computer. *"Do you wish to continue to the next level?"*

"Hold program," Worf said, eyeing his fallen enemy. Despite the raw, unfettered ferocity of the fight, he knew the victory was hollow, taken as it was from a computer-generated simulation and within an environment that carried no real risk. For a moment, he considered instructing the program to remove the holodeck's safety protocols, but doing so would be in defiance of Starfleet policy with respect to simulation training scenarios as well as Captain Picard's own standing orders. In the past, such as when he had served as a lieutenant aboard the *Enterprise*-D, Worf on occasion had disengaged the holodeck safety measures for the set of calisthenics programs he had created as a personal fitness regimen. After all, Klingon honor required no less than a genuine threat to one's own safety if a fight was to be worth undertaking.

When Picard had learned of this practice, he at first had said nothing, other than to offer his understanding of what Worf was trying to accomplish. Still, he did instruct that the fail-safe parameters were to be enabled should anyone else attempt to navigate the program. This respect of Klingon culture and heritage was but one of the many reasons Worf had admired Picard from his first day aboard the *Enterprise*; a sentiment that only had strengthened during the intervening years.

Later, as he evolved into his role as security chief following the death of Lieutenant Tasha Yar, Worf realized that despite the demands of his Klingon birthright, he needed to present a proper, disciplined role model for the men and women in his charge and that meant not disregarding orders or undertaking undue risk when a situation warranted no such action. With that in mind, he saw to it that the scenarios used to train the security detail were as real and unrelenting as they could be without causing actual wounds or death. The risk of being stunned, knocked out in hand-to-hand combat, or even suffering minor injuries remained, and it was a sufficient motivator for his officers so far as completing the training sequences were concerned. In years past, Worf himself had fallen prey to such pitfalls within the different simulations, thanks to some rather inventive programming on the part of two former *Enterprise* shipmates, Data and Wesley Crusher.

"Lieutenant Šmrhová is requesting entry to the holodeck," reported the computer. *"Should I allow her access?"*

Worf frowned. There had been no alert sounded or other summons from the bridge apprising him of a situation requiring his attention, and it was atypical of Aneta Šmrhová to call on him unannounced. "Access granted."

Behind him, the computer-generated façade of a dilapidated stone structure morphed to reveal the arched doorway of the holodeck's main entrance. The doors parted to admit Šmrhová, dressed in exercise attire as might be worn in the ship's gymnasium or recreational areas. Her clothing and hair were damp with perspiration, and Worf noted that her face was flushed, indicating she had just completed some form of exertion.

"I'm sorry, Commander," she said in greeting. "I hope I'm not disturbing you."

Shaking his head, Worf replied, "No. What can I do for you, Lieutenant?"

The security chief did not answer at first. Instead she cast her gaze to the dirt covering the ground of his holodeck simulation, as though considering her next remarks.

"I feel odd, sir, about not accompanying Doctor Crusher on her mission."

"Odd? In what way?"

Šmrhová shrugged. "I'm the security chief. The safety of the ship and the crew is *my* responsibility. When a team's sent into a potentially hazardous situation, I should be there, with them."

Frowning as he regarded her, Worf asked, "Do you believe Lieutenant Konya was an incorrect choice to send with Doctor Crusher? Are he and Lieutenant Cruzen not qualified to carry out the assignment given to him?"

"Of course he's qualified," Šmrhová replied. "This has nothing to do with him or Cruzen or whether they're up to the job. I guess this is just me, worrying." She reached up to rub the bridge of her nose. "Commander, I have to be honest with you when I say that there are times when I feel as though I'm still figuring out how to be an effective chief of security." Noticing his questioning look, she held up a hand. "I don't mean the tangible things like ship's operations and protocol or leading and training my people, or even facing the risks that come with my position." She sighed. "I seem to have trouble knowing when it's my place to lead and when to stand by and let others do their jobs."

Assigned originally to the *Enterprise* as a tactical officer, Aneta Šmrhová had proven herself on multiple occasions in the years since then. Her service during the Borg Invasion and the aftermath of that devastating assault had been exemplary, earning her a reputation as a smart, capable officer who thought fast on her feet and did not shrink from challenges or additional responsibility. She had been promoted to her present billet following the death of the ship's previous chief of security, Jasminder Choudhury.

As still happened when thinking of his late lover, Worf felt within him a pang of emptiness; an almost palpable ache in his chest at her absence. The feeling was only exacerbated here and now as he stared into the face of her successor, and Worf reminded himself that Šmrhová did not deserve to be the target of any negative feelings he might still harbor over Choudhury's loss.

Owing to the sensitive nature of the mission Crusher had undertaken, Worf had suggested to Captain Picard that Šmrhová not even be told about it or Konya and Cruzen's roles. Picard had convinced him otherwise, making the valid point that the security chief deserved to know the truth when it came to the risks her people were being asked to face.

"It is not unusual to question one's abilities," he said. "Indeed, it is a healthy practice, as it often prevents one from slipping into complacency or even mediocrity."

Nodding, Šmrhová replied, "Agreed, sir."

In truth, Worf understood and even sympathized with her feelings. There was a time when he—as chief of security or simply a junior member of the operations staff—might well have doubted the wisdom of superiors choosing to exclude him from a duty to which he seemed ideally suited. However, time and experience had given him a broader perspective, in particular with matters pertaining to the proper knowledge and utilization of those in his charge. It was but another set of lessons he had learned while serving under effective leaders like Jean-Luc Picard, William Riker, Benjamin Sisko, and—for the brief time with which they had worked together—Natasha Yar.

"I have experienced similar doubts," Worf said, gesturing for Šmrhová to walk with him as he began strolling toward the nearest of the simulated ruins. "I was a junior officer on the previous *Enterprise* when Lieutenant Yar was killed in the line of duty, and Captain Picard promoted me to chief of security. I knew he would not have done so if he did not believe me capable of accepting the responsibility, but still there were those occasions when I felt unworthy of the trust he had placed in me. I faced similar uncertainty when the captain chose me to be his first officer after Admiral Riker received his posting to the *Titan,* but that was due to other reasons."

They passed through the remains of what was supposed to be an arched gateway leading to a small courtyard before the front wall of a castle. The computer had seen to it that the

Peaceable Kingdoms   69

ancient structure appeared to tower above them, extending much higher than the ceiling of the holodeck's interior. Worf never ceased to be impressed with the amount of care and detail that went into simulations of this sort.

Šmrhová said, "I know of the difficulties you experienced during your time on Deep Space Nine, including the reprimand Captain Sisko was forced to enter into your service record. I'm sure overcoming that was its own challenge."

"It was," Worf replied. "Captain Sisko himself told me that I likely would never earn a promotion to captain or command of a starship."

"I can't believe that," Šmrhová countered, "not after everything that's come since, and that's before Starfleet takes into account the ongoing need for good, experienced officers to take command postings. We're still recovering from the Borg attack, after all. Besides, if you thought you had no future career prospects, why stay with Starfleet? You were an ambassador for the Klingon Empire. Why leave that behind to put your uniform on again?"

"Diplomacy and I are not a good mix," Worf said, pausing as he cast a wry look in Šmrhová's direction. When she smiled at his subtle attempt at humor, he added, "Truthfully, that also was something of a learning experience, but ultimately my place is here, in Starfleet, serving Captain Picard and the *Enterprise*." His selection as the ship's first officer had—he knew—raised a few eyebrows at Starfleet Headquarters, but Worf was told that Picard had held firm in his decision, refusing to be swayed by anyone in the command hierarchy. Worf harbored no doubt that his career in Starfleet, whatever might happen in the years to come, was a result of Picard's unwavering support and trust. The Klingon would die before he allowed that confidence to be dishonored to even the smallest degree.

"Sir," Šmrhová said, "if you don't mind my asking, what do you think about being left behind, especially considering that Doctor Crusher could end up in danger? I have to think Captain Picard hates the idea, but we both know he'd never show it. What about you?"

Worf said, "Like you, I felt that my place was with her on the mission, but if I had left with her, others would become suspicious. By staying here, I not only maintain my proper role and responsibilities, but I also protect Doctor Crusher and Konya and Cruzen." He eyed the security chief. "You are doing the same, Lieutenant."

"Frustrating, isn't it?" Šmrhová asked, more to herself than him. She gestured to her clothing. "I thought I could work off some of it, but kickboxing dummies or even willing friends just doesn't cut it." Pausing, she glanced around the ruins and at the bodies of the five opponents the computer had sent after Worf. "You seem to have found a method that works."

"Indeed," replied the Klingon. "I find training scenarios like this to be more . . . fulfilling . . . than conventional exercise."

Šmrhová smiled at that. "And I've interrupted you for long enough. Thank you for your time, Commander. Our talk helped."

"I am happy to hear that," Worf said. After a moment's consideration, he added, "You are welcome to join me in the next iteration, if you wish."

Her eyebrows rose in response to the offer. "Really? You don't mind the intrusion?"

"Not at all." Worf turned and walked to one of his vanquished opponents, a Hirogen soldier he had added to the training program based on xenobiological and cultural data collected by the *U.S.S. Voyager* and other ships that had explored the Delta Quadrant. He reached down to retrieve the long sword carried by the computer-generated alien warrior before its demise at Worf's hands. "I think you will find the regimen more rewarding. For one thing, the fighting is more satisfying when facing the enemy alongside a worthy ally."

"Anything else I should know?" Šmrhová asked.

"Yes." As he hefted the sword and tested its weight and balance, Worf was unable to suppress a small grin. "Here, there is no need to pull your punches."

Eight

It had been many years, more than he cared to count, since his days as a cadet, but for some reason he could not identify, Will Riker always felt an odd compulsion to run rather than walk across the grounds, as though he was late for class. Even the fingers of his left arm seemed to be tingling, as if to remind him that a padd containing his course notes might still be sitting on the desk in his dormitory room.

Damn.

On the other hand, there definitely was a new sensation he was experiencing during this, his first visit to the Academy since his promotion. As he traversed the walkways winding around, across, and through the impeccably manicured grounds and gardens while wearing his admiral's uniform, he was struck by one very obvious observation: Many of the men and women around him, most on their way to some unknown destination or perhaps enjoying a brief respite while sitting on a bench in the sun and fresh air, were *young*. It was hard to judge in all cases, of course, owing to the diversity of species represented by the Academy's current crop of students, but that did nothing to alter his perception.

Was I ever that young? Perhaps it was his imagination, but Riker was sure he now could hear his very bones creaking as walked, and he visualized his beard growing grayer with every step. Were she here with him, Riker imagined that

Deanna would be enjoying his reaction. He was not *that* old, was he? What had she once called him during a conversation where he had been lamenting about how time seemed to be passing him? Seasoned?

That would do, Riker decided.

Rounding a bend in the walkway that took him past one of several reflecting pools scattered across the Academy campus, he saw a figure sitting on a bench overlooking the small, artificial pond. Leonard James Akaar, dressed like Riker in his Starfleet admiral's uniform, rested with his hands clasped in his lap, his back ramrod straight, and locks of his long, stark white hair resting atop his broad shoulders. At one hundred eighteen years as measured on Earth, the Capellan looked more like a human of advanced middle age. Aside from his muscled physique, Akaar's most intimidating feature was his eyes, which seemed to miss nothing and were—if the admiral was of a mind to do so—capable of inciting dread upon whomever they were fixed. Riker himself had been the target of Akaar's foreboding gaze more than once, and it was something to be avoided if at all possible.

On this occasion, as Akaar turned at Riker's approach, the admiral instead offered a small smile. "Will. Thank you for coming." He raised a hand and gestured as though to indicate the open area around them. "I thought this might be a better place to talk. Given how often we've been meeting in either of our offices, it seemed a change of venue might help to throw off suspicion."

"Good idea," Riker said, taking a seat on the bench next to Akaar. They had been conducting frequent clandestine meetings at Starfleet Headquarters in recent days, each time taking precautions to ensure neither of their offices was being subjected to covert monitoring. Riker suspected that President Ishan had to have somebody keeping an eye on him as well as Akaar, but if their movements or conversations were being tracked, then whoever was shadowing them was very good at his job. So far, neither admiral had found any evidence of such surveillance, but they knew that Ishan would not stand idle while they harbored suspicions about him. Though they possessed no evidence to substantiate their theories, the president pro tempore had to know that they were continuing to search for such proof and that they also would enlist trusted friends to assist them in the endeavor.

Which is why Jean-Luc is stuck at Ferenginar. Riker needed Picard, but orchestrating a ruse to justify moving him and the *Enterprise* from the so-called "diplomatic mission" for which Ishan had dispatched the flagship to the Ferengi homeworld was proving difficult. Still, Riker was formulating a plan of his own.

"When you requested a meeting," Akaar said, his gaze focused on a small flock of ducks floating at the pond's opposite end, "you said there had been a development."

"Yes, sir. You know that I've continued to have my people working to find a way to monitor President Ishan's communications." At Akaar's request and after the admiral had provided him with critical information with which to begin his unsanctioned investigation, Riker had asked trusted members of his crew aboard the *Titan* to target a secret, encrypted subspace communications array apparently in use either by the president or his chief of staff, Galif jav Velk. It had been a task fraught with risk; discovery of their actions likely would result in arrest and court-martial for treason. With the possibility of collecting incontrovertible proof of Ishan's or Velk's illegal activities, Akaar had accepted the danger, as had Riker and those members of the *Titan*'s senior staff with whom he had entrusted this information.

"I've kept my people at it," Riker continued, "in the hopes that Ishan might lead us to wherever Velk's being held." With the interim president's former chief of staff in the custody of the Federation Security Agency and being held at one of their detention facilities, Riker knew that time was running out for the Tellarite. At the moment, Velk represented the one key piece of evidence that could prove Ishan had knowledge of the president's assassination. Whatever value he might hold for Ishan *had* to be connected to that and covering up his own tracks. No doubt Velk also was a vital component in the interim president's bid to finish out the late Nanietta Bacco's term.

"I take it your people are still looking," Akaar said, when Riker paused.

Riker replied, "That's right, sir. Ishan's only apparent contact with Federation Security has been through normal channels, and my people haven't found anything that even hints at an update about Velk. So far as we know, he's still being held in detention and awaiting the council's special board of inquiry, and Ishan seems to be going out of his way to keep his distance from the whole thing." That Velk had been arrested on charges of usurping the Starfleet chain of command and ordering unauthorized covert operations was enough to send him to prison for the rest of his life, but there still was the matter of his alleged involvement with the True Way and Nan Bacco's murder. Riker could bring forth no public accusations on this front against Velk, let alone Ishan, without evidence he did not possess. Ishan knew this, which meant that the president pro tem had to be plotting some means of eliminating the ticking time bomb that was Galif jav Velk. So long as he was in custody, removing him without raising suspicion was an obstacle, but Riker had no doubt Ishan was plotting a solution to that problem.

We need to work faster than he is.

"Finding Velk is the priority," Akaar said. He seemed ready to continue but paused, and Riker glanced over his shoulder to see a pair of cadets—a human male and Vulcan female—walking past them. Both admirals waited until they had disappeared from view, then Riker counted off an additional ten seconds before saying anything.

"If Ishan's already got spies embedded within the Academy-class ranks, we're in big trouble."

Akaar offered a grunt of mild amusement. "As I was saying, we definitely need to find Velk, and sooner rather than later, but we also need to track down Ishan's contacts within Starfleet Command. Someone is working for him, behind my back."

"You're sure?" Riker frowned. "I know there was that issue with Commander Sarai, but I thought you handled that." He recalled what Akaar had told him about Commander Dalit Sarai, an Efrosian officer assigned to Starfleet Intelligence and staffed to headquarters. Akaar had discovered that she was funneling information to Velk and Ishan without his authorization, circumventing him and undermining his authority, and that was before taking into account any possibility of her colluding with the president and his chief of staff to take part in any illegal activities. After discovering what Sarai was doing, the admiral transferred her from Starfleet HQ to a posting on Luna, where she hopefully would do no further harm. This did not preclude Ishan having other officers working for him in the upper echelons of Starfleet's command hierarchy, but Akaar's efforts to find those individuals so far had been fruitless.

"It's possible Ishan is communicating directly with whatever cadre of officers he's assembled to assist him," Riker said. "People like Captain Unverzagt of the *Warspite,* for example. And let's not forget Seth Maslan from the *Lionheart,* the one Velk sent to kill Julian Bashir. But, hell, Admiral, some of these people likely don't even know they're being duped. After all, there aren't many starship captains who would refuse a direct order from their commander in chief."

Akaar replied, "No, but I would expect at least some of them to inquire to their superior officers as to the irregularity of receiving orders that sidestep several links in the chain of command." He shook his head. "Of course, if these officers are receiving eyes-only directives with orders not to share their information, this problem could be larger than we thought, but I suspect it's not Ishan doing it himself. He almost certainly has someone working within Starfleet Command; someone with access to security protocols. That shortens the list a bit."

"A bit," Riker repeated.

Rising from the bench, Akaar blew out his breath. "I need to get back to my office. I would not put it past Ishan to have someone keeping track of my comings and goings. Yours, too, for that matter."

It was an unsettling thought, to be sure, Riker conceded as he stood along with the Capellan. He had no desire to go on living and working like this. The time had come to resolve this business, once and for all. "We'll find the leak, sir. It's just a matter of time."

"Don't take too much time, Will," Akaar said as he moved to the path for his walk back to Starfleet Headquarters. "I don't know how much of it we may have left."

Nine

All around her, Beverly Crusher heard and saw the suffering. She willed herself to ignore it and focus on the problem directly in front of her.

Not problem, she chastised herself. *Patient. Focus on your* patient, *Doctor.*

The wounded were strewn on beds or tables or just left on the stretchers upon which they had been carried into the *Sanctuary*'s already-cramped primary trauma center. Reports from the other treatment areas across the ship were communicating similar conditions, and the captain already had notified the medical teams that more injured were coming.

"We're running out of places to put them," called out Lieutenant Rahadyan Sastrowardoyo, one of the *Sanctuary*'s trauma nurses, as he helped to move a patient from one of the treatment tables to a clear space on the deck. "At this rate, we'll be stacking them on top of each other."

Crusher did not answer. The room was littered with wounded, Starfleet and Cardassian alike, and a peek through the doors leading from the trauma center told her that the situation in the corridor was pretty much the same as in here. She knew that the hospital ship's captain already was enacting emergency procedures designed with the express purpose of handling unusual situations like the one the *Sanctuary*'s crew now faced. Cargo bays, briefing rooms, any space large enough to accommodate patients, medical personnel, and equipment for treatment were at this moment being set up as triage stations, with the most serious cases being sent to the ship's main hospital and satellite trauma centers. Other patients were still on the planet's surface, filling the make-shift emergency aid station set up by members of the *Sanctuary*'s first response away team. Those injured parties also would be transported to the ship at the earliest opportunity; perhaps just as soon as a transporter pad or even a large enough expanse of open deck became available.

So, Crusher mused as she reached for a hypo spray and tried to forget just how tired she was after hours of almost nonstop work, *it's like that.*

The diagnostic scanner positioned over her current patient's chest confirmed what she had seen with her own eyes, with the Cardassian having suffered four broken ribs and a punctured lung as a result of shrapnel from an explosion at the supply depot on Fradon II. Its location in proximity with the border separating Federation and Cardassian space was attractive from a strategic perspective. Starfleet had established an outpost here to serve as an interim facility until such time as a proper starbase could be constructed in order to support starship operations in this region.

This plan had not set well with the Cardassians.

"I still don't understand why they'd attack here," Sastro-wardoyo said as he set to work on another patient. "We're well within Federation territory."

With most of her attention on the unconscious Cardassian before her, Crusher said, "They were probably trying to send a message." Fradon II represented a significant tactical advantage for Starfleet in this area, something the Cardassians would not allow to go unchecked. "I just wish the intelligence people had crunched their numbers and statistics and probability predictions a little better." Reports from Starfleet

Intelligence had predicted the odds of a direct attack on the depot as being quite low.

"I just wish they were here," Sastrowardoyo replied. "We could use the help."

Crusher grunted, nodding in approval at the observation. The analysts and other experts responsible for the reports that had been so wrong of course were not here, just as they had not been present when Cardassian vessels arrived in orbit above the planet, delivering ground troops with the goal of seizing the outpost and its materiel. The Starfleet vessels detailed to the outpost had managed to keep the attacking ships from inflicting too much in the way of damage from orbital bombardment, while personnel on the ground were able to repel the initial assault. The holding action had succeeded long enough for Starfleet reinforcements to arrive, after which began the process of tending to the scores of casualties.

"What I don't understand is why they didn't just obliterate the entire base from orbit." Sastrowardoyo's voice was punctuated by the sound of his medical tricorder as he waved its accompanying diagnostic scanner over a female Starfleet officer who—so far as Crusher could tell—had suffered severe burns to one leg and her right torso. "Why go to all this trouble? What kind of statement does that make?"

Crusher stepped back and allowed two of her nurses to finalize their preparations for moving the wounded Cardassian from the diagnostic table. "I don't know, unless they just decided they could use the planet themselves. All the supplies and equipment down there probably looked pretty enticing, too." One of the nurses, a young Bolian female whose name Crusher could not remember, looked to her, and Crusher nodded. "He's stable for now. Prep him for surgery and keep an eye on his medication, but he can wait until after the critical cases are done." The Cardassian's injuries, though serious, were not life threatening, earning him a place in the waiting line.

For a brief moment, Crusher wondered how that simple judgment call on her part would be viewed in the days to come once a full recounting of this incident was made to both Federation and Cardassian government leaders. Despite Starfleet's doctrine of providing medical treatment to enemy casualties in a combat zone, she knew something as straightforward as prioritizing the injured based on the severity of their wounds rather than the uniform they wore often earned the Starfleet Medical Corps scorn from parties on both sides of the conflict. Still, it was a time-honored tradition, going back centuries on Earth, and strict adherence to this policy was one of the reasons medical starships, be they Starfleet or Cardassian, were allowed to operate in dangerous areas with the understanding that they were not to be targeted as combat vessels. So far, both parties to the protracted conflict had respected that rule of engagement.

An alarm from behind her made Crusher turn to see Sastrowardoyo and another nurse, now working on yet another patient deposited on one of the other treatment tables, scrambling around their stricken charge as alert indicators on the bed's diagnostic scanners blinked and flashed harsh crimson.

"He's gone into cardiac arrest!" Sastrowardoyo shouted, already maneuvering into position the equipment necessary to treat the new complication. Though she knew she was needed elsewhere and the nurse was more than qualified to handle the situation without her help, Crusher still stepped forward to assist him.

"Doctor Crusher!" called a new voice, this one from the trauma center's entrance, where two more orderlies were maneuvering another anti-grav stretcher into the already crowded room. "Head injury! She needs emergency surgery *now*!"

"Get her prepped!" Crusher ordered, leaving Sastrowardoyo and the other nurses and doctors to their own patients. At the same time, she once more attempted to push away the tendrils of fatigue doing their damnedest to ensnare her. How long had she been working? How many more patients were there still left to treat?

When would it all end?

A hand on her arm almost made her jump out of her skin, and Crusher whirled to find herself staring into the face of a Cardassian who mere moments before had been lying unconscious on her diagnostic table. His eyes, though open, were reddened, and there was no mistaking the expression of pain he was doing his best to hide.

"What the hell are you doing?" she asked, recalling after a startled moment the extent of this patient's injuries. Taking hold of his arm, she snapped, "You need to lie down. Your wounds . . ."

"Are not that extensive," the Cardassian said. "I am still able to function. There are others who require more immediate aid."

Crusher tried to guide him back to his stretcher. "I won't argue with you on that, but I don't have time to argue with you about anything right now. We're shorthanded and up to our necks in casualties. You need to . . ."

"I can help," he said, cutting her off once again. "Doctor, I too am a physician. I can assist you with treating the wounded Cardassians."

Despite her initial misgivings, Crusher was not about to turn down any offer of help. "If you're sure you're up to it." She gestured to a nearby nurse. "Get him started on the Cardassian injured. He can triage them faster than we can." Pausing, she turned back to her mysterious new benefactor. "Thanks for pitching in."

"To do otherwise would be unconscionable, I think," the Cardassian replied.

"I'm Doctor Beverly Crusher, by the way. Welcome aboard the *Sanctuary*."

"Ilona Daret, at your service."

Ten

"**D**octor Crusher?"

Jerking herself upright in the narrow bed, Crusher blinked several times, pushing away the mental fog and the reminiscences captivating her attention. How long had she been lost in her own thoughts? It took the doctor a moment to realize that her pulse was racing and that her breathing was fast and shallow. She frowned, turning toward the sound of the voice that had intruded on her recollections, and fixed on the concerned gaze of Lieutenant Rennan Konya.

"Are you all right?" asked the young officer, his expression one of mild concern. "I thought you might be dreaming, but your eyes were open."

Crusher swung her legs off the bed. "More like daydreaming," she said, pushing away the decades-old memories.

"Whatever it was," Konya said, "you seemed a bit upset."

"It was a long time ago." Forcing a smile, she asked, "Was it that obvious?"

Konya shrugged. "Even to me." Despite lacking the same degree of telepathic ability born to most of his fellow Betazoids or even Deanna Troi's capacity to read the emotional states of other beings, the lieutenant still possessed a knack for gauging people that even he often struggled to define.

Placing her hands on her hips, Crusher tried to stretch the kinks out of her back. The small, semi-enclosed bunks that served as berthing space aboard Starfleet runabouts were functional, but they were no substitute for her own bed. That, and she never could shake the feeling that she was sleeping in a coffin, which was why she tended to leave open the privacy screen.

"I actually came back here because you asked me to let you know when we were outside the range of the *Enterprise*'s sensors." Stepping back toward the open hatchway leading from the berthing area as Crusher pushed herself from the bed, Konya added, "I've already run a sweep, and so far as I can tell, we're all alone out here." He shrugged. "I suppose there could be a cloaked ship out there, but if that's the case, then we likely have bigger problems than somebody just spying on us."

"Are you always this cheerful, Lieutenant?" Crusher asked, smiling in order to take the sting out of the remark. "So, you think we're okay to execute the course change for Jevalan?" She had never been one for subterfuge or other clandestine assignments. On those few occasions in which she had undertaken such missions, she always had felt out of place, despite whatever preparation she had received. In those situations, she tended to rely on the other members of her team with the requisite training and experience.

"I don't see why not. Cruzen's already input the course. We were just waiting for your order."

"Let's do it," Crusher said. "I'm also going to need to use the comm system."

"Commanders Worf and La Forge briefed us on the situation before we left, Doctor," Konya replied. "We've got you covered. I've already set up the frequency and encryption protocols. You can use the station in the mess area."

He said nothing else, but Crusher still heard the unspoken question lacing his words. For security purposes, she and Jean-Luc had chosen not to inform Konya and Cruzen as to the real reason for their assignment, at least until such time as the *Dordogne* was well away from the *Enterprise*.

"I know you have a lot of questions, Lieutenant," she said, feeling uncomfortable with his scrutiny. "To be honest, so do I. My friend Ilona Daret only gave me the bare essentials, as he also was worried about eavesdropping. He's waiting until we get to Jevalan before he tells us everything."

Konya said, "Commander Worf said you might not be able to tell us much, at least not until we get to the planet." He smiled. "As you might imagine, Kirsten and I are pretty curious. All we know is that it's classified and possibly dangerous, and we're supposed to keep a low profile even from our own people. Captain Picard is running cover for us so that people think we're heading to Deep Space Nine, and he's hoping he can keep certain unnamed and oh-so-mysterious individuals off our backs until we get to Jevalan and your friend tells us this whole, odd story."

"Now you know almost as much as I know," Crusher said. "Once I talk to Ilona, I hope to know more, and whatever I learn, I'll share with you." She smiled. "Promise."

"Good enough for me, Doctor," Konya replied.

She knew from past experience that the lieutenant was being genuine with his response. Rennan Konya was an experienced security specialist and no stranger to classified missions and the "need to know." He had not balked at his captain or first officer informing him that details of his assignment would be kept from him and Cruzen until the appropriate time. Crusher knew that other people, and perhaps even Konya himself, might be not so ready to trust their superior officer if he was any other person, and it was a testament to the trust and loyalty Jean-Luc Picard commanded that Konya had raised not one question or doubt. That same confidence had without hesitation been extended to Crusher, as well.

Stepping back across the threshold and into the narrow

corridor leading from the bunk area, Konya asked, "Can I get you anything else?"

"I'm fine, thanks."

"I'm heading up front, then. I promised Cruzen a break." With that, Konya disappeared, his footsteps fading as he made his way toward the *Dordogne*'s cockpit.

Tea, Crusher decided. *Tea would be good.*

In the dining area of the crew compartment in the runabout's aft section, she instructed the replicator to produce a cup of her favorite tea, a blend she had come to love thanks to Marthrossi zh'Thiin, a professor with whom she had worked for a time during the *Enterprise*'s visit to Andor, just prior to the incidents that had resulted in the planet's secession from the Federation. Even now, three years after those events and after all the turmoil Andor's withdrawal had caused, zh'Thiin still saw to it that a shipment of the tea leaves made its way to Crusher on occasion. It had taken some time to perfect the replicator's re-creation of the blend, which served well enough when she lacked the actual tea leaves.

The sacrifices one must make for duty.

After a moment, a cup and saucer materialized in the replicator's alcove, and Crusher paused to inhale the tea's sweet aroma, sighing with contentment. Jean-Luc, she decided, could keep his Earl Grey.

As Konya had promised, the computer station in the crew cabin's far corner was active, with a status message on one display screen informing her that the communications protocols she had requested were input and standing by. Settling into the workstation's lone seat, Crusher paused for one sip of her tea before calling out, "Computer, open a hailing frequency and activate communications program Crusher Sanctuary Five Seven Alpha."

"Working," replied the computer's feminine voice. *"Communications parameters established. Enabling subspace transceiver protocols and transmitting hail message."*

The station's primary display screen shifted from its image of the Federation seal to a field of static, which faded after a moment to reveal the face of a Cardassian male, Ilona Daret. As she had noticed after viewing the short, pre-recorded message Daret sent her, Crusher saw again that he looked much older than the last time she had seen him. Their communications over the past twenty years had been infrequent, but during those earlier conversations Daret seemed to be wearing his advancing age with grace. Now, however, he looked tired, almost haggard. His once deep black hair had gone gray, though she still saw in his eyes the intelligence and compassion she had first come to know all those years ago on the *Sanctuary*.

"Ilona," she said, smiling, "it's good to see you again."

On the viewscreen, Daret replied, *"It is good to see you again as well, Beverly. It truly has been too long. I only wish we could be communicating under more agreeable circumstances. Hopefully, once these matters are behind us, we will have more time for more pleasant conversations."*

Aware that despite all of Konya's assurances, any communications from the *Dordogne* might well be subject to monitoring, so Crusher wanted to keep this conversation short. Just after their departure from the *Enterprise,* Konya had debated with her the wisdom even of trying to contact Daret before reaching Jevalan, but the unusual circumstances that had put into motion her current mission had not allowed her to depart with any more information than her friend had provided on the data chip. She had to know more before they arrived at the planet, if for no other reason than to get some idea as to whether she might want to contact Jean-Luc to send more help.

"So, what's the big mystery, Ilona?" she asked, leaning forward in her seat. "We're going to an awful lot of trouble to avoid attracting any unwanted attention."

"I know, but I believe these precautions are necessary. You'll

*understand once you see the evidence we have collected, Beverly.
One of my colleagues, who left here on a mission to share this
information with a trusted confidant on Bajor, has disappeared.
I fear the worst for him, and for us, if the wrong people realize
the scope of what we've found here. So, please forgive me if I seem
overzealous in my desire to protect not just the information, but
also my safety. Yours, too, for that matter."*

"Safety?" Crusher frowned. "You mean from Ishan?
How? Does this have to do with why you're on Jevalan?
What are you even doing there, anyway?"

Despite the continued speculation that the Federation's
interim president might well have some involvement in the
assassination of Nanietta Bacco and the Bajoran's insistence
on seeing to it that the movements of key Starfleet vessels—and their commanders—were closely monitored and
even controlled in the case of the *Enterprise,* nothing yet had
pointed to Ishan Anjar posing an actual, credible threat.
Then again, that people like Ishan were able to work their
way into positions of power was due in no small part to their
ability to carry out all manner of dreadful deeds without
raising suspicion.

Sighing, Daret said, *"You were witness to the role this
world played during our oppression of Bajor. As one of several
continuing efforts to heal the grave wounds we inflicted upon
their people, we have committed to helping with the location
and identification of those who died at labor camps here on Jevalan and other worlds. I joined the team here almost a year ago
now. It is slow, painstaking work, with thousands of missing
Bajorans still waiting to be found, but we have achieved some
success."*

Crusher frowned. "What does any of this have to do with
Ishan?"

*"It is a matter of record that your president is a survivor of the
ordeal inflicted here upon him and his fellow Bajorans, though
very little is known about his activities at the time of the final*

uprising and Cardassian evacuation." Daret paused, reaching for a glass of some unidentified beverage. To Crusher, it was obvious that her friend was uncomfortable discussing this dark chapter in his people's history. *"There are stories of mass killings leading up to the revolt, and rumors persist to this day of a handful of Bajorans collaborating with the Cardassians. As you know, such traitors have been hunted and prosecuted by the Bajoran government—as well as vigilantes—in the years since the Occupation."*

"What are you saying, Ilona?" Crusher asked, already sensing what her friend was about to reveal, but not wanting to believe it. "Do you think Ishan was a collaborator during the Occupation?"

Daret at first did not say anything, though his own expression told her that he saw her skepticism and uncertainty. Crusher watched him look around the confines of whatever room he was using for this conversation, as if verifying that no one might be nearby, eavesdropping. He then reached to something she could not see, but she did hear a string of telltale beeps indicating he was interacting with a computer or other console.

"You are certain your communications frequency is encrypted?"

"Of course," Crusher replied, though she still looked at her own workstation to confirm that the scrambling and encoding protocols Konya had prepared were still active. She knew the lieutenant was monitoring sensor readings and would notify her if he suspected any sort of attempt to tap into the secure communication.

After another brief interval spent in silence, Daret leaned closer to his own comm station's visual pickup. *"Forensic analysis of remains that recently were uncovered here by one of our excavation teams have been identified with veritable certainty as those of a Bajoran laborer named Ishan Anjar."*

Eleven

"**H**ey, what do you know? It's raining."

Turning from the large transparasteel window set into the guest suite's rear wall, Lieutenant Chen regarded Picard with one of her trademark sardonic grins. "Was the weather mentioned in the travel brochure? Because if it wasn't, then I think we owe it to ourselves to visit the nearest tourism office and lodge a formal complaint."

"Perhaps we'll do that after we're done here for the day," Picard said, sitting at a table positioned before the window and sipping from a cup of tea. "It's not as though you have to walk around in it."

Like most of the major population centers scattered across the planet, Ferenginar's capital city was protected from the incessant storms by a giant dome. Lightning streaking across the cloud-riddled sky reflected off the dome's transparent surface, resulting in a constant, beautiful light show that had captured Picard's attention for the past several minutes.

"But it sure does put a crimp in my sunbathing plans for after lunch, sir," Chen replied. She made a show of offering an exasperated shrug. "I guess that means I can go to the afternoon conference."

Picard smiled, setting his tea back onto its coaster. "If I can't get out of it, you have no chance of avoiding it."

"I'm well aware that rank has its privileges, sir," the lieutenant said, moving from the window to take a seat in one of the chairs opposite Picard, "but is torturing your subordinates listed among them?"

"It's one of my personal favorites," Picard replied.

"I knew it." Saying nothing for a moment, instead casting her gaze around the ornately appointed suite that had been given to the captain as a place where he could take a break between the conference sessions or even conduct private business. All of the fixtures were gold, and gold also was prominent in the tapestries adorning the walls as well as the area rugs beneath their feet and the curtains framing the windows. A crystal pitcher sat at the center of the table with a set of glasses, and Picard already had watched Chen scan them with her tricorder to determine that the table setting had been fashioned from a rare mineral native to Ferenginar that was quite valuable.

"This place is incredible," she said after a moment. "It's nice to look at, of course, but hardly practical."

Though the unchecked materialistic display did nothing for Picard, he still could appreciate its aesthetic beauty. "The Ferengi aren't typically known for their appreciation of the arts, but it does exist, even if it still lends itself to their more typical, capitalistic pursuits." Over the years, he had seen several paintings and sculptures by renowned Ferengi artists, though common tastes for such things tended to run to the "sophisticated," as others might label it. Picard had noted the odd, even lewd fixtures in the guest suite's lavatory and made a mental note not to bring René down here for a visit.

Before Chen could offer a rebuttal to his observation, the chime for the guest suite's door sounded.

"Are you expecting anyone, sir?" Chen asked.

Picard shook his head. "Come," he called out, and the door slid aside to reveal a Romulan dressed in dark, ceremonial robes that contrasted with his pale, yellow-green complexion. His dark hair was cut in the familiar style worn by most Romulan males, and his eyes, peering out from beneath his pronounced brow, seemed to bore into Picard as he regarded him from the doorway.

"Captain Picard," said Ambassador Teclas, nodding his head in greeting. "I hope I am not intruding."

Though surprised by the unannounced visit, Picard nevertheless decided to play it as though he had been expecting his caller. Rising from his seat, he said, "Good afternoon, Ambassador. I was only taking a brief respite before returning to the conference. What can I do for you?" So far as he knew, this was the first time any member of the Typhon Pact's diplomatic delegation had ventured behind the conference room or their own guest suites since arriving on Ferenginar.

Teclas waited until Picard directed Chen to take her leave before he entered the suite. His curtailed stride and restrained gait coupled with the length of his robes and how they covered even his feet gave him the appearance of floating across the carpeted floor as he moved farther into the room.

"Before we proceed any further," Teclas said, "I wish to correct an oversight I made at the beginning at the conference. On behalf of Praetor Kamemor, I offer condolences on the loss of President Bacco. Her death was a tragedy, not just for the Federation, but also for the peace that exists between all our people. I have expressed this sentiment to your diplomatic representatives, but Ambassador Sherwood seemed . . . less than convinced of my sincerity."

Picard replied, "Don't take it personally. Ambassador Sherwood normally is less than convinced of my sincerity, as well. However, you can be assured that I will pass on your sentiments to President Ishan and the Federation Council at my earliest opportunity. I know that Praetor Kamemor and President Bacco worked tirelessly to forge a lasting peace between our peoples." He paused, offering a small smile.

"For what it's worth, I greatly respect your praetor and what she strove to accomplish."

"I felt the same way about President Bacco," Teclas replied. "Captain, I know this meeting is unusual, but your reputation is that of an individual with an open mind and a predilection for diplomacy over military action. Your standing as one of Starfleet's senior and most-respected officers gives you a perspective and perhaps even an attention not afforded to your contemporaries. I suspect that your status also serves you well with respect to gaining an audience with your superiors."

"I do well enough," Picard said. Prior to attending the first conference sessions here on Ferenginar, he had reviewed what information was available on Teclas and came away thinking he—like most Romulans—was patient and analytical, preferring to listen rather than speak: a trait uncommon to diplomats, in Picard's experience. Indeed, he had said little during the previous conference sessions, allowing his colleagues to engage in the debate with representatives of the Ferengi government. However, Starfleet's intelligence file on the ambassador was thin, giving Picard little insight into Teclas' background other than what he presented while engaged in activities such as these negotiations.

Picard indicated for the ambassador to have a seat at the table. "Would you like something to drink?" he asked as he ordered a fresh cup of tea from the room's replicator.

"No, thank you," Teclas replied. He waited in silence as Picard retrieved his tea and took his own seat at the table before saying, "Captain, there has been much speculation that the Typhon Pact is somehow culpable in President Bacco's assassination. In particular, some faction from within the Tzenkethi Coalition is believed responsible, at least according to a handful of your own government leaders. Despite whatever ideological differences may exist between us, we would never condone such a barbarous act. Further, we stand ready to offer any possible assistance in bringing the assassins to justice, whoever they may be."

Taking a sip of his tea, Picard asked, "Do you have any information as to the identity of the perpetrators?"

"I do not. What I do know is that our praetor has made it a priority to determine whether anyone within the Romulan Empire may have been involved in the plot. It is my understanding that the other Pact members are conducting similar investigations, but as you no doubt realize, these sorts of matters tend to be handled with varying degrees of . . . *commitment* . . . depending on the party in question."

"Indeed I do, Ambassador," Picard replied. While there existed little evidence implicating the Tzenkethi or any of the Typhon Pact's other members in President Bacco's assassination, it was heartening to hear that the Pact itself—or, some of its elements, at least—seemed determined to prevent the heinous incident from sparking open hostilities between it and the Federation. Similar resolve between Praetor Kamemor and President Bacco had prevented war between the two powers following the destruction of Deep Space 9 two years earlier. Kamemor already was on record denouncing Bacco's murder almost from the moment the news had spread across the quadrant. Was it all a ruse, a desperate attempt to cast suspicion away from the Pact and perhaps even the Romulan Empire itself? Of course, Picard had no intention of sharing with Teclas the information he possessed regarding the culpability of the True Way for Bacco's assassination. There was no real proof to substantiate the allegation, for one thing, but Picard also figured there was no harm in allowing the Pact members to think they—or yet another rogue element within the upstart coalition—were suspected by the Federation of having at least some involvement. If nothing else, it might foster greater communication between the two powers as both sides worked to avoid war.

Movement at the doorway leading to the suite's other

room caught Picard's attention, and he looked over to see Chen standing at the entrance, her expression one of nervousness.

"Yes, Lieutenant?"

"I'm sorry to interrupt, Captain, but I've just been contacted by the *Enterprise*. Commander Worf is reporting that Admiral Riker needs to speak with you immediately. He's ready to route the connection down here at your order, sir."

Rising from his chair, Teclas said, "I have taken up too much of your time as it is, Captain. Thank you for meeting with me. Perhaps we can do so again, under more pleasant circumstances."

"I appreciate you coming to see me, Ambassador," Picard replied as he stood. "As I said, I will see to it that what you've shared with me is forwarded on to President Ishan and the council."

Teclas bowed his head. "I am most appreciative, Captain. Good day." With a nod to Chen, the Romulan turned and exited the room, leaving Picard alone with his subordinate.

"Well, that was interesting," he said. Retrieving his tea, he moved from the table to the comm station situated in the wall on the room's far side. "Lieutenant, did Commander Worf indicate why Admiral Riker might be calling?"

"No, sir," Chen replied. "He just said it was important."

"Very well. You're dismissed, Lieutenant. I'll call for you when I'm finished here." As Chen turned to depart the suite, Picard tapped his communicator badge. "Picard to *Enterprise*."

"*Enterprise*. *Worf here*."

"Patch Admiral Riker down to me, Number One." Taking the lone seat positioned before the suite's communications station, Picard was just getting settled when the single display monitor activated, followed by a scrolling stream of Ferengi text that then was replaced by a Federation seal and the caption ENCRYPTION PROTOCOLS ENABLED. CODE

47AT-1. Picard nodded in approval at that, knowing it meant Commander La Forge had succeeded in employing security parameters that would ensure the conversation was not being monitored by outside parties. The code designation La Forge had appended to the message was the chief engineer's way of authenticating to Picard that the protective measures were active and—for the moment, at least—uncompromised. La Forge also had told him that Riker was employing a similar strategy at his end, with the assistance of his trusted chief engineer from the *Titan*.

A moment later, the graphic was replaced by the face of Admiral William Riker. Picard noted the small green icon in the screen's lower left corner, another indicator supplied by La Forge to indicate the frequency's secure status. He knew that Worf would be monitoring the connection—though not the actual conversation—to guard against possible infiltration.

"Jean-Luc," Riker said, smiling. *"Good to see you, as always."*

"Likewise, Admiral."

Riker's smile widened. *"We've been friends long enough that I think we can dispense with the formalities, don't you? At least now, while we're on a supposedly secure channel?"*

"Very well, then, Will." Picard held up his tea in salute.

"Have you heard from Beverly?"

"Still on her way to Deep Space Nine, at last report." Picard knew that Riker was asking the question under the guise of "catching up" and perhaps using the feint to determine whether their communications actually were being monitored. Glancing to the display screen's bottom corner, Picard noted that the icon there remained a steady green. "She's due to arrive there in a day or so, if my math's right. René misses her terribly, of course."

"I can imagine. Deanna sends her best. Natasha is growing like a weed."

"As is René."

"*My father always told me that kids grow up too fast. Now I know what he meant. How's Ferenginar?*"

"Wet, and boring." After sipping from the tea, Picard set the cup aside. It was time, he thought, to test the limits of their secure connection. "Will, you and I both know the *Enterprise* being here is a colossal waste of time."

"*Not for long. I've got a new assignment for you. We've just done some reshuffling of sector patrol routes and there's a gap, which the* Enterprise *has been ordered to fill. You'll be relieving the* Sutherland."

"Patrol duty?" That was perhaps the last thing Picard would have expected Riker to say. "You can't be serious?"

"*I am, and so is everyone else.*" Riker paused, sighing. "*Ordinarily I'd think it was a misuse of the flagship and her captain, but with tensions heating up and all the posturing taking place with both the council and the Typhon Pact, it's felt that we need to 'enhance our visibility' along the borders, particularly with respect to the Pact's more prominent players.*"

"The Romulans?"

"*For starters, though for obvious reasons we're also beefing up patrols along our border with Breen territory. However, you and the* Enterprise *will be heading for the Neutral Zone.*"

Picard considered that for a moment. "Starfleet has a habit of sending me to the Neutral Zone whenever they want to get me out of their hair for a while, don't they?"

"*I guess they figure you have a long way to travel if you want to cause trouble.*" Riker's smile returned. "*However, these new orders also allow me to give you something else to take care of on your way out there. Remember the last thing I told you?*"

Picard's gaze once more shifted to the screen's bottom edge and the indicator that continued to glow a steady green. "Indeed I do," he said, recalling the veiled message Riker had dispatched soon after his own confrontation with President Ishan.

Sometimes the enemy hides in plain sight.

Riker now was convinced that President Ishan—perhaps guided by his former chief of staff, Galif jav Velk—had somehow conspired with the True Way to perpetrate Nanietta Bacco's assassination. Riker was pursuing that angle from his end, but he had intimated the presence of obstacles hindering his efforts. The two men had not been able to converse on this subject since then, for fear of their communications being monitored.

"Well, I have reason to believe the circle is larger than we think," Riker said, *"and that involved players are . . . closer to home. I've been researching recent orders cut for various ships and starbases to see if anything sticks out. I haven't found too much yet, but there are some patterns emerging. As for your next assignment, I need you to go to Starbase Three Ten and pick up a shipment of supplies for the colony on Acheron."*

Frowning, Picard said, "Starbase Three Ten? That's a bit out of our way so far as traveling to the Neutral Zone."

"I know, and to be honest, there already was another ship scheduled to make that delivery, but I need you to take a look around while you're there and see if anything strikes you as unusual. The starbase commander's a friend of yours, right?"

"Yes," Picard replied. "Admiral Rhaast and I went to the Academy together." He paused, realizing what Riker might be suggesting. "I've known her for decades, Will. You don't think she's involved in any of this, do you?"

Riker held up a hand. *"I have no reason to believe that, Jean-Luc. However, some of the ships that have been given assignments that took them to Starbase Three Ten for one reason or another trace back to directives handed down from someone very high up."* He stopped there, but his expression was enough for Picard to complete the thought.

Ishan, or someone in his inner circle. Velk, perhaps. The president pro tempore's chief of staff already had made his presence known during the interim administration, particularly in his dealings with Admiral Akaar and Riker himself.

"What I want you to do," Riker continued, *"is simply try and look around and see if you can determine whether anything odd might be going on, which we then might be able to trace back. Maybe Admiral Rhaast has noticed something. With all the ship traffic that starbase gets, it's a good chance something's stuck out for her."*

Considering how he might go sneaking about the installation in command of one of his oldest friends still on active Starfleet duty, Picard said, "And if I find something? What then?"

Riker shrugged. *"One step at a time, Jean-Luc."*

Before Picard could say anything, something on his monitor caught his attention, and he saw that the green icon had turned red. If La Forge was right, then that only could mean one thing.

Someone's listening. He had no way to know who might now be monitoring the conversation, and he could only hope that his chief engineer was at this moment attempting to trace to its source whatever signal he had detected.

"Very well, Admiral," Picard said, forcing himself not to sit straighter in his chair or do anything else that might tip off possible eavesdroppers that their presence was known. He saw in Riker's eyes that his friend had received the same warning from his own people. "Once the afternoon session is concluded and I can take my leave of the Grand Nagus, we'll make course for Starbase Three Ten. I'll have the estimated time of arrival and departure for Acheron with my next report."

"Excellent, Captain," Riker replied, playing his part. *"I know the detour is a bit outside the norm, but the* Enterprise *is the only ship in the vicinity that's large enough to handle the entire consignment and get there in a timely fashion. Once that's concluded, you'll be free to head for the Neutral Zone to relieve the* Sutherland.*"* He smiled. *"Thanks for adding the extra stop. I owe you dinner the next time you're back this way."*

"A debt I shall most certainly collect, Admiral. Picard out."

His smile faded as the image shifted from Riker to the Federation seal before reverting to the official symbol of the Ferengi Alliance. Picard watched as the red icon lingered on the display for an extra moment before it, too, faded.

Had someone, either Ishan or one his confidants, heard enough of the conversation to damage whatever plan Riker had put into motion? There was no way to be sure, though Picard trusted La Forge's technical expertise when it came to defeating electronic eavesdropping. The only course of action would be to stick to the scheme Riker had plotted and carry out both his legitimate assignment as well as the more clandestine tasks the admiral had given him. As his former first officer might say, whoever else had entered the game would be keeping their cards close to their vest, waiting for the right moment to play their hand.

Picard just hoped that his crew—and Beverly, for that matter—would be able to cover that bet.

Twelve

Grateful for the momentary respite, Beverly Crusher dropped onto the bench along the starboard side of the shuttlecraft *Justman*'s cargo compartment and slumped against the bulkhead. She blew out her breath and closed her eyes, already feeling the first tendrils of sleep teasing her exhausted mind and body.

I don't need much, she thought. *Just a month, or so. I think I'm starting to get a little old for this kind of thing.*

How long had it been since their arrival? A glance to the chronometer on the cockpit's console told her almost nine hours had elapsed since the *Enterprise* had entered orbit above this world. The time between then and now was but a blur, with Commander Riker leading the first away team in order to give Captain Picard a hands-on assessment of the situation here on the planet's surface. The Cardassians had left devastation in their wake before evacuating the planet with its collection of encampments and other outposts, strip mining operations, scores of bedraggled slave laborers, and even a significant number of Cardassians. It was the latter part of the entire tragic equation that had struck Crusher harder than anything else. After all, it was expected that the Cardassians would treat Bajorans as disposable, but their own people? Seeing that, and how some of them had been treated at the hands of those who had risen up to throw off the shackles of their oppression, had all but made her ill.

There had been precious little time for such personal failings, as no sooner had she and Riker delivered their initial reports to the captain than Picard and the commanders of the other two starships that had accompanied the *Enterprise*—the *Farragut* as well as the hospital ship *Centaur*—had begun mobilizing response teams to send to the surface. Now it was nine hours later, and Crusher was certain that she and her medical and other support personnel—to say nothing of the comparable teams from the other starships—had only just begun to have any appreciable impact on the number of refugees being routed through their processing and treatment facility.

"Well, that was a great rehearsal," a voice said. "I think we're ready for the real thing. Can't say I'm looking forward to the reviews, though."

Crusher turned to see Lieutenant Miranda Kadohata, one of the *Enterprise*'s junior operations officers, standing at the foot of the shuttlecraft's rear ramp. Her thin smile was humorless, though her expression warmed as Crusher acknowledged her.

"Opening nights are always the hardest," she said, leaning forward on the bench. "Do I look as tired as I feel?"

Frowning, Kadohata asked, "I don't know. Do you feel dead?"

"I wish I felt that good."

"Then you look great."

The quick banter elicited a small chuckle as Crusher stood from the bench and tried to stretch tired muscles, doing her best to ignore the dirt and dried blood that spattered the medical smock she wore over her uniform. As for Kadohata, the gold fabric of her uniform was dirty, and her boots and legs were covered with mud. Strands of her dark hair, normally held in a tight bun at the back of her head, hung loose about her face and shoulders. There were circles beneath her brown eyes and smudges of dirt—or something else—on her cheeks.

"Do you want some coffee?" Crusher asked, stepping across the *Justman*'s cargo compartment to the small replicator in the forward bulkhead.

Shaking her head, Kadohata grimaced. "I've had enough coffee for one day, I think. Maybe even the next three or four." Then, she shrugged. "Oh, to hell with it. Cream and sugar, please."

After providing the appropriate instructions to the replicator, Crusher turned away from the mechanism. "What have they had you doing? Come to think of it, why are you even down here, anyway?"

Kadohata replied, "I've been asking myself that same question all day. The simple answer is that bodies are needed whenever we're short staffed down here. Commander Data detailed our section to help out the engineering teams with infrastructure repairs."

Two cups materialized in the replicator's alcove, and Crusher retrieved them. Handing one to Kadohata, she said, "Lucky you."

"Don't I know it." Pausing to take a sip of her coffee, she held up the cup in salute. "Thank you, by the way." She reached up to push aside a lock of hair that had fallen across her forehead. "Now that the surviving refugees have been moved from the Tabata labor camp, I've been overseeing repairs over there. The power generators and water filtration system were destroyed during the final attack. I guess I should be thankful I wasn't assigned to remains handling. According to a friend of mine who's on that detail? They've catalogued nearly a thousand bodies." She shook her head. "I honestly don't know what the Cardassians were trying to do when they pulled out of here. From the reports I've read, they had more than enough firepower to level all the camps and everyone in them. Were they hoping to just leave any survivors here to die from starvation or exposure?"

Crusher sighed as she sipped her own coffee. "The official statement from the Cardassian government is that the detachment assigned here fled because they feared for their lives in the face of a massive resistance effort on the part of the Bajorans." It had sounded ridiculous when Captain Picard had briefed her and the rest of the *Enterprise* senior staff on the Jevalan situation, and Crusher considered it ludicrous now that she had spent the day wading through the aftermath of the Cardassians' evacuation. "I think they just cut their losses and got the hell out of there, but not before making one last statement before running away like a bunch of cowards."

More than a week had passed between the Cardassians' departure and the arrival of the first Starfleet vessel, a small scout ship without the resources to provide any meaningful aid to the hundreds of survivors in the seven different labor camps scattered across the planet. The *Enterprise, Centaur,* and *Farragut* had arrived within hours of each other, and Starfleet was sending additional ships to assist in the relief effort for the next day or so, but the three starships and their crews would bear the brunt of the work involved. Not wanting to overtax any of the vessels with survivors, initial treatment and processing centers had been established in hasty fashion in areas adjacent to the three largest labor camps, which were situated far enough away so that the emergency facilities would not be overrun by hordes of frantic survivors. Refugees were beamed in groups to receiving areas for initial processing and examinations before being transported to the medical stations set up at one of the three main hubs. The camp established by the *Enterprise* groups had been teeming with incoming survivors at a steady though not overwhelming rate, owing in large part to the triage and other efforts of those satellite locations.

Elsewhere, temporary housing sites were being constructed to billet those Bajorans who had no desire to return to the labor camps, though a significant number of the former slaves were taking matters into their own hands, building interim shelters within the existing compounds. With rumors of the Cardassians preparing to withdraw from their occupation of Bajor, it was not unreasonable to assume that the refugees from this and similar camps on other worlds would be returned to their homeworld, but what would be waiting for them there? Large sections of Bajor had been strip-mined, while others had borne the brunt of ecological damage at the hands of Cardassian oppressors. It would take years to repair the wounds—both physical and otherwise—inflicted upon Bajor and its people, if indeed such healing even was possible.

Crusher's communicator badge chirped.

"Data to Doctor Crusher," said the voice of the *Enterprise*'s second officer.

Setting aside her coffee, Crusher grunted as she exchanged knowing glances with Kadohata. "So much for break time." Tapping her badge, she said, "Crusher here. What can I do for you, Commander?"

"I am sorry to disturb you," the android replied, *"but a new group of refugees has just arrived at the medical station, and your presence has been requested."*

"Is there an emergency?" Crusher frowned, moving toward the *Justman*'s ramp.

"Not that I am aware of, but some of the new arrivals are Cardassian."

Crusher grunted. "Understood, Commander. I'm on my way. Crusher out."

"I was wondering if we'd be getting any," Kadohata said as Crusher stepped off the ramp and they both set off toward the medical station. "Most of the Cardassians we've found so far have been beamed up to the *Farragut*."

"Which is probably why they're still alive." Crusher knew that in the wake of the mass exodus from Jevalan, those Cardassians left behind had been at the mercy of the surviving Bajoran workers. Early reports from the first Starfleet vessel to reach the planet, as well as those submitted by Commander Riker and other survey teams taking stock of the situation, detailed how many of those Cardassians had not been treated with anything resembling compassion. There also were reports of Bajorans protecting small bands of Cardassians from retribution, for reasons that at this point remained unknown. Were the Bajorans collaborators, or perhaps they merely were acting in what they perceived to be the best interests of the remaining workers in the event their Cardassian overlords returned?

All questions for somebody else to answer.

Crusher and Kadohata made their way to the security checkpoint that served as the entrance to the medical station. A protective perimeter had been established around the temporary encampment, consisting of portable force-field generators. Four checkpoints were set up around the barricade, each manned by a two-person team from the *Enterprise*'s security detachment. As she and Kadohata drew closer, Crusher saw that other members of the security cadre were working to organize the newest group of arriving refugees into columns for orderly movement into and through the processing station. Two lines of people had formed to either side of the checkpoint, one consisting of Bajorans and the other containing Cardassians. While the Cardassians were standing in silence, some with their heads bowed while others glared with defiance either at the Bajorans or the Starfleet officers, the former labor camp workers were making their displeasure known. Verbal assaults filled the air, and once or twice Crusher saw a rock or clump of mud thrown in the Cardassians' direction.

"Well," Kadohata said, keeping her voice low, "this looks

like fun." Crusher glanced down to see that while the lieutenant had not brandished her phaser, her right hand now hovered near the weapon.

Despite the shouting and gesturing, *Enterprise* security personnel, most of them wielding phaser rifles, seemed to have the situation under control. The entrance to the checkpoint was clear, and Crusher and Kadohata were waved in by a female lieutenant whose face Crusher recognized but whose name escaped her. She had only a moment to consider the small lapse before she entered the medical station's receiving area to find Data waiting for them.

"Good evening, Doctor," the android said. "I know that you were resting, but it appears we have an unusual situation with one of the new arrivals."

"The Cardassians?" Crusher asked as she moved toward the entrance to the main treatment area. "What's wrong?" Though she had done her best to make sure that every member of the *Enterprise*'s medical contingent was capable at least of diagnosing injuries and illnesses in numerous species from across and even outside the Federation, she knew there always would be some abnormality that might at first defy classification. She further expected that to occur in situations involving members of races that her people might not encounter on a regular basis. So far as she was aware, she possessed greater experience treating Cardassians than anyone else on her staff.

Gesturing to an area of the treatment center that had been cordoned off with privacy screens, Data replied, "We were preparing this group of Cardassians for transport to the *Farragut*, but one of them insists on speaking with you first."

"Is he someone in authority?" Kadohata asked. "If so, then Lieutenant Worf or Commander Riker is going to want to talk to him."

"No, Lieutenant. He claims to have been assigned to the Olanda labor camp during the Occupation, which the

U.S.S. Centaur is overseeing for refugee processing, but he asked to be sent here." Looking to Crusher, Data added, "He specifically requested to speak with you, Doctor. He says that he is a physician."

"Wait, what?" Crusher asked, her eyes widening in realization. "A doctor? You're sure?" She knew it was a silly question to ask Data of all people, but she could not help the reflexive response. Hastening her pace, she asked, "Is he hurt?"

"He has suffered only minor injuries, Doctor," Data replied, following her as she reached for the privacy screen and pulled it aside to reveal a cot and a chair, and Crusher could not help but smile as she recognized the Cardassian male standing before her. There were cuts and bruises on his head and face, his hair was dirty and mussed, and the clothing he wore—not the typical heavy armor of a soldier, but instead a simple gray jumpsuit—was torn and dirty.

"Ilona," she said, reaching out to take the extended hands of Ilona Daret. "I can't believe it."

Daret returned the smile. "Beverly Crusher. I think it would be beneficial to both of us if we ceased meeting like this."

Thirteen

Jevalan, Doltiri System

Standing at the edge of the ridge that acted as the western boundary of the joint Bajoran-Cardassian temporary settlement, Beverly Crusher studied the remains of the Tabata labor camp. Even though more than half a kilometer separated her from the site, she still was able to identify the different structures as well as the network of connecting paths that cut patterns through what once had been the central courtyard. While the area at that time had been well manicured due to the thankless efforts of Bajoran workers, unchecked grass and other vegetation had long since reclaimed the expanse of open ground. Such was the case with the rest of the encampment, with the bases of the perimeter fence stanchions as well as the towers that once had held armed guards now obscured by weeds and other local flora. The odd member of the indigenous wildlife could be seen wandering around the deserted camp, searching for food or shelter.

A chill gripped Crusher as the wind kicked up, and without thinking, she hugged her arms close to her chest. Her hands brushed against the rough material of her top, and she looked down to inspect the clothing she now wore in lieu of her Starfleet uniform. It was Lieutenant Konya who had suggested they wear civilian attire—specifically, clothing favored by Bajorans—in order to better blend in with the personnel living and working here and at the nearby excavation sites. It was a weak ploy, Crusher knew, unlikely to fool anyone tasked by President Ishan to track them, but if it gained them even a few moments' worth of advantage or surprise over any would-be followers, then it was worth the effort.

For the same reasons, Konya and Lieutenant Cruzen had taken steps to conceal the runabout that had brought them to Jevalan. Rather than keeping the craft here on the surface, he had programmed the *Dordogne*'s onboard computer to maintain a fixed orbit over the planet's northern magnetic pole in order to better conceal it from sensors. Crusher had smiled upon hearing the lieutenant's suggestion, asking him if he had learned that trick from Admiral Riker, to which Konya had replied, "You can't go wrong with the classics."

Footsteps behind her made Crusher turn to see Ilona Daret walking toward her, following one of the narrow paths leading up from the archeological and forensic expedition's small base camp. The Cardassian's gray hair moved with the breeze wafting across the ridge, and he was a bit stoop shouldered as he walked. Still, his pace was impressive for one of his years, though when he arrived at the top of the ridge to stand beside her, Crusher noted that his breathing was somewhat labored. He gestured past her toward the plateau and the abandoned encampment.

"I imagine it looks much different than the last time you saw it. Current plans call for the entire area to be turned into an historical monument, you know."

Crusher replied, "So I've heard." She watched as he straightened his posture and took a deep breath. The simple action seemed to calm him. "The fresh air seems to agree with you."

"I haven't been this active in ages," Daret said, smiling. "I've done more meaningful work in the year I've spent here than the last five spent in clinics and laboratories." Seeing her expression as she eyed him with skepticism, he added, "Oh, don't misunderstand me. I miss my patients from my practice on Cardassia Prime, and I did not come here without first ensuring all of them were to be well cared for by my replacement." He gestured toward the abandoned labor camp. "This, however? There's a chapter of history—not just our history but also that of the Bajorans—that needs to be preserved and remembered, for all time. That's why I'm here and why I've spent so much time over there."

The aged Cardassian pointed past the main camp to another, larger compound just visible beyond a row of trees, which featured buildings and other structures similar to the closer location. Even from this distance, Crusher could see figures moving about, a few walking alone, but most of them working in clusters of four or five. Land vehicles maneuvered over the broken terrain as well as along narrow paths pressed into the barren earth that allowed the vehicles access to different excavation sites.

"That is where the real story of this world is to be found," Daret said, "beneath earth and rubble, beneath sweat and blood, beneath tears and lies." He paused, shaking his head. "There are many things about my people in which I take great pride, but what happened here will never be one of them."

Crusher reached over and placed a hand on her friend's arm. Ilona Daret always had been something very different from the other Cardassians she had encountered during her career. While she had met ones similar to Daret who seemed to possess an awareness about morality and their people's place in the interstellar order of things, it was her experience that such individuals tended to get lost amid the quite valid perception of the Cardassian Union as a militaristic state. This, despite the Cardassian people's rich history of appreciating science, literature, and the arts. Much of that was long past, of course, owing to the growth of the Cardassian military industrial complex, numerous conflicts with rival interstellar powers, and an ill-fated alliance with the Dominion. Cardassia Prime still suffered the scars of those choices and the attitudes that had allowed them to occur in the first place. The path to healing would be long and littered with obstacles both known and unforeseen.

But with the help of people like Ilona, they at least have a chance.

"Your companions have returned from your ship," Daret said. "They are securing your equipment and . . . other items . . . in my cottage."

Crusher's eyes narrowed at her friend's euphemism for the weapons Konya and Cruzen would have brought with them from the *Dordogne*. "It's just a precaution, Ilona. I don't think we can be too careful, about any of this, and you haven't even told me the whole story yet."

"I know," Daret replied. "It is well past time that I show you what I've been safeguarding, and for what I now need your assistance."

Leaving the ridgeline, Crusher followed the Cardassian back to the small settlement that—according to Daret—had started here as a collection of emergency shelters nearly two years earlier. Over time, it had grown to encompass more than two dozen buildings of varying size, arrayed in haphazard fashion around an open field that was treated as the community's "town square." The buildings themselves were the sort of prefabricated structures designed for easy assembly and removal. To Crusher, the scene resembled any number of new colony outposts she had visited over the years, including the small villages in which she had lived as a child with her grandmother on planets like Arvada III and Caldos II. Those colonies on those two worlds eventually had grown and thrived into cities and other communities scattered across their respective planets, both of which now were full-fledged members of the Federation. Would something like that happen here, one day? It would be interesting if representatives from Bajor and the Cardassian Union, especially given their people's joint, tragic history, elected to found a permanent home here.

Stranger things have happened, Crusher conceded.

Dozens of Bajorans and Cardassians, as well as a handful of humans and members of other species, moved about the various buildings. Everyone was dressed in some variation of simple attire designed for working hard and getting dirty. Not a uniform or other indicator of a government or Starfleet or other military presence was visible. In this respect, at least, Crusher and her team now blended with the rest of the population. According to Daret, transports and other private vessels made routine stops at the planet, either to transfer personnel or with new supplies and other equipment, so the arrival in camp of three new faces would—in theory—not attract undue notice.

Navigating the walking path leading across the square, Crusher followed her friend to the simple, one-story structure that served both as his domicile as well as his primary workspace when he was not visiting one of the excavation sites. As they entered the building's foyer, Crusher once more saw the collection of diagnostic and forensic equipment arrayed around the small laboratory. While another, larger mortuary facility had been designated for the delivery, processing, and examination of remains, it was staffed at all hours of the day as new discoveries were retrieved from the camps or the graveyards that sat adjacent to those compounds. Daret and a handful of the project's senior members had set up their own work areas in order to escape the morgue's constant activity, allowing them to work in relative quiet and privacy.

Lucky for us.

Footsteps echoed from a narrow passageway connecting the foyer with rooms farther inside the building, as Konya and Cruzen walked into view. Over their own simple work attire, both security officers wore light jackets, which Crusher suspected was a means of concealing whatever weapons with which the security officers had chosen to arm themselves.

"Everything settled in?" Crusher asked.

"Yes, Doctor, and the *Dordogne* is parked in its polar orbit. I've programmed the onboard computer to maintain a lock on our comm badges." Konya opened his jacket to reveal his own communicator, pinned to his chest as if he still was wearing his Starfleet uniform. "It'll respond to normal verbal commands, but if something happens and you need a fast beam-out, just tap your badge twice. That'll activate the emergency extraction directive I've given the computer."

"Are you expecting trouble, Lieutenant?" Daret asked.

Cruzen replied, "We always expect trouble, sir. It's part of our job description."

The aged Cardassian smiled. "Prudent." He turned to Crusher. "Since you're all here, I see no reason to delay this any longer." After first tapping the keypad near the entrance, which Crusher saw was the control to engage the door's lock, Daret gestured for her and the others to follow as he led them into his lab. A computer workstation resided atop a small desk in one corner, but it was the only piece of equipment Crusher recognized, save for the examination table occupying space at the room's center. The table sat atop a cabinet with two large drawers running its length, and a display monitor was mounted to its far end. Crusher saw from the unit's construction that contents from the drawers could be moved out of storage and into position atop the table without having to touch the body or remains in question.

"Do the drawers act as stasis chambers?" Cruzen asked.

"Indeed they do." Daret nodded, as though approving of the lieutenant's astuteness. "Each unit is self-contained so that it can be moved from this table via anti-gravity implements back to the mortuary while protecting its contents from possible contamination."

Konya said, "I read about your work. I'm amazed at the

number of . . . recoveries . . . this expedition's been able to make. I would've thought more of the Bajorans who died here, particularly those killed in the final attacks, would've been vaporized."

"The commander presiding over all of the camps, Gul Pavok, was more benevolent toward the workers than others in his position. He allowed the Bajorans to bury their dead in accordance with their customs." Daret paused, then released a small sigh. "Of course, he had his own idiosyncrasies, and he was not above ordering harsh punishments—including executions—if he felt it necessary. As for the attacks that came with my people's withdrawal, the evidence we've found was that the damage inflicted by the departing ships seemed aimed more at infrastructure than people. Because of that, most of the fatalities, while numerous, were due more to trauma from shrapnel, or being crushed inside collapsing buildings, or buried within the mines, and so on." He stopped again, reaching up to wipe what Crusher saw was a single tear from his left eye.

Clearing his throat, Daret stepped to the monitor at the table's far end and tapped it. When the screen flared to life, he touched one of the controls on the unit's interface keypad, and the door to the bottom drawer slid up, allowing a metallic case to slide out. The case moved up along the unit's embedded tracks and raised itself to the table. Now Crusher could see that the case's top was a form of dark glass or composite material, and there was a low yet noticeable hum from the internal power generator that supported the case's stasis system. Such units had been in use for decades, but most designs with which she was familiar were more streamlined than this version. This piece, on the other hand, was of a more ruggedized design, better-suited to environments such as this remote settlement where repairs and other maintenance would be carried out by the people who used the equipment, rather than relying upon engineers or other specialized technicians.

Daret touched another control on the monitor and the opaque tint of the stasis unit's top surface began to clear, revealing what Crusher recognized as something resembling the body of a humanoid. Bones and fragments of bones had been arranged inside the container in such a manner as to present the appearance of a person, as though the individual in question had been assembled from miscellaneous components. The skull, along with several sections of both arms and legs, was missing.

"These remains were discovered in an area of what was the Olanda labor camp," Daret said. "That section of the compound was excavated about six months ago. As is common practice with the identification protocols we've established, we ran comparisons of the subject's genetic structure against all known databases of such information on Bajor. We also engaged Federation and Starfleet resources, hoping to find genetic matches to family members." He shook his head. "Such records aren't complete, of course, and a lot of that information was lost during the Occupation, but protected archives still exist on Cardassia Prime. Every Bajoran in Cardassian custody was identified via retinal and genetic scans, particularly if they were sent to Terok Nor or to labor camps or other destinations away from the Bajoran homeworld."

Crusher remembered something about this from a file detailing the status and medical treatment of slave workers employed aboard Terok Nor, the massive Cardassian space station that had orbited Bajor during the Occupation. Doctor Julian Bashir once had shared the file with her during one of the *Enterprise*'s rare visits to Bajor, after the station had been repurposed to serve as Federation Station Deep Space 9. Of course, now that station was gone, replaced by a state-of-the-art Starfleet facility, and Bashir was a criminal facing court-martial for violating Starfleet and Federation law while working to help the people of Andor. Though he likely had saved that planet's civilization from eventual extinction, there could be no arguing the illegality of the methods he had employed to bring about that laudable achievement. Crusher sympathized with her friend's plight, but the doctor's status was sure to be a key debate now that Andor had been readmitted to the Federation. He almost certainly would be surrendered to the authorities for trial, to answer for whatever charges Starfleet and the Federation Council had drawn up against him.

Good luck, Julian.

"How conclusive are such comparisons?" Konya asked.

Daret replied, "As you might imagine, it is a slow, painstaking process, which often yields failure—or, as some of my associates and I prefer to view it, more challenges." He gestured to the subject. "However, we also enjoy our share of successes, such as with this individual."

Crusher stepped closer to the table. "You're telling us that this person is . . . ?" She allowed the rest of the question to hang in the air between them, unspoken, and Daret's gaze met hers.

"This person, according to every record available to us, is Ishan Anjar."

Cruzen was the first to react. "Wait, what?" Her features closed with confusion; she looked first to Daret before turning to Crusher. "Is he serious?"

Nodding, Crusher replied, "Yes, he's quite serious."

"You're saying that the Federation president is . . . what?" Konya asked, making no effort to hide his disbelief. "An impostor? That he took the identity of another Bajoran?"

Daret replied, "Based on the available evidence, it seems so."

"I can see getting away with that here, during the Occupation," Cruzen said, "but later? Are you suggesting he avoided any further checks of his identity?"

Konya replied, "No, that's impossible. There would've been any number of physicals after the Occupation and more when he began serving in public office. Hell, the background checks to be elected to the Federation Council would be enough to uncover any sort of deception."

"He had help," Crusher said.

His mouth frozen in the midst of his next sentence, Konya blinked and turned to Crusher before nodding. "Yes, exactly. He would've needed help somewhere along the line. At the very least, he would've needed access to sensitive information."

"That may be the more likely scenario," Cruzen said. "From the bio I read when he was appointed president pro tem, he worked for a time as a civil servant in the Bajoran provisional government. Back then, with so many people needing help and so many issues to tackle after the Cardassians' withdrawal, the new government was filling positions as fast as applicants presented themselves. It took months just to get everything organized." She paused, as though considering the ramifications of what she was saying. "Someone looking to manipulate or falsify whatever records or databases remained after the Occupation could have done it any time in those first couple of years."

"It's just a theory," Konya snapped, and Crusher watched his expression change as he looked to the floor, shaking his head. In a quieter voice, he added, "But I suppose it's possible. Crazy, but possible."

"Any crazier than Changelings replacing prominent leaders during the Dominion War?" Cruzen asked. She gestured to the body on the table. "If this really is Ishan Anjar, then the impostor's had years to cement his cover. Are we thinking he's some kind of sleeper agent? For who? The Cardassians?"

Crusher said, "Maybe, but that raises a lot of other questions. Is the impostor—if that's what he truly is—simply a turncoat Bajoran, or a Cardassian or some other individual surgically altered to appear Bajoran? Any of those scenarios would require the sort of records falsification he would need to preserve his identity."

"If he is an undercover operative," Daret said, "then he certainly had assistance establishing his cover, even in the early days of the Bajoran provisional government. It would have taken a great deal of time to insert him, and it may well have been a process that began here, though there are no records of any such operations taking place. Even if it was a scheme to alter his identity for another reason—such as concealing his activities as a collaborator—the records kept here for the Bajoran laborers could have been manipulated well before the evacuation and Starfleet's arrival. Assuming he possessed the appropriate resources, opportunity, and assistance, such a deception could be furthered with relative ease."

"But why?" Crusher asked. "I mean, I understand wanting to cover his tracks after the Occupation if he was a collaborator, but what about after that? If he was hoping to keep a low profile and avoid prosecution by the Bajoran government, taking a position on the Federation Council and running for president seems counterproductive."

Daret's expression grew somber, and Crusher heard him clear his throat before he said, "Beverly, you will recall from our conversation while you were en route here that I made mention of a colleague. He was a Bajoran, Doctor Raal Mosara, and he was the one who identified this subject as Ishan Anjar, working from the archived records kept on Cardassia Prime. He spent three months confirming this, keeping it a secret even from me for most of that time. Only when he had removed his final doubts did he share what he had found, along with his intentions to take what he had learned to visit a close personal friend who serves in the Bajoran government. He prepared copies of all his findings and accompanying notes and sources and departed on a transport for Bajor more than two months ago."

"And you haven't heard from him since then?" Konya asked.

"No, even though we had established a schedule for contact." His gaze seeming to fix on something before him that only he could see, Daret began to pace a slow circuit around the examination table. "Mosara would not even tell me the identity of his friend on Bajor, so my ability to attempt locating him was severely limited, and that's before you take into account any danger he might have faced with the knowledge he possesses."

"You said he prepared copies of his notes," Crusher said as Daret came around the table and walked toward her. "Does that mean the originals, or other copies, are still here?"

Again, Daret sighed. "That is my understanding, though none of that data is here, or in Mosara's residence or laboratory. He told me before he left that he had taken care to hide those materials." He placed a hand atop the stasis unit. "Along with portions of the remains he recovered from the excavation site. According to Mosara, there is enough evidence to prove without doubt that this is Ishan Anjar."

"So where did he hide the evidence?" Cruzen asked.

"I do not know," Daret replied. "He insisted it was for my own protection, at least for the moment, but if anything happened to him that I would know what to do."

Konya grunted, "If he said that, then he's left some clue he's expecting you to find, something in his house or lab, or something you'd be able to figure out because you know him well enough."

"Yes," Daret said, "that was my thinking, as well, but I am at a loss to divine what Mosara might have meant."

"A puzzle," Crusher said. "Wonderful. Whatever we're going to do," she said, "we need to do it fast."

On the one hand, she could understand the precautions Raal Mosara had taken to protect not only himself but also Ilona. But Raal's disappearance would only hamper efforts to retrieve the stunning evidence he had amassed, and Crusher already was operating on borrowed time. How much longer could she hope to evade suspicion or detection? Would Captain Ro Laren be able to cover for her absence on Deep Space 9, or did President Ishan—whatever his real name—have someone on the station to alert him when Crusher failed to arrive for duty? Once that was known, attention would be cast on Jean-Luc and the *Enterprise* crew, who also were attempting to provide protection for her whereabouts and activities.

"About your friend," Crusher said. "Maybe Captain Ro or Captain Sisko can help us with that. Surely they have contacts on Bajor who might be able to help find him."

"That'll be a waste of time," said another voice from behind them, startling Crusher. Its familiar baritone tenor filled her at once with surprise and relief, and she turned to see the imposing figure dressed in dark civilian attire standing in the doorway leading from Daret's lab. Her initial astonishment only deepened when she realized the man before her was both a friend and a stranger. His dark hair possessed more gray, and there was a weariness to his normally intense, bright blue eyes. The beard he sported was unkempt and also littered with gray, almost but not quite covering a thin scar.

Oh my god. It can't be . . . ?

"Raal Mosara is almost certainly dead," said Thomas Riker, "and we will be, too, if we don't find his evidence and get it back to Earth."

Fourteen

"While I can't say I don't appreciate the help, Captain, I cannot help thinking that sending the *Enterprise* on a cargo run seems a little beneath you."

From where he stood at the viewing port overlooking the flurry of activity taking place on the main floor of the starbase's primary cargo transfer center, Picard affected what he hoped was a convincing air of muted resignation. With a sigh that to his ears sounded a bit forced, he turned from the window and regarded the station's commanding officer, Admiral Joris Rhaast.

"It's no trouble at all, Admiral. The *Enterprise* is heading in that general direction, anyway, and a brief stop at Acheron won't impact our schedule." In truth, the cargo run to the colony world was but one part of the ruse Admiral Riker had engineered as a means of giving Picard maneuvering room while the captain carried out a different, clandestine mission.

Rhaast smiled, and when she did so her white teeth seemed even brighter when contrasted against the deep hue of her blue skin. "Spoken like an accomplished diplomat. Even that assignment seems a bit odd for you. Security patrols along the border?"

"Not given the problems we've experienced with some of the sensor systems upgrades," Picard said. "I'm thankful for a bit of dull patrol duty. And that reminds me: Thank you for letting us borrow your station chief to assist my chief engineer with the diagnostics. I know Commander La Forge is grateful not only for the extra set of eyes and hands, but also the perspective of someone who's not used to looking at our ship's innards every day."

"No need to thank me. Chief Vitali is grateful for the change in routine." Casting another glance down to where Picard counted seven different cargo consignments being moved to different locations around the massive processing facility, Rhaast added, "As he told me, it is not often that he receives the opportunity to crawl around inside a *Sovereign*-class vessel. After all, our repair facilities aren't large enough for something the size of *Enterprise*."

"Still, I imagine the chief is rather busy, so any time he can spare to help us is appreciated." In point of fact, Picard was happy to have one of the admiral's people working aboard his ship, as it lent an air of legitimacy to his request for help diagnosing the supposed issues with the *Enterprise*'s sensor systems. La Forge had "invented" the problems in order to provide cover for the real assignment given to him by Picard: sweeping the ship for anything that might be some kind of covert surveillance equipment, as well as scanning the computer memory banks for sniffer software. As of the chief engineer's last cryptic status report, he had found no such attempts at furtive reconnaissance.

Rhaast said, "What I don't believe is them sending you out to run a security patrol, while you're dealing with such issues." She shook her head. "There are times when I question Starfleet Command's decision-making abilities. Then again, I made the decision to accept promotion and command this starbase, rather than keeping my captain's rank and my ship. I think you may be smarter than all of us, Jean-Luc."

Picard allowed his expression to soften. "Oh, they're still after me, Joris. I've lost track of how many times they've chased me with a promotion, but for the moment I'm able to outrun them. I just don't know how much longer I can keep it up."

Her eyes widening as she feigned shock, the Bolian chuckled. "This, from the first freshman cadet to win the Academy marathon?"

"First, and only," Picard corrected. "At least, as far as I know. I should probably check on that, one of these days." He recalled that day, so long ago, and the elation he had felt as he passed four other runners, each of them upperclassmen, on his way to the finish line. Even now, he was hard-pressed to explain from where he had summoned the will and the energy for that final, decisive burst of speed.

"I would have beaten you if I had not tripped." Rhaast leaned closer, her voice lowered. "And I never did get that rematch. What are you doing later today?"

"With any luck, bidding a tactical retreat," Picard replied. "I know a sucker bet when I see one." It was true that Joris Rhaast appeared almost too thin for her flag officer's variant of the Starfleet duty uniform, with its jacket seeming to hang from her shoulders. Due to her slight physique as well as her age, a casual observer might even dismiss her as weak, but Picard knew better. In addition to the various awards and accolades she had won over the years for record-setting marathon wins at events held across the Federation, the Bolian also was a noted martial arts enthusiast. She excelled in several disciplines and had taught a specialized unarmed combat course for a time at Starfleet's training school for new officers and enlisted personnel who had chosen the security division as their career path.

Rhaast shrugged. "Then dinner, perhaps? You and your family can be my guests." Then she chuckled again. "Jean-Luc Picard, father; I say it out loud, and I still can't believe it."

"There was most definitely a transition," Picard said, "but one for which I've enjoyed every moment." His response elicited another small laugh from his old friend.

"Even that sounds improbable." She reached out, patting him on his arm. "Though I must say that you shoulder fatherhood well. You always were a father figure or mentor of sorts, once you settled down after the Academy. I have never met anyone who knows you and would not follow you anywhere you might lead, and I cannot wait to meet the child who will benefit from having a man of such character in his life."

Becoming uncomfortable with the effusive praise, Picard cleared his throat. "I'd love to introduce you to René, but it will just be two of us. His mother has taken a temporary assignment at Deep Space Nine as their interim chief medical officer."

Nodding, Rhaast said, "A fine mess, that. I do not know all the details, of course, but I know enough. Are the rumors true that Doctor Bashir and Captain Dax are to stand court-martial?"

"I don't know," Picard replied. "The matter is being kept under wraps, at least for the moment." He had tried to get more information from Riker, but his former first officer and trusted friend had been unable to provide any details. Even discussing the issue might attract unwanted attention, something Picard was keen to avoid for as long as possible.

"Secrets seem to be the status quo, these days," Rhaast said. "I cannot say it is something that brings me great comfort." She sighed, gazing through the viewport into the cargo center and the activity taking place there. "Indeed, there is very little within the upper echelons of Starfleet Command and the Federation that brings me comfort."

Frowning, Picard asked, "What do you mean?" When Rhaast at first said nothing, he pressed, "Joris, we've known each other since our first day at the Academy. You've always been someone I could trust, and I'd like to think you believe the same of me." Even as he spoke the words, he tried to ignore his own recriminations over his decision not to tell the admiral about La Forge's ongoing hunt for surveillance devices aboard the *Enterprise*. Instead, he said, "It's in the spirit of that trust that I ask you: What is it that you see happening around us?"

Rhaast glanced around them, as though to ensure that no one might be eavesdropping, but they were alone here. In a low voice, she said, "I must be honest with you, my friend: I do not like the more aggressive stance we—Starfleet *and* the Federation—seem to be taking. Defending ourselves against known threats is one thing, of course, but it seems that we are looking for fights where none exist, even with those parties with whom we have legitimate grievances."

After a moment, Picard offered a slow nod. "Agreed."

"Of that I had no doubt," the admiral replied. "And to be sure, not everyone in Starfleet or on the council shares this desire, but at the moment President Ishan's will seems unwavering." Once more, she glanced over her shoulder before adding, "I worry what might happen should he win the upcoming election, for he does have his share of supporters. What strikes me is the level of tenacity I am seeing in some of the newer officers. I do not mean recent Academy graduates, but those new to command positions. It is almost as though they are out to prove that something like the Borg invasion will never happen again, now that we have a leader like President Ishan, along with a 'fresh perspective' with respect to Starfleet's role as an instrument of Federation policy."

Picard had seen a bit of that, himself. Following the tremendous losses it had suffered during the final Borg invasion, Starfleet was forced to promote numerous officers regardless of their time in service, level of experience, and even duration at their present rank. Mid-grade officers with no real practical fleet experience were finding themselves pushed through accelerated training regimens so that they might be given command billets aboard starships or at starbases or other critical facilities across the Federation. This "new generation" of leaders, most if not all possessing the requisite drive and potential to excel in their new roles, still were lacking in significant field experience. Veterans like Picard and his contemporaries who remained in the service often were viewed with reverence if not awe by their fresh counterparts, a situation that always had unnerved him.

Then, there were the other sentiments.

"I've heard rumblings here and there," Picard said, "a few odd comments dropped in your officers' lounge, that sort of thing. Nothing too outlandish, but a few observations that those of us from the 'old guard' failed to prepare for what many saw as the Borg's inevitable full-scale invasion."

"I have been made aware of similar comments. I believe 'ideological entrenchment' was the phrase my yeoman heard; an inability to adapt to ever-evolving threats from beyond the Federation's borders. That can no longer be tolerated, of course, and such sentiments now have a champion, in the form of President Ishan."

"I've seen some of those editorial features on the Federation News Service," Picard replied. He was troubled by many of the claims made by the people hosting those programs. "The notion that the Federation and Starfleet must put forth some unquestioned display of strength and resolve seems to be of particular importance now."

"In some respects, I can agree with that," Rhaast said. "With the Typhon Pact seemingly lurking within every shadow and their long-term agenda still a mystery, a certain level of vigilance seems required, perhaps even more so than what some might consider 'traditional' when compared to Starfleet's accepted role."

Picard grunted. "To a point, yes." There were those, both within the Federation Council and Starfleet's highest command echelons, calling for a more aggressive policy toward the Pact, and there were even a few extreme suggestions that waiting for the upstart coalition to make their move was a grave mistake in the making.

Ishan, of course, while not going so far as to advocate such a bold strategy, still was looking for any reason to tie the Pact, specifically the Tzenkethi, to President Bacco's murder. However, a special-operations team, dispatched originally to track down the assassins, had instead come across new evidence implicating the True Way. Elements of the Cardassian extremist sect had been acting at the direction of someone within the Federation government. Admiral Riker had suspected President Ishan and Galif jav Velk of collusion with the terrorists, but any chance of proving that had faded after the special-operations team was sent to find the band of rogue agents. All of the Cardassians were killed during the operation meant to capture and return them to the Federation for trial, but not before the startling revelation that the True Way's mission to kill President Bacco had come from President Ishan's chief of staff. Before Velk could be charged with that crime, he had been taken into custody, apparently after confessing to Ishan his role in the unsanctioned covert action to eliminate the True Way assassins. With Velk and Ishan seemingly insulated from any possible accusations of complicity in Bacco's death, rumors once again were circulating that the entire operation somehow had been sanctioned if not coordinated by the Typhon Pact. Despite the utter lack of anything resembling credible evidence to support such allegations, Ishan already was using the rumors—which Riker suspected him of leaking in the first place—to further cement his hawkish stance against the upstart coalition.

As it was, damage elsewhere remained to be felt. Once made public, the startling revelation of the True Way's involvement in Bacco's murder would deal a devastating blow to the tenuous peace agreement between the Cardassians and the Federation. Whether this fragile bond survived that disclosure remained to be seen.

And that's without taking into account anything Beverly might find on Jevalan.

"Joris," Picard said, and this time it was he who looked around them to ensure they were not being overheard. "This starbase is a key hub for ships coming and going between several Starfleet security patrol routes through this sector. Have you noticed anything . . . *unusual* . . . with respect to the ships that have made port here?"

Now it was Rhaast's time to frown as she regarded her friend. "Unusual? What do you mean?"

It was a good question, one Picard had been contemplating since his last conversation with Riker and following the admiral's request to be on the lookout for indications of coercion, collusion, or corruption that could, through even the most indirect means, lead in some way back to President Ishan. While he was working with little more than suspicions and gut feelings, Riker already was tightening his inner circle of close, trusted friends. The small group, at least so far as those officers and others in a position to help him on Earth, was being supplemented by Picard and a small cadre of others scattered across Federation space. Though Picard had cultivated his own very short list of friends and contacts over his lengthy career—among whom he listed Joris Rhaast—Riker still had warned him to tread with care when approaching anyone about Ishan or any of the policies and actions the president pro tem had enacted during his brief tenure in office. Ishan, it seemed, had eyes and ears everywhere, or at least was in the process of establishing such a surreptitious network. How far had his reach extended? Would he already have made it out this far, and if so, how powerful was his influence? As he regarded Rhaast, Picard knew that it was prudent to wonder if the charisma and sway Ishan had demonstrated was strong enough to undermine a friendship going back six decades.

No, he decided. *It most certainly is not.*

"I don't think it would be anything too overt," Picard said. "Have you noted anything you might consider out of the ordinary with respect to requests for supplies or personnel? Perhaps ships are heading to or returning from destinations not in keeping with their normal duties?"

Rhaast sighed. "Given our location, it would not be unusual to service a ship that had been given a classified assignment. There have been occasions where I've been tasked with supporting covert missions, but those orders always are delivered to me from Starfleet Command. I also am quite certain that vessels have come here while in the midst of carrying out such assignments, the details of which were not shared with me." After a moment, the admiral stepped closer and again lowered her voice. "Where are you going with all of this, Jean-Luc? Do you think someone at Headquarters is conducting secret missions for President Ishan?"

"The thought has crossed my mind," Picard replied. While he himself had supported and even undertaken similar covert assignments in the past, the current administration's apparent preference for such activities was troubling. In his mind, it only strengthened the doubts he had about President Ishan's true motives. "If these missions are legal, then their classified nature is an issue that can be addressed at a later time."

"*If* they're legal?" Rhaast asked. "Are you suggesting the Federation president might be doing something *illegal*?"

Though Rhaast had broached the subject, Picard was unwilling to drag her too far into this mess, fearing whatever reprisals might come her way if Ishan somehow were to get wind of the *Enterprise*'s real reason for visiting Starbase 310. "Joris, all I'm suggesting at this point is that something unusual is taking place and that we need to remain vigilant, particularly now. Our enemies are watching how we navigate the upheaval we've endured and the challenges we face as we try to regain some semblance of normalcy."

"Your words are not dissimilar to those uttered by Ishan and his supporters," Rhaast said. Then, her expression softened. "However, I suspect you are not considering preemptive strikes against our enemies."

Despite the serious nature of their conversation, Picard could not help the small chuckle that escaped his lips. "I wasn't planning on it just yet."

Rhaast crossed her arms and regarded him in silence for what Picard estimated was almost an entire minute before she said, "I've known you long enough to know when you're up to something, Jean-Luc." She nodded toward the cargo processing bay. "All of this is a cover, isn't it? What are you trying to do? Find some clue that Ishan or someone loyal to him has been somehow corrupted? Are you looking for some kind of threat?"

"I'm also looking for friends, Joris," Picard replied.

"Well, you know you have one. The question now is: How many more do you think you will need?"

Picard sighed. "I don't know, but one's a start."

Fifteen

Reports, memorandums, maintenance logs. Personnel and materiel requests. Intelligence and security briefings. All of it lay scattered before him, each piece waiting for his tired eyes and—he imagined—increasingly addled brain to give it his undivided attention. Looking at the array of administrative flotsam cluttering the top of his desk, Riker released a tired sigh, which was punctuated by the now-dreaded tone of his computer workstation alerting him that a new message had been added to his queue. He glanced to the station's display screen, noting that it was not a single message that had just arrived, but thirteen.

No wonder admirals are always so grumpy.

Riker did not even know how the backlog had grown so large in such a short amount of time. It was as though the messages and padds provided to him by his aide, Lieutenant Ssura, multiplied whenever he dared to step outside his office. Admiral Akaar had wasted no time redirecting to Riker's office the constant stream of correspondence, for which the newly minted admiral had been directed to read, absorb, and recommend action. Riker's first order of business was to put to work three junior officers who formed his administrative staff, ordering them to prioritize everything. He was most interested in intelligence and security matters, of course, but he also wanted quick looks at anything pertaining to

Starfleet personnel and ship matters. The triage operation helped to reduce the data overload he had experienced during those first few days in his new role, but even the culling process still left him with a virtual mountain of reading. The situation only worsened when he spent any appreciable time away from his office. His recent trips to the *Titan*—working in secret with his ship's senior officers to decipher the covert communications channel and encrypted messages discovered by Akaar and belonging to Galif jav Velk—all had provided opportunities for his workload to suffer exponential increases.

As though mocking him, his workstation beeped, announcing the arrival of another half dozen messages. Riker pictured the computer terminal catching the rays of the morning sun as they filtered through his window toward San Francisco Bay.

Relax, Admiral, he cautioned himself. *Remember why you're here.*

In addition to helping him complete a crash course in the current status of nearly every active starship in the fleet, reviewing the regular barrage of reports also afforded Riker an opportunity to search for patterns and other trends that might indicate something untoward taking place. Though he suspected that President Ishan or a member of his inner circle already had someone within the halls of Starfleet Command seeing to it that no truly sensitive materials made it to this office, Riker was hoping that the sheer volume of information might allow something to slip through. There was also the possibility that he might discover who, if anyone, might be censoring the material delivered to him and perhaps even find another link to Ishan. Riker wondered if that latter goal might be too ambitious, given the interim president's demonstrated talent for covering his tracks and casting suspicion onto other parties. It was doubtful anything truly damaging would cross his desk, but Riker had nothing to lose by looking, anyway.

The door chime sounded, followed by Lieutenant Ssura's voice filtering through the intercom system. *"Admiral Riker? Apologies for the interruption, sir, but you have an urgent call from Admiral Akaar."*

Frowning, Riker had only a moment to consider what Akaar might want or need, when the still-open communications channel erupted with several new voices.

"Remain at your desk, Lieutenant," said an unidentified male, followed by another voice issuing similar instructions to what Riker surmised were the other members of his staff occupying his suite's outer offices. Then his own doors parted, and a pair of uniformed officers bearing the rank and insignia of the Federation Security Agency's presidential protection detail entered the room. A Bajoran female and a Vulcan male, they said nothing as they moved into the office.

"What the hell is this?" Riker asked, rising from his chair.

The female Bajoran, on her way toward the door at the rear of the room that led to the office's private lavatory, stopped and glared at Riker. "Standard security sweep, Admiral."

"Standard for what?" New movement from the doorway made Riker turn to see Ishan Anjar, his dark, full-length Bajoran robes flowing behind him as he entered the room. His long, fast strides carried him across the office to stand before Riker's desk in just a few steps. His expression was flat, though Riker saw irritation and perhaps even suspicion in the eyes of the president pro tem. Given how they had left their last meeting, Riker knew he should not be surprised by Ishan's confrontational demeanor.

"Mister President," Riker said, straightening his posture. "I wasn't aware that you'd be in San Francisco today, sir." He had last seen Ishan mere days earlier, in the president's office in Paris, with Riker pressing him about his hawkish stance toward the Typhon Pact. To say that the meeting had not

gone well was, Riker decided, something of an understate-
ment. He schooled his features, offering his best poker face
as Ishan fixed him with an accusatory glare. "What can I do
for you, sir?"

"You can tell me why the *Enterprise* is not en route to
the Neutral Zone to commence its patrol rotation. Admiral
Akaar informed me that you changed its assignment. I want
to know why."

I guess this is what Akaar wanted to talk about.

Feigning confusion, Riker replied, "I don't understand,
Mister President. As I reported to Admiral Akaar, I redirected Captain Picard to Starbase Three Ten in order to take
on supplies and other equipment for the agricultural colony
on Acheron. It's not too far off the *Enterprise*'s scheduled
route to the border, and it's one of the closest and fastest
ships in the sector."

He resisted the impulse to ask whether the president
really had received his information from Admiral Akaar or
instead had come to possess it thanks to other, less savory
means. It had taken his people aboard the *Titan* little time
to determine that Riker's last subspace conversation with
Captain Picard had been monitored. Despite detecting the
intrusion and being able to warn Riker, his team so far had
been unable to locate the source of the infiltration, though
he had confirmed the interception had taken place only after
the discussion was under way for several minutes. Because of
this, Riker was confident that nothing damaging had been
overheard, but he still had opted to take greater care as to
how he would continue to pass information to Picard and
other trusted allies from this point forward.

Ishan made no attempt to hide his dissatisfaction and
its accompanying disbelief of Riker's explanation. "It's my
understanding that another ship had already been given that
assignment. Why the change?"

Rather than further annoy the president by asking him

how or why he even should care about such mundane details, Riker instead replied, "The *Enterprise* is also large enough to transport some of the heavier equipment the colony needs. The colony's had additional equipment failures due to some extreme weather events." He shrugged. "Apparently, spring monsoon season is something you have to experience to truly appreciate." Reaching to his desk, he retrieved the padd he knew contained a record of the reports and other information he had compiled regarding the situation, and he held it up for Ishan to see. "Admiral Akaar approved my recommendations, and I issued Picard modified orders." When the president did not offer an immediate response, Riker decided to press, just a bit. "The captain said he'd be able to accommodate the revised timetable and the extra stops, and I've already contacted *Sutherland* to inform her captain that the *Enterprise* will be a day or so late relieving them."

"That's not Picard's decision to make," Ishan snapped.

"He didn't make the call, Mister President; I did."

The president stepped closer, his eyes narrowing. "It wasn't your decision, either."

"I've been detailed to Starfleet Operations under Admiral Akaar, Mister President," Riker said. "One of the responsibilities I've been given is monitoring the status of all deployed Starfleet vessels and effectively allocating them as necessary to respond to whatever situations or crises might arise."

"Your responsibilities are whatever I tell you they are, Admiral," Ishan countered, a hint of menace creeping into his voice, and it was obvious to Riker that the president had not put behind him their last meeting. "Starfleet answers to the properly elected civilian authority. Do not ever forget that. Some of your predecessors had difficulty with the concept."

Riker, keeping his tone level and his expression flat, replied, "Yes, sir. The properly elected civilian authority." The verbal jab, delivered as it was without inflection, took an extra moment to assert itself, at which time he saw the barest flash of fury in Ishan's eyes. To the Bajoran's credit, he almost succeeded in maintaining his composure, but Riker saw the all-but-imperceptible tell as Ishan's jaw clenched just the slighted bit.

I hope for your sake that you don't play poker, Mister President. So far as Riker was concerned, Ishan had overplayed his hand, coming here asking after the *Enterprise.* In addition to setting a poor precedent with respect to presidential protocol, it also was a poor tactical move, revealing his unusual and even obsessive interest in the starship's whereabouts. Was he that worried about Jean-Luc Picard? For the captain's own protection as well as his own, Riker had not pressed his friend for details regarding this odd mission Beverly Crusher had undertaken and for which Riker had constructed such an elaborate ruse to help cover her movements. Picard had provided no clues, and during their last communication Riker had gotten the sense that even the captain was operating somewhat in the dark while Crusher was off the ship. Officially, she was en route to Deep Space 9, and Riker knew the time limit on that deception was running out.

To his surprise, Ishan smiled, though it was by no means an expression of warmth. "Don't get me wrong, Admiral; I appreciate and even admire initiative. It's a hallmark of any good officer, and I know from experience that taking charge of a situation instead of waiting for orders to come down the chain of command sometimes is the only way to get desired or even necessary results." The smile faded. "The secret to success with such tactics is knowing when and where to employ them and when it's better to utilize restraint."

Now it was Riker's turn to smile. "Thankfully, I've had good teachers."

"Yes, you have." Ishan glanced toward the padd Riker still held. "When is the *Enterprise* scheduled to depart Starbase Three Ten?"

"According to the last report I received, within six hours. They should be at Acheron eleven hours after that."

The Bajoran released a small sigh. "Very well." He paused, and Riker hoped Ishan might ask about Beverly Crusher, if for no other reason than to reveal that he also was monitoring that situation with excessive interest. Instead, he said, "Keep Admiral Akaar informed."

With that he turned and headed for the doors, exiting the room with the same purposeful strides that had brought him to Riker. His protection detail waited until he had gone before taking a final look around the office as they made their own retreat. Riker moved not the slightest muscle until the doors slid closed, once more leaving him alone. Only then did he release a pent-up sigh.

He knows something.

There was no way to surmise what information Ishan possessed, but there could be no doubt that his network of informants and other accomplices had been hard at work. Not for the first time, Riker had to wonder if the president somehow had managed to recruit or insert a spy aboard the *Enterprise,* or if he had been shrewd enough to have someone track Crusher's runabout. If that was the case, then he likely knew the itinerary taking her to Deep Space 9 was at best a diversion and at worst outright deception on Riker's part. And what about the *Enterprise* and Crusher? Were they in danger? How much longer would Ishan entertain whatever game he was playing, and at what point would he relieve Riker—and Akaar, for that matter—of duty?

Riker suspected it would be sooner, rather than later.

Whatever the hell you're doing, Beverly, I hope you do it fast.

Sixteen

"I wonder what Jean-Luc would think about this."

Navigating a narrow path that had been carved out of the dark, unforgiving soil, Beverly Crusher walked alongside Ilona Daret as they descended into the vast shallow pit that had become the former Tabata labor camp's most prominent feature. The crater, no more than a few meters below ground level at its deepest point, had consumed the camp's center, bordered by huge sections of destroyed buildings and other debris, all of which contrasted with the vegetation that had begun reclaiming the savagely altered landscape.

"I only recently remembered that he is an archaeologist," Daret said as he and Crusher walked past one of several small canvas shelters scattered around the work site. He waved to a female Bajoran, smudges of dirt on her face and grunge covering her clothing, sitting in the shade the tarpaulin provided. She was working at a portable computer resting atop a field table, and she offered a tired smile as Crusher and Daret passed her. At this point in the late morning, the area was alive with activity. Daret nodded greetings to Bajorans and other Cardassians, some of whom Crusher recognized from breakfast at the camp dining facility. In addition to the forensic scientists working about the site, there also were several engineers and other heavy-machine operators guiding loaders and other excavation equipment to move great chunks of earth and wreckage. A series of air cleaners that had been deployed around the crater's perimeter helped to clear away the worst of the dust and dirt kicked up by the heavy earth-moving equipment.

"It's been a passion of his for as long as I've known him," Crusher said. "He's spent years studying ancient or extinct civilizations. It appeals to his meticulous nature, I think. He can spend hours immersed in books or documents or studying artifacts and writing his own papers and journals about whatever it is he's found. He has volumes of notes he's kept, going back to his childhood." She shook her head. "Sometimes, I think he missed his life's true path, and at least one of his professors thought the same thing."

Crusher sighed. Not for the first time, she had considered trying to convince her husband that he might be better suited to such a life, now that there was René to consider. The idea of following Jean-Luc from planet to planet and bearing witness as he instilled in their son an appreciation for history and other cultures, free from the confines of starship corridors, artificial gravity, recycled air, and replicated food, held a definite allure. But, she knew that commanding a starship—commanding the *Enterprise*—still was something that called to him. That he excelled at it was immaterial, at least to her; instead, it was the supreme dedication he brought to the duties and people entrusted to his care that drove him, she knew, just as she was certain it would take an extraordinary set of circumstances to remove Jean-Luc Picard from the bridge of that ship.

It was just one of the many things Crusher loved about him.

A familiar face stepped around a group of workers standing near another shelter, and she smiled as Lieutenant Kirsten Cruzen walked toward them. Her brunette hair was tucked beneath a drab brown cap, and she wore a black jacket over a rumpled tan jumpsuit. Crusher figured the security officer could pass for one of the expedition members with no difficulty.

"Doctors," Cruzen said, raising her right hand and tapping the brim of her cap as though offering an informal salute.

Nodding in greeting, Crusher asked, "Where are Lieutenant Konya and Tom?"

Cruzen gestured past them, toward the expedition camp. "Mister Riker suggested that a casual stroll through the landing area might be a good idea. They're checking out the other ships, looking to see if anything sticks out." She paused for a moment. "I swear, just looking at him is weird. He looks so much like Admiral Riker, but they're so different in so many ways."

"I was unaware that Admiral Riker had a twin sibling," Daret said.

"He's not a twin," Crusher replied as the trio resumed walking through the work site. "And calling him a 'clone' really isn't accurate, either. However, Tom Riker is an exact duplicate of William Riker, created by a very bizarre transporter accident more than twenty years ago." She remembered the shock she had felt upon first meeting Will Riker's "twin brother" after the *Enterprise*-D's visit to Nervala IV. Riker at the time was a lieutenant assigned to the *U.S.S. Potemkin,* which had been dispatched to the planet to evacuate the Starfleet science team posted there. The last to be beamed back to the *Potemkin,* Riker's transporter beam was affected by the planet's odd atmospheric distortion fields, resulting in a perfect replication of his transporter pattern and the creation of a second William Riker, identical in every conceivable way. This duplicate, unknown to the *Potemkin*'s crew, remained marooned for eight years on Nervala IV until the *Enterprise* had arrived to carry out a data-retrieval mission. His existence came as a shock to everyone, but none more so than Will Riker. Following his rescue, the uncanny doppelganger had elected to start using his and Will's shared middle name, Thomas.

Time and fate had not been kind to the other Riker, however, with him opting to join the Maquis resistance movement, taking on both the Federation and the Cardassian Union in opposition to the policies that had ceded colony worlds to the Cardassians in the wake of the conflict that had ended nearly two decades ago. His actions against Cardassian military interests ultimately had seen him taken into custody and sentenced to life in prison on the labor camp world of Lazon II.

Though it was believed he had died on that planet during the Dominion War, rumors of sightings had filtered to the *Enterprise* in the years before William Riker's promotion to captain and his assignment as commanding officer of the *Titan*. Crusher had believed Tom dead right up until the moment he appeared in Daret's lab, after which he had updated her and the others about his status as an unofficial field operative for Starfleet Intelligence, and the odd circumstances that had seen him recruited for the covert-operations team sent to find Nanietta Bacco's assassins. He, along with Commander Tuvok and Lieutenant Commander Nog, nearly had died during that mission; they were deemed collateral damage in a bid to cover up President Ishan and his chief of staff's involvement in Bacco's murder.

Following that mission, Tom had dropped out of sight for a short while, during which he had been attempting to gather information for his "brother," Will. The nature of that information was something Tom was not sharing, at least for the moment, citing a desire to insulate Crusher and her team from any repercussions should his activities draw the wrong kind of attention. Now he was here, having arrived aboard the civilian transport that had made planetfall the previous day, and he had spent the ensuing hours reconnoitering the camp and the associated dig site. Blending in with the mechanics and other technical personnel at the landing port had proven a simple exercise for someone with his background in covert actions.

"It's certainly an amazing story," Daret said after Crusher explained the incredible incident, as well as Tom Riker's difficult years following an aborted attempt to resume his Starfleet career. "I must admit that he certainly gives me pause. I still don't understand how he was able to defeat the locks on my home and laboratory."

"He's picked up a few tricks here and there," Cruzen said, "thanks in large part to the 'friends' he made when he was with the Maquis. Still, Admiral Riker vouches for him, and that's good enough for me." Pausing, the lieutenant glanced around the work site. "Where are we going?"

Daret waved at some indistinct point farther along the path. "I received a message this morning from one of the teams working an area we just uncovered. They have found both Cardassian and Bajoran remains, and one of my Bajoran counterparts always notifies me when such a find is made."

"Doctor Daret," Cruzen said, "I know the recovery effort has been under way for more than a couple of years now. How long did it take to dig out all of this?"

"Several months," the Cardassian replied. "It's a painstaking process, as we're taking great care not to damage or destroy any remains we might find during the excavation." He gestured toward the middle of the pit. "This portion of the camp suffered a direct hit during the final assault," Daret said. "The barrage leveled every building, and estimates at the time counted more than three hundred casualties. The overwhelming majority of which are Bajoran, of course."

Crusher asked, "What about the Olanda camp?"

"We will head there tomorrow," Daret said. "The team working that site is much smaller, as we believe most of the remains have been recovered from there. It was the first camp we began excavating, and the devastation inflicted during the withdrawal was much more severe, with a greater number of casualties." He stopped walking, and when Crusher turned to him she saw that his expression had turned to one of sadness.

Noticing her attention, he cleared his throat. "I am sorry. I was just . . . thinking." He paused, reaching up to wipe the corners of his eyes. "The Olanda camp is where the majority of those Bajorans with families were interred. Many of those killed during the final assault were children." He released a long, slow breath. "I am not proud of many things perpetrated by my people—against the Bajorans or anyone else—and that certainly was a most shameful act."

Crusher reached out and placed a hand on her friend's shoulder. "It's because of people like you that there's hope for us all to somehow get past all of this."

"I want to believe that's possible," Daret said. After a moment, he straightened his posture. "While we may not be able to change the past, we can work for a better future, yes?"

"Sounds like a good plan to me," Cruzen replied.

With Daret once more leading the way, he along with Crusher and Cruzen followed the walking path toward the pit's far end. Three more of the temporary shelters also stood here, though their field tables and other equipment were unattended. A large earth-moving vehicle sat near a mound of soil that was littered with displaced vegetation as well as chunks of metal and other building materials. Beyond the pile was what looked to be the entrance to a partially cleared tunnel.

"This is one of the entry points for this section of the mine," Daret remarked as they drew closer. "As I recall, most of the work had shifted to a point a few kilometers from here, so this passage was used mostly as a transfer point for workers and equipment, due to its proximity to the camp."

"Pretty damned creepy, if you ask me," Cruzen said.

Pointing toward the entrance, Crusher asked, "The prisoners walked underground from the camp to the work area?"

"Most of the tunnels are wide enough that large num-bers of workers could be moved on foot in rapid fashion. It also reduced the ability of anyone attempting any sort of insurrection or other distraction." Daret released a dis-approving grunt. "One of the common threats against the workers was that they would be sealed inside the tunnels if they attempted rebellion: buried alive. Such a situation was made worse by the minerals impeding sensor scans below-ground. The mineral ore at the lower levels is so dense that scans cannot penetrate."

"Charming," Cruzen said.

From the dark mouth of the tunnel, a male, dark-haired Bajoran appeared, dressed in clothing similar to that worn by other members of the expedition. Upon seeing Daret, Crusher, and Cruzen, he began waving in frantic fashion.

"Doctor Daret? Please, we need your help! There's been an accident!"

Without thinking, Crusher started toward the tun-nel, Daret jogging alongside while Cruzen followed. They crossed the expanse of cleared soil toward the Bajoran, who was dividing his attention between them and the tunnel. "What happened?"

"We were working in the new section," the Bajoran said. "There was a collapse, and one of our team members was caught by falling dirt and debris. We were able to free him, but he's unconscious, and we cannot revive him. I think he may have a head injury."

"Is he bleeding?" Crusher asked.

"No," the Bajoran replied before turning to lead them toward the tunnel, with Daret following close behind them as they moved past the mine's entrance. Crusher noted the dim illumination here, provided by a series of field lights sus-pended on a thick, insulated cable that had been fastened with steel bolts driven into the rock wall on both sides of the passageway. Though it was a narrow path leading from the mouth of the tunnel, she saw that it began to widen within just a few meters, opening into a larger chamber. The ceiling here was higher, and a series of brighter work lights suspended from metal stands were arrayed around the cavern. Several smaller tunnels appeared to branch out from the chamber, leading in different directions farther underground. At each of the tunnel openings was a sign bolted to the rock and featuring text inscribed in Cardassian, Bajoran, and Federation Standard, indicating distance and direction to some other areas of the vast subterranean mine.

"This way," the Bajoran said, gesturing for them to follow him as he ran to the left tunnel opening.

Cruzen called out, "Is there any emergency medical equipment in here?"

"Another of our team members has an emergency medical kit," the Bajoran replied, glancing over his shoulder, "and there are larger kits and stretchers at emergency stations throughout the work site."

Daret said, "Those are sufficient for light injuries, but we'll need to get him back to the aid station. Have you summoned help from them?"

"I lost my communicator during the cave-in."

Looking past the Bajoran, Crusher saw another, smaller chamber, its stone walls also illuminated by the same type of work lights. Their guide stepped through the short, narrow passage and into the larger area with Daret trailing close behind. She heard movement from the cave and caught glimpses of what she thought might be someone sitting or lying on the ground ahead of them.

She flinched as the Bajoran spun on Daret, shoving his left forearm beneath the Cardassian's chin and forcing him backward until he slammed against the wall. At the same time, the person lying on the cave's stone floor—another Bajoran with blond hair—sprang to his feet, an ugly-looking weapon in his hand.

"Get in here!" he snapped, aiming the blunt weapon at Crusher. Holding up her hands, Crusher felt a knot of fear tighten in her belly as she moved as directed to stand against the wall. The Bajoran waved Cruzen to stand next to her. With his arm extended, the weapon's muzzle was less than a meter from her face.

"What are you doing?" Crusher asked, fighting to keep her voice from trembling.

"Quiet!" Looking to his companion, who still had Daret pinned against the wall, he said, "They said he'd be alone. What are we supposed to do with these two?"

His forearm pushing against Daret's throat, the dark-haired Bajoran looked over his shoulder. "Kill them." His eyes bored into Crusher's, and she saw no hesitation or compassion there. "Make it quick."

"He doesn't know anything," Cruzen said, her voice hard and firm. "I'm the one you want."

What the hell are you doing? It took every scrap of will-power Crusher possessed not to turn her head or even move her eyes to see the lieutenant. What could she be thinking?

Frowning, the blond Bajoran growled, "What is she talking about?"

"Nothing," his companion said. "We're here for him. Hurry up and finish it."

Cruzen pressed, "I'm telling you I can take you to what you want. He doesn't know anything about it."

Now it was the dark-haired Bajoran's turn to scowl. "Who are you supposed to be? I don't recognize you, or her, for that matter." He nodded toward Crusher. "You're not part of the recovery group."

"We've been working at the Pencala camp," Crusher said, having decided it might be better to play along with Cruzen's ruse, wherever it might be going.

The blond Bajoran was glancing back and forth between them and his companion. "What if they do know something?" he asked, the pitch of his voice raising an octave. "Maybe we should take them with us." He turned to his friend, his eyes leaving Crusher and Cruzen.

It was not much—a mere instant—but that seemed to be enough for Cruzen.

The momentary lapse of attention was all the lieutenant needed as she lashed out with her foot, kicking the Bajoran in his groin. His initial howl of pain only grew louder as the security officer stepped in for her next attack. The flat of her boot struck the side of his left knee, and Crusher heard bone snap. By now his companion was moving, having released his hold on Daret as his other hand reached for the weapon concealed inside his jacket. Crusher was scrambling to retrieve her own phaser, but Cruzen beat them both. A high-pitched whine echoed around the chamber as a bright orange energy beam struck the Bajoran in the chest. His body went limp, and he slumped against the cave wall before sliding to the ground.

"Ilona!" Crusher cried, stepping around the fallen Bajoran to her friend who still leaned against the wall, rubbing his throat. "Are you all right?"

"Yes."

Still conscious, the blond Bajoran was lying on the ground, holding the knee Cruzen had injured and perhaps even broken. His expression was a mask of pain as he glared up at them, his breathing coming in short, rapid hisses between gritted teeth.

"Who are you?" Cruzen asked, stepping closer and aiming her phaser at his head.

Crusher knelt beside the Bajoran. "I'm a doctor," she told him. "I promise, we won't hurt you."

"They were going to *kill* us," Cruzen said.

"And that's not going to happen now, is it?" Crusher countered. "His knee is broken."

Cruzen stepped closer. "He might have friends, Doctor." To the Bajoran, she said, "It's obvious you're not professionals, so who hired you to grab Doctor Daret?" When the Bajoran offered no response save a strained grunt through his obvious discomfort, the lieutenant looked to Daret. "Do you recognize these men?"

The Cardassian replied, "I believe I have seen them around the camp, but I do not know their names."

"That means somebody's going to miss them, sooner or later." Lifting her phaser, Cruzen aimed it at the wounded Bajoran and fired. He went limp, now lying unconscious on the floor of the cave.

Shocked, Crusher turned on the lieutenant. "Why did you do that?"

"He wasn't going to tell us anything, and now that he's stunned, we'll have an easier time moving him." She returned the phaser to where she had concealed it beneath her jacket. "Besides, we've got bigger problems. When these two don't show up wherever they're supposed to take Doctor Daret, somebody's going to come looking for them, and him. We need to stay ahead of that."

"What are you suggesting?" Daret asked.

Crusher, though still uncomfortable with the casual way Cruzen had treated the wounded Bajoran, at least now was able to examine his injuries. Having assessed the fracture below his left knee, she looked around the cave and spotted a length of old, pitted wood she decided would do well enough as a temporary splint. "The camp has a security contingent, right?"

"Yes, but they're not professional law enforcement or military personnel," Daret replied. "In fact, most of them are volunteers who help the two full-time security officers. They have a small collection of weapons and a holding cell, but it's mostly used for those who drink too much and get into fights."

"It'll have to do," Cruzen said.

After tearing away a portion of the Bajoran's shirtsleeve, Crusher now was using the material to secure her makeshift splint to his injured knee. It would do, she decided; at least long enough to get him to the camp's medical station. "If we can get them there without too many people noticing," she said, "that should buy us some time."

Daret frowned. "Time for what?"

Rising to her feet, Crusher reached out and gripped her friend's arm. "Ilona, you heard what they said: They wanted you to take them to something. What else could it be? Whoever sent these two after you knows you've got access to the evidence and information your friend Mosara collected. Wherever it is, we need to find it and get you away from here."

"And fast," Cruzen added, gesturing to the pair of unconscious Bajorans. "These two may have dropped the ball, but you can bet whoever sent them won't."

"Kirsten," Crusher said, "contact Konya and Riker, and tell them what's happened. These two knew we didn't belong here, so somebody might be getting suspicious about them, too."

Cruzen nodded. "Whoever sent these clowns is probably trying to keep a low profile, but once they don't show up, or it gets out that they're locked up? Those people—whoever they are—will be coming for us."

Seventeen

"Incoming encrypted communication. Please enter access code."
Leaning forward in his high-backed chair, Admiral Declan Schlosser tapped a control on his desk's embedded keypad, which engaged the locks on his office doors and severed the room's links to the rest of the building's internal communications system. Another control increased the tinting on his office's windows, obscuring the room's interior from anyone who might be attempting visual surveillance from one of the neighboring buildings. Then, before entering the command string to activate the protected communications link, he entered one more instruction to the terminal, this one designed for his own private use. As he had learned over the course of his long career, one never could be too careful when it came to matters of security. Still, even his own compulsive observance of such practices paled in comparison to the person with whom he was about to speak, as evidenced by the multi-step process in which he now was engaged.

"Computer, identify Schlosser, Declan, Admiral. Authorization code Beta Seven Three Sierra Nine Alpha. Enable."

"Working," replied the feminine voice of the headquarters' central computer. *"Authorization code accepted. Activating security and isolation protocols."* It took the computer an additional few seconds before indicating that all of the secu-

rity measures for the use of this most irregular and unusual mode of communication were in place.

The image on his screen—that of a helix spinning before a black background—dissolved as a humanoid figure coalesced and solidified before him. A moment later, Schlosser found himself staring into the face of President Ishan Anjar.

"Mister President," Schlosser said. "Good evening, sir."

Ishan nodded, his expression fixed. *"Admiral. I trust you have enabled all of your security protocols?"*

"Indeed I have, sir."

More than two decades serving in various divisions of Starfleet's tactical and intelligence departments had honed Schlosser's ability to lie without effort. In open defiance of the president pro tem's orders, he was recording this conversation just as he had all of his previous communications with Ishan as well as his chief of staff, Galif jav Velk. After Velk had been arrested—ostensibly following a confession to Ishan citing his sole responsibility for violation of numerous laws and the use of Starfleet resources and personnel to conduct unsanctioned covert operations—Schlosser was forced to wonder if the Tellarite had sacrificed himself in order to protect Ishan from being implicated in however many illegal activities to which he had confessed. There was no evidence of the president's having possessed knowledge of Velk's unlawful pursuits, of course, which Schlosser suspected was the point. With the president reaching out to other parties to assist him in continued clandestine operations, Schlosser had no intention of being caught without some kind of insurance for his own benefit should circumstances lead him to a situation similar to the one in which Velk had found himself.

Leaning back in his chair, Schlosser said, "How may I be of service, Mister President?"

"I need a ship with a sizable security detachment sent immediately to the planet Jevalan, in the Doltiri system, for a sensi-

tive mission." Ishan's expression was unreadable, though the simple fact that he wanted this to happen told Schlosser all he needed to know about how serious the president viewed this matter.

The admiral said, "That system is in Cardassian space, as I recall." As he spoke, he used the workstation's manual interface to instruct the computer to call up data on the system and the planet Ishan had specified. It had been some years since he had read or heard anything about that region, but half-buried memories were beginning to assert themselves. "A mining planet, and the Cardassians used slave labor to extract and process dilithium and other minerals during their Occupation of Bajor." Though he did not say it aloud, Schlosser also recalled that Ishan himself had once lived there while Bajor still was under Cardassian rule.

"Correct," Ishan replied, and this time Schlosser thought he heard the barest hint of irritation in the president's voice. *"I didn't call you for a briefing about how my people were conquered and oppressed by the Cardassians, Admiral. I'm quite familiar with that chapter of Bajoran history, thank you. What I need is a starship detailed to that system at once."*

Though he bristled at Ishan's abrupt change in tone, Schlosser offered no outward sign that the stinging words were having any effect. "I'll need to review our current deployment to see which ship's closest and available for reassignment."

"You're not understanding me, Admiral," Ishan snapped. *"I need a ship routed there now. I don't care what else it might be doing. This is an urgent security matter, and time is of the essence. Am I making myself clear?"*

"Very much so, sir," Schlosser said. He had dealt with overanxious individuals often enough not to let such histrionics faze him. His reputation for remaining calm under pressure, coupled with what he admitted was his own slight, stark countenance, had earned him a nickname early in his career: Warhawk. The name was bestowed on him by the captain of the first starship on which he had served, following an intense engagement with a trio of Tzenkethi vessels where Schlosser had been forced to take over the ship's tactical bridge station after his immediate superior was killed during an exchange of fire. Despite his junior rank and lack of actual combat experience, Schlosser had—as his citation later would read—engineered a devastating counterattack resulting in the destruction of two enemy ships and severe damage to the third. His conduct during the engagement led to awards and a promotion as well as his captain's moniker, which would follow him from assignment to assignment as he continued to climb the rank ladder. These days, only close friends called him by the nickname; in the decades since that fateful day, his icy, composed demeanor only had strengthened. Compared to what Schlosser had faced during his career, an exasperated superior was nothing.

"I will see to it immediately. May I ask the nature of the reassignment?"

"Not at this time. As I said, it's a sensitive matter, but rest assured that the ship you send will be acting on a matter of the utmost importance to Federation security interests. I need the ship on station as quickly as possible, and any other priorities under which its captain may be operating are rescinded." The president moved closer so that his face all but filled the workstation's display screen. *"This is a classified operation, Admiral, so I want all proper compartmentalization protocols in place and enforced. Once you've found the ship and routed it to Jevalan, inform her captain to expect further instructions directly from me."*

"Sir, I'm happy to act as your liaison in this matter. I do have a top-security clearance, and I can certainly help with making sure that the ship's rerouting doesn't attract any undue attention."

"I expect you to do all of that, anyway, Admiral. After all,

you're supposed to be someone who can accomplish great things under pressure, 'Warhawk.' I hope that reputation is well-earned. Let me know when the ship is on its way. Ishan out."

The communication ended before Schlosser could say another word, leaving him alone with the now-blank computer screen and a growing number of points to ponder. Something about this planet, which so far as he knew had no strategic value other than as a source of dilithium—which belonged to the Cardassians, anyway—was some kind of irritant to the president pro tempore. Without more information, there was no way for Schlosser to form any sort of coherent hypothesis, other than the fact that the order itself was just another in a string of odd directives handed down by Ishan as well as his chief of staff before him. On the surface, the orders of which Schlosser was aware possessed no links or commonalities, other than being of great interest to the president. To this point, Schlosser had refrained from attempting to find any such connections out of concern that his actions might be discovered by Ishan, resulting in his own set of problems with the president. No, the admiral decided, prudence was the wise course, but something about this new request still intrigued him.

"Computer," he said, directing his attention once more to the desktop workstation, "access current status of all Starfleet vessels operating in or near Cardassian space that can reach the Doltiri star system. Order search results in ascending order of transit time to that system from their present location, and display to my screen."

"Stand by," replied the computer, and in a moment, the terminal's screen began to list what ended up being eight starships of different classes and capabilities, along with the names of their captains and current spatial coordinates. Also included were travel times, listed in hours, to the Doltiri system. Based on their vessel classes, only four of the ships met President Ishan's criteria of having a "sizable security detach-

ment," which Schlosser chose to interpret as being required in order to engage some kind of military target or perhaps to locate and take into custody one or more persons of interest. As for the latter scenario, the admiral had no idea who that might be or what they might have done to earn the president's attention.

Tapping his desk as he mulled possibilities, Schlosser said, "Computer, information on planet Jevalan, located in the Doltiri system. What is its current status?"

"Jevalan is a mining planet belonging to the Cardassian Union. It is the former location of labor camps used by Cardassians overseeing indentured Bajorans. The camps were abandoned in 2369 just prior to the end of the Cardassian Occupation of Bajor. Currently, the planet is the site of a joint Bajoran-Cardassian effort to locate, identify, and return to Bajor the remains of Bajorans who remain unaccounted for since the end of the Occupation."

That seemed benign enough, Schlosser decided, to say nothing of being a relevant and timely cause, given the ongoing effort to solidify relations between the Cardassians and the Federation, of which Bajor now was a member. Aside from its history, which could not be considered pleasant or noteworthy by any sane definition, what on this otherwise unremarkable world could possibly warrant Ishan's acute attention?

It was an intriguing question, Schlosser decided, and the answer promised to be equally fascinating.

What are you up to, Mister President?

Eighteen

Everything about the cooling unit just sounded so *wrong*.

"Where in the world did you get this thing?" asked Commander Geordi La Forge, shouting to be heard over the unit's internal generator as the sounds of its coughs and sputters spilled forth from its open access panel. "I didn't even know they still made this model anymore."

Standing next to him while he finished his inspection of the unit's innards, Vernon Wilmer, the colony's chief mechanic, offered a smile of unabashed pride. "They don't, but since most of their internal systems can be adapted to comparable replacement components from other hardware without too much trouble, they're popular with colonies like ours." His hands were jammed into two of the deep hip pockets of his tan coveralls, which were soiled and frayed at the cuffs and shoulders. This, La Forge knew, was a man who had no trouble getting his hands—or the rest of him—dirty to accomplish a task, and he looked as though he might enjoy every moment of his work.

From where she leaned against the master control console overseeing the unit's operation, Captain Sonya Gomez added, "Colonies and remote Starfleet outposts, too. Just about anybody can fix them, given time and the right tools."

"Even me," Wilmer said, "and you have no idea how much of a blessing that is."

Gomez replied, "Not the first time I've heard a version of that story, and not the first time I've seen one of these. We've definitely run into our share of them over the years."

"I'll bet you have," La Forge said, reaching for the control pad and pressing the key to close the cooling unit's maintenance hatch. "I've seen a few here and there, myself." As the cover slid back into place, there was a notable reduction in the noise. "Well, despite what my ears are telling me, my eyes and my tricorder say this beast is functioning within the guidelines." In addition to the scans provided by his tricorder, the chief engineer also had brought his ocular implants to bear, surveying every centimeter of the cooling unit's power systems using the full visual range afforded by his artificial eyes, and he found nothing out of the ordinary.

Wilmer said, "It may not be pretty, but it's liable to outlive us all."

"I think I've read stats to support that," Gomez added.

"Tell me about it." Upon the *Enterprise*'s arrival at Acheron and after getting his first look at the array of agricultural and other equipment the colonists had brought with them to establish the initial settlement, La Forge had taken the time to refresh his memory on some of the older, non-standard machines and other devices he had found. The cooling unit for the colony's central power generator was the latest iteration of a model introduced more than five decades earlier, descending from a design first developed by another group of Federation settlers on Tau Cygni V. La Forge and his engineering staff aboard the *Enterprise*-D—which, at the time, had included a bright young ensign named Sonya Gomez—first became acquainted with the design during the relocation of that colony nearly twenty years ago. He had recalled that earlier encounter during his review of the Acheron colony's equipment, noting that the model in use here was somewhat newer—less than twenty years old—yet still possessed many of the same internal components.

"Well, Chief," he said, "everything checks out here. We'll set you up with some extra components, just in case, but I can't find a thing wrong with it."

Wilmer extended his hand. "Thanks for taking the time to give it the once-over. It never hurts to get a second opinion, particularly out here, where we don't get too many of them to begin with."

"No problem at all," La Forge said as they shook hands. "Get with my assistant, Commander Taurik, before we leave, and he'll make sure you have any other parts or tools you think you might want."

"I appreciate the offer," the mechanic replied, "and don't think I won't take you up on it. I know a good deal when I hear one." Something beeped in one of his jumpsuit's chest pockets, and he retrieved a small rectangular device that La Forge recognized as a civilian communicator. Wilmer studied its compact display and frowned. "I forgot that I promised to take a look at one of the water pumping stations at the other end of town." Looking up from the communicator, he smiled. "I need to head that way. Need me to guide you out?"

"Don't worry about us. We can find our way."

"Thanks again for your time and help." Wilmer smiled. "Feel free to pop over there if you get a chance."

La Forge shook his hand again. "We might just do that. Take care, Chief."

"You, too." Turning to Gomez, he said, "And you, Captain."

Waiting until Wilmer had left, La Forge stood for another moment, listening to the cooling unit's labored chugging. "Hearing something like this on the *Enterprise* would drive me nuts."

Gomez laughed again. "That's the trouble with you chief engineers and your spit-and-polish starships. You've forgotten what it's like to roll up your sleeves and do some real work."

Grinning, La Forge reached for the satchel he had

brought with him from the *Enterprise*, and he returned his tricorder to it. "Spit and polish? Ouch. Are you really the same ensign who used to work for me?"

"A lifetime ago," Gomez replied. Then, she frowned. "Well, half a lifetime ago, anyway. Wow. Has it *really* been that long?" Unlike the bright, young officer who first had come to the *Enterprise*-D, Captain Sonya Gomez was a confident, mature woman, with her impeccable captain's uniform and its accompanying rank insignia, a shorter hairstyle that revealed her neck, and the lines around her eyes that seemed to carry within them uncounted memories and stories both uplifting and tragic. She had begun her career toiling in relative obscurity, only to emerge as one of Starfleet's finest officers.

"Time flies when you're having fun," La Forge said, slinging the satchel over his shoulder. "Or, saving the galaxy three or four dozen times, or rebuilding after a Borg invasion." He blew out his breath. "Sometimes, I wonder if I should've taken up another line of work."

"You and me both."

La Forge said, "Then I think about how I'd probably have ended up being bored. You can call life on the *Enterprise* a lot of things, but boring sure isn't one of them."

"Same with the *da Vinci*." Gomez made a show of rolling her eyes. "I don't think I've even *used* the word 'boring' since I first stepped aboard that ship."

Sonya Gomez had been a freshly minted officer, newly graduated from Starfleet Academy and her follow-on engineering school, when La Forge had welcomed her to the *Enterprise*-D's engineering team twenty years ago. As it was for many cadets, her assignment to the Federation flagship had been a dream realized, though La Forge remembered fearing that she might not be prepared for the responsibilities that came with such a posting.

Her trial by fire had come very soon after her arrival

aboard ship, when the *Enterprise* found itself flung across the galaxy by the omnipotent being who called himself "Q" and into the first of what was to be several fateful encounters with the Borg. Eighteen crewmembers were lost during that initial meeting, and La Forge recalled how rattled young Ensign Gomez had been as she fought to compartmentalize her emotions and concentrate on her duties. Her own ability to adapt to the chaotic, even terrifying situation, along with a gentle mentoring nudge from him, had allowed her to carry out necessary tasks as the engineering staff fought to repair damage inflicted on the ship by that first Borg cube.

After that harrowing initiation to the dangers that were accepted aspects of starship life, Gomez had continued to distinguish herself aboard the *Enterprise* before heading off to new assignments, eventually receiving a promotion to commander and a transfer to the *U.S.S. da Vinci,* a *Saber*-class vessel supporting a detachment from the Starfleet Corps of Engineers. In addition to leading that team, she also had served as the ship's first officer. Five years ago, she was given command of the *da Vinci* after its captain, David Gold, had elected to retire following his own rather lengthy and distinguished Starfleet career.

"From what I've read from the *da Vinci*'s mission reports," La Forge said, moving to the control room's main console, "I don't see how you even had time for boredom, or anything else, for that matter. Come to think of it, how did you even have time to *write* those reports?"

"I bribed one of the enlisted personnel to write them for me." Gomez watched as he studied the control panel, giving each of its displays and rows of status indicators one final look. "You just can't leave well enough alone, can you?"

La Forge chuckled. "I can't help this nagging feeling that the second we leave, that thing is going to blow up or something."

"Well, if that's how confident you are in your own maintenance work, then may I suggest that we make a hasty retreat out of here?"

"Right behind you." He followed Gomez to the exit, and they navigated their way through the building that housed the colony's main power systems. They traversed cramped corridors and across a pair of narrow catwalks until La Forge spotted the door he remembered entering an hour or so earlier, and he and Gomez emerged into the fresh air and bright sunlight of early afternoon in this region of Acheron.

"Well," Gomez said as they began walking in the direction of the colony's administration offices, "now that we've delivered all those supplies and equipment and given proper, Starfleet-certified inspections, what *are* we to do?"

"Captain Picard asked me to give the colony's main computer systems a look before we go," La Forge replied. He gestured toward the path they were following and to the administration building, where the rest of the teams from the *Enterprise* and the *da Vinci* were coordinating their various efforts. "To be honest, that's really something better suited to your people."

Gomez shrugged. "Well, like Chief Wilmer said, it can't hurt to have another pair of eyes." Then, with a wry grin, she added, "Especially if they're yours."

"They are rather dashing, aren't they?"

Giggling, the *da Vinci* captain offered him a playful punch on his arm. After a moment, she asked, "So, the rumor mill says you're seeing somebody these days."

La Forge felt himself blushing, if only a bit, in response to the question. "Rumor mill, huh? You never can stay ahead of that, can you? As a matter of fact, I've been dating someone. Tamala Harstad, one of Doctor Crusher's assistant medical officers. Been with her for a while now, actually." Just thinking of Tamala brought a smile to his face, one that Gomez did not fail to notice.

"Good for you, Geordi. You deserve to be happy."

"What about you? Anybody taking up any of your precious little free time?"

"There was someone for a while, about a year ago," Gomez replied. "It went bad, and we were both hurt, so I've sort of sworn off the whole romantic thing for a while." They walked without speaking to each other for a moment or two, acknowledging greetings from the handful of colonists they passed, before she cleared her throat and drew a deep breath.

"Okay, topic change: Where are you and the *Enterprise* heading after this?"

"Starfleet's sending us to the border to relieve the *Sutherland*. I don't know exactly how long we're supposed to be there. A month, maybe." The orders as conveyed by Captain Picard had offered no clue, and he had admitted that the estimate was his own. Given the current state of affairs, La Forge figured they might be out on patrol duty for much longer than Picard's guess.

Gomez shook her head. "I can't believe they're wasting you on something like that." When La Forge said nothing, she eyed him. "Come on, Geordi. You know how fast scuttlebutt travels. Word is that somebody in Starfleet—Admiral Akaar, maybe—has been told to keep the *Enterprise* on a tight leash. Sitting on your butts for weeks while the Ferengi and the Typhon Pact dance around each other, and everybody knowing there's no way any sort of trade deal was going to happen? Milk runs to colony planets? Border patrol? Something weird's going on there." She frowned. "Something weird's going on in a lot of places."

That got La Forge's attention. "What do you mean?"

"You've been getting odd orders and assignments, right? So have we." She paused as they passed a pair of colonists, each wearing light, comfortable-looking clothing, as they worked on a piece of equipment positioned outside one of the smaller structures along the settlement's perimeter. When she resumed speaking, it was in a lower voice. "A few days ago, we're on our way to Starbase Seventy-five because we're due for a baryon sweep, but we get rerouted by a new set of orders. All classified, all hush-hush, 'captain's eyes only' and everything. We're directed to rendezvous with a civilian colony transport so that we can take on passengers and carry them to another rendezvous where we hand them off to another long-haul civilian transport." She released a long, slow breath. "I've never been asked to do anything like that before."

"If all this is classified," La Forge said, "then why are you telling me? We can both land in a brig somewhere if anybody finds out we're talking about this." Despite his warning, he could not help but be curious, as this sounded exactly like the sort of thing Captain Picard had briefed his senior staff on regarding any interaction they might have with members of the *da Vinci* crew or even the colony's leadership and administrative staff. In particular, Picard had asked La Forge to be mindful of his conversations with Gomez, hoping that their long friendship might provide an opening to the discussion of any sensitive topics.

Like this one?

"Because all this sneaking around for no apparent reason bothers me," Gomez said. "I heard the reports about the special-operations team that was sent to find the people who assassinated President Bacco. That mission was ordered and authorized by Ishan's chief of staff, and they supposedly were successful, right? This group we picked up from the freighter? My orders said they were civilian engineers heading out to some remote Starfleet outpost." She scowled. "No way."

"No way what?"

As he posed the question, La Forge became aware that they were beginning to encounter more people as they continued their route through an area of the colony's commercial district on their way to the colony's administration center. Touching Gomez on her arm, he motioned for her to follow him to a patio outside a small tavern. The sign next to the door advertised that the establishment would not be open for a few more hours. On the patio seven sets of tables and chairs were arranged, and La Forge selected a seat that allowed him to place his back to the café's storefront.

"Okay," he said, placing his satchel on the table as Gomez took the chair across from him, "you think you were giving some spec ops guys a ride?"

"Had to be. For one thing, I had a check run on both ships, and the flight plans they'd filed didn't match up with their respective course trajectories to and from the rendezvous points. I can see a mistake for one ship, but both?"

"What about the people? The engineers?"

"They weren't like any engineers I've ever run into, and you know I've run into a lot of them, including some pretty eccentric characters." Rolling her eyes, Gomez added, "Hell, I've got a whole shipload of those. These guys were nothing like that. They carried themselves like soldiers. I don't think they were Starfleet, or maybe they used to be, but at some point, they wore somebody's uniform."

La Forge considered what he was hearing. "Some special ops personnel don't follow the standard uniform regs. They're authorized to modify their clothing, hair, and whatever so that they can pass as civilians, which comes in handy in certain situations." In his experience, it was the rare special-operations officer who successfully could modify his or her demeanor so as to conceal all "giveaways" or "tells" that might reveal them to be something other than a simple pilot, mechanic, or other civilian working on a freighter. The sort of elite training that produced such effective operators often did not lend itself to fostering humility or a lack of self-confidence.

"I thought about that," Gomez replied, casting a casual glance over her shoulder as they heard a colonist walking past the tavern's patio. "But there was something else about these guys; something I couldn't put my finger on. They were . . . I don't know . . . unpolished? Rough around the edges, somehow? One of them even had a scar down the left side of his face. Who does that?" She held up her hands as though trying to wave away her words. "I know. It sounds weird, right?"

La Forge shrugged. "It's not the strangest thing I've ever heard." Still, he shared his friend's curiosity as to why a special-operations team—similar to the one dispatched to apprehend President Bacco's killers—might be deployed in such a covert manner. Who had deployed them, and for what purpose? Was this yet another aspect of President Ishan's secretive scheming? "I can ask Captain Picard to make a few discreet inquiries." If anyone could get Admiral Riker to do some digging about this, it was the captain.

"Discreet is probably the key word here," Gomez said.

"You're not kidding." Picard's briefing on what Admiral Riker had asked of him and a small cadre of close, trusted colleagues still rang in La Forge's ears. The idea that the Federation's interim president might be involved in Nani-etta Bacco's murder was still hard to believe, but it already had been demonstrated that Ishan was willing to circumvent the truth and the law in pursuit of his goals, some of which remained known only to him.

His combadge beeped, the indicator tone followed by the sound of Commander Worf. "Enterprise *to Commander La Forge.*"

"La Forge here," the chief engineer answered after tapping the communicator.

"*We have received new orders from Starbase Two Eleven,*" the first officer said. "*They picked up a distress call from a civilian freighter and have requested the* Enterprise *to investigate. All away teams are being recalled, and we are to depart immediately.*"

"Mysterious new orders," Gomez said, keeping her voice low so as to avoid being picked up by the open frequency. "That's certainly odd, isn't it?"

Trying not to be distracted by her suspicions, La Forge replied to Worf, "On my way. La Forge out." As the communication ended, he rose from his seat, adjusting his satchel.

"Well, what do you think about that?" Gomez asked.

"I think it's a distress call," the engineer said. "But I also think it's a bit odd that a starbase would call us to go check it out. Starbase Two Eleven has five starships assigned to it."

"Exactly."

"Or, you could just be paranoid," La Forge countered.

"Maybe," Gomez said. "Maybe you should be, too." She stepped closer, wrapping her arms around him. "Good luck, Geordi, and be careful."

Returning the embrace, La Forge considered her comments, at the same time trying to remember an old saying about such thinking. How had it gone?

Just because you're paranoid, doesn't mean they're not out to get you.

Nineteen

The first thing Beverly Crusher noticed upon entering Ilona Daret's home was the stench of something burning.

"Ilona?" she called out, stepping farther into her friend's quarters. When there was no answer to her call, Crusher retrieved the phaser concealed inside her jacket and verified its power setting. "Ilona, are you here?" The only response she received was the echo of her own voice along the narrow corridor leading from the domicile's main entrance. The doorway to Daret's lab was closed, and as she drew closer, she heard the sounds of someone moving about within the room. Phaser held out before her, she advanced to the entry and keyed into the control pad the code Daret had given her, and the door slid aside.

Smoke drifted through the open doorway, and Crusher stepped to one side, using for cover the wall beside the door as she peered into the lab. "Ilona!" she called out.

"I am here, Beverly," the Cardassian replied, and when Crusher moved to look farther into the room she saw him standing before the examination table at the lab's center. He held in his hands what she figured had to be a portable fire extinguisher, but his attention was on the table and the stasis unit sitting atop it. The smoke now filling the room was coming from the table.

"What happened?" Crusher asked, lowering her phaser and stepping into the room.

Daret replied, "That is an interesting question." Moving away from the table, he returned the extinguisher to a mounting bracket on the lab's rear wall.

Outside the room, Crusher heard the sound of the front door opening, followed a moment later by the sound of Rennan Konya calling out, "Doctor Daret? Doctor Crusher?"

"In the lab, Lieutenant," Crusher replied, and a moment later the security officer and Kirsten Cruzen appeared in the doorway. Both of them had their phasers drawn, relaxing only a bit upon seeing that Crusher and Daret appeared to be alone.

"A fire?" Konya asked, his tone one of doubt.

"Looks that way," Crusher said.

Cruzen stepped into the room, moving to one side and giving the various cabinets and other equipment a visual inspection. "Any idea how it started?"

"The stasis unit's internal power systems are still functioning," Daret said, having moved back to the table. Crusher stepped closer as he tapped several series on the unit's control pad. After a moment, he frowned. "Its self-diagnostic program indicates a failure in the temperature regulation system."

Konya gestured to the stasis unit's top, which now was charred black. "That's one way to put it. Dare I ask what was inside?"

Nodding, Daret sighed. "This unit was housing the remains we believe belong to the real Ishan Anjar."

"There's a coincidence," Cruzen said, turning from her once-over of the lab's other equipment. "You found it like this?"

"Yes." Daret gestured to the table. "The interior already was being consumed by fire when I entered the lab. I was able to extinguish it, but by then it was too late."

Reaching into one of her jacket's other pockets, Crusher extracted her tricorder and activated it before sweeping it across the top of the ruined stasis unit. "I'm picking up residue from some kind of flammable compound inside the chamber and remnants of materials that aren't part of the unit." Something about the reading was off, somehow, but how or why eluded her. "This wasn't an accident or a malfunction. Somebody rigged this thing to burn." Eyeing the tricorder's display, she realized what about the scan was bothering her. "Whatever they used, there was more than enough here to destroy the unit."

"You're sure?" Konya asked.

Crusher shrugged. "I'm no detective, but the presence of the foreign matter's enough for me, particularly considering our present situation."

"After our little adventure down at the excavation site," Cruzen said, "I'm okay with being a little suspicious."

Konya, who had moved to the room's opposite side, had pulled his own tricorder and was conducting a scan. "Not a bad idea. Look at this." He moved aside a large piece of lab equipment to reveal a small container on the floor beneath it.

"What is that?" Crusher asked.

Adjusting the setting on his phaser, Konya aimed at the package. "Some kind of improvised incendiary device. It's packed with the same compound as the stasis unit." He fired at the package, the phaser's bright orange beam engulfing the small container and vaporizing it.

"Found another one," Cruzen said. After a third such device was found and destroyed, the lieutenant returned her weapon to her jacket. "Somebody wanted the whole lab to go up. It's a good thing you got here when you did, Doctor Daret."

The Cardassian, who had taken a seat at his desk in the room's far corner, released an irritated grunt. "Not early enough, I'm afraid." He gestured once more to the devastated stasis unit. "The fire was more than sufficient to obliterate all of the samples." Tapping controls on his computer workstation, he scowled. "According to the system access log, someone performed a search of all my data files, and the alarm system has been disabled, not just the fire alert."

Moving to stand behind her friend, Crusher crossed her arms. "You're sure?"

"Absolutely. The entire security protocol was deactivated." Daret tapped another control, and the data he had been reviewing vanished. Reaching past the workstation, he retrieved a wooden, hand-carved framed photograph of himself and a Bajoran. The image depicted the two figures standing at what looked to be the lip of a large, shallow crater. "I am sorry, Mosara." Then, as though realizing Crusher was watching him, he looked up at her and smiled. "He gave this to me after our excursion to the Olanda labor camp. He even made the frame himself." She watched him trace the image with his fingertips, pausing to tap the photo on an area of the landscape in the distance behind him. "We found a makeshift temple here, buried beneath the ground. It was never discovered by the guards."

"They must have gone to great lengths to protect it," Crusher said.

"Yes, though the inability of scanners to work at those levels was a great aid in that regard. Still, it is shameful that such actions were necessary. At least now, we're trying to address the wrongs we perpetrated." He smiled again. "Mosara always was certain that Bajorans and Cardassians, working together, could find a way to put the past behind us. He believed in this project more than anyone I know." He sighed. "I have failed him."

Crusher placed a hand on his shoulder. "Not yet, you haven't."

Rising from his chair, Daret placed the photograph back on his desk. "Why didn't whoever did this just vaporize the stasis chamber and the samples? Why attempt to destroy the entire lab? Were they trying to make it look like an accident?"

"That's exactly what they were doing."

Crusher and everyone else looked up at the new voice to see Thomas Riker standing just inside the room's entrance. She had not heard him enter the lab; it was though he had just materialized out of thin air.

"Your friend does seem rather talented at employing stealth," Daret said. "Disturbingly so, in fact."

"No kidding," Crusher replied as the group converged on the ruined status unit.

Overhearing the remarks, Tom smiled. "Sorry, Doctor. It's an old habit. When you spend enough time around some of the people I've fallen in with over the years, you learn to be light on your feet. And fast, too." His expression turned serious. "I've checked with the security detachment. No one's come asking after the two Bajorans we gave to them."

"That might be telling us something," Konya said. "They're locals, right? Whoever put them up to trying to nab Doctor Daret doesn't care about them. They've been hanging back, trying to keep a low profile, but I'd bet they're the ones who set up the lab to burn."

Crusher gestured toward the exam table. "They took care of this, anyway."

"Right," Tom said, "but they don't know what else Doctor Daret might have. You said they checked your computer files. Did they find anything?"

Shaking his head, Daret replied, "No. I kept none of Mosara's notes there. Everything that he prepared he hid, along with additional samples of the remains belonging to the real Ishan Anjar."

"Which means whoever did this very likely knows or at least suspects what you and your friend have here," Crusher said.

Tom said, "Or, they've just been hired to collect or

destroy your work, in addition to getting their hands on you. The two Bajorans wanted to take you somewhere, most likely to someone who knows what you and Doctor Raal have learned. In addition to making sure you stay quiet, they'll want to know that any data you've collected won't be found or used by anyone else. But, they still need you to help them get it."

"After which," Daret said, "they will want to kill me."

"It's what I'd do." When that earned him disapproving looks from the rest of the group, Tom shrugged. "Sorry. I meant that if I was them, of course."

Crusher stepped next to Daret, placing her hand on his arm. "Mosara knew what he'd discovered was dangerous, which is why he went to such lengths to protect the evidence, and you."

"He may have done too good a job," Cruzen said. She looked to Daret. "He didn't offer you any clues as to where he might've stashed everything?"

The Cardassian sighed. "Mosara told me nothing before he left."

"Sure he did," Tom countered. "We just need to figure out how he did it."

To Crusher, it looked as though an earthquake had been unleashed within Raal Mosara's home. Furnishings and personal effects were scattered across the floor of the small, unassuming residence. Clothing had been torn from closets and bureaus, books and other items swept from shelves, and foodstuffs, cookware, and utensils had been pulled from storage cabinets in the cramped galley. Even the refrigeration unit, which to Crusher appeared as though it may have been emptied by Mosara prior to his departure, had been pulled from its mounting and allowed to fall to the floor.

"I'm going to go out on a limb here," Konya said, "and guess that Doctor Raal was a better housekeeper than this."

Cruzen, stepping over a chair that had been tipped over and its cushion torn from the frame, said, "I think my Academy roommate came through here."

Ignoring the security officers and their commentary, Crusher turned to Daret. "Do you have any idea when this might have happened?"

"Within the past two days," the Cardassian replied. "I was here tending to Mosara's plants, and everything was in order."

Tom Riker crossed the room, scrutinizing every centimeter. "So, after you made contact with Doctor Crusher while she was on her way here from the *Enterprise*?" He frowned as he regarded her. "I guess that could answer the question of whether anyone may have followed you."

"We maintained constant sensor scans the whole way here," Konya said. "Nobody was following us."

Grunting, Tom said, "If only they made some sort of device that might . . . I don't know . . . *cloak* a ship's movements. That sort of thing could really come in handy, don't you think?"

"You're suggesting a cloaked ship followed us here?" Crusher asked. "Wouldn't that narrow the possibilities to a Klingon or Romulan vessel?"

Again Tom offered a cynical snort. "Yes, because as we all know, a lofty organization like Starfleet would never equip their ships with such dastardly gadgets."

"Well," Cruzen said, "if President Ishan—or whatever the hell his name is—is sending someone to make sure his secrets stay buried, there's no telling what resources he or somebody working for him might be channeling to such people."

The lieutenant's unspoken accusation troubled Crusher. "You're not suggesting that somebody from Starfleet is doing all of this?"

"Somebody loyal to the president?" Tom asked. "That

could be anyone. Starfleet, civilian, hired gun; who knows? We know the man has friends. I almost learned that lesson the hard way on Nydak II. It stands to reason that a few of them have pull with someone." He gestured around the room. "What I don't get is why they didn't cover their tracks here but went to the trouble to stage an accident at your place."

Konya said, "Maybe they didn't know that Doctor Daret comes here every so often. They weren't expecting anyone to find this; not the way a fire would attract attention. Not that it really matters anymore. They know we're here, and they probably know we're onto them."

"But we don't know who they are," Crusher said. She touched Daret's arm. "Mosara wouldn't have left anything here, would he?"

"I highly doubt it," the elderly Cardassian replied. "He was much too careful, but you think he left a clue for me here?"

Tom replied, "Here, or your place, or both. Somewhere the two of you had in common, and likely something not noticeable to anyone who didn't know you very well."

"He always was so creative," Daret said. "And so much smarter than me. I don't even know where to look."

Cruzen stepped around a small table that had been upended and left propped against a shelving unit. "He'd want you to find it, but limit the possibility of someone else figuring it out. It's probably something personal, something you're both familiar with, or have worked on together, or exchanged."

With Konya and Cruzen taking up a security watch near the front entrance, Daret, Crusher, and Tom inspected the remainder of Raal Mosara's home, including that portion of the residence which, like Daret's, had been configured as a laboratory space. Much like the main room, the rest of the domicile was in similar disarray. Whoever had ransacked the rooms and their contents had been quite thorough, in Crusher's estimation.

"Can you tell if anything's missing?" Crusher asked as they were finishing their check of the lab.

"Nothing obvious," Daret replied, moving past a work-table running the length of the room's far wall to stop before a small metal desk. "So far as I know, Mosara kept nothing of any intrinsic value here. Only his work and a few mementos." He lowered himself to one knee and reached beneath the desk to retrieve an item. When he returned to his feet, Crusher recognized the object as a broken frame encasing a photograph. The frame was wood, similar in style and texture to the one Daret had in his own lab, and a closer look confirmed her suspicion that it contained a copy of the same image of Daret and Mosara at the Olanda excavation site. Daret fumbled with the frame as though trying to mend it.

"We probably don't have much time," Tom said, his back to them as he studied the emptied cabinets and their contents that had been scattered across the floor. "Whoever did this, assuming they didn't find anything, is probably looking for you right now." He turned to Crusher. "You, too, Doctor, and likely Lieutenant Cruzen, as well. If we're lucky, they might not know about me, and maybe not Lieutenant Konya, but we have to keep assuming the worst." To that end, he had directed Daret to pack whatever belongings he felt necessary before leaving the doctor's own home, having convinced Crusher and the others that remaining here in the camp invited too much risk.

"And we haven't had any luck tracking down who might be after Ilona," Crusher said. "It could be anyone."

"Yeah. Konya and I have been surveying the main camp as well as the excavation site, looking for anyone who might not fit in for one reason or another. The trouble with that strategy is that someone who knows what to look for knows we don't fit in, either." He shrugged. "Still, it beats waiting around here for someone to try and ambush us."

"Beverly."

Turning at the sound of Daret's voice, Crusher saw that her friend still stood at Raal Mosara's desk, holding the broken picture frame. His expression was one of surprise.

"There's something I think you both need to see."

He waited until Crusher and Tom joined him at the desk, then he pointed to the computer screen, upon which was displayed several icons. Crusher saw that each represented a different image, including several that appeared to be similar to the photograph in the broken frame.

"I was looking through Mosara's personal files, to see if anything had been accessed. All of these images were reviewed, but nothing appears to have been altered or destroyed."

Tom leaned closer, gesturing first to the screen and then to the photograph next to Daret's right hand. "These all look to have been taken around the same time. Are they significant?"

"Beyond what I already told you about the site and that we found the temple?" Daret asked. "No. We recorded these images to mark the occasion of the discovery. Mosara had been keeping detailed notes about his work, not just for the official reports but also because he was considering writing a book chronicling the entire effort. We even had discussed a collaboration, to ensure both Bajoran and Cardassian viewpoints were represented. It seemed a prudent approach, given the sensitivity of the subject matter."

Tom asked, "Where are those notes?"

"I don't know. They're not here, so I assume Mosara either took them with him when he left for Bajor, or else he left them with the rest of his notes and other materials." Daret tapped one of the icons displayed on the monitor, and the image expanded to fill the screen. Crusher recognized it as the same photograph framed and occupying space on both Daret's and Raal's desks, with the two of them standing at the edge of the wide, shallow crater that was the Olanda labor camp excavation site.

Something's different.

"Hang on." Crusher frowned at the sudden thought, leaning closer to the desk in order to study the picture.

"You see it, too." Still holding the broken picture frame in his hand, Daret placed it on the desk, angling it so that the photograph it contained could be studied alongside its digital counterpart. On the screen, the area behind Daret and Raal depicted a section of the exhumed labor camp ruins with debris and equipment scattered across the swath of upended soil. As for the picture in the frame, it depicted the two scientists in the identical pose, but in the distance behind them at the bottom of the crater's opposite side, a small dark opening was visible.

Pointing to that section of the photograph, Daret said, "That is the entrance to the temple. It's visible in other images, but not in any of the ones featuring us." He reached up to tap the monitor, and a series of images from the dig site began to display in sequence, with each image remaining on screen for several seconds before advancing to the next picture. When a photograph without Daret or Raal presented itself, Daret paused the playback. "See?"

Tom grunted. "I'll be damned."

"Yeah," Crusher said, staring at both images. "Ilona, can you tell if any of these images have been copied from here?"

"So far as I'm able to determine, nothing was copied." Daret turned from the desk to face Crusher and Tom. "That's it, isn't it? The message Mosara left me."

"Why else would he alter that image?" Crusher asked.

Daret studied the smaller picture in its broken frame. "Now that I see the two versions side by side, it seems so simple and obvious."

"Sometimes simple and obvious is just what's needed,"

Tom countered, "particularly when you're trying to be sneaky. There's a good chance whoever's after you missed that completely. What's the condition of the area where you found the temple?"

"After cataloging its contents and verifying that no remains were there," Daret said, "Mosara and I saw to it that the area was sealed off. The Bajoran government has expressed its desire that the site be protected, at least until such time as a final disposition is determined for the camps and any plans for historical markers or other monuments are finalized."

"Is it being guarded?" Crusher asked.

"There seemed to be no need. Everyone here is treating the entire excavation with utmost care. None of us would intentionally damage or destroy anything we found here."

"Can't bet on that anymore," Tom said. "Still, it's not an obvious place for anyone to look if they're not familiar with your routines, or who hasn't read any of Doctor Raal's notes. Whoever's after you is probably keeping a low profile for the moment, waiting for us to make the next move."

"What *is* our next move?" Crusher asked. She gestured to the images. "We can't just lead whoever's watching us to the dig site."

"No," Tom replied. "We're going to have to flush them out."

Footsteps behind them made them turn to see Konya standing in the doorway, his expression grave. "I think we may have a problem. I didn't get the hourly advisory message I programmed to be sent from the *Dordogne*'s onboard computer, and I can't reach it with my communicator." He sighed. "I think our friends may either have taken control of the runabout or just destroyed it."

"Is there any way to verify that?" Crusher asked, trying to ignore the uneasy feeling in the pit of her stomach.

"Not without making contact with the computer or trying to locate it with some other sensor array or getting up to it."

"The administration building over at the docking facility would have the necessary sensor equipment to let you track your vessel," Daret said, "assuming you could provide it with the necessary information to work around whatever security protocols you had established for your ship."

"Okay," Tom said, "Konya and I will work on that, but to be honest, I was expecting them to take care of the runabout by now. We'll just have to find another way to get to the Olanda camp."

"What about our friends?" Crusher asked. "The ones you want us to flush out? They still have their own ship."

Tom smiled. "Not for long."

Twenty

Standing in the middle of the holodeck, Will Riker waited as the *Titan*'s temporary captain, Commander Christine Vale, tapped a series of commands on the control panel set into the archway at the chamber's entrance. A string of beeps emanated from the panel, after which Vale turned to Riker, who was standing at the center of the room with Commander Tuvok, Ensign Torvig Bu-kar-nguv, and the holographically generated mechanical form of the Sentry artificial intelligence, White-Blue.

"Security protocols are in place, Admiral. The room is completely isolated from the rest of the ship's onboard systems."

Riker nodded in approval. The secure holodeck chamber already had proven its usefulness in the weeks since he had ordered its creation, wanting a protected area in which he could talk freely with members of the *Titan*'s senior staff without having to worry about someone attempting to monitor his conversations. Having such meetings at his office on Earth was out of the question, and even most areas aboard ship were vulnerable to eavesdroppers if one possessed the requisite skills, equipment, and opportunity. And while he was loath even to consider the notion, Riker could not rule out the possibility of President Ishan, Velk, or one of their supporters having managed to recruit as a spy a member of his crew.

"All right, then," Riker said, exchanging glances with each of his three companions. "You said you had something for me?"

Vale replied, "Indeed we do, sir. Commander Tuvok and Mister Torvig have been busy these past several days, and we've had a few breakthroughs."

Nearly three weeks previously, Riker had come to this small, trusted group of officers and given them a special mission: monitor a top-secret, heavily encrypted subspace communications array that had been designed for the sending and receiving of encoded message traffic in such a manner as to not be detectable by conventional tracking systems. Special equipment—some of it fashioned by Ensign Torvig by cannibalizing components from disparate shipboard systems and perhaps a few caches of scrap parts about Riker wished to possess no knowledge—coupled with a complex suite of software written by the *Titan*'s cryptolinguist, Ensign Y'lira Modan, to target the decompiling and translating of the intensely packed and scrambled data streams had been used to crack the classified channel. This effort eventually had led them to the secret orders as well as personnel and resource reassignments made by President Ishan's chief of staff, Galif jav Velk.

All in a day's work, I suppose.

"You've got a line on whoever Ishan's been talking to behind the scenes?" Following Velk's arrest, Riker had directed his team to continue their efforts to monitor and decode any further secret communications, in the hopes of finding some concrete link between Ishan and those who perpetrated Bacco's assassination.

Vale replied, "We think so." She gestured to Torvig, and the diminutive Choblik began tapping the padd he held in one of the cybernetic arms extending from his torso. Before them, a ball of energy coalesced into existence, the effect similar to that of a transporter beam. The sphere grew and stretched until it acquired the shape of a humanoid's head and shoulders, and seconds after that, the holographic projection solidified to depict a human male with dark hair slicked back and away from his face. A long, narrow nose was flanked by dark blue eyes that seemed to bore through Riker, and a small, thin mouth accented a pointed chin. Though only the man's upper torso was visible, it was still enough to show that he wore a Starfleet flag officer's uniform with a rear admiral's rank insignia affixed to his high collar.

"I know him. Admiral Declan Schlosser. He's one of the deputy chiefs at Starfleet Security." Riker studied the holomodel. Though he only had encountered the admiral perhaps twice in the short span of time since his own promotion, he decided that the holomatrix had done a fantastic job of capturing Schlosser's severe, almost pained expression.

Thank God I don't have to work for him.

Tuvok said, "He also has been receiving direct instructions from President Ishan and—before he was arrested—Galif jav Velk."

"You're sure?"

"I/We are," replied White-Blue. "President Ishan and Admiral Schlosser have taken extraordinary steps to limit and encrypt their communications. I/We were able to interface with the software used to manifest the encryption and establish that Schlosser has been contacted by the president's office on three occasions in the past five days."

Tuvok added, "There were other instances in the weeks prior to Velk's arrest, during which we believe it was he who was communicating with the admiral. Those interactions were scrambled, of course, and our deciphering efforts so far have yielded nothing."

Riker crossed his arms. "Ishan kept records of these conversations?"

"Yes, Admiral," Torvig replied, "though his copies of the records are on a secure server within the Palais de la Concorde that is not connected to the larger Starfleet or Federation government—restricted data network."

"No luck getting in there, I'm guessing," Riker said.

White-Blue replied, "Not to this point, Admiral, but our efforts continue." The product of a merging by Torvig between its own software and that of a holographic program designed for secure communications and employed by Galif jav Velk, the Sentry's original AI had evolved before Riker's eyes, becoming an amalgam of both entities' core processes. The true potential of this integration was still being explored, but so far it appeared to be reaping all manner of dividends.

"However," Torvig said, "Admiral Schlosser also kept records of his exchanges, with President Ishan as well as Velk. We can access those, but they are encrypted."

"One more thing on the To-Do List," Vale remarked.

"No kidding," Riker said. "Schlosser might be a lot of things, but he's definitely no fool. Ensign, can you at least get dates and times for the exchanges?"

"Yes, sir," the Choblik replied. "We are cross-checking them against all personnel transfers, starship reassignments, and other resource allocation directives for the previous ninety days. So far, we have traced communications to the starships *Bastogne, da Vinci,* and *Tonawanda.*"

Vale added, "This is our guy, sir. We need a bit more time to connect all the dots, but this has to be him."

Stroking his beard as he listened to his officers' reports, Riker asked, "What about the captains of these ships? Are they working for Ishan or just following orders?"

"At this time," Tuvok replied, "we have no reason to suspect that the captains of these vessels are or were knowingly colluding with President Ishan or Velk. We will verify this, of course, as part of our continuing investigation."

"What about Velk?" Riker asked, his gaze still locked on the computer-generated representation of Admiral Schlosser. "Has there been any chatter about him?"

White-Blue said, "I/We have not yet found anything. The notable lack of such communication suggests extraordinary measures are being taken to ensure no connection exists between Velk and the president."

"Makes sense," Vale said. "Ishan can't afford any perceptions of impropriety; not now, after he gave that big speech about Velk confessing everything and surrendering to him. The best thing the president can do right now is to keep as far away from Velk as he can get until the Federation Council convenes their board of inquiry."

Turning from where he was standing next to the hologram, Tuvok clasped his hands behind his back. "It is logical to assume that President Ishan will take whatever action he feels is appropriate to ensure that inquiry never takes place. Indeed, it is possible that Velk already is dead."

"Maybe," Riker replied. He had been considering this possibility since before his meeting with Admiral Akaar on the grounds of Starfleet Academy. "However, we know that Velk was turned over to Federation Security after he surrendered himself to Ishan. Federation News Service reports show him being taken into custody and removed from the president's office. Assuming none of that was faked, it means that Velk is in a secure holding facility awaiting the council's decision. If Ishan tries to move on him, somebody's going to know about it." He shrugged. "That might buy us some time, but not much. Torvig, you and White-Blue keep following that thread, wherever it goes."

"Aye, sir."

"What do we do about Admiral Schlosser, sir?" asked Vale.

"For now? We just keep an eye on him." Riker's first thought was to confront the other admiral head-on, using the information his people had collected as a means of leveraging answers and cooperation. He had decided that the smarter course was to allow the admiral to continue unimpeded, in the hopes that he—or Ishan, or another of his supporters—would make a mistake. "Keep tracking all of his communications, with a priority on finding Velk and any orders he might be sending off to other starships. I want to know where he's sending them and why."

"There is an additional item of interest, Admiral," Tuvok said. "Another string of communications using the subspace array—though not from Admiral Schlosser or President Ishan's office—to someone on Cardassia Prime. We do not yet know the nature of the messages that were sent, but we have been able to identify the target: Rakan Urkar."

Riker, his attention once more focused on Schlosser's holoimage, snapped his head to glare at the *Titan*'s second officer. "Urkar? You're sure?"

"Yes, sir," the Vulcan replied, his eyes narrowing. "Are you familiar with him?"

"Only his name," Riker said. "My brother, Tom, sent me a list of True Way members he'd acquired from one of his underground contacts, all of whom seemed to disappear in the weeks leading up to President Bacco's murder." He eyed Tuvok. "You and Nog met some of them."

Tuvok's right eyebrow arched. "Indeed."

The admiral recalled the list of names Thomas Riker had given him soon after departing the *Titan* at Delta Leonis and making contact with one of his "associates" there. "Yeah, but one or two of them, like Urkar, are still unaccounted for."

"Assuming President Ishan is the one responsible for initiating the communication, this may well constitute a tangible link between him and those who carried out President Bacco's assassination."

Riker looked to Torvig. "Have you found anything indicating that?"

"Not yet, sir."

Damn, Riker thought. *So close.* "If you're right, then we've got our smoking gun." Still, something seemed wrong.

"But if it is true, that seems like a stupid move for him to make. Why would he do something like that, after playing it smart and safe to this point? Something doesn't make sense here."

Before anyone could answer, White-Blue turned once again to face Riker. "Admiral, I/We are decrypting a directive sent by Admiral Schlosser to the *U.S.S. Tonawanda*. Vessel redirected from colony support mission . . . and ordered to proceed with all due haste to the Doltiri system."

Once more, Riker was caught off guard. "The Doltiri system? Jevalan? When?"

Consulting his padd, Torvig replied, "The order was issued just two days ago, Admiral. Does that planet have some significance to you, sir?"

With the exception of Deanna, Riker had not shared with anyone his knowledge of Beverly Crusher's secret mission to Jevalan, as he had been unwilling to chance any undesired parties learning of the doctor's whereabouts. How had Ishan or someone working for him learned of Crusher's activities? Had she been followed from the *Enterprise*? Considering the lengths Ishan was willing to go to in order to protect his secrets, nothing he might do seemed too far-fetched, so far as Riker was concerned.

"It does mean something, Ensign," he said after a moment, "and I'll explain all of that shortly." He turned to Vale. "I need a secure communications link to Captain Picard on the *Enterprise,* right now."

Twenty-one

U.S.S. Enterprise

Stepping out of the turbolift and onto the bridge, Picard took in the image displayed on the main viewscreen, getting his first look at the Andorian freighter *Cereshta*. The image was less than ideal, with signs of interference or other disruption visible as the picture wavered or was inundated with static every few seconds. He noted how it listed to starboard, its bow oriented down and away, and its engine ports facing the *Enterprise*. Like other classes of Andorian military and civilian vessels, the freighter was long and narrow, its warp nacelles mounted on support struts to either side of its primary hull. The struts themselves had been constructed so as to carry additional cargo pods, and Picard saw that the vessel had two such sections. No running lights or other signs of energy output were evident. Picard's first thought was that the vessel had to have been abandoned. In the distance, the brilliant red-purple haze of the Drazen Nebula contrasted against the utter blackness of open space.

"Report, Number One."

Worf, occupying the captain's chair at the center of the bridge when Picard arrived, already had risen from his seat. "We have closed to just outside transporter range and are maintaining yellow alert with our deflector shields up." He nodded toward the screen. "The nebula is interfering somewhat with our scans, but so far we are able to compensate."

Turning from the engineering station at the rear of the bridge, the second officer said, "Sensor scans are showing that their warp core's sustained serious damage. Shields and other safety protocols look to be holding, but I don't like it, Captain."

Picard made his way to the command well and moved to stand in front of his chair before glancing over to his chief of security, Lieutenant Aneta Šmrhová. "Any luck hailing them?"

From where she stood at the tactical console to Picard's left, Šmrhová said, "We've received no response, sir, or any indication that our message is being received. Life signs are faint and indeterminate, perhaps due to environment suits or something else they're wearing to protect themselves." Pausing a moment to consult her console, she shook her head. "I'm picking up two life signs, but I'm not even able to confirm that they're Andorian."

"I've run a search of our data banks," Worf said, "and according to the available information, the *Cereshta* has no non-Andorian crewmembers. However, as it is a civilian vessel, such information may not be up-to-date. That, or they took on passengers."

Picard eyed his first officer. "I presume you've already looked into their flight plan?" Worf looked to Šmrhová and nodded.

"Yes, sir," she said. "A cross-check of its registry shows that the *Cereshta* departed the Kondaii system eleven days ago, bound for Arcturus with a shipment of erinadium. They're scheduled arrival date is the day after tomorrow."

La Forge said, "I don't think they're going to make it."

"Indeed." Picard began pacing the perimeter of the command area on his way toward the viewer. "Even with their difficulties, it would seem they're a bit off course if they're headed for Arcturus. Of course, anyone doing business on Arcturus might well be engaging in other activities for which they'd wish to avoid attention." The planet Arcturus was a non-aligned world located on the fringes of Federation space. Its reputation for "anything goes" with respect to law and commerce was well earned. Picard himself had visited the planet only twice over the course of his career, and Starfleet tended to give it and its home system a wide berth.

Worf said, "There are several colonies and other ports of call along the prominent civilian trade routes through this region. It is possible that they intended to make an unscheduled stop at one of those destinations."

Despite the current situation, Picard could not help eyeing the Klingon with a small, wry grin. "You used to be more suspicious than this, Commander. Are you finally beginning to mellow, even just a little?"

Straightening his posture, the first officer nevertheless allowed a small gleam of amusement to soften his otherwise implacable features. "Perhaps a small bit, sir. Please do not inform Admiral Riker of this development."

"I'll take it to my grave, Number One."

The brief moment of levity now passed, Worf's expression once again turned serious. "There is something worth noting: The ship's three escape pods have all been jettisoned. There are no indications of other craft carried aboard the ship, and we've picked up no trace of the pods anywhere in our sensor range."

"So they may have evacuated." Picard crossed his arms, studying the image of the freighter. "Which could mean those two life signs were the unlucky souls who didn't make it out of there." His words conjured several rather unpleasant images as he considered the fate of anyone stranded aboard the wounded freighter.

"I'm downloading their memory banks and sensor logs, Captain," said Lieutenant Dina Elfiki, the *Enterprise*'s senior science officer, from where she sat at the science station along the bridge's starboard side. "There may be a clue to what happened to them somewhere."

Nodding in approval at her initiative, Picard said, "Good. What about the damage to their warp core? Do you have any readings on interior radiation levels?"

"Definitely elevated, sir," Šmrhová replied. "I wouldn't attempt to go aboard without environment suits."

"Given the condition of their warp core," La Forge added, "I don't know that I'd recommend sending anybody at all. Its instability is increasing; slowly, but getting worse by the minute. At this rate, I'm estimating a full breach within two hours. We want to be somewhere else when that happens."

Šmrhová's tactical console emitted a string of subdued beeps, and the security chief tapped a few controls. "We just received a response to our hails, sir. Audio only, but it's something."

Picard ordered, "On speakers, Lieutenant." A moment later, the ship's intercom system flared to life with a litany of hisses and static.

"*. . . freighter* Cereshta, *requesting immed . . . suffered catastrophic da . . . core failing . . . elp us!*" A sharp pop punctuated the final word, after which the channel fell silent. Picard looked to Šmrhová, who shook her head.

"That's all there is, sir. Their comm system looks to have failed."

"Transporters," Picard said. "Beam them out of there."

Seated at the ops station, Glinn Ravel Dygan replied, "Interference from the nebula and the warp core damage is hampering transporters, sir." The young Cardassian officer, serving aboard the *Enterprise* as part of a shared officer utilization program between the Federation and the Cardassian Union following the latter party's signing on to the Khitomer Accords three years earlier, tapped several controls on his console before shaking his head. "We're unable to establish a lock, Captain."

"What about a tractor beam?" Worf asked. "Moving the

ship away from the nebula might reduce the interference enough for us to compensate."

La Forge held up a hand. "I don't recommend that. With the shape their warp core's in? Any disruption could cause it to fail completely, and we'd be way too close when and if that happened."

Already uneasy with how the current situation was continuing to evolve, Picard now did not like how options were being removed, leaving him only with the obvious alternative and the one with which he felt the least comfortable. He released a small, annoyed sigh. "Geordi, are you certain about your estimate?"

"As certain as I can be, sir," replied the chief engineer. "I know what you're thinking, and I think we can get over there, get the crew, and get out in plenty of time." He stopped, looking past Picard to the viewscreen. "In fact, we may even be able to repair the damage and stabilize their warp core. I won't know for sure until I get a good look at it, but it might be worth a try. That erinadium shipment would be a tough loss for whoever's waiting for it on Arcturus."

Picard recalled what little he knew about the mineral that—so far as was generally known—existed only within the confines of the Kondaii star system. Erinadium, a rich substance that rivaled dilithium for raw energy potential, had seen its usage within the Federation grow during the past century as relations with the system's indigenous race continued to evolve. The mineral, which was very stable in its processed form, was a preferred element of large-scale clean energy production on worlds throughout the quadrant, but its present limited availability made it a valued commodity.

"Well," the captain said, "if you think you can avoid that loss, I'm sure the mineral's intended recipient would be most appreciative. Take a minimal away team; only those you need to make the necessary repairs." He turned to Worf.

"However, the priority is rescuing any stranded personnel. I want you out of there at the first sign of trouble."

The first officer replied, "Understood, sir."

At the tactical station, Šmrhová said, "Captain, there's something else. I've scanned the ship's docking port, and it's showing signs of damage. I don't think a shuttle would be able to link up there safely."

Worf frowned. "If that's true, then we have no way of getting to . . ." His words faded into silence, and when he turned to regard Picard, there was no mistaking the Klingon's disapproval as realization dawned.

"Surely there must be some other option. *Any* option."

This time, Picard forced himself not to smile, but La Forge grinned as he reached out to clap the first officer's shoulder. "Come on, Worf. Let's take a walk."

Using his environment suit's maneuvering thrusters to orient himself, La Forge closed the remaining gap separating him from the *Cereshta's* hull and allowed his own momentum to carry him the final few meters. Handholds positioned at various points along the freighter's hull provided ample targets, and within seconds, he felt his gloved hand closing around one of the metal support grips. With practiced ease, he turned himself so that his feet made contact with the hull, and he pressed the control along his left thigh to activate the magnetic grips built into his boots.

"Touchdown," he called out, his voice along with his breathing echoing inside his helmet as he felt his boots affix themselves to the hull plates. Looking around him, he watched as the rest of the away team arrived at the freighter, each of them taking up similar positions and securing themselves to the vessel's hull. "Everybody okay?"

"I'm fine," Šmrhová replied as she adjusted her stance. When La Forge caught sight of her face through her helmet, he saw her small smile. "It's nice to go outside for some fresh air once in a while."

"That is a matter of opinion," countered Worf from where he had sat down behind the security chief.

Behind La Forge, Lieutenant Commander Taurik said, "I have made the transit without incident, Commander."

Per the captain's instructions, La Forge had opted to keep the away team to no more than four people, and the time-sensitive nature of their task had inclined him to go with seasoned officers. Worf and Šmrhová would see to locating and extracting anyone still left aboard the freighter for transfer back to the *Enterprise,* where they would receive any needed medical attention. At the same time, La Forge and Taurik would see to the *Cereshta*'s ailing warp drive and—with luck—repair any damage and prevent the vessel's destruction.

A quick inspection showed that the ship's external docking port had indeed suffered some kind of damage. The visual evidence was obvious, with the port having been subjected to some kind of collision. Hull plating around the entry point had been warped and pushed inward, making any kind of safe link with another ship or even an emergency-docking collar dangerous if not impossible.

"My tricorder is registering a loss of atmosphere in the compartment behind the port," Taurik reported, holding up for emphasis the scanning device in his left hand. "However, that section has been sealed off from the rest of the ship."

"Good." Between that and the six airlock entrances scattered around the vessel, La Forge did not anticipate any problems gaining entry. With careful, deliberate steps, he began making his way across the hull toward the nearest of those portals. "We've got about an hour. Let's get inside and get this done." According to the estimate he had refined prior to their departure, the freighter's warp core would fail in just over ninety minutes, and he had given the team a thirty-minute cushion before they were to evacuate and return to the *Enterprise*.

The P-38 magnetic door seal converters from their tool satchels allowed La Forge and Taurik to make quick work of the airlock's reinforced outer hatch. Once inside and past the airlock itself—which of course required waiting for the proper atmosphere pressurization and equalization protocols to complete—La Forge could feel the omnipresent hum of the freighter's main engines reverberating up through the deck plating and into the soles of his boots. That was a good sign, he thought, but what bothered him was the lack of internal lighting within the passageways and compartments. They had been extinguished, and though their environment suits provided suitable illumination, the effect on the narrow, darkened corridors was enough to give La Forge a momentary chill of uncertainty.

"Artificial gravity appears functional throughout the ship," Taurik said, his attention focused on his tricorder. "As is environmental control, but given the leakage from the warp core, I do not advise removing our helmets."

"Don't worry," Šmrhová replied.

"The freighter's communications system remains inactive," Worf said. "Maintain your own open frequencies at all times, and report anything unusual you might encounter."

La Forge nodded in approval. Though the first officer had not said as much, the stark reality was that the away team had only one another on which to rely should anything odd happen. Captain Picard had ordered a security team to stand by for transfer to the Andorian ship in the event of an emergency, but La Forge and the others knew they would not likely be able to make the transit from the *Enterprise* in time to be of much use. For all intents and purposes, the away team was on its own.

Let's get this over with.

La Forge turned his head so that that his helmet lights offered him a look down the corridor stretching in both directions from the airlock. Comparing what he saw to the internal schematic transferred from the *Enterprise* sensor array to his tricorder, he oriented himself with respect to their desired destinations within the freighter. "Scans show the two life signs somewhere in the main cargo section. We'll try to get the lights back on as soon as possible. Good luck."

"And to you," Worf said before he and Šmrhová set off down the corridor, the Klingon leading the way with his tricorder in one hand and his phaser in the other.

Consulting his own tricorder, La Forge and Taurik maneuvered down the passageway that—according to his scans—would send them to the freighter's engineering section. Their route through the ship took them past the main cargo hold, which La Forge knew was filled with containers of processed erinadium ore. They also passed crew quarters and what the chief engineer guessed to be passenger-berthing compartments, as these areas appeared to lack any clothing, possessions, or other items a crewmember might use to decorate his or her personal space. La Forge noted how each of the crew berthing spaces looked to have been left along with their contents. Whatever had caused the crew to abandon the *Cereshta* had happened with little or no warning, and seemingly no time to address whatever crisis had befallen the ship.

"Here we are," he said as he and Taurik turned a corner in the passageway and found themselves standing before a large hatch. Aiming his tricorder at the massive fortified door, La Forge frowned. "Its magnetic safety locks have been engaged. That's likely a consequence of the warp core damage, which means the ship's computer probably has a safety protocol that'll prevent us from opening this thing."

"A logical protective step," Taurik replied. "My tricorder readings show that this hatch's proximity sensors have been disabled. Even if we are able to defeat its safety seal, we will have to open it manually."

A beep echoed in La Forge's helmet, followed by the voice of the Enterprise's first officer. *"Worf to La Forge. We have arrived at the primary cargo bay, but there are no immediate signs of the remaining crewmembers. Also, there is evidence to suggest the freighter was transporting some form of smaller craft; a shuttle or other compact transport vessel. The cargo bay contains diagnostic equipment for servicing small warp-capable craft, and its control console indicates recent use."*

La Forge frowned at the report. "There was nothing like that on the ship's manifest. On the other hand, this is a civilian ship, and it *was* headed for Arcturus, which is a popular hub for smuggling. For all we know, there may be compartments and access tunnels crammed with contraband and shielded from our sensors."

Over the comm link, Šmrhová said, *"Now we're talking."*

"Stand by, Worf." La Forge turned to Taurik, who still held his tricorder. "Are you able to pick up the Andorians?"

The Vulcan's right eyebrow rose. "Scans continue to show them in the main cargo compartment."

Over the communications link, Worf said, *"We are continuing to search."*

"Why don't I like the way this is going?" La Forge asked, more to himself than to Taurik or anyone else. "La Forge to *Enterprise.* Are you monitoring our communications?"

"We're hearing everything, Commander," Captain Picard replied. *"What's your assessment of the situation?"*

"I'd still like to take a look at the warp core, sir."

The captain replied, *"Understood. Watch yourself, Geordi. Evacuate if you think you need to. If we lose the freighter, then so be it."*

"Aye, sir." Returning his tricorder to the holder at his waist, La Forge retrieved the P-38 from his tool satchel and applied it to the engineering hatch. As he keyed the device to interrupt the magnetic seal keeping the door locked, he heard the pneumatic hiss as it deactivated and the hatch began to cycle open. "La Forge to *Enterprise.* We've got the hatch unsealed. We're proceeding into the engineering section." It was not until he felt his hand closing around the pommel of the phaser on his hip that he realized he even had reached for the weapon.

"Acknowledged, Mister La Forge," Picard answered. *"Proceed with caution."*

Taurik said, "Perhaps it is advisable to wait for Commander Worf and Lieutenant Šmrhová to return."

Though his initial reaction was to dismiss the notion as being a bit on the silly side, La Forge instead found himself pausing to consider his colleague's suggestion. Everything about this little field trip rubbed him the wrong way, and he knew Worf was not happy about the way the situation seemed to be evolving. There was no telling what the captain might be thinking, though La Forge guessed Picard at this moment was giving serious thought to ordering the away team to abandon its mission and return to the *Enterprise*.

"There's nobody else in this part of the ship," La Forge said, stepping up to the door. "I think we'll be okay." He and Taurik each wedged the fingers of their free hands into the slot between the reinforced doors, exchanging nods before both men pulled on their respective halves of the hatch. With the magnetic seal deactivated, opening the doors proved a simple task, with both doors sliding into their sides of the threshold. The hum of the ship's engines was loudest here, resonating even through La Forge's helmet. Leaning around the doorframe, he cast his helmet lights into the chamber behind the entrance, catching sight of several workstations, all active and with their displays providing what little illumination the room possessed. At the rear of the large compartment was what La Forge recognized as a warp core in common use aboard civilian Andorian vessels. Its internal components pulsed with life, but La Forge's practiced ear told him the system was in rough shape.

Sounds terrible, but let's see if we can't save this old bucket, anyway.

Twenty-two

Very little about their present situation made sense to Worf, and the longer he and the away team stayed aboard this vessel, the more intense that sensation was becoming.

"Someone's definitely been servicing a small transport or something similar," said Lieutenant Aneta Šmrhová from where she stood at a workstation sitting atop a wheeled pedestal positioned near the center of the Andorian freighter's immense primary cargo bay. "Maybe a pair of them. There's certainly enough room here to park a couple of them side by side, and they tried to erase the service logs, but they did a pretty poor job of that. It's almost like it was a backhanded effort before whoever did it decided it was time to leave, and they didn't care if they failed. Odd."

In addition to the workstation, three different tool lockers as well as optical cabling and other diagnostic and repair equipment—only some of which Worf recognized—had been positioned at various points around the open area, which was surrounded by immense containers that he knew contained vast amounts of the processed erinadium ore. It was the arrangement of the storage implements that had caused Worf and Šmrhová to believe that at least one small ship—possibly two—had occupied the cargo bay's otherwise clear deck, with the tools and other equipment arrayed around it while members of the *Cereshta*'s crew—or other, unidentified persons—serviced said craft.

"According to the data banks," Worf said as he made his way down the length of the cargo bay's interior bulkhead, "this ship carried no smaller vessels aside from its escape pods. Perhaps the transport or shuttle was itself an item being delivered to another party."

Šmrhová frowned as she looked up from the console. "Why not just have it flown to its destination? I mean, I suppose protecting some kind of smuggling operation might be the answer."

"We will ask the remaining crewmembers about that," Worf replied, using his tricorder to guide him along one bulkhead. "Assuming we can find them, of course." The Andorian life signs had remained faint but steady since *Enterprise* sensors had first detected them. Upon entering the cargo space, Worf's tricorder had indicated the readings to be coming from somewhere deeper in the chamber, but upon his and Šmrhová's entering the bay, no one had come running to meet them. No one had answered their repeated shouts alerting anyone to their presence. So far as Worf could tell, the life signs had moved not one iota. Were they trapped or incapacitated? While that might explain their lack of action in the face of imminent rescue, it also made Worf consider how such a situation may have come about in the first place.

The tricorder readings were leading him to a hatch that, according to the technical schematic provided by Commander La Forge, accessed a smaller storage space. He heard footsteps behind him and turned to see Šmrhová crossing the bay toward him, her own phaser and tricorder once more in her hands.

"This should be it," said the security chief. Returning her tricorder to its holder at her waist, she reached into a pocket on the thigh of her environment suit and produced a P-38, which she affixed to the hatch. She activated the device, and Worf heard its string of telltale beeps before that sound was replaced by the hiss of the hatch disengaging its magnetic seal. Out of habit, Worf stepped to one side as the door began to slide open, rather than allow himself to be framed in the open hatchway and perhaps become a target, whether by a frantic Andorian survivor or anyone else who might be waiting for them.

No one was waiting for them.

"Hello?" Šmrhová called out before stepping around the edge of the doorway and shining her helmet lights into the smaller compartment. The beams played off the collection of storage lockers, boxes, other containers of varying sizes and shapes, and assorted items Worf did not recognize. "Is anyone in here? We're from the *U.S.S. Enterprise,* and we answered your distress call."

"The life signs are in this room," Worf said. Taking point, he stepped into the room, following the readings on his tricorder until it led him to a storage locker that was too small to accommodate even a single person, let alone two. His unease growing with every passing second, he reached for the locker's door and opened it, his eyes locking on the single item it contained. The tricorder, a civilian model Worf had seen used by merchant freighters and construction engineers, lay at the bottom of the locker, active and emanating a low, barely audible hum. In his hand, his own tricorder was telling him what he already knew.

"Faked?" Šmrhová asked. "Are you kidding me?"

"It is not a joke," Worf said, reaching for his suit's communicator link. "Worf to La Forge! This is all a trap! Evacuate the ship! Now!"

His next words were drowned out by the wail of an alarm siren erupting across the cargo bay. Startled by the abrupt noise intrusion, he saw that Šmrhová flinched, as well.

"What the hell is that?" she snapped. Before he even

could give the order to move, Worf felt the security chief grab him by his arm and pull him from the storage compartment. As they plunged back into the main cargo bay, he now saw alert indicators flashing the length of the chamber.

"Worf!" La Forge's voice erupted from his communication link. *"Some kind of booby trap's been triggered. The warp core is going to breach any minute! We need to get the hell out of here right now!"*

Rising from his chair, Picard stepped toward the main viewscreen, hardly daring to believe what he was hearing as Geordi La Forge's voice conveyed his frantic report.

"What happened?" he asked, looking to Ensign Abigail Balidemaj, the security officer overseeing the tactical station while Lieutenant Šmrhová was off the ship.

"Unknown, sir. So far as I can tell, the triggering of the alarms came after Commander La Forge gained access to the freighter's engineering section."

A deliberate act, Picard decided, but to what end? If it was a ruse, had it been set for whichever vessel answered the distress call, or had the *Enterprise* away team, and perhaps even the ship itself, been the specific intended target?

Not now.

"How much time do they have?"

Without looking up from her console, Balidemaj replied, "Less than two minutes, sir, and we still can't get a transporter lock."

Another alarm sounded across the bridge, and Glinn Dygan turned in his seat at the ops station. "Captain, the freighter has activated a tractor beam and directed it at us."

"What?" Picard heard the astonishment in his own voice, his attention now divided by the viewscreen and the young Cardassian. On the screen, a thin green beam of energy now was visible, emanating from the *Cereshta's* forward section and reaching across space. From the image's perspective, the beam seemed to be aiming at a point just above the edge of the screen's frame.

"Confirmed, sir," Dygan replied. "The beam isn't being used to pull the *Enterprise*. The freighter is being drawn closer to us."

"Adjust our position to keep them at maximum transporter range. Stand by phasers. I want that tractor beam eliminated." Stepping between the conn and ops stations, Picard called out, "*Enterprise* to away team! Get off that ship immediately!"

Over the open communications link came the sound of La Forge's labored breathing as he shouted, *"We're on our way, Captain!"*

At the conn station, Lieutenant T'Ryssa Chen reported, "Adjusting our position, sir. They're still coming."

"Phasers standing by," said Dygan.

"Fire."

Picard watched as the first pair of orange-white energy beams lanced across space, appearing from the viewscreen's bottom edge to strike the freighter near its bow, but there was a visible disruption just before the beams made contact with the ship itself. Energy erupted in the void as the phasers impacted against the otherwise invisible barrier.

"The tractor beam emitter is shielded," Dygan said. Without waiting for Picard's order, the Cardassian repeated the firing sequence, and he did so a third time before the phaser beams penetrated the deflector shield and reached the *Cereshta*'s hull.

Balidemaj called out, "That's got it. Tractor beam is down."

Nodding at the report, Picard said, "Bridge to transporter room. Are you able to scan the away team?"

"Transporter room. Lieutenant Nader, sir. I scan them, but I can't get a lock!"

"Maintain scans until further notice, Lieutenant."

"Captain," Balidemaj said, "without transporters, there's no way we'll be able to get the away team out of there and get away ourselves before the freighter's warp core breaches."

Picard, his gaze fixed on the viewscreen and the image of the *Cereshta,* offered only a single nod. "One thing at a time, Lieutenant. Conn, continue adjusting our position relative to the freighter and keep us just within transporter range. Place phasers and a full barrage of quantum torpedoes on standby, and prepare to fire at my command."

Dygan cast a tentative look over his shoulder, "Sir?"

"You heard my order, Mister Dygan. Make it so." Folding his arms, Picard continued to stare at the freighter, which now was little more than a drifting bomb in space, much too close to the *Enterprise* for his comfort, and much too far away—for the moment, at least—for him to do anything to help his people in danger.

One damned thing at a time.

As fast as his confining environment suit allowed him to do so, La Forge covered the last few meters of corridor leading to the airlock used by the away team to board the *Cereshta,* following the telltale glow of the lights on the helmets worn by Worf and Šmrhová. The first officer and the security chief were waiting for them, and La Forge knew that even his Klingon friend's normally severe, even unreadable expression showed signs of worry as he and Taurik arrived.

"I'd like to go on record as saying this little field trip was a really bad idea," Šmrhová offered by way of greeting.

"No argument from me," La Forge said, holding out his arms and motioning her and the others toward the airlock's outer hatch.

"Do you know what happened?" Worf asked.

"Later!" La Forge snapped. After sealing the inner hatch, he took one last look to verify that the rest of the team was in position—crouching near the door with arms raised to protect their helmet faceplates—before setting the controls to override the compartment's depressurization sequence. "Okay, here we go!" he barked just before slamming his fist against the airlock control.

He had just enough time to hunch down into something resembling a protective stance before the lock's outer hatch cycled open and the air trapped in the small chamber exploded for the opening, carrying the away team with it into the void. On his way through the door, La Forge grunted in momentary pain as his left boot struck the edge of the hatch, but no alarms sounded within his suit to alert him of any loss of internal atmosphere. Within seconds he was in open space. Worf and the others were drifting in similar fashion, their momentum carrying them all away from the *Cereshta.*

"I'm not sure this is better or worse than staying aboard the ship," Šmrhová said.

Using his suit's thrusters, La Forge brought his tumbling under control while trying to re-orient himself. He now faced the *Cereshta,* but he could not see the *Enterprise,* which almost certainly had been moved to beyond transporter range.

"Commander!"

La Forge sensed the hand on his arm before he felt himself being turned away from the Andorian ship, and he saw Šmrhová holding on to him as she keyed her suit's thrusters, maneuvering them both closer to where Worf and Taurik had brought their own wayward flights under control. All four of them now were continuing to pull farther away from the *Cereshta,* and La Forge was counting off seconds in his head.

We should be dead any time now.

"Enterprise *to away team,*" called out the voice of Captain Picard, resonating in his helmet. "*Stand by for transport.*"

"Look!"

Feeling the tug on his arm, La Forge turned his head to

see that Šmrhová was pointing away from the freighter, and then he caught sight of the *Enterprise*, growing larger with every passing second as it closed the distance.

"What the hell are they doing?" was all La Forge had time to ask before twin beams of energy erupted from the ship's forward phaser arrays, lancing past the away team and passing overhead on their way to slam into the *Cereshta*. The continuous beams were followed by pairs of pulsing blue-white orbs launching away from the *Enterprise*, each one targeting the wayward freighter. Plowing into the unprotected vessel, the torpedoes bored through hull plates and into its depths before detonating, sending plumes of debris into space. Instinct made La Forge throw up his hands in what he knew was a futile effort to defend himself, but then bursts of energy erupted before him as the chunks of shrapnel impacted against something unseen.

"The *Enterprise* extended her shields to protect us!" he heard Worf call out over the communications link.

Watching the violent conflict between mass and energy unfold before him, La Forge at first did not sense the welcome, familiar tingle of a transporter beam forming around his body. Then his view of the *Enterprise* framed by distant stars and the nearby Drazen Nebula vanished, replaced with that of the starship's transporter room. Like the rest of the away team, he materialized in standing position, his arms held before him as he had been doing seconds earlier.

"Is anyone injured?" Worf asked, his voice at first sounding in La Forge's helmet before becoming muffled as the Klingon removed his own suit's headgear.

No one even had time to answer before the entire ship seemed to shudder around him. La Forge tried to steady himself as the deck heaved beneath his feet, but he ended up tumbling from the transporter platform as the lighting flickered and alarms began wailing. He dropped to the deck, and Šmrhová fell on top of him, and he heard her grunt of surprise as she rolled away. La Forge heard the sound of the *Enterprise*'s warp engines fluctuating, and even as the drone stabilized, he could tell that something was wrong.

"All stations, damage reports!" said the voice of Glinn Dygan over the intercom system. *"Internal sensors registering a hull breach on Deck Seventeen."*

"The *Enterprise*'s proximity to the freighter may have subjected the ship to greater damage than our shields could sustain," Taurik said as he rose from one knee and stepped from the transporter platform. "Closing to a distance where the shields could be extended to protect us may have compromised them, as well."

Lieutenant George Nader, the transporter room's officer on duty, picked himself up from where he had fallen behind the transporter console and moved toward the platform. "Is everyone okay?"

"I think so," La Forge said, accepting the lieutenant's offered hand to help him to his feet. Looking behind him, he saw that Šmrhová, Taurik, and Worf also were rising from where they had fallen.

"Worf to bridge," the Klingon called out to the intercom system. "The away team has returned safely."

Through the speakers Picard's voice said, *"Glad to hear it, Commander. Mister La Forge, you've likely gathered that your expertise will be required in engineering. Our shields overloaded from protecting you and the ship against the freighter's explosion. Reports are coming in from all departments, and we've apparently suffered damage to the warp drive."*

Šmrhová said, "Considering the goal likely was to destroy the *Enterprise,* I'd say we got off lucky."

"It seems a logical conclusion," Taurik said. "Everything we encountered aboard the freighter suggests subterfuge."

Ignoring the side discussion, La Forge kept his attention on his conversation with Picard. "What happened, sir? Did the freighter's warp core breach?"

"No," the captain replied. *"When we saw the overload had been triggered, we moved in and destroyed the ship before that could happen. Unfortunately, that meant getting close enough to protect you with the shields until a transporter lock could be obtained. You have Lieutenant Nader to thank for getting you out of there when he did."*

La Forge reached out to clap the transporter officer on the shoulder. "Drinks are on me the next time we're someplace where I actually need to buy them." To Picard, he said, "Taurik and I are on our way to engineering now, Captain."

"Very well, Commander." There was a pause for several seconds before Picard said, *"Mister Worf, I'll need you and Lieutenant Šmrhová on the bridge. We have a new development."*

"Acknowledged," Worf replied. "May I ask what's happened, sir?"

"We may have a sensor lock on whoever laid that trap for us, Number One."

Pacing around the bridge's perimeter stations, Picard sensed the tension radiating from his crew. After the close call with the *Cereshta,* the near loss of the away team, and the strong suspicion that the *Enterprise* had been the deliberate target for destruction, his people wanted answers—and justice. Picard wanted that, too, but those things would have to wait, at least for the moment. For now, there only was one goal.

"I want that ship," he said, moving to stand once more between the conn and ops stations. On the main viewscreen, the small, angular vessel that had emerged from the Drazen Nebula and gone to warp was continuing to make a bid at escape. Its profile was low and narrow, with a pair of warp nacelles tucked in close to its primary hull in a manner similar to a Starfleet shuttlecraft. Picard already had ordered pursuit, knowing even as he issued the commands that the *Enterprise,* having suffered damage as a consequence of the

Andorian freighter's destruction, might not be up to the task. "Who are they? Can you identify the vessel?"

At the tactical console, Ensign Balidemaj replied, "It's a civilian ship, Captain. Scout class or personal transport, but it's had some serious modifications. It's got a warp drive on par with one of our runabouts and comparable weapons and shields. If I didn't know any better, I'd swear it was a Starfleet ship."

Struck by a thought as he recalled what Worf and Lieutenant Šmrhová had reported during the investigation of the *Cereshta,* he glanced over his shoulder at the young tactical officer. "Ensign, how big is that ship? Too big to fit in the cargo space of that freighter?"

Balidemaj eyed him for a brief moment, her confusion evident, but then Picard saw realization dawn and her eyes narrowed. "No, sir. I think it would've fit rather nicely inside that cargo bay."

That mystery could be solved later, Picard knew, but only if they were able to catch the fleeing vessel.

"Engineering to bridge," said Geordi La Forge over the intercom. *"Captain, I'm only just getting a look at the damage we took. We're not going to be able to keep up this speed much longer. Whatever you're doing, you need to do it faster."*

"Understood, Commander," Picard said. He of course sympathized with his chief engineer's concerns, but letting this ship get away was out of the question.

"They're really making a run for it, sir," said T'Ryssa Chen from where she still manned the conn station. "They're increasing speed to warp seven."

Balidemaj said, "I think that's their limit."

"We'll see about that," Picard said. He had questions, and that ship held the answers. "Increase speed. Maintain pursuit course until we catch them or our engines come apart."

Twenty-three

From where she crouched in the evening darkness, Beverly Crusher watched as Lieutenant Rennan Konya and Tom Riker each peered at their target through the viewfinders of their tactical binoculars. The transport ship, so far as she could tell, was not that different from the other, similar craft occupying berths at the landing port situated to the south of what once had been the Tabata labor camp. According to Ilona Daret, the port had been a hub of activity during the Cardassian Occupation, with dozens of personnel and cargo transports arriving and departing the planet each week. Now the docking and servicing facility saw but a fraction of that traffic. Still, enough vessels came through the area that the single ship might not attract too much attention, particularly if its crew was taking steps to avoid such scrutiny. Only an unduly suspicious party, or someone who knew what to look for, might notice that something was amiss.

Fortunately for Crusher and her team, Tom Riker was both well trained and suspicious.

"That's them, all right," he said, keeping his voice quiet as he lowered the binoculars.

"You're sure?" Crusher asked.

"Yeah. We've been watching these guys since yesterday. They've done a pretty good job trying to blend in, working around their ship and engaging the port staff for maintenance requests and so on. If you were a casual observer, you'd never notice anything odd."

"How many do you think we're dealing with?" Crusher asked.

Cruzen replied, "At least eight, we think. Could be a couple more, but not many, judging from the size of that ship."

Taking the binoculars Tom offered, Crusher put the viewfinder to her face, studying the enhanced view of the small transport craft and what she counted as three male figures walking around it. "So, what is it that's odd about them?"

"No loading or offloading of cargo or passengers," Konya said. "No one's come calling on them about that, either. The way I see it, they've got to be getting close to the point where they'll start arousing suspicion even with the less-observant people walking around here."

Tom leaned against the nearby wall. "I followed one of these guys from the ship back to the main camp. He didn't go to security, but I managed to overhear him talking to a group of maintenance workers at the depot where they store the excavation equipment. Anybody want to guess who he was asking about?"

"A couple of missing Bajorans?" Konya asked.

"Give that man a prize."

Trying to swallow the nervous lump that had formed in her throat, Crusher did not at first realize that she had folded her arms and was gripping herself. These were the people who had ransacked Ilona's home as well as that of Raal Mosara, and they may well have murdered Raal, as well. They now were hunting Daret, and her, and the rest of her team. If they were responsible for Raal's death, then how far would they go to get what they wanted? More important, did they have friends who to this point had escaped notice?

Let's hope not.

Crusher handed the binoculars back to Tom. "What about port security? Wouldn't they think something's up after a while?"

"There's no real security to speak of," Tom replied. "They've got a couple of guys tracking who's coming and going, but they're also part of the maintenance staff, and they've got their hands full overseeing loading and unloading and answering any service requests. One small ship that's not causing much trouble and not bugging the maintenance staff can probably get away with it for a day or two." He shrugged. "But Konya's right. They'll have to make some kind of move, soon."

They already have, Crusher reminded herself. After a covert visit to the landing port's administration facility, during which they had utilized the operations center's sensor suit to scan the nearby space above Jevalan, Konya and Tom had been able to determine that the *Dordogne* was nowhere within the equipment's scanning range. Whether that meant the runabout had been captured or destroyed by their unwanted stalkers remained a mystery, but for the moment, the answer to that question was irrelevant. What mattered now was that the ship was unavailable to them, either for support or escape. They somehow would have to make do without it.

Wonderful.

Even at this time of night, Crusher could see workers and ship crews still were present, moving and working about several of the vessels making use of the port's facilities, though activity seemed to have begun tapering off as the hour grew later.

"So what do we do?" she asked.

Tom exchanged with Konya what Crusher took to be a knowing glance before turning to her, and she realized that in an odd, eerie way when he smiled as he now was doing, she imagined that he looked even more like his "brother," Will Riker, than even a perfect clone could manage.

"We make a move first," he said.

After finalizing a plan and sending Konya back to retrieve Lieutenant Cruzen and Ilona Daret, Crusher and Tom maintained their hidden positions, keeping watch on the ship. Though workers and other personnel passed it on their way to other landing berths, no one approached or left the vessel. At Tom's insistence, Crusher did her best to avail herself of a brief catnap while sitting on the hard ground with her back against the wall. She did not recall nodding off, and when she jerked herself awake, it was only to smack the back of her head against the wall behind her. Wincing in momentary pain, she only just managed to avoid giving voice to her discomfort, and she forced herself to contain her reaction to a simple hissing intake of breath as she closed her eyes.

"Ow."

"You okay?" Tom asked, and when she opened her eyes, she saw him next to her.

"This hotel leaves a lot to be desired," she said, pulling herself to a kneeling position. "How long was I asleep?"

"About ninety minutes. It won't be light for another couple of hours."

"What did I miss?"

"Nothing. Pretty boring, so far." He indicated the communicator badge pinned inside his jacket; a civilian model like the ones he had given to Crusher and the others so as to avoid using their Starfleet communicators. "I just heard from Konya. They've made it to our designated rally point, and they'll stay put until we join them, or something more exciting happens."

"I guess that's our cue, then." Moving forward while still remaining in the shadows of the dark corner of the landing port's service area where they had chosen to maintain their temporary observation post, Crusher tried to make herself part of the walls as she studied the nondescript transport.

Nestled in its landing berth and illuminated by an array of maintenance lights, the ship appeared to have been powered down, though she still felt the low hum of its warp core even from this distance. The only light cast off by the craft itself came from the frame of the access hatch on its port side, set into the sloping hull above the warp nacelle that, along with its companion on the vessel's other flank, served as the ship's landing gear. In this respect, the transport was very much like a Starfleet shuttlecraft or runabout.

"Think anybody's home?" she asked, keeping her voice low.

His own gaze remaining fixed on the ship, Tom nodded. "I'd bet on at least one being in there. With any luck, the others are out trying to find us. Hopefully your security people are on their toes." Earlier in the evening, it had been decided that Lieutenants Konya and Cruzen would safeguard Ilona Daret, while Crusher accompanied Tom to the landing port. At this moment, the security officers had moved Daret from his home and had secreted him in another part of the settlement, waiting for Tom and Crusher to return before the five of them set out for the Olanda labor camp.

"They are," Crusher replied. "Don't let Rennan's rank fool you. He's got more experience than most officers with more pips on their collars. He's been through a lot, particularly in the last couple of years. Jean-Luc wouldn't have sent him to look after me if he wasn't one of the best people for the job. He'll look out for us."

"If he's good enough for Jean-Luc Picard, then he's good enough for me." Drawing a deep breath, he turned to look at her. "Ready?"

"Yes." Despite her answer, Crusher had a hard time keeping her nervousness in check. Seeing Tom's concerned expression, she attempted to force a small smile. "Sorry. This sort of thing isn't really my specialty."

Tom patted the satchel he wore slung from his left shoulder. "Don't worry. I'll take care of the dirty stuff. I just need you to watch my back." He gestured to the phaser in her hand. "Will's told me you're pretty good with that."

Glancing at the weapon she held, she recalled the times she and Jean-Luc had challenged each other to marksmanship contests on the *Enterprise*'s phaser range, and even those occasions years ago when Guinan—of all people—had accompanied her during her regular requalification tests. Those had been training exercises, of course, though she had been in her share of scrapes, including a few with Tom's brother. "It's different when the targets shoot back."

"It sure is," Tom replied. "You'll be fine. We only need a couple of minutes. We're in, we're out." He shrugged. "I've done this sort of thing before, you know."

At his behest, Crusher took an extra moment to ensure her hair was secured at her neck and that the resulting ponytail was tucked down the back of her jacket. As Tom had said, there was no sense giving anyone something easy to grab on to in the event they surprised anyone aboard the transport.

Now I feel even better about this.

"Okay," she said. "Let's do it."

At this time of morning, an hour or more before sunrise, there was almost no one out and about, making easier their approach to the transport ship. Crusher saw only a single person walking around the docking area; a maintenance worker apparently on her way to one of the cargo vessels moored at the facility's far end. Waiting until her route had taken her well away from their target, Tom and Crusher stepped from their hiding place and proceeded across the tarmac. For his part, Tom was affecting a pace and gait suggesting that he had every reason to be here at this time of morning, and Crusher did her best to follow his lead. He held a tricorder in his hand, low and against his leg, and she could hear the device emitting a subdued whine as it worked.

"No sign of any surveillance or alarm system," he said as

they approached the transport. "At least, none my tricorder can find. That's either good news or bad news."

Keeping her voice low, Crusher asked, "You think they could have some kind of monitoring process that your tricorder can't pick up?"

"Possible," Tom replied. "This tricorder's been modified beyond typical Starfleet specs, but I imagine any kind of special-operations team might have similar equipment." He offered her a wry grin. "One way to find out, I guess."

They arrived at the transport, which Crusher was happy to see did not explode at their approach, and neither did any alarms sound or weapons emerge to confront them. It seemed odd to her that any precautions against intruders might not be in use. "I doubt they're stupid," she said. "Overconfident, maybe?"

Tom said, "Maybe more of the latter. They may think that a Starfleet doctor and a couple of relatively low-ranked security officers aren't actively trying to hunt them down. I'm pretty sure they still don't know about me, so I guess it's time for an introduction."

He reached into his satchel and retrieved another tricorder-sized device Crusher did not recognize. Placing the device on the bulkhead near a recessed panel featuring an unlabeled keypad with a small display, Tom pressed a control to activate the unit and entered a command sequence to its own interface. As the unit began doing whatever it was supposed to do, he turned and bobbed his eyebrows.

"Think of it as master passkey."

"Dare I ask where you came across something like that?"

Offering another of those smiles that reminded her of Will Riker at his mischievous best, Tom replied, "You're probably better off not knowing."

After a few moments of watching the device's display flash a steady stream of text—much of it a blur to her eyes—and during which she was sure the owners of the transport either would appear from the shadows or else open the hatch themselves, Crusher breathed a sigh of relief when the activity stopped and a steady green light illuminated along the unit's top edge. This corresponded to a similar indicator activating on the hatch's locking mechanism, and she heard a click before the hatch slid aside to reveal an airlock.

"Bingo," Tom said, retrieving the device and returning it to his satchel before unlimbering his own phaser from his jacket's inside pocket.

To her relief, Crusher saw that the airlock's inner hatch already was open. At least now they would not have to repeat the lock-picking procedure while running the risk of being trapped within the airlock itself.

Small miracles, and all that.

Leading the way, Tom entered the craft and waited until both of them were through the airlock and inside the ship itself before once more activating his tricorder, and this time Crusher noticed that he had taken the precaution of completely muting the telltale whine that normally accompanied its operation.

"No life signs," he said after a moment, though Crusher saw his frown.

"What's wrong?"

"Not sure." Closing the tricorder, Tom returned it to one of his jacket pockets. "This is starting to feel a little too easy. Let's get this over with and get out of here."

The transport was small enough that it took only a moment to reach the cramped command deck, which was not dissimilar to the cockpit of a runabout and consisted of two chairs positioned before a U-shaped console, along with a third chair angled toward the port bulkhead before a workstation of its own. Without saying anything, Tom lowered himself into the left seat and immediately began pecking at the console's array of controls and keys.

"Do you know what you're doing?"

"I know enough," Tom replied, not looking up from the console. "I'm just checking to see if there's any kind of lockout. There is, but I think I can get past it." After a moment, he released a mild, satisfied grunt. "They've been monitoring Starfleet communications frequencies, so they've tapped into the conversations you and the others have had over your comm badges. So far as I can tell, they haven't yet figured out that we might be talking via other means." He had warned them about this possibility when providing them with the civilian versions they had been using for what they hoped were their covert discussions. The other communicators had been modified to operate on very low frequencies that fell outside the typical monitoring range of Starfleet equipment, and the group had continued to utilize their Starfleet badges for normal interaction as a means of convincing any would-be eavesdroppers that they were listening to all of their targets' conversations.

After a few more moments spent working at the console, Tom turned in his chair and gestured to the third seat. "If you use that console, you may be able to download their flight log to your tricorder. I've already set it up."

He continued to work as Crusher carried out her own task. As promised, he had enabled an interface to the ship's computer and the data banks storing the navigational data. It took her only a moment to transfer that information to her tricorder, and when she finished, she turned in her seat to see Tom affixing a package to the underside of the forward console. He repeated the action with the station she occupied.

"That should be enough to take care of their flight control and sensors," he said. "It'll take only a minute or two to plant the others, and then we're out of here."

Despite their initial temptation to simply destroy the transport while it was moored in its landing berth, Tom and Konya had discarded that notion out of concern for possible collateral damage or injury to innocent bystanders. Instead, they had opted for a more controlled action taken against vital areas inside the ship. Using materials provided by Daret as well as a few "special items" Tom had brought, a set of improvised explosives was fashioned which—if all went to plan—would be sufficient to incapacitate the ship's cockpit as well as render useless the small arsenal and supply compartment Tom had found near the crew quarters. All of the packages he had prepared contained burst receivers, to which he would send a signal via his communicator.

"That's the last one," Tom said as he finished placing the last explosive, setting it so that they would destroy the ship's small yet impressive weapons locker. Securing his satchel over his shoulder, he led the way down the transport's main corridor and back to the hatch they had used for access. Because he was in front of Crusher, he was the first one to exit the airlock and step out onto the small boarding ramp as the phaser blast lanced out from the darkness and struck the side of the ship's hull, centimeters from Tom's head.

"Look out!" Crusher cried, grabbing onto his arm and pulling him back into the airlock. She ducked as another phaser beam flashed past her head, chewing into the bulkhead behind her and inside the outer hatch. By now Tom was reacting, bringing up his own weapon and snapping off a single shot in the direction from where the attack had come. Without looking, he reached behind him and gripped Crusher's jacket.

"We need to get out of here," he said. "Even if there's only one shooter out there, he's probably already called his friends for help."

"What do you want to do?"

"Make a lot of noise," Tom replied, leaning around the edge of the airlock's outer hatch and firing once more into the darkness. This time, he did not stop after a single shot but instead continued firing, altering his aim with the weapon's every discharge. "Come on!" Grabbing her wrist, he pulled her behind him and they both dropped to the ground. He maintained his covering fire as they dashed away from the transport, heading for the meager cover afforded by a collection of massive cargo pods arrayed in haphazard fashion upon a large gravel field. Pausing at the corner of the closest container, Tom guided her to relative safety before turning and releasing another string of fire.

"I don't know if I hit anything," he said, reaching inside his jacket, "but I guess it won't matter in a minute." He extracted a small, palm-sized device with a black finish and a burnished gold cover, and Crusher recognized it as an obsolete style of Starfleet communicator. Flipping it open, he pressed one of the unit's control buttons, and a moment later Crusher heard the first muffled explosion from inside the transport. It was followed in rapid succession by the additional charges detonating, and she saw several of the craft's external running lights flicker before going dark. Elsewhere in the depot, alarms began to sound, and at least one person shouted in the distance.

"That should do it," Tom said, moving past her on his way deeper into the collection of cargo pods. "We should keep moving. The others are waiting at the rally point, and I want to get a jump on heading for the Olanda camp before these guys figure out what we're up to."

"No argument here." Getting to the labor camp would not be a simple task, now that they had been denied the assistance of the *Dordogne*'s transporter. Other transporters were available, of course, but using them meant leaving behind a possible record of their transit and their destination, information that could be found and exploited by their still-unidentified adversaries. Konya and Cruzen, in addition to safeguarding Ilona Daret, also were exploring alternative modes of transportation.

With Crusher following Tom, they worked their way to the cargo pod's far end while trying not to make too much noise as they traversed the gravel beneath their feet. Slowing at the container's corner, Tom peered around its edge. Angled as he was and trying to look to his left, he did not see the shadow cast on the wall of the adjacent container. Crusher did.

"Tom!"

A dark figure dressed all in black emerged from hiding and slammed into Tom, sending them both into the pod's metal bulkhead. Tom grunted in surprise and momentary pain, and Crusher heard something metallic dropping to the gravel. She saw his phaser lying at their feet, but Tom's assailant was fast, kicking away the weapon before Tom could retrieve it. Crusher raised her own phaser, looking for a clear shot, but the men were too close to each other.

When the attacker raised an arm and advanced, Tom stepped into the attack, throwing up his left arm and blocking the other man's downward swing. His opponent moved with practiced ease, pivoting and ducking beneath Tom's arm and lashing out with his other fist. The punch sank into Tom's side and he growled, but Crusher realized it was more in anger than pain.

What followed was a series of rapid strikes, each aimed at a vulnerable spot on the other man's body. The attacker was able to block some of them, but Tom's hands were almost a blur, lashing out and catching the other man in the throat, the groin, and even one solid punch to the face. Staggering backward, the assailant tried to reset himself and prepare for a new attack, but by then Crusher had leveled her phaser and pressed its firing stud. The bright orange beam hit the man, and he sagged against the wall of the cargo pod before slumping to the ground, unconscious.

"Are you all right?" she asked, stepping closer and verifying that the other man was stunned.

Leaning against the neighboring container as he tried to catch his breath, Tom nodded. "Yeah, I think so. Thanks for that." He grimaced as he rubbed his right side. "I thought he might have had me for a minute there."

Crusher knelt next to the fallen attacker, whose face was covered by a black balaclava. She pulled away the mask, revealing what at first appeared to be a Bajoran male. "Recognize him?"

"No," Tom said, moving closer, "but that doesn't mean anything. If this guy's some kind of mercenary or special-operations agent, his identity's likely classified."

"You're probably right," Crusher replied, "but I'm taking a DNA sample and a retinal scan, anyway. We might get lucky." Using her medical tricorder, she quickly gathered a blood specimen and recorded a scan of the unconscious Bajoran's eyes. "Putting a name to him would definitely help shed some light on whoever had sent him here, along with how much danger Ilona and the rest of us are facing." She hoped that she might have an opportunity to transmit this information to the *Enterprise,* along with the data regarding Ishan Anjar. It had been decided not to attempt contacting the starship from Jevalan for fear of their communications—no matter how encrypted—being intercepted by unwanted eavesdroppers.

Keeping his attention divided between her and the different avenues of approach to them from between the cargo containers, Tom asked, "Are you sure you want the answers to those questions?"

Crusher sighed.

Not really.

Twenty-four

It required physical effort for Jacob Barrows not to kill the security officer where he stood. With every passing moment, he considered and discarded another in a series of effective ways to dispatch the interloper and dispose of his body. Of course, that now would be problematic in broad daylight, the sun having risen less than an hour earlier.

Maybe next time.

"A disturbance such as this is most unusual," said the officer, a Bajoran who had identified himself as Sikra Lyros. "We received reports of weapons fire at undetermined locations in this vicinity just prior to the incident aboard your ship. Do you know anything about that?"

With practiced ease, Barrows affected an expression of surprise as he stood on the tarmac before the transport's open hatch, and with no effort whatsoever crafted a simple lie. "No, sir. None of my people reported hearing anything like that. Most of us were sacked out in our bunks just before the explosions, and then things got pretty hectic. It was all we could do just to contain the fire and make sure nobody was hurt." Frowning, he added, "Are you saying someone was fighting out here?"

Even as he spoke, he ignored the onlookers watching the exchange from what they probably thought was a discreet distance near the far end of the tarmac or near the main thoroughfare cutting through the center of the landing facility and flanked by ship berths. Morning had brought out all manner of maintenance personnel as well as the crews from other docked vessels, but Barrows did not recognize Crusher or her Starfleet team among the various faces gathered around the facility at this early hour.

Seemingly oblivious to his audience, Sikra shrugged. "We have had disagreements between the crews of different vessels in the past, but it is a fairly uncommon occurrence." He paused, examining a data padd he held in his left hand. "As for your own difficulties, those do not sound ordinary, either. Have you experienced anything like them before?"

"No, sir," Barrows replied, "I mean, we've had systems malfunctions, of course, but nothing like this. We're overdue for drydock and some major refitting, but I was hoping I could stretch it until the end of the month. I've got a couple of time-sensitive charters I can't afford to miss, that sort of thing." He shook his head, reminding himself not to overplay his dejected air. "So much for that idea. It's going to take me months to recover from this."

There was no hiding the explosions that had been unleashed aboard the transport. Barrows's only recourse had been to describe the incident as some kind of internal accident, which of course would invite an inspection by the dock quartermaster to determine the transport's priority with respect to receiving support services and personnel to aid with repairs. That did not bother Barrows; he and his team would be able to employ whatever deception was required to appease the quartermaster as well as Sikra. It was the time they were wasting with these activities that bothered him.

The Starfleet team—possessing far greater covert action skills and assertiveness than Barrows had credited them—had successfully rendered the ship all but useless. Hardest hit had been the cockpit, in particular the helm console. While flight control could be rerouted to another station elsewhere on the ship, it would make navigating and overseeing the transport's key systems problematic. Of more immediate concern was the loss of the vessel's sensor array as well as its arsenal and supply caches. The saboteurs had been quite thorough on that front, depriving Barrows and his team of most of their weapons and other field equipment save for those few items carried on their persons or stored elsewhere on the ship. Obtaining replacements for all but the most illicit components of their gear would be addressed through simple scrounging if not outright theft around the landing area and the neighboring settlement, though a reconnoiter of the outpost and its accompanying cadre of scientists and support personnel had revealed little in the way of weapons.

One thing at a time, Barrows reminded himself. *Deal with the immediate problem first. Get rid of this idiot.*

"I have already spoken to the dock quartermaster," Sikra said. "She is working to free up personnel, but she anticipates not being able to supply you with a repair team until the day after tomorrow, and she apologizes for the delay and resulting inconvenience."

In truth, there was no point spending time or resources trying to effect repairs to the damaged systems. For the moment, locating and securing Ilona Daret was the priority, after which Barrows could concern himself with finding alternative transportation from Jevalan.

These thoughts flashed through Barrows's mind as he regarded Sikra with a look of restrained irritation. "I guess if that's the best she can do, there's no sense complaining about it. We can get by with our own repairs for some of the damage while we wait."

This seemed to satisfy the officer. "Very well, then. If you will excuse me, I have to look into the other incident. Contact my office or the quartermaster if we can be of further assistance." Despite the words, Barrows sensed the Bajoran still harbored skepticism regarding the predawn excitement that had been visited upon his normal, quiet makeshift community. If he had any instincts at all, the security officer would not be satisfied with the explanation he had been given, and he likely would continue his investigation. That might be hazardous, Barrows decided.

There's nothing you can do about it now without attracting attention. Deal with it if and when you have to.

"Thank you for your time," he said, offering a respectful nod before Sikra turned and made his way across the tarmac in the direction of the quartermaster's office and the dock's administration facility. Barrows waited until the Bajoran was out of sight before releasing a long, exasperated breath.

"Damn, I already hate this place."

Hearing footsteps behind him, Barrows turned to see one of his team's other human members, Tobias Paquette, exiting the transport and dropping to the ground. The man looked tired, with grime smeared across his forehead and left cheek; his hands and clothing also were dirty. As the team's designated mechanic, it fell to Paquette to affect any emergency repairs to the ship in the event better-equipped facilities were unavailable.

"You want the good news or the bad news?" he asked, propping himself against the access hatch's lower edge before reaching up to wipe his face. The action left a fresh streak of dirt along his nose.

Barrows grunted. "There's good news?"

"Not really." Retrieving a rag from the back pocket of his dark blue coveralls, Paquette began cleaning his hands. "The helm is shot to hell. No way I can fix it without a full repair crew. Same with the sensors, and the weapons and supply lockers are a total loss." He sighed in apparent disgust. "According to my tricorder, whoever did this used a Klingon explosive compound called *qo'legh*. It's created using three chemicals that are inert when separated. Covert agents like it because the individual components don't show up on a lot of scans."

Frowning, Barrows said, "I've heard of it, but it's not something you just have in some starship supply locker. I doubt a Starfleet security officer would even know about it, unless they were trained in a broad range of demolitions."

"Exactly. This doctor and her security detail are getting help from someone, and that someone is one sneaky bastard."

This was surprising news, but not particularly worrisome, Barrows decided. As a covert operative for Starfleet Intelligence, he had been trained to expect that missions always encountered setbacks, as well as to endure and adapt to all manner of eventualities. The years since that initial training and the experience he had gained both during and after his time in uniform—including the year he had spent as leader of the covert action team and its top-secret designation Active Six—only served to solidify what his instructors had sought to teach him: "Always expect the unexpected."

More concerning to Barrows was his poor assumption that he and his team had arrived at the planet well ahead of anyone sent to retrieve the Cardassian doctor and whatever information he had been given by his Bajoran friend Raal Mosara. This was not the case, and the situation had been complicated by the Starfleet contingent's ability to evade several attempts at surveillance and pursuit by the Active Six's nine-member team. Much of their rivals' success seemed to stem from the assistance they were receiving from a fourth member of their group, who remained unidentified and whose background information was not included in the dossiers provided to Barrows and his companions. So far as the team had been able to determine, this mysterious fourth individual was not a member of the *Enterprise* crew and had not accompanied Crusher and her people to Jevalan.

Whoever he is, he had good teachers, too.

Both men grew quiet as Barrows heard the sound of footsteps approaching from the tarmac. He turned to see two of his team's Bajoran members, Fredil Pars and Contera

Hilbis, walking toward them. Barrows noted that Contera still walked with a slight limp, perhaps owing to the injuries he had sustained in his earlier fight with the unidentified human accompanying Crusher. As for Fredil, she looked as she always did: angry, and wanting to hurt someone.

"What's the story?" Barrows asked in a low voice as his companions moved closer. Fredil's initial response was to offer a derisive snort while rolling her eyes.

"They're gone," she said, reaching up to rub her right earlobe, something she did out of habit whenever she refrained from wearing her traditional Bajoran earring, a symbol of her faith. "We checked the Cardassian's home and lab, but they'd already left. From the looks of things, he packed light."

Barrows already expected that development. "What about Raal's house?"

"Nothing there, either," replied Contera, "though we got the sense that they may have been there before taking off, too."

Paquette said, "Probably looking for the same thing we are, whatever the hell that is. I knew we should've stuck closer to Crusher."

"We couldn't do that without attracting their attention," Barrows countered. "Or anyone else's, for that matter."

"I think that plan's pretty much run its course," Paquette said, continuing to wipe his hands with the dirty rag. "These people aren't stupid. If they're not here, then they may already have found another way off planet, and if that's the case? We have no way in hell of knowing where they might end up—at least, not until they pop up on the Federation News Service."

"There's no way they could've found whatever it is Raal hid for Daret and be out of here already. Crusher and her people haven't been here long enough, and though they've managed to sneak around here and there, they haven't been out of our sight long enough to have made any major discovery. If they'd found something in the last day or so, they'd have left, but even that would've been difficult without their runabout, and we've been monitoring all the ship traffic from here, anyway." Barrows gestured to Contera. "Instead, they hung around long enough to trash our ship and knock you around." Pausing, he regarded the Bajoran, who bore fresh bruises on his face and neck from his skirmish with the unidentified human. "Speaking of which, are you okay?"

Contera scowled, reaching up to gingerly touch where his wrinkled nose sported bruises and gave him the appearance of having two black eyes. "I'll recover."

"Did you get a look at him?" Paquette asked.

"He was a human, with a beard, but it was dark, so I didn't see much more than that. He had some Starfleet unarmed combat training, but his fighting style was a mixture of different techniques." Contera touched the swollen area beneath his left eye and winced. "I'll be wanting a rematch."

"We'll see what we can do," Barrows replied.

Fredil said, "So they're still here, and they're still looking for whatever Raal left for Daret. We don't know what that is, which means they're still at least one step ahead of us."

"That won't last," Barrows countered, "not if they don't have a ship." The Starfleet team's runabout had been dispatched thanks to Fredil's tireless efforts to access the ship's onboard computer. Its pilots had done an exceptional job establishing an encrypted lockout algorithm, but their skills were no match for the Bajoran's technical prowess. Though it had taken her several hours to defeat the protection scheme without triggering any alerts or other notifications to Crusher or her companions, Fredil ultimately had succeeded in penetrating the security protocols, providing her with access to the runabout's helm and navigational systems. This had allowed her to set the ship on a course that would remove it from use by the Starfleet officers, sending it as she did into the Doltiri system's sun. Without the ship and whatever supplies and other equipment it might have carried, Barrows hoped that its loss would hamper Crusher and her team. For the moment, at least, they seemed to be adapting to that turn of events.

"We know from the reports of Raal's interrogation that he left evidence and other information here, somewhere," Paquette said. According to those same reports, the Bajoran had resisted even the most unforgiving interrogation techniques before escaping his restraints and attempting to overpower his guards. Raal had died in that attempt, taking to the grave whatever secrets he may have harbored.

"Whatever it is," Paquette continued, "he obviously didn't leave it in his own house or the Cardie's. It has to be someplace they both know. A lab or office, or one of the dig sites, but a place Raal knew Daret would look."

Contera scowled. "We've been over all of this several times."

"No," Paquette snapped, "we haven't. At least, we haven't been over it enough times to figure out what it is we're missing. We've been approaching this whole thing all wrong, assuming these people are just lab rats who don't have any common sense or ability to be sneaky or scheming. I don't think it's an insult to say that no Bajoran or Cardassian who lived through the Occupation didn't figure out how to do something without getting caught. Hell, it was a survival tactic for any Bajoran with half a brain, and it's standard operating procedure for any Cardie, and anybody who's done any kind of sneaking around knows that the simpler your plan, the easier it is to get past someone looking for evidence of you being up to something."

"Whatever we're looking for, it's hiding in plain sight." Barrows had believed that to be true from the beginning, but was it possible that Raal Mosara and Ilona Daret still had managed to get something over on him and his team?

He turned to Fredil. "Go back over everything we

recorded from both their homes and labs. Every picture, every data file, every journal entry." To Paquette and Contera, he said, "We'll start with their work away from the settlement. Contact the others, and have them do another pass through the whole camp." The other Active Six members had spent the evening hours making a covert reconnaissance of the labor camp as well as the support settlement and had reported finding nothing. Barrows did not expect that to change with another sweep. "We might get lucky, but something tells me whatever they're after isn't here."

"One of the other camps?" Contera asked. "Olanda or Pencala?"

"There also are a few other, smaller outposts scattered across the planet," Fredil said. "I should be able to get into the central data banks where the scientists and other workers here have been entering their information and see if Daret or Raal have been to any of those locations."

Barrows nodded, liking her idea. "Do it. Get us a preliminary list of targets. Weed out any place they haven't visited within the last six months. We'll start with whatever that leaves us, and go from there."

"What do you think it is they found?" Paquette asked. "What is it that's got so many people upset enough to send us all the way out here to this rock?"

"I don't have the first damned clue." As was standard procedure for a mission of this type, Barrows and his team had been given no specifics regarding the information Ilona Daret was supposed to be safeguarding. Active Six only had been told that the Cardassian and whatever materials he held in his possession were of vital importance to his employer, as well as to someone higher up in the food chain. Though Barrows had lobbied for more insight into the specifics—if only to aid him in locating the prize he had been sent to obtain—the person giving him his orders had refrained from sharing that information, instructing Active Six to apprehend the

Cardassian and prepare him for transfer to a location to be named later.

That mission now had expanded to include at least four more targets, and his lack of knowledge regarding specific details made Barrows's task that much harder. He had to wonder what the people directing his team's actions were going to say or do if and when Active Six succeeded in uncovering whatever secrets Daret was protecting. Were the answers to such riddles worth killing people to keep them from being answered? What about those sent to retrieve whatever information might shed light on such dark matters? Were such parties also expendable?

Barrows was certain such questions soon would be answered.

Twenty-five

Picard sat in his command chair, arms folded across his chest while ignoring the status indicator on the seat's armrest display informing him that his ship's engines were threatening to give out. Instead, his gaze remained focused on the main viewscreen and the image of the small ship displayed upon it, framed as it was against the curtain of distant stars and the unyielding black of open space. Though the image appeared not to have changed since the beginning of the pursuit, reports and other information given to him by his officers told him a different story.

Almost there.

"Continuing to gain on them, sir," reported T'Ryssa Chen from her post at the flight controller position. Was it Picard's imagination, or did he detect a slight hint of fatigue in the lieutenant's voice? Like most of the bridge crew, she had refused relief from her station. Only Lieutenant Šmrhová had asserted rank, replacing Abigail Balidemaj at the tactical console, but even the ensign had remained on duty, moving to the secondary tactical station. Like Šmrhová, Worf also had reported to the bridge within moments of the away team's return to the *Enterprise*, delaying only long enough to don a regular-duty uniform before resuming her post. Given the current circumstances, he knew that all of the officers around him would remain on station until such time as he ordered them from the bridge or they caught their quarry: whichever came first.

"They're maintaining warp seven," said Šmrhová, "but I'm starting to pick up fluctuations in their warp engines, and I'm detecting power being rerouted from other systems."

Though the *Enterprise* normally was capable of speeds greater than its current velocity, Picard had weighed the decision of attempting to overtake the fleeing vessel against causing further and perhaps even irreparable harm to his own ship's engines.

"Hail them again," he ordered. "Advise them that we are aware of their engine status." He knew that the other vessel's crew likely was scanning the *Enterprise,* as well, and that their crew knew of the starship's own issues. "How much longer until we're in weapons range?"

Šmrhová replied, "At this distance, less than one minute, sir. They are continuing to ignore our hails."

"Place phasers and quantum torpedoes on standby," Picard said. "Target their propulsion system. I want them disabled only."

"Aye, sir."

The signal for the intraship communications system sounded, followed by the voice of Geordi La Forge. *"Engineering to bridge. Captain, we're starting to redline down here. If we don't drop out of warp soon, we're going to have big problems."*

"Maintain speed, Mister La Forge," Picard replied, his eyes still locked on the viewscreen. "We've almost got them." The longer the chase endured, the more irritated he was becoming. The other crew by now had to at least be thinking escape was impossible, or were they gambling that the *Enterprise*'s own engine difficulties and damage would force it to break off the pursuit before their own ship's engines overheated, or worse?

"We're doing everything we can, sir," La Forge said, *"but*

I can only reroute so much. We've got real damage that needs repairing, and the longer we push it, the worse it's going to be."

"Do whatever you have to, Commander, but do not reduce velocity until so ordered. Picard out." In his peripheral vision, he sensed Worf studying him, and he glanced in his direction. "Something on your mind, Number One?"

The Klingon replied, "Only that as your first officer, I am obligated to point out that Commander La Forge's concerns are valid, sir. We risk considerable damage to the *Enterprise* if we continue this action."

"Are you suggesting we break off and let them escape?"

Without hesitation, Worf said, "No, sir. They attempted to destroy a Federation starship, and that cannot go unanswered." He paused, and Picard heard him draw a deep breath. "There also are other questions for which I wish to have answers, as well."

At the conn station, Chen called out, "Sir, we're now in weapons range."

"Phasers and torpedoes ready, sir," Šmrhová added. "I've got their engines targeted."

"Fire," Picard ordered, rising from his chair as the first phaser beam leapt across space, accompanied by a pair of quantum torpedoes, all of which impacted against the fleeing scout vessel's shields. Šmrhová followed that strike with a second barrage, and within seconds the assault on the other ship's shields was repeated. It was not until the third salvo that Picard caught sight of an impact against the other craft's port warp nacelle. There was a momentary flash of energy as internal components suffered whatever damage the torpedo had inflicted.

"Their shields are down, and they're dropping out of warp," Chen said, her fingers moving across her console. "Adjusting our course and speed to compensate."

"Maintain weapons ready status," Picard said, wondering if the wounded ship might now turn and try to make a fight of it. "Close to transporter range. Number One, you and Lieutenant Šmrhová take a security team to transporter room one and prepare to escort our new guests to the brig."

Worf rose from his chair and nodded to Šmrhová. "Aye, sir."

As his first officer and chief security disappeared into the aft turbolift, Picard stood at the center of the bridge, his hands clasped behind his back, eyeing the damaged vessel that—allegedly, he was forced to admit—had caused them so much trouble.

Maybe now we can get some answers.

Waiting until the security guard had returned to his station, Picard turned and gave his full attention to the two men standing at the center of their holding cell. Neither man had said anything since their arrival, and the ensign on duty from Lieutenant Šmrhová's security detail had informed him that they in fact had remained silent since materializing on the platform in the transporter room. Despite their disheveled wardrobe, beard stubble, and unkempt hair—at least in the case of one man, as his partner was bald and possessing of a rather nasty scar running down the left side of his face—Picard's practiced eye noted the way each man carried himself: their stances, or the way their arms were allowed to hang loosely at the shoulders. Only their eyes moved, studying every detail of their cell and the room beyond the energy barrier containing them.

Soldiers, of one sort or another, Picard decided. At least, at one time. They were human, according to the preliminary scans taken upon their arrival, but there was no way to know which military or government they represented. An attempt at identification already had been made, but no match had been returned from Šmrhová's database search.

"My name is Captain Jean-Luc Picard," he said after a

moment. "You're aboard the Federation *Starship Enterprise,* but of course you know all that already."

Neither man said anything.

"Your vessel was scanned leaving the Drazen Nebula immediately following our destruction of the Andorian freighter. Our sensor logs reveal that you transmitted an encrypted burst transmission to that ship, just prior to the triggering of the computer command that enabled its warp core failure. That protocol also called for attempting to lock onto my ship with a tractor beam, ostensibly for the purpose of holding us close enough to be caught up in its warp core breach." The revelation had come from Lieutenant Dina Elfiki, after her review of all the sensor logs recorded from the moment the *Enterprise* had rendezvoused with the *Cereshta.* Delivered as it was via a very low, oft-ignored frequency, the transmission had escaped the science officer's notice at the time. Doubtless the frequency had been selected just for that purpose.

Though both men remained silent, the bald man's eyes narrowed as he heard Picard's words.

"Based on this admittedly preliminary evidence," he continued, "I'm forced to conclude that you attempted to destroy a Federation starship and its crew. That will be the charge with which I'll remand you to Starfleet, along with fifteen hundred counts of attempted murder." He paused, allowing just the trace of a smile to tease at the corners of his mouth. "I doubt all that will stick, of course, but I'm fairly certain there will be sufficient evidence to ensure you're imprisoned for the rest of your lives."

"You've got nothing on us, Captain," said the bald man.

His companion turned to glare at him. "Shut up."

"Who are you working for?" Picard asked. "We've already tried to identify you through official channels, and so far we've found no record for either of you. Either you're not Federation citizens or anyone who's ever done any business with any

Federation entity, or else your identities have been concealed or classified in some manner." For the first time, he moved, taking one step closer to the force-field barrier separating him from the prisoners. "However, my people are continuing their efforts. They will find out who you are, eventually." In truth, he had hesitated to order any overt attempts at identifying these two strangers, fearing that such efforts would attract attention from parties he wished for the moment to avoid.

The bald man grunted. "You won't find anything, Captain."

"Be quiet!" snapped his partner.

Ignoring the second man, Picard stepped toward the one who had spoken first. "Tell me what I want to know, and I'll do what I can to have any charges against you dropped."

"You keep your mouth shut," growled the other man.

Before Picard could further press the matter, the doors to the brig section parted, allowing Worf and La Forge to enter the room.

"Captain," said his first officer, offering a nod of greeting. Picard watched his gaze shift to the two men behind the force field.

"Status of your repairs, Mister La Forge?"

The chief engineer replied, "We're getting there, sir. Most of the damage to the warp drive was circuit burnouts, but we also had some buckling in the antimatter containment pods. We came pretty close to an automatic jettisoning of the warp core, and you know how much I enjoy those."

"Indeed," Picard said, recalling the last time the *Enterprise* had been forced to eject its warp core in order to contain a subspace tear resulting from the detonation of an isolytic burst weapon deployed by a Son'a vessel in the unstable region of space known as the "Briar Patch." At the time, ejecting and exploding the core to seal the tear had been the only course of action available to La Forge and Will Riker, still serving at that time as the *Enterprise*'s first officer.

Though the drastic action had worked, it left the ship requiring a tow to the nearest starbase so that a new warp core could be installed.

And we certainly can't risk needing such repairs right now.

"How much time until we're back to one hundred percent?" Picard asked.

La Forge said, "About three hours, sir. We can get under way now, but I'd recommend going easy on the warp drive until I finish my final checks."

"Understood." Noting that Worf was continuing to stare at the prisoners, and seeing that his scrutiny was beginning to have an effect on the two incarcerated men, Picard said, "What have you learned, Number One?"

Bringing himself to his full height, Worf looked away from the prisoners as he replied, "Our inspection team is continuing their investigation of the vessel. It is a civilian craft, though it possesses several upgrades and components not typically available to private ships."

"Starfleet issue?"

"Yes," La Forge replied. "Some of the propulsion and weapons upgrades in particular are Starfleet-grade and most definitely not available on the open market. Still, stuff like it has been known to turn up on black markets and non-aligned planets from time to time."

"What about their flight log?" Picard asked.

La Forge sighed. "Wiped clean, but I've got Elfiki and Chen going through the onboard computer, seeing if they can reconstruct the deleted portions of the data banks." He glanced from Picard to the prisoners as he was about to say something else, but instead said nothing, his mouth dropping open and his eyes widening in obvious surprise.

"Oh my god."

Frowning at the chief engineer's sudden emotional outburst, Picard asked, "Geordi? What is it? Do you know these men?"

"No, sir," La Forge replied, shaking his head as he stepped closer. "I . . ." He stopped himself, looking first to Picard, then to Worf, then returning his gaze to the prisoners. "Captain, I need to talk to you in private."

The three of them stepped into the hallway outside the brig, and La Forge waited until the doors had slid closed before saying, "I think those men are mercenaries or some kind of special-operations team."

"I suspected much the same thing," Worf said.

Picard asked, "As did I, but you obviously have something more to go on than gut instinct, Commander?"

"Yes, sir. It's something Captain Gomez told me back on Acheron. The *da Vinci* had received some unusual orders to take on passengers from a colony transport ship and take them to rendezvous with another transport. One of the things she mentioned was that even though the passengers were supposed to be engineers, she was sure they were some kind of soldiers or mercenaries." He paused, gesturing toward the doors leading back to the brig. "Captain, she said one of them had a scar running down the left side of his face."

That caught Picard by surprise. "You're certain?"

"Absolutely. Sonya said the whole situation seemed off to her, but she was operating under classified orders. Eyes only, the works."

"If these men are part of a secret-operations team working under orders from someone at Starfleet Command," Worf said, "then this may be the work of President Ishan, or someone working on his behalf."

Given what already had transpired as a consequence of the president pro tem's questionable actions and decisions, Picard had prepared himself to accept such revelations if and when they presented themselves. Despite that readiness, he still found himself at first rejecting the implications of his first officer's statement.

"If that's true," he said, "then we must tread carefully. It's likely that our attempts to identify those men already have triggered some kind of alert to someone working for Ishan. Inform Lieutenants Šmrhová and Elfiki to cease their efforts on that front. We'll have to proceed on our own for the time being."

Before he could continue his line of thought, his communicator badge chirped.

"Chen to Captain Picard."

Tapping his comm badge, the captain replied, "Picard here. What is it, Lieutenant?"

"You asked to be informed if we came across anything interesting in the data we retrieved from the Andorian freighter or the scout ship's memory banks. I think what we've got qualifies."

Exchanging glances with Worf and La Forge, Picard said, "What've you found?"

"The crews on both ships tried to wipe their navigation logs, but we were able to salvage some information from the Cereshta's computer. Comparing their course data to our star charts, it looks like they rendezvoused with another civilian transport before proceeding to the nebula. I've run a background check on that other vessel, and its flight logs place it near the Acheron system."

"So," Worf said, looking to La Forge, "Captain Gomez was right."

"Looks that way."

Chen said, *"There's more, sir. We also determined, based on the amount of coolant and other expendables carried in the freighter's cargo bay, that the crew serviced two small transport craft. One of them was the one we captured, but the other one was already gone before we got here. According to flight data we managed to dig out of the Cereshta's computer and reconstruct? It was headed for the Doltiri system."*

"Uh-oh," La Forge said.

Picard forced himself not to dwell on what this news might mean for Crusher and her team. As much as that tore at him, there were other, more pressing matters still to address. "Indeed. Thank you, Lieutenant Chen. Continue your investigation, and immediately report anything else you might find."

"Aye, sir," replied the young officer. *"Chen out."*

As the communication ended, Picard turned and proceeded back into the brig, crossing the room in measured strides until he stood before the holding cell containing their two guests. The bald man had made himself comfortable on one of the cots mounted to the cell's rear bulkhead, while his companion had taken a seat on the floor with his back against one wall. Both men looked up at Picard's approach, though of course neither of them said anything.

"We know from your navigation logs and other corroborating information that you've been in contact with at least one Starfleet vessel and that you have friends who likely are on their way to the planet Jevalan. Who are you working for, and what have you been ordered to do?"

The bald man lifted his head from the cot. "When's lunch?"

Behind him, Picard heard Worf stifle a menacing growl. The prisoner heard it, too, and his expression betrayed the façade of indifference he was trying to affect.

"Perhaps I should allow Commander Worf to continue this line of questioning," Picard said. "He's really rather effective at obtaining the information I want."

The other man looked up from where he remained sitting on the floor. "Nice try, Captain, but we know your record and reputation pretty well. You might break the rules on occasion, but you have lines you won't cross."

"Do I?" Picard asked, allowing himself a slight expression of surprise. "And which of your handlers told you that?" When neither man said anything, he stepped closer to the barrier, gripped by an abrupt new realization. "You knew when the freighter failed to destroy us that we'd catch you

after you fled the nebula. Why run?" Rather than wait for
an answer, he said, "You were acting as a diversion, trying to
hold our attention. Why? To keep us from changing course
and heading for Jevalan? What are your friends supposed to
do there?"

Once more, he received silence.

Unwilling to tip his hand so far as any information he
might possess regarding President Ishan, Picard felt his teeth
gritting as he regarded the prisoners. "I don't know who you
are, but I do know that whoever you work for has gone to
great lengths to make you appear invisible, no doubt as a
consequence of the type of missions you're given. It's unlikely
anyone will make a fuss if you were to disappear without a
trace."

"You're bluffing, Captain," the bald man said, but Picard
saw in his eyes that he did not fully believe his own words.
"You're a Starfleet officer, bound to duty. You know how this
works. We all answer to someone."

For the first time since engaging the prisoners, Picard
smiled. "Yes, that's correct. We all answer to a higher authority, but I imagine that your superiors won't worry too much
if you were never to be heard from again, especially if it prevents me from going through you to get to them." The smile
faded. "And that is precisely what I will do if anything happens to my wife on that planet. If she's harmed to even the
slightest degree, I will make it my mission to expose you and
anyone connected to you."

"And while he does that," Worf added, "it will be my
honor to ensure that you are as uncomfortable as a human
can be while still remaining conscious." He leaned closer to
the force field. "You will beg me for death."

Their earlier bluster gone, both men eyed the Klingon
before returning their attention to Picard. "You won't order
him to kill us."

"There are times when even my ability to control members of my crew can falter," replied the captain. "I haven't decided yet if this should be one of those occasions." He let his gaze linger on the prisoners for an additional moment before turning and exiting the brig. Worf and La Forge followed him into the corridor, and once the doors closed behind them, Picard heard his engineer release a loud sigh.

"Worf, have I told you lately how happy I am you're on our side?"

The first officer grunted. "I was beginning to wonder if you had forgotten."

Despite his mounting concerns for Crusher's well-being, as well as that of Lieutenants Konya and Cruzen, Picard allowed a small chuckle at the banter. Then, he tapped his comm badge. "Picard to bridge. Plot a course for Jevalan in the Doltiri system and engage at our best speed."

A moment later, Lieutenant Chen replied, *"Course plotted and laid in sir. We're getting under way now. Estimated time of arrival at our current speed is fourteen hours, fifty-six minutes, but engineering is continuing to advise us about repairs in progress."*

Turning to La Forge, Picard said, "Geordi, I'm sorry, but you'll have to conclude your repairs en route. I need everything you have to cut down that estimate, and whatever else you can find."

"Understood, sir," replied the chief engineer. "You'll get it."

"Make it so."

His officers left to see to their respective duties, leaving Picard in the corridor, alone with but a single thought.

Whatever you're doing, Beverly, be safe.

Twenty-six

"I have to say, as labor camps go, this looks like it could've been one of the nicer ones."

Positioned on a rise overlooking the remnants of what once had been the Olanda labor camp, Beverly Crusher turned to regard Tom Riker, who offered only a shrug as defense for his remarks. "I'm just saying, as someone who's seen the inside of a Cardassian prison, that things here could've been worse."

From where he stood next to Crusher, Ilona Daret said, "Rest assured, Mister Riker, that there were facilities here that would make you reevaluate your estimation of the lodgings we afforded to prisoners and laborers." He turned to face them. "As a physician, I did more than tend to injuries suffered by workers in the mines. I saw and treated the results of some rather malicious acts inflicted upon our Bajoran charges. Though there were regulations and protocols for the handling of prisoners, those are only rarely enforced in a place such as this, far away from the prying, judgmental eyes of Central Command." Pausing, he offered a tired sigh, and Crusher could sense his shame. "History itself will forever be the one true witness to all that transpired here."

As with the other two labor camps, Olanda also featured a settlement that served as a transitory home and base of operations for the scientists and other personnel living here.

The settlement was similar in size to the one supporting excavations at the Pencala site, without many of the creature comforts and larger facilities that had been established at the Tabata camp. From her vantage point, Crusher was able to see people moving about the camp itself as well as see the billeting area and its collection of makeshift tents and temporary shelters. There also was a landing area for cargo operations, though it lacked extensive service and repair capabilities. Several of the parking berths were unoccupied, but Tom had cautioned against using them.

The journey from the Tabata labor camp had proved a challenge, given Lieutenant Konya's continued inability to make contact with the *Dordogne*. It was Tom Riker's contention that the runabout was lost, either seized or destroyed by the same people who now hunted them. Using the camp's small field transporters carried with it the risk of leaving behind entries in system logs that could be traced. The group therefore had been forced to acquire alternative means of travel, but stealing a ship only would attract attention they did not need. Even requisitioning such a craft carried a risk, but the group was running short on viable options. For the moment, at least, they stayed a step or two ahead of their pursuers, but how long would that last?

We just need a little bit longer.

"It'll be dark soon," Tom said, kneeling at the edge of the rise and peering through his field binoculars. "Looks like people are winding down for the day. We should be able to make our move soon."

The plan so far had been for the group to bide its time and wait for nightfall before making any attempt to escort Daret to the excavation site. Both Daret and Tom decided it would be risky to let the Cardassian be seen by any of the other personnel working at the camp. Besides just wanting to avoid attention while they worked, there also was the distinct possibility that their pursuers might have colleagues or informants among the small cadre of people working at the site. Instead, Crusher had sent Konya and Cruzen ahead to scout the area and determine what level of security might surround the area of the dig where it was believed Raal Mosara had secreted his cache of information and other evidence. The security officers had been gone for more than an hour and had not yet checked in, and Crusher now was beginning to feel the first twinge of worry.

"What do we do with the shuttle?" she asked. Daret had requested the small transport craft from the dock master at the Tabata landing facility, which in turn had required filing a flight plan. After considering their options, Daret had submitted a falsified report detailing the shuttle's travel to a remote outpost in the planet's southern hemisphere. The disadvantage of that tactic was that they now could not avail themselves of the landing facility without arousing suspicion.

Tom replied, "I don't think it matters. Our friends will figure out we gave the dock master back at Tabata a fake flight plan. Once they realize we gave them the slip, they'll likely check the Pencala camp since that one's closer to where we said we were going, but it won't take them long to end up here."

The settlement Daret had listed as his destination was a satellite camp, manned by fewer than two dozen Bajoran and Cardassian scientists. They were working on the excavation of what once had been a secluded mountain lodge used as a retreat by the camp's Cardassian officers; a temporary diversion from the day-to-day demands of overseeing the trio of labor camps. It was far enough away that—assuming their pursuers fell for the feint and went looking, they would be well away from both the Pencala and Olanda labor camps before realizing they had been duped. At Tom's insistence, Daret even had conversed with the dock master about attempting to conceal the nature of their journey, pretending to be concerned that no one should know where he was going.

"I know the dock master told you he wouldn't pass along anything you gave him," Crusher said, "but that doesn't mean the people chasing us won't just ignore the flight plan and anything he says and come straight here."

"Definitely a possibility, but there's nothing we can do about that." Tom pointed a thumb back over his shoulder. "Just like the shuttle. We're committed now. The best we can do is get down there, find whatever it is Mosara hid, and find a way off this rock as quickly as possible, and preferably without having to deal with our friends along the way." He sighed. "Why do I think I'm not going to get my wish?"

Crusher felt a buzzing from inside her jacket and reached to retrieve the civilian communicator Tom had given her. "Blue One," she said, refraining from using proper names as Konya had suggested.

"Blue Two here," Konya replied. *"We've found the target. No one's working that area, at least not today. It's been cordoned off and security's monitoring it, but no more than anything else here. We shouldn't have any problem getting what we need."*

Tom moved closer. "Can we get in there tonight?"

Konya replied, *"Affirmative, Blue Four. We're setting up a workaround for the security measures and should have that addressed by the time you get here."*

With Daret leading the way and Tom covering their rear, the trio maneuvered along a circuitous route that led them the long way around the site's perimeter. Aided by darkness and the lack of a moon in the early evening sky, they were able to bypass most of the work sites established within the area of the old labor camp as well as the settlement where at least most of the excavation team was congregating now that their workday was ending. At one point, Crusher noted that the dim illumination cast off by work lights scattered around the site only partially obscured the stars that now were visible in the night sky.

It's beautiful. Too bad we can't enjoy it.

Staying away from the established walking paths reduced their chances of encountering anyone, but they still had to seek cover once to avoid being seen by a pair of workers exiting the dig site. A Bajoran and a Cardassian walked past them, taking a shortcut from the excavation at the camp's south end. The beams from their flashlights were focused on the ground ahead of them, and so enamored were they with their own discussion, they were oblivious to the three strangers lurking in the tall grass mere meters from them as they passed. It took nearly forty minutes to make the transit to the site's western edge, and as they approached the wall of the shallow crater that had been created in this part of the camp, Crusher recognized Konya emerging from a work tent and waving at them.

"Nice night for a walk," he said, smiling as they approached, though something about his demeanor seemed off to Crusher. Had something happened?

"What's the story?" Tom asked.

His eyes shifting to look past them as well as toward the rest of the compound around them, Konya replied, "The excavation site itself isn't guarded, but areas that have been cordoned off for safety or other reasons are being monitored by passive sensors; motion and infrared detectors, that sort of thing." He gestured past them to where the temporary settlement sat at the site's eastern end. "All of the data's being sent back to one of the temporary huts up at the camp. We can bypass those without disabling them, which should let us get inside the area Doctor Daret indicated without too much trouble. Once you're inside the tunnels and moving to the level where the temple's located, you should be fine. Cruzen and I checked and, yeah, there are a lot of areas where tricorders don't work worth a damn down there, at least not for more than a few meters. The temple is right smack in the middle of one of the heavier ore concentrations. Anybody looking for us from the surface would need either a tactical-grade sensor package or a starship helping them with the search."

"Eluding our pursuers is just part of the problem," Crusher said. "We still have to find whatever it is Mosara hid." Daret already had told the rest of the group that the underground area where the Bajoran temple had been constructed was littered with tunnels and small ancillary chambers, a consequence of the ceaseless mining efforts that had consumed this and the other labor camps on Jevalan. That the temple had escaped the notice of the camp's Cardassian overseers still was something Crusher found hard to believe, even with the assistance from tricorders or other scanning devices. "Are we even sure he put it in the temple itself or somewhere else down there?"

"There's only one way to find out," Tom said. "Let's get started. If we're careful—and lucky—we should be able to work through the night without anyone knowing we're down there."

Konya cleared his throat, hunching his shoulders and stuffing his hands into the pockets of his jacket as though overcome by a sudden chill. "I've been thinking about that. It might be better to wait, at least until we're sure we can bypass all of the camp's security measures. I wouldn't mind tapping into their feeds; they might be helpful keeping an eye out for our friends."

"We're on borrowed time as it is," Tom said. "The people following us aren't slouches. They will *find* us, and we have to be ready for that. Either we find Mosara's materials and get out of here, or we get ready to defend ourselves when the others show up." He turned to Crusher and Daret. "I'm sorry. I don't mean to sound like I'm trying to take over your show. I'm here because Will asked me to help you. I just don't want us to get caught unprepared or out in the open."

"Too late," Konya said, and Crusher flinched as the security officer lunged forward, all but tackling her just as a bolt of harsh red energy spat forth from the darkness and struck the tent behind him. Grunting in shock as she was driven to the ground, Crusher saw the ugly hole burned into the side of the temporary shelter, its edges glowing as the material caught fire. In her peripheral vision she noticed Daret lying beside her, rolling over as Tom used his own body to protect the elderly Cardassian.

"Stay down!" Konya said, pushing away from her just before another energy beam pierced the night air, screaming overhead and striking the crater wall behind the tent. She saw the phaser in the lieutenant's hand as he rolled up onto one knee and aimed toward the incoming fire's source. He did not fire only once but instead loosed several shots, moving the muzzle of his weapon as though able to see his target in the darkness.

"Over there!" Tom shouted, pointing with his free hand somewhere behind Crusher. Shifting onto her stomach, she reached for her own phaser before crawling across to where Daret still lay prone in the dirt. "There's two of them!"

How the hell did they find us so fast?

"There could be others," Konya said, scrambling from his kneeling position and running toward an empty cargo container that had been cast aside near one of the narrow walking paths crisscrossing the compound. A crimson beam chewed into the ground behind him, throwing dirt into the air as he reached the makeshift cover. Tom fired at where the beam had originated, and Crusher heard him curse, knowing he had missed his quarry.

More weapons fire in the distance sliced through the night air, only now Crusher realized it was coming from a Starfleet phaser. Two salvos of bright orange-white energy highlighted a figure emerging from a small cavity in the shallow crater's wall, then the new arrival passed beneath the soft glow of a freestanding work light and Crusher recognized Kirsten Cruzen. The lieutenant fired again and this time her weapon found its mark. A surprised groan reached Crusher's ears and she thought she was able to make out another figure falling to the ground as Cruzen approached it.

"Hang on!" Konya shouted before breaking into a sprint in Cruzen's direction across the compound.

Another weapon's report—this one close enough to make Crusher cringe—roared past her, and then she heard Tom cry out. She turned to seem him falling to the ground, but he had not been struck; somehow he had managed to avoid being hit, and now he was rolling to one side in a desperate bid for cover. Disruptor fire or whatever it was followed him as he rolled into a narrow ditch, and only then did Crusher notice that he had dropped his phaser. The weapon was out of his reach as well as hers, but she was already moving in that direction when she heard footsteps approaching from behind her.

"Get up," someone said before Crusher felt a hand gripping her arm and pulling her to her feet. She brought around her phaser but gasped when something smacked it from her hand. Turning her head, she saw a figure dressed all in black, including a balaclava that covered his head and most of his face. Only his eyes were visible, along with the wrinkled bridge of his nose. Her attacker was a Bajoran.

"No!" Daret cried, pulling himself to his feet, but Crusher's assailant turned toward him, aiming his weapon at the Cardassian.

"Don't even think about it," the Bajoran ordered. Pulling Crusher with him, he began moving toward Daret, the muzzle of his disruptor pistol trained on the doctor's face. "All right, move," he said, his head turning from side to side as he searched for threats. In the distance, Crusher could make out Konya and Cruzen standing over a fallen form. Something caused Konya to look over his shoulder, and then Crusher saw him and Cruzen turning toward her, brandishing their phasers.

The Bajoran muttered something under his breath, shoving Crusher in front of him before firing his disruptor toward Konya and Cruzen. Both security officers were forced to scramble for cover, and Crusher used that opportunity to attempt freeing herself. Jerking her arm out of the Bajoran's grip, she stomped her boot down on the top of his foot. She reached over her shoulder with her other hand, her fingers searching for her assailant's eyes, throat, or some other point of vulnerability. The Bajoran growled in pain, and then light exploded in Crusher's vision as something slammed into the side of her head.

"Do that again and I'll kill you," the Bajoran hissed between his teeth, reaching out to renew his grip on her arm. Something jabbed Crusher in the right side of her neck as he pulled her closer to him, and she felt him pushing it harder against her skin. The disruptor's muzzle was pressing against her carotid artery. To Daret, he said, "Move."

Whatever he might have said next was lost as the Bajoran emitted an abrupt gasp of pain and disbelief, and Crusher felt his entire body jerk. His grip on her loosened, the disruptor fell away from her neck, and then she heard him collapsing to the ground. He slumped onto his left side, his body limp and his weapon lying next to his open hand. Dim light reflected off something metallic along his back, and when she bent closer, Crusher saw the hilt of the knife.

"You okay?" a voice called out, and Crusher looked over to see Tom Riker coming toward her. His face and the front of his clothing were wet and covered with mud, a consequence of his rolling into the ditch behind him.

Looking first to Daret, Crusher nodded. "We're fine. How about you?"

Tom glanced down at himself. "Nothing a bath, dinner, and a decent night's sleep wouldn't fix. Maybe a bourbon. Or three." He gestured toward the fallen attacker. "I'm sorry about that. I didn't want to kill him, but I didn't have anything else, and I thought he might decide he didn't need you once he had Daret."

Crusher felt a lump in her throat. "I understand." Logic told her Tom was right and that her captor likely would have killed her. That did not alleviate the sadness she felt at the taking of another life, but she reminded herself that these were unusual, even desperate circumstances. "Thank you."

Movement in the corner of her eye made her turn to see Konya and Cruzen walking toward them, escorting another person dressed all in black. One of the security officers had removed the attacker's balaclava, revealing the face of a human male. The man, his hands bound before him with a pair of wrist restraints, did not look happy.

"Party crasher," Cruzen said by way of greeting.

Eyeing the rest of the group, Konya asked, "Is everyone all right?"

"We're fine, Lieutenant," Crusher replied. "You?"

"I'm happier now." Konya pushed the other man ahead of him. "When Cruzen and I were scouting the dig site, we started thinking that our friends might well split up, hoping to catch us at one of the labor camps. I had Kirsten hide out inside one of the tunnels where she could keep watch on me while I worked with the sensor array."

Cruzen added, "After Rennan contacted you, we noticed a couple of guys wandering around the site, not really working on anything." She tapped the other man on the shoulder. "Here's a tip: The secret to blending in is actually *blending in*. That outfit of yours kind of defeats the purpose. Try harder next time."

The man said nothing, though Crusher saw his eyes fix on the body of his fallen companion, and his jaw clenched.

"How many more of you are there?" Tom asked. "Did you split up and head to the different camps and other outposts?" When the man remained silent, Tom shook his head. "You have to be spread pretty thin, and that's before we count your buddy on the ground over there." He stepped closer, his voice lowering and taking on an edge of menace. "Want to join him?"

Almost too fast for Crusher to follow, the man sprang forward, something in his hands reflecting in the subdued glare of the nearby work lights. She saw the small blade even as the man closed the distance separating him from Tom. Cruzen and Konya, surprised by the abrupt move, dove toward him, but by then it was too late.

Tom stepped into the attack, using his left arm to arrest the downward swing of his opponent's restrained hands. Both men grunted at the sudden impact, and the operative attempted to pull himself free, but by then Tom was lashing out with brutal force to score a single strike to his assailant's throat. The other man's eyes bulged, and he staggered from the blow, a dreadful gurgling escaping his lips. Tom pressed his attack, landing a second punch to the man's face and toppling him to the ground. It was over in mere seconds, with Crusher covering her mouth in horror before training and instinct kicked in and she rushed to where the agent had fallen.

"Oh, my," Daret said, his voice trembling as he moved to assist her.

"Was that *really* necessary?" Crusher snapped, not even bothering with her medical tricorder as she pushed the fallen man onto his back. His eyes, open yet unseeing, stared up at her, and she shivered at the abrupt chill coursing down her spine.

Tom, standing behind her, replied in a flat, dead voice. "I'm sorry. When I saw the knife, I reacted. I didn't mean to kill him. It was just . . ." He let the rest of the sentence trail off.

Despite her choice of profession and the oaths she had taken throughout her career, on occasion Crusher had been forced to kill in self-defense. Such unfortunate instances tended to weigh on her, despite knowing the actions she had taken on those occasions were justified. She saw in Tom's eyes that same regret, but there also was something else; resignation to the idea that the killing not only had been necessary, but perhaps also deserved.

You're imagining things. Somewhere in there, he's still Will, and Will Riker would never . . .

"I'm not Will," Tom said, his gaze boring into her as though he had just read her mind. "I can see it in your eyes. I'm not him, and I'm sorry for that, too, but there's nothing I can do about it." He gestured to the man whose life he had ended. "It was him, or me. I'm okay with how it turned out."

He's right. And he saved your life, too.

Neither of them said anything for a moment, until Crusher noticed Konya and Cruzen standing nearby, remaining silent until she looked in their direction. "What is it?"

Konya held up an unfamiliar device. "I found one of these in each of their pockets. They're communicators, though they're a model I'm not familiar with. They've got some extra components built into them that look like encryption hardware. I think I may be able to figure out a way to defeat it, but it'll take some time."

"But if we do," Cruzen added, "we may be able to monitor any communications from the rest of their team."

"You mean we could know when they're coming?" Daret asked.

"That'd definitely be helpful," Crusher said, setting aside her discomfort over the events of the past few minutes. She made eye contact with Tom and offered a small, reassuring smile.

Shrugging, Konya replied, "I guess we'll see."

"We should try to find their ship, too," Tom said. "If nothing else, we might be able to verify how many of them are already here." He sighed. "Not that it matters. Once these two don't report in, the rest of the group will be dropping down on us like a damned hammer. Still, we can at least do something to get ready for them." Turning to Daret, he said, "But you've got the most important job, Doctor."

The Cardassian exchanged knowing looks with Crusher. "Yes. Let's find whatever it is that Mosara left for us."

"Right," Crusher said, nodding. "And then let's get the hell out of here."

Twenty-seven

U.S.S. Enterprise

Picard hated waiting.

He long ago had come to terms with the unforgiving reality that was the life of a starship captain, a role that often required him to stand by while others carried out tasks at his behest. Though he had spent the bulk of his adult life in a position of authority over others, there were occasions where he wanted to toss aside protocol and dive headfirst into a problem. His feelings had nothing at all to do with the trust he placed in his crew to accomplish whatever orders he gave them. On the contrary, Picard harbored no doubts that those he commanded were of the highest caliber Starfleet could offer, each of them committed not only to him but also the *Enterprise* and their shipmates. Of greater importance, he knew, was their knowledge of his belief in them and their abilities. The men and women who looked to him for leadership must accept as bedrock, inviolable fact that his confidence in them was unwavering. This, he felt, was of particular significance now, when their current situation carried with it such a heavy personal toll for Picard himself. Though he was certain his crew understood his anxiety, they were better served by him allowing them to do their jobs, rather than casting aside protocol in order to take matters into his own hands.

Such thoughts hovered like a dark cloud over Picard

as he entered the engineering section. The deactivation of the *Enterprise*'s warp engines had cast an odd pall over the vessel, characterized by the notable lack of the drive's low, omnipresent hum. Its absence was more palpable here, deep within the heart of the starship. At the center of the expansive chamber, the massive warp core was dark and inert, its innards exposed thanks to the removal of several access panels that now revealed the maze of circuitry, EPS conduits, and optical data cabling. Members of the engineering staff were immersed in their duties, standing or kneeling at the different access panels or hovering over workstations. Those who noticed their captain's arrival nodded in greeting but did not stop what they were doing, in observance of Picard's established order that activity in the ship's work areas not cease simply because he chose to visit them.

Standing next to an open access panel adjacent to the warp core, Commander La Forge was immersed in his study of an isolinear optical data chip he had removed from the station and inserted into a diagnostic tool. The chief engineer frowned before handing the chip to an ensign.

"Replace that one, too, just to be on the safe side."

The ensign took the chip. "Aye, sir."

As the younger man moved off to tend to his task, La Forge turned to see Picard, and his expression softened, as though he was embarrassed. "Captain," he said in greeting.

"Mister La Forge," Picard said, "do you have an update?" It had been an hour since the engineer's last report, and almost two hours since the *Enterprise* had been forced to drop out of warp. The reduction in speed had come in response to dire warnings that continuing to drive the starship on its headlong flight to Jevalan was risking damage to the vessel beyond the ability to fix without a starbase facility. With great reluctance, Picard had ceded to La Forge's frantic request, shifting to impulse power while engineering crews affected final repairs.

The engineer replied, "We're almost there, sir. The rup-tured EPS manifolds have been replaced. We're just giv-ing everything one more look before I initiate the start-up sequence." He cast a look over his shoulder where Lieutenant Commander Taurik was supervising activities near the warp core. Other members of the engineering team were closing various access panels and entering commands to their work-stations, and Picard noted that several status indicators on or near the warp core now were activating. Though he was not an engineer himself, he possessed enough familiarity with the *Enterprise*'s systems to recognize the preliminary steps that required completion before the warp core itself could be brought back online.

La Forge blew out his breath. "I have to tell you, sir: It was close. Another minute or so, and we might've been float-ing around out here, or worse."

"And now?" Picard prompted.

"Once we bring the warp core back online, I should be able to take you all the way to warp nine." La Forge paused, his attention caught by one of the status monitors positioned next to the open access panel. "I may even be able to push it a little more, if we're lucky." He paused, as though considering his next words, before adding, "I know how important it is to get to Jevalan as soon as possible."

"Important for all of us, Geordi," Picard replied, though he appreciated the commander's unspoken sentiment. "Excellent work, Commander. I know it wasn't easy, given the circumstances."

"If you don't mind my asking, sir, how's René doing?"

For the first time since entering engineering, Picard smiled. "As one might expect from a four-year-old: He misses his mother." As part of the informal "inspection tour" that he was conducting as a means of keeping himself from hiding in his ready room or fidgeting in his chair on the bridge, he had visited his son in the ship's child-care facility. René had been absorbed in play with the handful of other children under the watchful eye of Hailan Casmir, the Argelian charged with supervising the center. His daughter, Taro Katín, and René were separated in age by only a few months, and they had become fast friends. Content to watch his son and the other children without interrupting them, Picard had taken a few moments of comfort as he observed René at play. Picard would have preferred to remain a while longer, but duty would not wait for him to indulge his personal desires.

Returning his full attention to La Forge, Picard asked, "What's your estimate for getting us back under way?"

"Twenty to thirty minutes at the outside, if everything goes right with the start-up sequence." The engineer paused as one of the ensigns working with Taurik handed him a padd, and he consulted its display. "We're just about ready, sir." Looking up from the handheld unit, he asked, "Was Worf able to get anything more out of our guests?"

"No. Whoever they are, they're well-trained, and well-supported." Worf and Lieutenant Šmrhová had exhausted every means at their disposal to determine the identities of the two men still residing in the *Enterprise* brig. With no other choices left to him, Picard had risked using the encrypted communications protocols devised by La Forge to contact Admiral Riker, enlisting his former first officer's aid in solving this mystery. Knowing any messages sent from the *Enterprise* were subject to monitoring, Picard had sent a brief, vague query describing the scout ship they had encountered and from where it was believed to have come, but made no mention of anything involving the Andorian freighter or the *Enterprise*'s course change to Jevalan. He hoped Riker would be able to glean what he needed before other parties deconstructed the missive.

"Excuse me, Captain," said a new voice, and Picard and the chief engineer turned to see Taurik standing nearby. The Vulcan looked to La Forge. "Commander, we are ready to commence the initiation sequence."

"Outstanding," La Forge said. "Let's get it going." To Picard, he said, "Almost there, sir."

Picard replied, "Make it so, Commander." He was moving so that he could watch the start-up procedures without being in the way, when his communicator badge chirped.

"Bridge to Captain Picard," said the voice of Commander Worf.

"Go ahead, Number One."

The first officer said, *"We are receiving an incoming subspace transmission from Admiral Riker for you. It is encrypted under voiceprint authorization, sir."*

"Very good," Picard replied. "Route it to Commander La Forge's office in engineering, Mister Worf."

Making his way to the workspace reserved for the chief engineer, Picard slid into the chair behind the narrow, angled desk and activated the computer interface terminal there. "Computer, enable secure encryption protocol for incoming communication. Authorization Picard Alpha Omega Three Nine Five Five."

"Secure link established," replied the feminine voice of the *Enterprise*'s main computer. *"Oversight procedures initiated. No external monitoring sources detected."*

The image on the desktop monitor shifted to show the visage of William Riker, who looked as though he had not slept since the last time he and Picard had spoken. His uniform and general appearance were as polished as ever, but there was no hiding the dark circles beneath the admiral's eyes. Even his smile—forced as it was—hinted at his fatigue despite his best efforts at hiding it.

"Hello, Jean-Luc," Riker said. *"For all our sakes, we should keep this short."*

"Indeed," Picard replied. "I'm guessing you wouldn't call if it wasn't important."

"You can say that again. First off, you need to know that another ship is on its way to Jevalan. Ishan or someone on his

senior staff has a contact inside Starfleet Command who's willing to do his bidding. This person rerouted the U.S.S. Tonawanda *from its patrol route to the Doltiri system. We think we know who that is, but I'm not ready to start yelling names over subspace just yet. We're still trying to find the orders or something official detailing what the* Tonawanda's *captain, S'hirethal Verauk, is supposed to do when she gets there, but so far we're coming up dry."*

"Someone within Starfleet Command redirected the *Tonawanda*? Without Akaar's knowledge or authorization?"

Riker sighed. *"Exactly. I've got people helping me look into this, but so far as we can tell, the orders cut for Captain Verauk are top secret, including for her to run silent until such time as she accomplishes her mission, whatever the hell that's supposed to be."*

Picard searched his memory. "I'm not familiar with Captain Verauk. What can you tell me about her?"

"She was first officer of the Rochambeau *during the Borg invasion and was among that group of commanders who received accelerated promotions to captain to help replace the ones we lost. She's been aboard the* Tonawanda *for two years. By all accounts, she's a capable officer, but her fitness reports indicate she's pretty outspoken, particularly when it comes to Starfleet's role in protecting Federation interests."* Riker paused, leaning closer to the visual pickup. *"She's from Acamar Three, Jean-Luc. She lost her husband and seven children when the Borg destroyed it."*

"Oh, my," Picard said, sadness welling up within him. Acamar III had been one of the first worlds eradicated by the Borg during what ultimately had been their most brutal—and final—attack on the Federation four years earlier. Though some few inhabitants of that world had managed to evacuate, thanks in large part to an all-but-futile defensive stand made by Starfleet vessels, the bulk of the Acamarian people had been lost during the brief yet tragic battle.

"Are you saying she's become more aggressive in her stance on such matters?"

Riker replied, *"No more than anyone else who suffered such a loss, I suppose. Still, she's on record as stating that Starfleet needs to become more proactive in response to possible threats, be it from the Typhon Pact or anyone else who might come looking for a fight. With the right motivation, she's just the kind of up-and-coming officer who might respond to somebody like Ishan."* He stopped himself, shaking his head. *"I don't mean to say she's corrupt or anything like that, but if Ishan's stirring up people to take more hawkish positions when it comes to Federation defense, someone like Verauk could fit the profile of a supporter, unwitting or otherwise."*

"She may not even be aware of the real reason she's being sent to Jevalan," Picard said. "Will, if someone within Starfleet Command is undermining Admiral Akaar's authority to issue orders like this, there's no predicting the damage they might do." Such a person, handing out secret orders and instructing the recipients of those directives to maintain a strict compartmentalization, might have no idea they were being manipulated for an ignoble agenda. "Whoever's doing this, they need to be found."

"We're working on it," Riker replied, *"and we're pretty sure we know who it is, but they know how to cover their tracks. Somebody high up has to be giving them support and cover. If we could contact the* Tonawanda, *this would be easy."*

Picard considered that. "Perhaps. On the other hand, it's possible Captain Verauk is operating under orders that prevent her from divulging the identities of anyone issuing her orders, as part of that same security envelope."

"Thinking about that just makes my head hurt." Riker tapped his desk for a moment, then said, *"Speaking of covering tracks, we haven't found anything on the two agents you have in your brig. DNA and retinal scans came back with no match. Whoever they are, they're like ghosts so far as Starfleet is concerned."*

"That's impossible," Picard snapped, refusing to believe the report. "Someone somewhere knows who these people are and who they work for."

"Agreed, but special-operations personnel operate in a completely different realm than the rest of us. Information is strictly need-to-know. Agent identities are kept secret as much for their own protection as anything else. Even Akaar doesn't have access to that information without approval from the Council's oversight committee, and he can't get that so long as Ishan is running the show."

Before Picard could say anything else, Riker frowned, reaching toward something off screen. *"Captain, I think we're getting some interference on this frequency."*

Stiffening at the code phrase they had agreed to use when any attempt at eavesdropping was detected, Picard offered his prepared response, "The problem may be on our end." He reached for the desktop monitor and tapped an onscreen icon, which the computer had been programmed to provide during any communication he might have with Riker. In response, the image on the monitor became inundated with static. "Commander La Forge informed me earlier that our communications array was affected by our close pass of the Drazen Nebula. He has a crew looking into it now, but he warned me there may be problems. We should be . . ." His sentence was interrupted by the sudden disappearance of Riker's image, which was replaced by the Federation seal and the message SIGNAL FAILURE. COMMUNICATION TERMINATED.

Another spy, attempting to track his movements. Picard felt his ire rising at the thought of someone within Ishan's inner circle and perhaps even within the halls of Starfleet Command stalking him in this manner, along with dispatching another vessel to Jevalan and whatever else they might be doing. Were Riker or Akaar in danger? That possibility could not be discounted, Picard knew, even though there was nothing he could do about it. Riker would continue his investigation, and the admiral already had given Picard enough to worry about.

He recalled what he could remember about the *Tonawanda,* a *Nebula*-class starship that had been in service for nearly three decades. The *Enterprise* was a superior vessel in most respects, and it held a definite advantage so far as weapons and defenses. Even as he considered such things, Picard felt a knot of worry forming in his gut. Was it possible he might have to face off against a fellow Starfleet captain?

Not if I can help it.

The lights in La Forge's office flickered for the briefest of moments, followed by a low, resonating hum beginning to emanate from the main engineering chamber. Looking up from the desktop monitor, Picard peered through the office's bay window to see that the warp core had flared to life, the reinforced column enclosing the matter-antimatter reactor now pulsing with energy. From where he stood at one of the workstations positioned next to the warp core, La Forge turned and offered a thumbs-up gesture to Picard.

"Inject reactants," the chief engineer said to Taurik, who was manning the console and controlling the core's initiation procedures. "And that should do it." Moving away from the workstation, he approached the office. "Captain, we're up and running again. Full warp power at your command."

Rising from the chair, Picard stepped from the office. "Excellent, Mister La Forge. Inform Commander Worf of ship's status and to continue on course for Jevalan at maximum warp." As the engineer turned to that task, Picard took another look at the warp core, which now radiated the raw, harnessed fury contained within. He already could feel the renewed life reverberating through the deck beneath his feet as his ship once more exuded power and purpose.

His first instinct was to attempt contacting Beverly and apprise her of the *Tonawanda*'s looming arrival, but the threat of their communications being intercepted gave him pause. If any message to Jevalan was picked up by unwanted listeners, it might increase the threat to Beverly and the rest of the away team. So far as he knew, Ishan only suspected what he and the *Enterprise* were doing; the interim president still had no actionable proof, and Picard wanted to hold on to that advantage for as long as possible.

This, Picard knew, left him for the moment with but a single course of action.

Waiting.

Twenty-eight

Torture was unnecessary, Galif jav Velk decided as he contemplated his evening meal. Continuing to feed him in this manner would suffice.

"What is this slop?" he asked, his voice echoing off the undecorated metal walls that formed three sides of his prison cell. "I've seen finer cuisine offered at a waste-reclamation center."

His comments earned him a smile from Lieutenant Eric Cone, the officer manning the control console outside the cell. A force-field barrier separated Velk from the human, who at the moment was reclining in a chair with his feet resting on the console. Cone wore a dark gray uniform possessing rank and branch insignia that identified him as a member of the special security detachment utilized by the president as well as the Federation Council.

"We've routed the disposal lines to the galley," said the lieutenant, not bothering to shift his eyes from whatever he was watching on one of the console's monitors, which Velk could not see.

Forcing a mocking laugh, the Tellarite shook his head. "Your humor astounds me, human. I see Federation Security is continuing to recruit the best and brightest to fill out its ranks. Let me guess: Your unequaled wit made you overqualified to join Starfleet?"

His gaze unwavering, the security officer replied, "Says the person on the wrong side of the force field. Are you still hungry? I can have them send you a second serving."

Grunting in irritation, Velk pushed away the unsavory meal, directing the plate and its accompanying tray into the replicator slot from which it had come. Unlike the devices used by those who did not find themselves incarcerated, the cell's replicator was programmed to deliver only those meals and other items as directed by the security staff. Though Velk was granted the ability to choose from a menu of foods compatible with Tellarite tastes and dietary requirements, the computer's preparation of his selection left much to be desired. Since the beginning of his confinement, he had lodged several complaints about the quality of the meals, but those grievances along with all the others had fallen on deaf ears.

"Things could be worse, you know," Cone said. "You're still breathing, after all. There's apparently a long list of people who'd like to remedy that."

Velk opted not to rise to the officer's baiting, choosing instead to move from the compact table and stool that were mounted on the cell's left wall to the unimpressive cot extending from the rear bulkhead. With an audible sigh, he rolled himself into the bunk and once more was greeted by the ceiling tiles above his head. The tiles featured a grid pattern, and he resisted the urge to begin counting the tiny squares on the section directly above him.

"I don't suppose I could have something to read?" he asked, already knowing the answer he would receive.

"Sorry, sir, but you know our orders specifically forbid any reading materials or access to a computer terminal, even for recreational purposes."

"Of course they do," Velk said, shaking his head in dis-

gust. The new orders regarding the nature of his imprison-
ment had been in effect for the past three days, if his count of
the meals he had consumed since his arrival at this detention
facility was to be trusted. He had been moved to this new
location following an extended stay at a high-security center located in Paris. As for his new accommodations, though
Velk did not recognize this detention facility, he suspected
that it, like the man sitting before him, also belonged to the
special protective detail. This meant that he could be anywhere on Earth, assuming he even still was on the planet.
Such information had been kept from him since the moment
he had been arrested in his own office. How long ago had
that happened? Velk had long since lost track of time,
another direct and intended result of the treatment he had
received from his jailers.

What a long, ignominious fall from grace it had been,
from his position as perhaps the most powerful individual in
the Federation to this, a nondescript occupant of an equally
bland prison cell. As chief of staff to the leader of the United
Federation of Planets—admittedly a temporary position, at
least until the coming elections made a final decision as to
the fate of Ishan Anjar, the current president pro tempore—
Velk had been in a position to affect any number of policy
issues. Following Nanietta Bacco's assassination and his
installation as interim president, Ishan had given Velk wide
latitude to affect the kind of change the interim president
believed was necessary in order to return the Federation and
Starfleet to a position of prominence and even dominance in
the Alpha and Beta quadrants. Recent events had done much
to undermine that place of distinction, and it was Ishan's sin-
gular goal to see to it that damage was repaired while warning anyone who might challenge the Federation that these
notions were, at best, foolhardy.

Such statements needed to be made, particularly now,
with the Federation still recovering from the staggering

damage inflicted by the Borg four years earlier. Starfleet was continuing to recruit and train new personnel and had largely replaced or rebuilt starships lost in the battle. Still, total strength remained at pre-invasion levels, and many of the officers now commanding ships and starbases had been promoted to fill the numerous vacancies resulting from the immense loss of life. A significant number of those people lacked proper command experience, though several of them had acquired battlefield wisdom as a consequence of being on the "front lines" during the invasion. Far too many young officers had been forced to grow up in rapid fashion in order to meet Starfleet's immediate and ongoing needs.

On Earth and other planets that had survived the onslaught, civilian government leaders continued to struggle with the harsh reality imposed by costly wars, first with the Dominion and then the Borg, as well as the persistent challenges being meted out by the Typhon Pact. The upstart coalition had proven on numerous occasions that it was intent on taking advantage of the Federation's weakened state. Velk was certain it was only a matter of time before the Pact initiated some kind of large-scale offensive against their interstellar rivals. After all that had come before—worlds destroyed or severely damaged to the point that they no longer could sustain life, entire civilizations extinguished—the Federation Council still had managed to convince itself that with sufficient time, an accord could be reached, allowing both powers to exist in harmony with each other.

Velk knew it was folly, just as it always had been, and his wife and children had paid for that naiveté with their lives.

While the council acknowledged the distinct possibility of more direct action being necessary should the Pact decide to escalate the existing tensions, only a few brave members seemed to possess the fortitude even to give voice to such thoughts. President Bacco, a charismatic and effective leader in peacetime, had found her limits tested during the Borg invasion. Despite some strong talk with Typhon Pact representatives in the early going, she had appeared reluctant to commit Starfleet forces to any prolonged action once it became clear—to Velk and other likeminded individuals, at least—that the Pact had no real interest in peaceful coexistence.

For the security and well-being of the Federation, a change in leadership was required. Despite an interest in politics that had caused him to change careers after a lengthy span of time spent in the private sector, Velk never had harbored any aspirations of holding political office. Instead, he preferred to act in a support and advisory capacity and had found particular satisfaction working for elected officials who not only inspired their constituents, but who also pushed through bureaucracy and complacency in order to solve real issues by all necessary means.

Ishan Anjar was just such a person, and Velk had taken an immediate liking to the Bajoran when fate saw fit to bring them both to the halls of the Federation Council within months of each other. Still mourning the loss of his family at the hands of the Borg when he began serving Ishan as the Bajoran was working his way up through the halls of power at the Federation Council, Velk finally had set aside his grief and immersed himself in his work. Like Ishan, Velk no longer was content to wait for the next interstellar power to come and put its boot on the Federation's figurative neck.

As Ishan advocated for stronger security, more ships, and installations to prepare for the next threats, Velk did everything in his power to ensure that the Bajoran's voice was heard. Already possessing a reputation as one who let no obstacle prevent him from doing or getting what he wanted, the Tellarite had pieced together an impressive network of informants, confidants, and others willing to work for him for the right fee and favors in return. As time passed, Velk's outlook changed, and his increasing approval for "the end justifying the means" took hold. Seeing that Nan Bacco seemingly was content to continue with the same sorts of policies that already had brought about mass destruction and now political turmoil in the form of the Typhon Pact, he began to posit ideas on how radical changes could be introduced. Bold action was vital, he knew, but what?

Though Ishan displayed a genial, even paternal façade, his outspoken views on security and defense were a welcome change of perspective in the months after the devastating Borg attacks. Velk remembered thinking Ishan possessed an almost Tellarite-like sensibility when it came to debate and refusing to acquiesce to weaker viewpoints. Working together, Velk had helped Ishan shape his message, acting as an advocate for vigilance and strength in the new, post-invasion Federation. Never again, Velk vowed, should anyone be forced to endure the heart-wrenching sorrow that had gripped him from the moment his family was torn away.

But, even Ishan Anjar had limits as to how far he was willing to commit to the cause. Yes, there were lines he was prepared to cross, but only at the expense of others, rather than himself. That always had been his nature. It was this character flaw that Velk had been able to exploit, but which inevitably had turned Ishan against even him, his closest and most trusted confidant.

When Velk learned of a Bajoran from some remote planet formerly under Cardassian rule sniffing about, inquiring into Ishan's background, he discovered the truth behind the Bajoran's identity and what he had done on Jevalan. After addressing that potential embarrassment and the Bajoran doctor who had brought it forward, Velk realized he now had at his disposal the ideal person to affect the sort of real, rapid change that was needed. After all, if Ishan, or whatever his real name was, could kill dozens or even hundreds of his own people to incite rebellion and save thousands, what was killing one more person if it might ensure the security of billions? Already an influence within the council, and now within the line of succession should circumstances require such changes in leadership, Ishan was in the perfect position to benefit from an abrupt shake-up at the highest levels. He and Velk simply had to possess the courage to take the final, bold step to put their plan into motion: Remove Nanietta Bacco.

The scheme had worked—flawlessly, in Velk's opinion. Now Ishan was poised to be elected to permanent high office, campaigning on a platform of peace through strength and the resolve to never again be victimized by outside forces. Meanwhile, Velk was rotting in this cell, waiting for whatever fate Ishan might decree for him. The Tellarite knew that the only reason he remained alive was because Ishan was still looking for a way to reap some political benefit from having removed the Tellarite from his post, though he likely still was seeking a way to separate the illegal mission to Nydak II from his own complicity in Bacco's murder.

For a while, at least, I remain useful.

The sound of a hatch sliding open intruded upon Velk's thoughts, and he looked up to see a human male dressed in the gold-and-black uniform of a Starfleet lieutenant commander entering the detention block's anteroom. The man was armed with a phaser holstered along his left hip, and he cast an indifferent glance in Velk's direction before turning his attention to Cone, who had stood at the commander's arrival.

"Good evening, sir," the lieutenant said. "What can I do for you?"

Holding out a thin blue wafer of translucent material that Velk recognized as an isolinear data chip, the other man replied, "I'm Commander Hayden from Starfleet Security. I have transfer orders for Galif jav Velk. He's being moved to a facility in Paris in preparation for his trial."

So, Velk mused, *I was moved from Paris, after all, but to where?* He had no idea how such information might be useful, but it still was a question worth pondering. How far had President Ishan seen fit to banish him?

Cone frowned. "I'm sorry, sir, but this is the first I've heard of a transfer."

"It's being kept low profile," Hayden said. "The trial's attracting a lot of media attention, and the president and the council want to avoid the whole thing turning into a circus." He shrugged, offering what Velk recognized as a smile intended to disarm. "You know how these things are."

Though it was doubtful the younger officer did know how "these things" were, Cone still nodded. "Yes, sir." Taking from Hayden the data chip, the lieutenant inserted it into a reader at his workstation and reviewed its contents. "Everything seems in order."

Velk said nothing as he endured the process of being fitted with a pair of wrist restraints, which then were secured to a magnetic belt cinched around his waist. It was not until Cone and Hayden escorted him from the detention area into the adjacent passageway before he cast a sidelong glance toward the commander.

"My trial's been scheduled?"

Hayden replied, "Not yet, but there have been some new developments with your case. Your defense lawyers want to talk to you, but they don't want to make the trip here, which is why I'm the lucky one who was sent to drag you back to them."

"And where is here, anyway?" As expected, his question received no reply.

They reached a turbolift, and Cone punched a command string into the security keypad embedded into the bulkhead next to the doors. The lift opened once the code was entered, and Hayden gestured for Velk to step into the car.

"Thanks for your help, Lieutenant," Hayden said, offering an informal salute as the doors slid closed and the lift began to move upward.

"So where am I being taken?" Velk asked.

Hayden turned away from the doors, and when he raised his right hand, Velk saw that the commander now held his phaser.

"Nowhere."

Twenty-nine

Jevalan, Doltiri System

Despite its crude construction, created as it was from whatever materials and other scrap could be scrounged, the temple, so far as Beverly Crusher was concerned, was beautiful.

"This is amazing," she said, stepping farther into the small, low-ceilinged chamber. Cut from solid rock, the walls, ceiling, and floor retained their rough, uneven texture. Much of that was hidden with crude tapestries fashioned from scraps of canvas or other materials, each presenting a unique, abstract design rendered with paint, charcoal, or whatever else their creators had been able to find. The familiar oval-shaped Bajoran symbol was a prominent feature of several of the tapestries.

"Workers went to great lengths to conceal the temple's entrance," said Ilona Daret as he entered the chamber behind Crusher. "As I said before, none of the guards ever suspected anything."

The temple's slight opening was nothing more than a hole drilled through a section of the tunnel where the rock wall formed a corner. With only small work lights providing just enough illumination to navigate the tunnel outside the room, the entrance itself was almost invisible. It was just large enough for an adult humanoid to step through, provided he ducked his head and shoulders. Daret already had shown Crusher the elaborate façade that had been placed in front of the entry, consisting of a large piece of rock cut in a manner that allowed it to be set into the bend in the tunnel in such a way that it appeared in the low lighting as just another section of the wall.

"Mosara learned of this place from one of the Bajorans who survived to be rescued from here," Daret said. "According to that person's recounting, it took six people to move the cover aside in order to access the temple. Mosara and I used an anti-gravity tool, of course."

Like other, similar shrines she had seen, the makeshift sanctuary was long and narrow. Metal poles, likely remnants from building materials used around the labor camp, had been placed in the rock floor along the walls and were mounted with a small flat platform, each sporting a candle of various size, shape, and color. The candles themselves were not lit, but Konya had taken a small work light from one of the other areas where excavation was taking place in order to provide illumination. Two pairs of low benches, fashioned from metal girders and supported with wide, stout wooden legs, were angled forward to face a raised platform sitting atop a piece of flat stone at the chamber's far end. Positioned upon the dais was a large box that—although it might once have been rectangular—had been modified so that its sides bowed outward, and some kind of elliptical colored glass or other translucent material was set into the container's side panels. The box also was adorned with painted etchings.

"It's a representation of an ark for one of the orbs from the Prophets," Crusher said, running one hand along the container's flank. "Someone made this?"

"It's a testament to the Bajorans' devotion and strength of will that they undertook such risk. If the guards had found this, they would have destroyed it and hunted down anyone who had a hand in creating it."

Stepping onto the dais, Crusher moved behind the box

and saw that its rear panel could be opened. Pulling it aside, she saw that within the cavity where an orb might reside inside an actual ark had been placed stacks of paper, parchment, cloth materials, and even thin pieces of wood, onto which were inscribed passages in what she recognized as native Bajoran writing.

"Some of the workers recorded excerpts of scripture," Daret explained, "recalling favorite or other appropriate passages from memory, and stored them here." He cast a gaze around the room. "I truly hope that this place will be left intact, as a permanent memorial. It deserves to be seen by anyone who wishes to understand the truth and the harsh reality Bajorans faced here every day, and of my people's role in their suffering. Perhaps it can serve as a reminder, so that such a travesty is never again perpetrated."

Crusher smiled. "You always were an idealist. Still, I can't think of a more fitting tribute to the Bajorans who lived and died here."

Movement at the front of the room made her look up to see Tom Riker stooping low in order to enter the chamber.

"Konya and Cruzen are making a sweep of the area," he said. "So far as we can tell, we're all alone down here, but it never hurts to be sure. The sun will be up in a few hours, so whatever we're going to do, we should do it fast." As Crusher had done upon first entering the temple, he paused at the threshold, allowing his gaze to take in the room before him. "Wow. This is something else." He gestured with his thumb to indicate the tunnel behind him. "And that camouflage for the entrance? Genius. It almost makes you want to go hunting through the whole mine, looking to see what else might be hidden away down here."

"Mosara and I did that, on occasion, and other members of our expedition did so, as well. We found no other temples, but we did discover a few caches where weapons and other equipment had been concealed." Daret shrugged. "After all, even here, the Bajoran resistance thrived as best it could. The weapons were removed, of course, but there still might be other hiding places. We'll find them soon enough and handle them in similar fashion, for safety reasons if nothing else." He gestured around him to indicate the temple. "However, this place has been left as undisturbed as we were able. Everyone working the site has respected its sanctity."

"Which makes it a good hiding spot for anything Mosara wanted to stash here," Tom replied. "On the other hand, it seems kind of obvious."

Crusher said, "Not necessarily, and not when you consider how much trouble Mosara went to provide Ilona with very subtle clues. We may be overthinking this." Looking around, she examined the temple's contents. The room itself offered precious few hiding places. A quick check behind the tapestries and other items affixed to the walls revealed nothing, as did the benches for visitors to the sanctuary. There was the dais and the makeshift orb ark, of course, which were the first things Crusher might investigate, but she already had examined them and had not found anything resembling a hidden door or panel, and the dais itself was too heavy to move.

Or, was it?

It can't be that simple.

"Ilona," she said, moving once more to the platform, "you said you and Mosara used an anti-grav lifter to push aside the rock covering the entrance?"

Daret replied, "Yes, we did the first few times we came here, when we were still searching this part of the underground complex. We have retrieved remains from the tunnels and other chambers nearby, but we found nothing in here. Once it was decided by everyone not to disturb the site, we stopped closing off the entry."

Retrieving her tricorder from her jacket pocket, Crusher activated the unit and aimed it at the dais. At first the device's readings were somewhat chaotic, owing to the rich concentration of raw mineral deposits embedded all around them in the rock. She adjusted the tricorder's sensitivity settings, and the resulting feedback calmed a bit. "The platform is a single, solid piece."

"Yes," Daret replied. "Mosara and I theorized that it was fashioned from a single slab of stone removed from a tunnel or other chamber opened up for mining purposes."

Another of her tricorder's readings made Crusher frown; there was a discrepancy in the way the unit was reporting the composition of the rock floor beneath the dais. It took her several attempts at adjusting the unit's readout before she realized what was causing the discrepancy.

"There's a pocket underneath this stone," she said. "It's small—less than a meter in diameter, but it's almost two meters deep. With all the interference from the minerals in the rock, it would be easy to miss." She looked up from the tricorder. "Think that's what Mosara might've had in mind?"

At the front of the temple, Tom was once again entering the chamber through the small opening, only this time he was carrying what Crusher recognized as a Cardassian version of an anti-grav lifter.

"There's a tool locker at the tunnel intersection," he explained. "Look what I found." Walking past Crusher and Daret, he moved to position the lifter atop the dais before activating it. He gripped its handle and pulled, and the stone platform rose from its resting place until it hovered a full meter above the temple floor. Crouching in order to afford herself a better look, Crusher smiled.

"Bingo."

Daret kneeled next to her, and they both saw the small, ragged hole that had been carved into the rock. Crusher got the impression that the cavity had been cut in haste and without precision, as though the person who had created it possessed no real expertise with the required equipment. Inside the hole rested a burnished metal box. Using the anti-grav to set down the dais, Tom then applied the tool to removing the box from its hideaway. The container, long and thin, was more than a meter in height, but Crusher saw from its design that it was intended to lie on its long edge.

"Why bury it on its end like this?" Daret asked as he and Tom worked to lay the box on its side.

Crusher replied, "Maybe because it presented a smaller profile if anyone came looking for it with a tricorder. The minerals in the surrounding rock do a pretty good job of masking it, but if it had been buried lengthwise in a shallow hole, it might still be detectable without having to make a scanning adjustment."

Moving to kneel before the container, Daret pointed to something etched into the metal lid's surface. "See this? It's Mosara's name, written in Bajoran. This is it." The box contained no locking mechanism, and he raised its lid. Inside, Crusher noted several storage cases of varying size, including one she recognized as similar in type to the stasis containers Daret had used in his lab. Each of the cases had been labeled in Mosara's handwriting.

"Remains," he said, lifting the stasis case from the box and setting it aside. "Just as Mosara said he had done." Crusher saw that the storage vessel also contained what looked to be the Cardassian equivalent to padd devices, along with several small, colored, translucent tubes that were a form of isolinear optical data storage rods. Each of the rods bore writing. Daret held up one of them. "His notes, I believe."

It took more than thirty minutes to inventory the storage box's contents, during which Daret began reviewing the information stored on several of the data rods. Crusher, working from some of the notes Mosara had recorded during his examination of the remains, was using her tricorder to scan the samples the Bajoran scientist had stowed in the small stasis unit.

"Mosara was right," she said after a moment of scanning

the remains with her tricorder. "This person was afflicted with Orkett's disease, a common enough ailment for Bajoran children during the Occupation. I'm also detecting traces of donated bone marrow, which would've been necessary for this individual to have survived to adulthood."

Daret frowned as he listened to Crusher's report. "Orkett's disease. Why is that familiar to me, somehow?"

"Like I said," Crusher replied, "it was fairly widespread among Bajoran adolescents, particularly on the Bajoran homeworld, but it obviously made its way to the different labor camp worlds, too." She gestured to the remains container. "This person could even have contracted it on Bajor before being transported here. After all this time, there's just no way to know."

Tom, reclining against the dais and watching the two scientists work, asked, "Did President Ishan suffer from this Orkett's disease?"

"I suppose it's possible," Crusher said, "but I don't know for sure."

Sitting on the stone floor next to the storage container, Daret held up another data rod. "Mosara was able to access a copy of your president's medical records; not a difficult task, given your government's odd practice of making such information available for public scrutiny. Based on his medical history, your president never suffered from the disease."

Crusher indicated the stasis unit. "There's something else. This person is much younger than President Ishan; at least a decade or more. Whoever he was, he was barely an adult when he died."

"According to a copy of the laborer identification database we were able to obtain from a contact of mine on Cardassia Prime, Ishan Anjar was listed as a young male, twenty-two Bajoran years of age. That is approximately twenty-nine Earth years, and far younger than the person currently serving as your president."

"It's not enough that we have proof this is the real Ishan Anjar," Crusher said, gesturing toward the stasis unit. "We need evidence as to the president's real identity: something irrefutable."

Daret said nothing, but Crusher noticed her friend was inspecting yet another data rod. Frowning, he reached for a reader device that had been included inside the storage container and inserted the rod into a receiving port.

"What is that?" Crusher asked.

His expression one of uncertainty, Daret replied, "Something I've not seen before: a visual transcript of an interrogation involving two Bajorans, on the same evening a bombing was carried out against a barracks building here in the Olanda camp. That attack was the precursor to the retaliatory strikes inflicted on the Bajoran camps, before the entire situation devolved and the Cardassians fled the planet." As he spoke, Crusher noticed how his features seem to darken, and there was actual fear in his eyes.

"Ilona, what is it?"

Looking up from where he was staring at the still-inactive data reader, Daret's voice was almost inaudible as he whispered, "I believe I was there."

Thirty

It was with restrained fury that Gil Rakan Urkar watched the quartet of guards push the two Bajorans into the interrogation room. That anger was laced with disgust as the prisoners were forced to their knees and his nostrils were assailed with an odorous blend of dust and mud from the mines and sweat. His first impulse was simply to execute them and return to his quarters and the young female waiting for him there, but Urkar knew that his work here was only just beginning.

"Where did you find them?" he asked, glaring in turn at each of the men.

One of the guards, Gorr Cadek, indicated the younger of the Bajorans with the muzzle of his disruptor rifle. "This one was apprehended outside the perimeter. He was alone, but we found the bodies of two others inside the fence." The guard moved the weapon to point at the older prisoner. "He was near the recycling facility. No work was scheduled there for tonight."

"I should kill you both just for being out of your barracks after curfew," Urkar said, moving for the first time to stand within arm's reach of the prisoners. "The fact that you both were armed only makes my decision easier, and it seems likely that either or both of you were involved in the attack on the barracks. Still, I know you were not working alone."

Reports from the blast site still were coming in, but early estimates indicated that no fewer than thirty Cardassians along with several Bajoran workers had been killed in the explosion that had decimated the barracks building, with dozens more injured. Almost a third of the Olanda labor camp's military contingent either was dead or wounded. The camp's commander, Gul Pavok, already had requested assistance from the Tabata and Pencala camps to supplement his sudden manpower shortage. As for any responsible parties, it was obvious to Urkar that the small yet committed and apparently well-organized resistance cell operating within the camp was behind the attack. Despite numerous searches and inspections and even the enlistment of spies within the Bajoran population, the group had been most effective at concealing their identities and activities. Lacking sufficient evidence to the contrary, Urkar was certain that the two Bajorans now kneeling before him were members of that faction.

Though they were not restrained, both men knelt with their hands behind their backs. The older Bajoran looked straight ahead, his eyes focused on a point behind Urkar, whereas his younger companion held himself ramrod straight and looked up at him, not with defiance or hatred or even confidence. Was it simple resignation to his fate? Urkar could not be certain.

Then, it occurred to him that he recognized the man.

"Ishan Anjar," Urkar said, allowing himself a small, satisfied smile as realization dawned. "I knew it was only a matter of time before one of you did something to implicate yourself." The man was one of several who had been identified as having possible involvement in resistance activities, at least according to the reports Urkar had reviewed. Until now, Ishan, like others immersed in such undertakings, had succeeded in concealing his ties to the insurrectionist movement. Having incriminated himself, all that remained was to find his associates. "Who else was involved in this attack?"

Neither man spoke a word, though the older one at least had the sense not to look at him in an insolent manner. The same could not be said for Ishan, whose eyes narrowed and jaw clenched as he stared at Urkar. Without warning, the Cardassian lashed out with his foot, planting the sole of his heavy boot onto the man's chest. Ishan toppled backward from the force of the kick, grunting as he fell to the floor. His hands clutched his chest, grimacing in pain though he said nothing. Cadek stepped forward, grabbing the prisoner by his neck and pulling him to his feet. The guard kept one hand on the Bajoran and held him in place. Two of the other guards reached for the older prisoner, yanking him up as Urkar moved to stand mere centimters from Ishan's face.

"You could not have carried out this attack on your own!" he hissed, his spittle striking the Bajoran's cheek. When his prisoner flinched, the gil turned his attention to the other man. "And what of you? Have you nothing to say?"

To his surprise, the older Bajoran chose to respond.

"What reason do I have to cooperate with you, Cardassian?" For the first time, his expression darkened. "You've already decided we're guilty. That's how your justice system works, isn't it?"

"Of course," Urkar countered. "A presumption of innocence is inefficient." Stepping toward the Bajoran, he glowered at the prisoner. "Perhaps you are hoping you can anger me enough to just kill you, before you're forced to betray your fellow resistance fighters." He shook his head. "Rest assured, that is a false hope."

Moving toward the small desk positioned before the interrogation room's rear wall, Urkar regarded the prisoners, studying their faces and body language. Ishan was struggling to maintain his bearing—an obvious consequence of his youth and lack of experience—whereas his companion once again had composed himself. Indeed, he seemed to lack even a hint of fear with respect to his current predicament. Had he already consigned himself to whatever fate might await him? If so, he would prove all but worthless as a source of information. However, the other prisoner already was showing signs of breaking. Questioning him would be quick, if not entertaining.

Urkar looked to Cadek. "Where is Lagrar? It was his men who captured these two. His statement will be required for my report." He had not seen his fellow gil since before the explosion. Lagrar had been the officer on watch for the evening, responsible for the guards on duty in the watchtowers and moving about the camp. He likely would have headed for the destroyed barracks building within moments of the blast.

"I do not know, sir. He was last seen running across the compound, reportedly in pursuit of saboteurs trying to make an escape." The guard gestured toward the younger Bajoran. "This one was captured near the area where Lagrar was heading." Cadek's report had a slight yet noticeable effect on the young prisoner. A flash of recognition seemed to cross Ishan's eyes, and Urkar glared at him with renewed suspicion.

"What do you know of this?" he asked, stepping toward the man. His fingers closed around the prisoner's throat and Urkar lifted Ishan off his feet. The man gasped in surprise, his expression for the first time displaying the first hints of fear.

"I know nothing!" Ishan said, forcing the words from his constricted throat and past his lips. His hands clasped Urkar's forearm in a futile attempt to loosen the Cardassian's grip, his eyes bulging and his face reddening. Cadek and another of the guards stepped closer, restraining Ishan's arms even as Urkar held him in his unwavering grip. Despite the need to question both prisoners in order to discover the truth behind the bombing, his desire to kill them and be done with this frustrating exercise mounted with every passing moment. It would be so easy, he knew. So, too, did Ishan, whose struggling was continuing to increase as his breathing became more labored. He stared down at Urkar, waiting as though knowing his end was near.

Urkar dropped him, and Ishan collapsed in a heap on the floor, coughing and sputtering as one hand reached for his throat. As guards moved to once more pull him to his feet, the gil moved back to the desk.

"Prepare them for full interrogation," he said, offering a dismissive wave in their direction. "Inform the physician that his services will likely be required."

As Cadek reached for his arm, the older Bajoran took a step toward the desk, earning him a chorus of surprised grunts from all of the guards. Cadek raised his disruptor rifle and aimed its muzzle at the back of the prisoner's head, but the man stopped after the single step, his hands held at his side and his gaze fixed on Urkar.

"Paxyirta kren otal jek."

Uncertain as to what he had just heard, Urkar scowled in apprehension as he regarded the Bajoran. "What did you say?"

The prisoner drew himself up, a renewed confidence now present in his voice and demeanor as he repeated the phrase in native Cardassian. Ishan, still recovering from his treatment at Urkar's hands, now stared at him with utter astonishment.

"What are you doing?" the younger man asked. His belief and growing dread appeared genuine, at least to Urkar. "Was that Cardassian? What did you just say? Are you a spy? A traitor?"

Ignoring the questions, Urkar kept his focus on the older prisoner. "What is your name, Bajoran?"

The man did not answer, instead glancing at Ishan before saying, "What about him? He does not know me."

"Neither do I," Urkar snapped, weary of the conversation. He had no intention of taking on faith that this prisoner had just given to him a personalized, confidential code identifying him to the camp's guard contingent as an informer among the Bajoran labor population. Though he did not recognize the man, it was common practice for all of the gils and many of the guards to cultivate spies while not divulging the identities of those individuals even to each other. Urkar had a small cadre of such covert personnel, though their number was few and he tended to err on the side of caution with respect to their usefulness and length of servitude before such informers met all manner of tragic fates as a "consequence" of the hazardous work performed in the mines.

As for this potential spy, it was obvious he did not want to reveal his name while standing before his luckless companion. After a moment, he seemed to realize that nothing would come from delaying—except perhaps his untimely demise if he continued to irritate his captors.

"My name is Baras Rodirya. Contact Gul Pavok. He will explain everything. I can tell you exactly who was responsible for the attack and where you can find them."

The first rays of the morning sun were beginning to chase away the darkness as a new day greeted Doctor Ilona Daret, but all it did was serve to cast new light on the scene of devastation dominating the compound. From where he stood in the courtyard outside the building that housed the camp commander and his staff, he could see guards and other Cardassians moving about the pile of rubble that was all that remained of the wounded barracks building's front half. Smoke from small fires still rose from gaps in the wreckage, and the noxious odor of scorched metal, thermocrete, and whatever else had been caught in the blast filled the air. Ash covered everything in proximity to the ruined building, including several of the people poring over the site. Daret heard the low-pitched whines of scanning equipment as workers searched for survivors.

Gul Pavok, the officer charged with overseeing the Olanda camp's operations, stood before the ruined structure, using it as a backdrop as he glowered at the group of Bajoran workers who had been assembled before him. The compound where the Cardassian contingent lived and worked was far too small to bring together all of the Bajorans in this manner, but Daret knew that such a gathering was not necessary. The demonstration Pavok was providing did not need to be seen by everyone; every member of the audience mustered here would waste no time communicating to others what they had been gathered to witness. Daret was familiar enough with Pavok to know that the commander was deriving no small amount of perverse pleasure from the stunned and horrified reactions his demonstration was garnering. It required all of Daret's willpower not to avert his eyes from the ghastly display.

A young Bajoran male—an adult, to be sure, but only a few seasons beyond adolescence—had been tied to a rectangular metal frame, his extremities lashed to each of the corners. His face was all but unrecognizable thanks to the severe beating he had endured. Dried blood traced paths down his front, staining his tattered clothing. The Bajoran hung limp from the rack, life having mercifully fled and leaving him in whatever state might pass for peace.

"Behold the price of treachery," Pavok said, addressing his conscripted audience via a public address system that carried his voice across the compound as well as throughout the rest of the labor camp. "We know there are those among you who seek to undermine our presence here. Though you may have enjoyed a few isolated victories, rest assured that your days are numbered, as this prisoner can attest."

Daret heard murmurings of shock, sorrow, and anger emanating from the group of assembled Bajorans, and he wondered if any of them had known the luckless prisoner who somehow had crossed the camp commander. Had the man been part of the resistance movement that had been festering within the laborer population, growing seemingly ever more bold with each passing day? On the Bajoran home-world, the crusade had propagated to the point where nearly a third of all Cardassians stationed either on Bajor itself or aboard Terok Nor, the space station orbiting the planet, were committed to fighting the uncounted resistance cells operating among the occupied population. Here on Jevalan, insurrectionist activities still were limited both in scope and the damage they were inflicting, but the rebels' efforts seemed buoyed by the successes being recorded by their brothers and sisters on Bajor. Gul Pavok was concerned about the mounting unrest and even had contacted his superiors on Cardassia Prime to request additional troops and support to deal with the problem. An ongoing hunt for the troublemakers had provided only marginal results, and the commander always was seeking ways to undermine whatever morale they might be instilling within the different labor camps. That likely was the prime reason he had orchestrated the gruesome display now being presented to the small group of stunned Bajorans.

"Have I not shown benevolence?" Pavok asked, though Daret could tell by the commander's tone that he was not expecting any answer to that question. The gul was enjoying this latest opportunity to remind the Bajoran workers that their fates were subject to his whim. "Have I not given you at least some comforts, and allowed you to retain a portion of your dignity, in the hopes that you will be content to make the best of your situation and serve Cardassia? Surely, you cannot argue that your life here is preferable to that endured by those assigned to camps on other worlds, to say nothing of that ball of mud from which most of you sprang. And how am I repaid? Disobedience, rebellion, sabotage, and murder." He paused, allowing his words to linger in the air before his audience. "Very well, then," he continued after a moment, gesturing to the body of the dead Bajoran. "For the insolence exhibited by the few, punishment will be visited upon the many."

He turned to one of the gils standing behind him, a ruthless soldier Daret recognized as Urkar, who oversaw one of the guard companies providing security for the camp. "Bring me the insurgents. All of them. We will string them up here, next to their collaborator, for all to see. As for anyone who might be harboring them? It's time they learn that such action also brings cost. See to it."

As Urkar moved off to carry out his orders and guards began ushering, directing, or herding away the group of assembled Bajorans, Daret moved toward the rack that still held the Bajoran's body. Drawing closer, the doctor heard Pavok and Urkar conversing in low tones.

"Throw the corpse into the recycling center," the commander was saying as Daret stepped up behind him.

Keeping his voice low, Daret said, "With respect, I do not believe that may be the wisest course. The Bajorans are already uneasy. As you explained to them, you have shown them an unprecedented degree of generosity, including allowing them to carry out funeral arrangements for their dead."

Pavok said, "And for that kindness, I have a destroyed barracks and dozens of murdered or injured soldiers. The time for compassion is over, Doctor. We are overdue for a reminder about who is in charge of this facility."

There was little doubt that the commander intended to make an example not only of those responsible for the attack, but also anyone who may have assisted them or who may have possessed knowledge of the plan. How many innocents would suffer as retribution was dispensed? Daret's heart sank as he imagined what the next hours and days would bring for the camp's Bajoran population. And what of those at the other camps? How far would Pavok take his reprisal efforts?

Eyeing the dead Bajoran and trying to contain his own

revulsion at the sight, Daret said, "It is not my place to question your command decisions, and I do not do so now. However, my perspective with respect to the Bajorans is somewhat different than yours, as I am in closer proximity to them on a daily basis."

"You coddle them," Pavok countered. "I have been told how much compassion you display as you treat their illnesses and injuries." Before Daret could respond, the gul paused, holding up a hand. "Forgive me, Doctor. That sounded more accusatory than I intended. I do not question your loyalty or your ethics as a physician."

Daret allowed himself a sigh of relief. "Thank you. What I am trying to say is that the Bajorans already are emboldened by the actions of this resistance movement. They know you are going to seek out and punish those responsible for the attack. Indeed, they likely have accounted for that response as a cost of taking action. However, if you expand such reprisals to include those who took no part in the plot, you will only bolster their resolve." He sighed as his gaze lingered on the wreckage of the barracks building. "They do outnumber us, after all."

"Such matters are my concern," Pavok replied, and Daret saw his expression harden as he, too, stared at the devastation. "However, I do appreciate your insights, Doctor." Without looking, he gestured toward the dead Bajoran. "You may take possession of the body. Return it to the Bajorans."

"Thank you," Daret said, reaching into the pocket of his coat to retrieve his data padd. "I will see to the details." Tapping on the padd's display, he opened a new file for his records. "What was his name?"

Looking away from the wreckage, Pavok's eyes narrowed. "Baras. His name was Baras Rodirya."

Thirty-one

Sitting on the floor of the makeshift temple with nearly three dozen isolinear data rods, data padds, and other records collected by Raal Mosara, Beverly Crusher held up one of the rods and shook her head.

"So, that's it, then," she said, eyeing the compact storage device and marveling at the simple yet staggering information it contained. "President Ishan's real name is Baras Rodirya."

"And Urkar?" asked Tom Riker from where he sat on an adjacent bench. "Rakan Urkar? I've heard that name. Recently. He's a major player in the True Way."

Perched on one of the improvised benches facing the dais, Daret regarded Tom with widening eyes. "The True Way? Are you sure?"

"As sure as you can be when you're dealing with unsavory information merchants on worlds that operate all sorts of shady business deals outside Federation influence. Deneb, Arcturus, Delta Leonis, and so on. One of my contacts gave me a list of prominent True Way members who've gone dark in recent months, since before President Bacco's assassination. We know what happened to a few of those—they were killed on Nydak II—but the others?" He shrugged. "No one knows."

"I cannot believe this," Daret said, holding his hands

clasped before him and squeezing them so tightly that Crusher could see the slight tremors in the muscles beneath his skin. "I simply cannot fathom that I was so close to the truth, and yet never suspected anything."

"You never saw the real Baras," said Tom Riker from where he sat on an adjacent bench. "No doubt that was by design. Once the identity switch was made, they would have moved him to another area of the camp to protect his status as an informant."

Crusher frowned. "But why bother with the identity switch at all? That doesn't make any sense."

"In a way, it does," Tom replied. "The real Baras Rodirya was a spy, working for the camp commander. It's possible that his name was known to resistance members as a potential threat. If it wasn't, then it likely would be once Baras was released from interrogation, because only spies and collaborators tend to survive those sorts of situations. His Cardassian handler may have simply decided to err on the side of caution and cover his tracks by eliminating the real Ishan Anjar and giving his identity to Baras."

Shrugging, though still not completely convinced, Crusher asked, "What about everyone at the camp who knew him?" Before Tom or Daret could answer, she realized she had overlooked the obvious. "The retaliatory strikes on the Bajoran camps following the barracks attack."

"According to the interrogation transcript," Daret said, holding up another of the data rods, "Baras supplied information to Gul Pavok that incriminated several dozen Bajorans as members of the resistance. Most of them were living in the targeted camps, so it's possible the strikes were intended as much for retribution as they were to provide cover for Baras's status as Pavok's personal spy. In that regard, it seems those attacks were most effective." Crusher saw his disgust. "I never had any reason to consider such a plot was under way. By the time they had completed their . . .

interrogation . . . of the real Baras Rodirya, they already had taken care of the identity switch, including any records kept at the camp's administration center. When I entered the final information into his file before making the preparations for his burial, all of the relevant data already was in place. I never suspected a thing."

Shifting his position on the bench, Tom said, "I can see why he'd change his identity. If he did all of that, he's a traitor to all other Bajorans. They've never been forgiving of anyone who collaborated with the Cardassians during the Occupation. What about the burial? Didn't anyone raise an issue then?"

"Due to the severity of the injuries he sustained during his interrogation, his burial vessel was sealed. Baras Rodirya had no family or relatives among the labor population. So far as I know, no one who attended his burial ceremony ever mentioned anything untoward." Daret paused, reaching up to wipe his face. "I had completely forgotten about him. By the time the revolt had escalated to the point that my people were evacuating the planet, there were far too many bodies to worry about a single individual with no familial ties. And now, after so many years? All of the names have long since become a blur, and that's assuming I even had an opportunity to learn their names in the first place."

Crusher was tempted to offer some kind of solace to her friend, but instead she remained silent. Ilona Daret, despite being a physician, still had participated in the oppression and indentured servitude of an entire world. She always had set him apart from other Cardassians she had encountered during her own Starfleet career. Even here, on a world whose sole purpose was to utilize Bajoran prisoners as slave labor for the enrichment of the Cardassian Union, Daret still had found a way to place his duties as a healer over whatever loyalty he might have to Cardassia Prime or its military. Crusher knew that her words would have little effect; whatever guilt Daret carried—deserved or otherwise—as a consequence of his service during the Occupation would stay with him for the remainder of his days.

"I can see the charade working here, on this planet, during the Occupation," Tom said, rising from the bench. "But now? With Ishan . . . sorry . . . Baras being elevated first to the Bajoran government before his time on the Federation Council until he ultimately is named as the Federation's interim president?" He scowled. "The only way his identity remains a secret is if he's had some kind of help, behind the scenes. That had to be Velk."

Crusher said, "According to the biography that's been released in the wake of his appointment as president pro tem, Ishan's listed as a survivor of the camps here, one of the few hundred or so who didn't die in the final attacks the Cardassians launched prior to evacuating the planet."

"What about the Cardassians?" Tom asked. "Obviously most of them survived, but what happened to them? In particular, what happened to the camp commander?"

"He evacuated the planet, along with most of the other officers," Daret replied, "but not before overseeing one final strike on the Bajoran compound. I do not know what became of him after the Occupation ended, but Central Command has never taken a kind view of those who abandon their duties. While I am sure some of his subordinates escaped punishment, Gul Pavok almost certainly did not."

"What if Ishan . . . *Baras* . . . maintained contact with any of them?" Crusher asked. "Or maybe Velk was the one who handled that. It's definitely worth a look." She would have to apprise Jean-Luc about this possibility—along with all of the other explosive information now in their possession—as soon as possible. However, there were more pressing matters requiring attention. "Our top priority is getting all of this out of here. Any thoughts on that?"

"One of the civilian transports," Daret said, "assuming your runabout is no longer an option."

Tom said, "I'm guessing our friends took care of that, and even if they didn't, it's a sure bet they're watching for that thing to show up on sensors, or they've got backup on another ship in orbit, or somewhere close by. Calling your runabout is a sure way to bring them and who knows what else down on our heads." He nodded toward Daret. "He's right. We need to find a way to sneak away."

"There's something else we should do," Crusher said, indicating the collection of data rods and other materials. "Make copies of all of this. If we have to split up, we'll have a better chance of getting the evidence to the *Enterprise*."

"Good idea," Tom said, moving to reach for one of the data readers included in the storage box. "A tricorder will hold all of this with no problem."

Before Crusher could say anything more, the communicator Tom had given her chirped, and she retrieved the device from her jacket. "Blue One," she said, continuing to use the call signs the group had instituted.

"This is Blue Three," said the voice of Lieutenant Cruzen, her voice sounding small and distant thanks to a low hiss of static permeating the connection. *"We've got something going on up here."* She and Rennan Konya had been maintaining a security watch on the surface, keeping a lookout for any signs of their pursuers. With their earlier dispatching of the two agents, Crusher knew it only was a matter of time before their companions came looking for them.

"What is it?" Crusher asked.

Cruzen asked, *"You're not hearing it? Some kind of alarm's been triggered up here on the surface, and there's been an announcement to clear the site. The report mentions some sort of gas leak, but I'm not picking up anything with my tricorder."*

Frowning, Crusher looked to Tom and Daret, both of whom were staring back at her with confused expressions, though she noted that Tom already had drawn a phaser from his jacket pocket.

"I didn't hear anything," Tom said.

Daret added, "Neither did I, but such alarms are not unusual. Our excavation efforts have taken us into areas of the mines where gas pockets have been encountered, necessitating evacuation of the underground sections." He paused, glancing about the room. "However, those alarms are supposed to be audible down here, as well."

"I knew it," Tom said, gesturing with his phaser to their collection of evidence. "Come on. We need to get this stuff out of here right now." To the communicator Crusher held, he said, "Blue Three, you and Blue Two know what to do. We'll join up with you at the rally point as soon as possible."

Upon their arrival at the Olanda camp, both Tom and Konya had decided on the need for a fallback position, someplace with limited, controlled avenues of approach that could be defended against anyone who might come looking for them. After studying a schematic of the underground tunnel system provided to them by Daret, the pair had decided on an area on one of the mine's lower levels. Its location deep within the rock would hamper any attempts to locate them with tricorders or other sensors, and it was possible that the team might be able to draw their pursuers into a tactical disadvantage.

"Acknowledged, Blue Four," Cruzen replied. *"We're shutting down this frequency. We'll link up on the first alternate."*

With that, the connection ended, and Crusher returned the communicator to her jacket before turning to assist Daret in gathering the data rods and other materials. Tom, rather than pitching in, had taken up a position near the temple's entrance.

As she worked, Crusher looked to Daret. "Ilona, you're sure you know your way around down here?"

"Yes. There are several routes from here to the surface."

"That's good," Tom said. "The last thing I want to do is give those bastards a chance to trap us. Still, with all the interference from the mineral deposits permeating the rock, we may have an advantage if they try to follow us through the tunnels."

"If it's all the same to you," Crusher said, "I'd just as soon deal with them above ground." She recalled one of the few times she had conducted a clandestine mission that had taken her deep under the surface of the Cardassian-occupied world Celtris III. The operation, during which she, Jean-Luc, and Worf were tasked with investigating the existence of metagenic weapons in the hands of the Cardassian military, had required them to infiltrate the secret underground base located on that planet. Though she did not suffer from claustrophobia, eluding Cardassian soldiers while being cut off from all possible aid as the team maneuvered far below ground had only served to exacerbate an already tense situation. This was before the operation had gone horribly wrong, resulting in Jean-Luc's capture. He eventually was released and returned to the *Enterprise,* but not before suffering extended physical and emotional torture at the hands of his Cardassian captors. Though she doubted the agents now following her and her companions would expend much time and energy in similar activities, Crusher knew without question that if found in the mine's depths, they never again would see the light of day.

So that means it's time to go. As she and Daret worked, and despite her best efforts, Crusher could not ignore the sudden feeling that the walls of the underground chamber now were closing in around her.

Thirty-two

Everything was being consumed by fire.

From where he crouched along a ridge overlooking the Olanda labor camp, Baras Rodirya watched the scene of destruction unfolding before him. With few exceptions, not a single building or other structure had escaped the wrath of the Cardassian ships strafing the compound and surrounding area. Clouds of smoke hung over the entire site, thick enough in some spots to obscure his view. The only thing that appeared to keep the vessels from utterly obliterating everything in their sights were the precious few acts of retaliation scattered around the camp. Bursts of weapons fire from disruptor rifles and pistols stolen from the Cardassians' own armories pierced the night air, lancing upward in desperate attempts to sway the ships from their attack runs.

"They won't be happy until they've killed everyone," said Helva Dras from where she lay in the grass next to Baras. Her voice cracked under the strain of fury and sorrow as she, like Baras, watched the unchecked annihilation of the hovel they had for years called home.

On her opposite side, their mutual friend, Myrosi Ghalj, said, "Gul Pavok's gone mad. There's no reason for this level of violence."

"Not from their perspective," Baras countered. In the weeks that had passed since the attack on the Cardassian troop barracks, reprisals instituted by the camp commander had escalated far beyond simple retribution. While the Bajoran labor population at first had reeled under the constant sweeps and arrests conducted by Cardassian soldiers, it had not taken long for members of the camp's burgeoning resistance movement to take up whatever arms they had been able to scrounge, steal, or fabricate and mount something resembling a defense. Though the resistance members were far outnumbered and outgunned by their Cardassian counterparts, they had on their side the knowledge that there was nowhere for them to go and nothing else for them to lose that had already not been taken from them.

This conviction had spread to the rest of the labor camp population, with first dozens and then hundreds of Bajorans rising up to revolt against their would-be masters. With members of the resistance providing the means and the opportunity, strikes against Cardassian buildings and vehicles had been on the rise, to the point that Gul Pavok had been forced to institute curfews to keep the Bajorans in check. Mining and ore production quotas were suffering, despite the lies propagated by the camp commander as to the effectiveness of the growing rebellion. Now mining operations had all but ceased in the face of what fast was becoming an all-out war spreading from the Olanda camp to the other compounds and installations across the planet.

For a moment, Baras considered the gravity of what he had done by providing information on the saboteurs responsible for the barracks attack. In truth, he had reasoned that Gul Pavok would use that information in order to launch direct action against the guilty parties. While Baras had suspected there might be additional casualties and other collateral damage, he had not imagined the scope of the camp commander's wrath. On the other hand, this disproportionate response on the Cardassians' part was spurring the Bajoran laborers, finally, to take action against their masters. Yes, there would be many more deaths as a consequence of this uprising, but at least now his fellow Bajorans would die fighting for their freedom, rather than waiting to meet a far-less-noble end in the mines or at a guard's whim. Surely, it was better this way? Perhaps the Cardassians would give second thought before considering future plans of conquest, and Bajorans would never again allow themselves to be enslaved.

History may even judge me a hero, one day.

"Before we escaped, I heard talk yesterday that the spoonheads might be pulling out," said Helva, not taking her gaze from the horrific scene unfolding in the distance.

"I heard something about that, too. If this keeps up, they might leave any day now." Baras gestured toward the embattled camp. "Maybe this is them getting in their last hits before they go."

The rumors had begun spreading throughout the small brig facility where he and his new friends had been housed. While Helva and Myrosi had been arrested on suspicion of being resistance members with knowledge of the attack on the troop barracks, Baras had been held as a means of safeguarding his cover as a spy for Gul Pavok. Following the execution of Ishan Anjar and the effort the camp commander had gone to to switch Baras's identity with that of the luckless Bajoran, Pavok had decided the best course of action was to keep Baras in detention until such time as any links to his real identity were severed. So, Baras had bided his time, waiting for his handler to release him back to the laborer population, until it became obvious that the gul seemed content to keep his mole under lock and key. Despite all efforts to seek an audience with Pavok, his every request had been denied.

Then, the attacks had escalated, on both sides.

Even as Cardassian soldiers descended upon the labor camps and the mines in search of dissidents, members of the Bajoran resistance were hitting back with everything they could muster. Soft targets such as mining equipment and vehicles were among the most frequent casualties, though the insurgents gained courage with each successful strike. Other buildings were targeted, with the resistance cells using a variety of improvised explosives to inflict damage across the camp. Word of similar uprisings at the Tabata and Pencala settlements soon began drifting through the Olanda populace, providing even more incentive to the Bajorans fighting to break the grip of their Cardassian overseers.

"I'm just glad we're not still caged like rats," Myrosi said, wincing as he rolled onto his side. "That hit on the detention center couldn't have come at a better time." Earlier the previous evening, he had sustained considerable bruising as well as a pair of fractured ribs from a beating he had suffered during his last interrogation at the hands of an overzealous guard. Having inspected the man's injuries, Baras was certain that another such session might well have proven fatal, but Myrosi was spared that possibility when a resistance cell assaulted the detention facility in the early morning hours. Caught unprepared, the three soldiers on duty in the cell block housing Baras and his companions were killed, allowing the twelve prisoners in that section to be freed before an explosive destroyed that area of the building. It was yet another in the aggravating series of attacks Gul Pavok had been forced to endure, and it—along with strikes on his own command center—appeared to have been the tipping point for the latest round of retaliatory moves against the Bajorans. So far as Baras could discern, Pavok was offering no leniency in the face of the worsening revolt.

"Look," Helva said, pointing down into the shallow valley housing the camp. "That ship's lifting for orbit."

Baras watched as the Cardassian vessel, an armored troop transport that had been firing on the compound, rose from its position over the camp and now was angling its nose skyward. The echo of its engines powering up rolled across the ground as the ship lifted ever higher, growing smaller with each passing second until it was swallowed by the clouds. Farther away, another ship was executing a similar maneuver, disappearing into the night sky and leaving behind the residual rumbling of its thrusters before that also faded. Elsewhere, Baras saw Cardassian soldiers retreating from the camp, most of them heading in the general direction of the compound reserved for their use but also toward the landing field where additional transports and other craft were staged. Many of those vessels were activating their engines and other systems, preparing for liftoff.

"It's an evacuation," Baras said. Could they be giving up? Had Jevalan been deemed a lost cause?

Let's hope they don't decide to just obliterate the entire planet from orbit.

"What do we do now?" Helva asked. "Even if they are pulling out, it's not going to happen all at once. This fight isn't over yet. I think we should try to link back up with our cell, because you know the Cardassians will be looking to capture any stragglers." She looked to Baras. "What about you? Where's your rally point?"

Baras pointed to the far end of the compound, which was ablaze in the wake of yet another air strike. "Near the secondary mine entrance. The problem is that it looks like it's one of the hardest-hit areas of the whole camp. I can't believe anybody from my cell survived." Of course, he knew that the area in question would be a prime target for the attack, as it was one of the locations he had provided Gul Pavok as being a hiding place used by those members of the resistance who had carried out the attack on the troop barracks. That simple action would brand him as a traitor to the Bajoran people, and anyone who learned of his collusion with the Cardassians would take great pleasure in seeing him pay for his crimes. Such restitution would be long and painful, but it only would be an issue if he managed to survive the coming days.

And I have every intention of surviving.

To that end, Baras had elected not to return to the Olanda camp. There still existed the possibility that someone there would see him and ask why he was still alive, as they had seen or heard that "Baras Rodirya" was dead. He did not need that complication. No, he had decided; he would take his chances and head for the Tabata camp. Surely there would be survivors, and he would be able to blend in there using the new identity given to him by Gul Pavok, "Ishan Anjar."

Before that could happen, Baras knew there was one potential complication that required immediate attention. Two complications, in point of fact.

While Helva's and Myrosi's attention remained fixed on the burning Olanda camp and the transport vessels that one by one were lifting away from the landing field, Baras drew from his jacket the disruptor he had purloined from one of the Cardassian guards killed during their escape, and he adjusted the weapon's power setting to maximum.

Thirty-three

Paris, Earth

The sound of his desk intercom paging him startled President Ishan Anjar from his troubling reverie, and he glared at the unit with no small amount of disdain. He did not answer the page, but instead drew several breaths to calm himself. Retrieving a crystal carafe of water that had been placed near one corner of his desk, he poured some of its contents into a matching glass, noting as he did so that his hand was shaking.

Calm yourself, Mister President.

Sipping his water, Ishan considered that it had been a very long time since he allowed himself to think of those final days of the Occupation efforts on Jevalan, to say nothing of his actions while under Cardassian rule. Indeed, he had spent years forcing himself not to dwell on his prior life or even to think of himself by his former name, Baras Rodirya. Though it certainly was true that he often revisited those events in an abstract sense, he could not remember the last time he had pondered the harsh reality that had forced him to commit such heinous acts.

The past cannot be changed. You survived. That is what is most important.

He swiveled his chair so that he could take in the wondrous, panoramic view of Paris afforded him by the large, curved window that formed his office's rear wall. The city was awash in the rays of the afternoon sun, highlighted by a brilliant blue sky accented only with a handful of scattered, wispy clouds. Pausing to contemplate the beautiful, centuries-old city, teeming as it was with life and activity, served to calm him and push aside, if only for a moment, the stresses of his office. Though he was only a handful of weeks into his term as president pro tempore—a position many might consider as little more than a figurehead until such time as the special election was held and a permanent replacement was installed as successor to the late Nanietta Bacco—Ishan had wasted little time turning with verve to the demands of the Federation's leader. Given the current volatile situation and the very real threats to the security of billions of people on hundreds of worlds, he could ill afford to sit idle and occupy a ceremonial station even for the sixty days between his temporary appointment and the election. The Federation deserved better than that, particularly now.

More than once, he had considered the notion that his emerging from the hellish existence that was life on Jevalan had been due to divine reason. Had the Prophets intervened, sparing him so that he might advance to the position he now held? If so, was it not incumbent upon him to make use of the reprieve death had granted him and see to it that such atrocities never again were allowed to be perpetrated upon anyone living beneath the banner of the Federation he had chosen to serve? Did he not now sit here, occupying the office of the most powerful person in two quadrants? How far he had come from his deplorable former life, toiling as a miner under the oppressive heel of the detestable Cardassians who had enslaved the entire Bajoran race. Surely, this evolution could not be happenstance?

Something else had to be responsible. It certainly sounded reasonable enough, though Ishan knew there were many who would disagree with his interpretation of the actions he had taken. Fortunately, most of those dissenters were dead.

Most, but not all. The thought taunted him, and it took effort for Ishan to force away the errant thought as the intercom sounded for the third time. Releasing an irritated sigh, he drained the contents of his water glass before reaching across his desk to slap the unit's activation control.

"What is it?" he snapped.

"I apologize for the interruption, Mister President," replied the voice of his personal assistant, Syliri Alvora. The nervousness in the young Bajoran female's voice was evident with every word. *"You are receiving an incoming call from a Starfleet officer, Commander Hayden. He provided your authorization code for personal communications. Shall I route the frequency to your secure workstation?"*

With a mixture of anticipation and apprehension, Ishan replied, "Yes, put him through." As he waited for Alvora to route the connection, he took the opportunity to refill his glass. The shaking in his hand had subsided. Perhaps that was a sign?

The tabletop computer workstation positioned on the left side of his desk activated, displaying the seal of the United Federation of Planets. Beneath the symbol, the caption SECURE COMMUNICATION appeared on the screen, followed by the voice of the Palais de la Concorde's central computer system.

"Incoming encrypted communication. Please enter access code."

Using the workstation's manual interface, Ishan entered the authorization protocol he had created just for this purpose, and which he dared not speak aloud to the computer. After all, it was not unreasonable to presume that even the office of the Federation President was not immune from eavesdropping.

"Authorization code accepted," reported the computer. *"Activating security and isolation protocols."* Ishan waited a moment until an indicator on the display screen flashed

green, apprising him that the office's protective counter-surveillance measures now were in operation. *"Your location is now secure. Internal sensors detect no indications of monitoring."*

Satisfied with the report, Ishan tapped another control on the terminal, and the image on the screen shifted to show a male human Starfleet commander, Joshua Hayden. A protégé of Admiral Declan Schlosser, Ishan's contact within Starfleet Headquarters, Hayden, like the admiral, was an ambitious officer who recognized that the status quo gripping Starfleet and the Federation was not sustainable. Survival in any meaningful sense required new perspectives and a willingness to take bold, even unpopular action. While many of the officers filling out Starfleet's senior ranks appeared to lack such conviction, those like Schlosser and the man now staring out at him from the computer screen showed great promise.

"Good afternoon, Mister President," Hayden said, bowing his head in greeting. *"You asked me to apprise you when my task was accomplished."*

"It's done?" Ishan asked, omitting any specifics. After all and despite his precautions, he wanted nothing left to chance.

"Yes, sir." Hayden paused, and Ishan noted the man's obvious discomfort. There was no doubting that the assignment he had been given had been difficult and even distasteful, and it was a testament to the man's character that he had seen the necessity behind the action he had been asked to undertake. Admiral Schlosser had given his personal assurance that the commander could be trusted, so perhaps it was just a case of residual nervousness on Hayden's part. *"Though I encountered no issues, I do have to wonder about . . . long-term consequences."*

"That's not your problem, Commander," Ishan replied. "I have others to see to those details." He knew that removing Galif jav Velk from the Federation Security Agency detention facility was a calculated risk, but he also had seen no other alternative. "Is there . . . anything that still requires your attention?"

It seemed to take Hayden a moment to comprehend the question's cloaked meeting. *"No, Mister President. Everything's been . . . resolved."*

"Very well, then, Commander. Thank you." He was of two minds about this matter, of course. He and Velk had started out as colleagues and allies, and it was the Tellarite who was responsible for Ishan's rise through the ranks of the Federation government. Ishan owed him everything, but their relationship had taken a distinct, irrevocable turn when Velk confronted him with his knowledge of Ishan's true identity. That he possessed such damaging information was a risk that could not be ignored.

Such is the way of things, my friend.

Ishan was about to dismiss the officer but paused in the midst of reaching for the control to terminate the communication. What was wrong with him? His expression was flat, but there was still something in his eyes. Uncertainty? Guilt? "Is there anything else? You seem . . . troubled."

Pausing a moment as though considering his answer, Hayden finally replied, *"No, Mister President. Is there anything else I can do for you?"*

"No, thank you. Report to Admiral Schlosser for further instructions." He severed the communication, and Hayden's image dissolved from the computer screen. Even as the Federation seal reappeared on the monitor, Ishan continued to ponder the commander's odd behavior. Was it possible Hayden was wavering in his convictions? Might he become a liability? Ishan made a note to discuss the matter with Schlosser at the earliest opportunity.

Eliminate one irritant, and another takes its place. Why must everything be so difficult?

It seemed that from the beginning of this entire insane plot, he had been forced to deal with problems and complications that continued to arise. Though Velk's dispatching of a covert-operations team had resulted in the elimination of Onar Throk and the other Cardassians who had perpetrated Nanietta Bacco's assassination, members of the team sent to carry out that assignment still were alive. As such, they posed a potential threat, as there was no way for Velk—or Ishan—to know if Throk or his companions had confessed anything to Commander Tuvok or Lieutenant Nog regarding Velk's involvement in the plot before their timely rescue from Nydak II by Admiral Riker and the *U.S.S. Titan*. Ishan suspected that Throk must have acknowledged his role as the assassin, giving Riker the confidence he possessed on the evening he had come to confront Ishan over the issue.

Anticipating this, Ishan had been forced to take the only action available to him: having Velk arrested and detained at a secure facility. He then had crafted a narrative highlighting his former chief of staff's "remorseful confession" for the unsanctioned orders he had given for the pursuit and execution of Bacco's assassins. It was not a long-term solution, Ishan knew, but at the time it was enough to insulate both him and Velk from their actual complicity in Bacco's murder. The action also was sufficient to keep at bay Riker and Admiral Akaar until Ishan could find a way to deal with them. In addition to the trouble they were causing, there also was the Federation attorney general with which to contend, who already had made inferences that she was considering her own investigation into Velk's activities. That, Ishan could ill afford. If it came to light that Velk had orchestrated the entire conspiracy, including the leaking of information to agents of the True Way regarding Bacco's schedule and protection detail to his cover-up attempts with the murder of the assassins at Nydak II, neither the Tellarite nor Ishan would be able to escape Federation justice.

The simple truth was that Velk had become a problem requiring resolution. Hence Commander Hayden and the assignment Ishan had given him.

Equally troubling was this business with Picard's wife sneaking off to Jevalan under the guise of transferring to Deep Space 9. There was only one reason for Beverly Crusher—or anyone else, for that matter—to travel to that distant world under false pretenses: She, or someone she knew, had found some evidence leading back to him and the truth of Ishan Anjar.

And Baras Rodirya.

The only thing Ishan could do was try to contain Crusher and whatever information she may have uncovered, and to that end he had instructed Admiral Schlosser to direct the *Tonawanda* to Jevalan with orders to arrest the doctor and anyone with her and to impound whatever data or materials she may have collected. What if Crusher resisted? What if she managed to communicate her discoveries—whatever they may be—to Picard? Was Ishan prepared to destroy the Federation flagship to keep his secret?

What then? Where would it end?

With a sigh, he pushed himself from his chair and began pacing the width of his expansive office. Not even the serene view of Paris beyond his window could assuage his tension. Velk, Riker, Akaar, Crusher, and possibly even Picard and the *Enterprise*; would they all have to be eliminated before Ishan was free to do what needed to be done?

Perhaps.

Leading the Federation back to its role as the unrivaled power in the quadrant was the only matter of true importance, and Ishan could not accomplish that goal so long as he was forced to continue cleaning up the mess Velk had created. The longer he dealt with these distractions, the less time he had to focus on preparing Starfleet and the Federation to defend itself, both from external adversaries as well as the onerous, stifling ideology that might well be its undoing.

Fools! Will they ever come to see their own transience, held before them in the grasp of our enemies as they conspire and plot and plan? What will it take to make them open their eyes?

Pausing before his window, Ishan allowed his gaze to wander over the scene before him. In the streets of Paris, life was playing out for the millions of people who called the city home, but he knew that beneath that supposed tranquility flowed an undercurrent of insecurity. That feeling was mirrored in cities across the planet and worlds throughout the Federation. The past several years of conflict and political turmoil had done much to undermine the quality of life promised to every citizen. The time had come to put to rest—once and for all—the question of the Federation's place in galactic affairs. Peace was the objective, of course, though such peace had to be buttressed not simply through perceived strength, but also a willingness to use that strength in order for the citizens of the Federation to be free to live without fear. Such peace had been denied for far too long.

No longer, Ishan vowed.

Thirty-four

U.S.S. Enterprise

Picard emerged from his ready room and looked to the main viewscreen, upon which was displayed an image of stars streaking past as the *Enterprise* continued on its course. All around the bridge, his officers were immersed in their respective tasks, and there was an air of renewed concern mixed with a slight yet still palpable tension. Worf, sitting in the command chair, rose upon seeing Picard.

"Report, Number One," the captain said, crossing the bridge to the forward conn and ops stations.

"Our sensors are detecting another vessel on a course for Jevalan, traveling at maximum warp," replied the officer, ramrod straight after moving to stand before his own seat to the right of Picard's chair. "Its transponder identifies it as the *U.S.S. Tonawanda*. We have attempted to contact it per your instructions. So far it has refused to acknowledge, though we can confirm that it is receiving our hails."

Drawing a slow, deep breath as he considered the situation and how it might evolve over the next several minutes, Picard nodded. "They're maintaining communications silence." Will Riker had warned him that this likely would be the case, in that the captain of the *Tonawanda*, S'hirethal Verauk, was operating under orders restricting her transmissions only to authorized personnel for the duration of this mission. "She'll continue to do that, unless we can find a way to convince her otherwise."

Having never met his counterpart on the other vessel, Picard's only knowledge of her was what he had been able to glean from a library computer search of her personnel file. Promoted well ahead of schedule thanks to the need to replenish the ranks of starship captains following the costly Borg invasion, Verauk's record was that of a solid, dependable officer. As Admiral Riker had intimated during their earlier conversation while apprising Picard of the *Tonawanda* being routed to Jevalan, Verauk had no qualms about airing her feelings with respect to what she perceived as Starfleet's role in ensuring the Federation's security. Picard harbored little doubt that her stance was motivated in no small part by the loss of her family and her entire planet during the Borg assault.

"Glinn Dygan, what's our estimated arrival time at Jevalan?"

Obviously anticipating the query, the young Cardassian exchange officer replied without hesitation, "We'll be entering the Doltiri system in twenty-seven minutes, sir, and will be in position to assume standard orbit twelve minutes after that."

"What about the *Tonawanda*?" Worf asked.

Dygan replied, "They will make orbit approximately fourteen minutes ahead of us, Commander."

Glancing over his shoulder to the tactical station, Picard said, "Lieutenant Šmrhová, try hailing the *Dordogne* again." Previous attempts to reach the runabout had been unsuccessful, and the *Enterprise* still was too far away to attempt contacting the away team via their personal communicators. Picard forced himself to say nothing, silently counting off the seconds he knew would be needed for the security chief to complete her latest attempt. He waited that interval and not a moment longer before once again looking to her, only to see the lieutenant shaking her head.

"No response, sir, and no indication they're even receiving our hails."

At the science station, Lieutenant Dina Elfiki turned in her chair. "Captain, if the runabout is on the surface in an area with a high concentration of particular mineral ore deposits, that may be affecting their communications, but we won't be able to confirm that until we're closer."

Stepping forward until he stood between the conn and ops stations, Picard crossed his arms. With the *Enterprise* still en route and without being able to contact Beverly and the others, it seemed there remained but one course of action. "Open a channel to the *Tonawanda*."

After a moment, Šmrhová reported, "Channel open, sir. I can confirm that they're receiving."

"*U.S.S. Tonawanda,* this is Captain Picard of the *Enterprise.* I know that you're traveling to Jevalan under classified orders issued by President Ishan and that those orders call for you to restrict your communications. I must inform you that the orders you've received are unsanctioned by Starfleet Command and may well be illegal. I'm requesting a conference so that we may discuss the matter person to person. Please acknowledge."

After several seconds had passed, Šmrhová said, "No response, sir. The *Tonawanda* is maintaining course and speed."

Moving to stand next to him, Worf said in a low voice, "It is doubtful that Captain Verauk will break comm silence without sufficient justification."

"Perfectly understandable, given the circumstances," Picard said, weighing those few options remaining to him. Louder, he called out, "Captain Verauk, I have reason to believe that your orders call for you to take into custody one or more Starfleet officers assumed to be on the planet's surface."

Once you cross this line, there may be no going back.

Glancing to Worf—whose stern expression told him that the Klingon, as always, would stand by him regardless of whatever might happen next—Picard returned his gaze to the viewscreen and its field of onrushing stars.

"Captain Verauk, if these are your orders, then you need to know that I am prepared to do everything in my power to prevent you from apprehending these individuals."

Jevalan, Doltiri System

Her lungs burned, her muscles ached, and she thought her heart might explode through her chest, but Beverly Crusher kept walking, one tired foot in front of the other. How long had they been moving at this rapid pace? Twenty or thirty minutes, she guessed. Though she followed a regular fitness regimen, exercising in the ship's gymnasium or on the holodeck could not compare to the sustained exertion required to navigate the narrow, winding, dust-choked tunnels of the mining complex. Then there was the added burden of assisting her friend Ilona Daret, older and frailer than she and who already was feeling the effects of their prolonged navigation of the underground passageways. She had one of the elder Cardassian's arms slung across her shoulders, and she was doing what she could to support his weight, but the effort was beginning to take its toll.

Maybe you're just getting too old for this kind of nonsense.

"How much farther?" she asked between sharp intakes of breath.

Ahead of them, a tricorder in one hand and a phaser in the other, Tom Riker replied, "Another few minutes, if I'm reading this thing right. Hang in there." Though his scanning device was all but useless at this depth, owing to the concentration of mineral deposits permeating the rock around them, Daret had taken the precaution of loading to the team's tricorders his copy of the mine's tunnel map. There also was the bundle of cables, wound together and suspended from the wall near the ceiling, which acted as something of a guide. The cables, used at this depth to power the work lights and other equipment, had to lead somewhere, right?

Looking over his shoulder, Tom asked, "Are you sure you don't want me to take him? You can lead the way."

"No, I've got him." If they encountered trouble while making their way to the rally point where Konya and Cruzen were waiting for them, she wanted Tom to be the one with the phaser and ready to engage. Crusher glanced at Daret, whose breathing now was even more labored than it had been moments earlier. "How are you doing? Going to make it?"

"Yes," replied the Cardassian, "thanks to you." He forced a small, tired smile. "A vacation would not go unnoticed or unappreciated, however."

"I'll see what we can do," Crusher said, looking up as they traversed a bend in the passageway. The tunnel was widening now, and there was a stronger source of light somewhere ahead of them. "Almost there, I think."

The tunnel gave way to a larger chamber, which to Crusher's eye looked to approximate the size of the *Enterprise*'s shuttlebay. Like the rest of the underground passages, the room had been carved from the dense rock and was supplied with illumination via power lines running through the tunnels to generators and routers located on the surface. Piles of rubble had been pushed against the walls, which ascended in order to form a high, domed ceiling. The remnants of mining equipment and other detritus littered the cavern floor; cargo containers and metal bins intermixed with clusters of rock and debris. The air here was cool yet stale, and she heard the sounds of water dripping somewhere in the distance. Studying the walls, Crusher saw where smaller ledges and tunnels had been cut into the rock, some of which were accessible from the floor by means of ladders or rope and pulley systems supporting an oversized metal cart. Positioned along the cavern's perimeter were a dozen rectangular structures resting on metal frames that served to elevate them several meters above the rock floor.

"Guard towers," Tom said. He pointed to one of them. "You can see the weapon mounts along the railing."

Movement from one of the other tunnels leading out of the chamber caught Crusher's attention, and she looked over to see Rennan Konya and Kirsten Cruzen waving at them as they approached.

"Might want to watch your step," Cruzen said by way of greeting. "We've been busy while we were waiting for you." Nodding to Tom, she added, "Mister Riker gave us some helpful pointers."

Tom asked, "Did you have any luck breaking the encryption on those communicators you took from them?"

"No," Konya replied. "Whatever they're using, it's top of the line. I've never seen anything like it. If I had access to the runabout's onboard computer, I might have a better chance at cracking the codes, but otherwise?" He shook his head. "Besides, I figure in a little while, it won't really matter." As he moved toward Crusher and gestured that he would help with Daret, the lieutenant smiled. "So, it's a good thing you're the ones who got here first."

"Why's that?" Crusher asked.

Slipping his arm around the elder Cardassian's waist, the security officer smiled. "We've laid out a few presents for our friends. Come on; we've got a nice perch all set up and ready to go."

With Cruzen keeping an eye on the tunnels leading into the chamber, Konya and Tom assisted Crusher and Daret onto one of the lift carts before working the ropes and pulleys to hoist the cart from the floor. It took only a few moments to raise the cart to one of the tunnel openings higher up on the wall, after which Cruzen used one of the ropes to make her own climb. That accomplished, they secured the lift cart before the security officers led them away from the exposed tunnel entrance to another area carved out of the wall. Crusher saw at once the desirability of the location, as it afforded a view of the entire cavern floor while offering a decent place of concealment.

"That's our emergency escape route," Konya said, hooking a thumb over his shoulder to indicate the tunnel behind him, which penetrated even deeper into the rock. "According to Doctor Daret's map, it'll take us to the surface at the north end of the camp, near where the Cardassians used to have their support base."

Crusher asked, "What if they use that path to get down here?"

"Then they're not going to like the surprise I left them," Cruzen answered.

Tom said, "They don't have enough people to cover all the exits, and they're going to want to take care of us without attracting attention. They'll want to find us down here, and that means they're going to want to *get* down here as quickly as possible. I'm betting they found their own copy of a map, too. It's what I'd do, and they may even figure out where we might decide to hide or make a stand. There aren't that many options, after all. What I'm counting on is them thinking of you as if you're Starfleet officers."

"They are Starfleet officers," Daret said. To Crusher, he asked, "You've not yet retired, have you?"

"Been thinking about it," Crusher replied. "Been thinking about it a lot, particularly over the last half hour."

Tom smiled. "What I mean is that if these guys think of you as Starfleet officers, then they may be expecting you to think and react in a certain way." He tapped his chest with a finger. "Me, on the other hand? They weren't expecting somebody like me, and I don't think they've quite figured me out just yet."

"What exactly are you, Mister Riker?" Daret asked.

His smile fading, Tom replied, "Trouble."

Alternating his attention between his tricorder and the tunnel intersection before him, Jacob Barrows grunted in approval.

"This is right on the money."

"Our sensors are still experiencing interference thanks to all the mineral deposits," said the voice of Captain S'hirethal Verauk, commanding officer of the *Tonawanda* and Barrows's unexpected new ally for this assignment. *"We can't pinpoint individual life signs, but we can detect the presence of anyone in the mining complex. It should still be enough to get you where you need to go."*

"Affirmative," Barrows replied. "I'll be in touch. Out." He tapped the control to sever the connection. He was surprised at first by the abrupt communication with the Starfleet captain, but Verauk had offered the correct security code: the one Admiral Schlosser had told him to expect when his courier made contact to take charge of Daret. Barrows had been expecting not to interact with the *Tonawanda* until they had captured the Cardassian and were well away from Jevalan, but he figured that circumstances of which he was not aware had changed. He did not care, as experience had taught him to be flexible during covert missions and to adapt to evolving situations even when he might not possess all key facts. For example, there had been no contact with the team sent to delay or disable the *Enterprise* with the Andorian freighter. Had they been successful, or had they encountered their own set of complications? What if the *Enterprise* crew had managed to evade the trap that had been set for them? There was no sense dwelling on such things, Barrows knew; he had his own issues with which to contend. For the moment, it was good that Verauk and the *Tonawanda* now were here and that their sensors were able to assist him in his search for Daret.

So, let's get on with it.

Tapping the control for the communicator pinned inside his jacket, Barrows said, "Alpha One to Alpha Two."

"Go for Two," said the voice of Tobias Paquette, just audible over the static-laden connection.

"I'm getting close to the large chamber on our maps. Where are you?"

Paquette replied, *"If I'm reading this right, we're within fifty meters of it. We've been following the schematic as well as the cables strung up everywhere. We should be there in a minute or so."* Along with Fredil Pars, the Bajoran using the call sign Alpha Three, Paquette was approaching the cavern from another tunnel based on information the team had retrieved by infiltrating the excavation crew's computer network. The other four members of his team, each divided into pairs, were advancing on the same position from different directions, with Barrows's plan being to surround the Starfleet interlopers.

"Good," Barrows said. "Hold up once you get there. We'll move in together." Repeating the status checks with the remaining teams only served to remind him that two members of his group, the Bajoran Contera Hilbis and her human partner, Miguel Aguilar, still were missing. Barrows had sent them ahead to the Olanda camp to scout the area while the rest of the Active Six contingent performed similar tasks at the Pencala camp and some of the smaller outposts scattered across the planet. When they had failed to make their scheduled check-in, Barrows had wasted no time collecting the rest of his team and converging on the Olanda camp.

Once there, it had taken little time to find the transport vehicle Ilona Daret had taken from Tabata. A casual investigation of the area and the people manning the excavation and forensics efforts had turned up a few people who recalled seeing humans and a Cardassian moving around the dig site and even the general area where they had been seen. Comparing this information with the data he had taken from the computer files belonging to Raal Mosara had led Barrows to believe that whatever materials Daret was protecting had to be located somewhere here in the remnants of the camp where he and his Bajoran companion had been working.

Finding them, in comparison, was proving to be quite the challenge.

The plan at first had been to conduct a simple sweep of the mine after staging a pretense to evacuate the surrounding area. Breaking into the computer network set up by the recovery team was easy enough, as was triggering the alarm warning the camp residents of a gas leak somewhere in the mine. Sneaking aboard one of the transports at the camp's landing port, they had used its sensors to determine the general location of five life signs inside the mine's underground tunnel network: four humans and a Cardassian. Armed with that information and the knowledge that there only were a handful of exits from that level of the mine, Barrows had split his group into pairs so that they could attempt to converge on the Starfleet team. Though the task had begun lacking any sort of real-time updates from the transport's sensor array, their efforts now were aided by the timely arrival of Captain Verauk and the *Tonawanda*.

The tunnel ahead of them turned downward before again leveling out, and as they reached a curve, Barrows slowed. According to his tricorder, the large chamber they sought was only a few meters beyond this point. He was getting close.

"Alpha Four to Alpha One."

Forcing his attention back to the matter at hand, Barrows activated his communicator. "Go for One."

"We're here," said the voice of Loras Galir, another of his team's agents. *"My tricorder's picking up indeterminate life signs, but there's definitely someone in here. Looks like our guess was right. This is a great place to stake out an ambush."*

"Okay, just hang tight. Once we all get set, we'll move in."

"Roger that. I'm thinking our best . . ." Something whined across the connection, drowning out Loras's voice, and it took Barrows a second to realize he had heard phaser fire. The sound was repeated as another voice, likely Loras's companion, Haruka Tomashiro, shouted something Barrows could not understand.

"Alpha Four, what's going on?" When no reply came, Barrows barked, "Alpha Five, come in! What's your status?" He growled in frustration, realizing that his people now were under attack. To his communicator, he called out, "Alpha One to all teams. Hold your positions until further notice."

He heard no other weapons fire as he approached the entrance to the cavern. Pausing while still cloaked in shadow, Barrows surveyed the scene, comparing what he was seeing with the schematic on his tricorder. Much of the chamber's floor was littered with rock and other debris, and from his vantage point he was able to see three of the raised guard towers positioned along the far wall. Another tunnel entrance also was visible, and according to the schematic, it should be the direction from which Paquette and Fredil should be approaching, though he saw no one there.

Something beeped behind him, and he turned to look for the source, his gaze falling on something set into the wall near the ceiling. The item was small and dark, almost invisible in the dim lighting, and it most definitely looked out of place. As he studied it, a single, small indicator flashed red.

Move! His mind was screaming the warning even as Barrows turned and sprinted out of the tunnel.

Thirty-five

The first explosive detonated mere seconds after the human emerged from the tunnel, running and diving for cover near a pile of excavated rock. Crusher felt the blast reverberating through the surrounding rock, and for a frantic moment she envisioned the underground cavern collapsing all around them. The explosion was brief, its echo already dying as dust and shards of rock belched from the tunnel opening. Despite what Tom had told her about the small size of the charges he had instructed Konya and Cruzen to place, the resulting blast was still sufficient to cast chunks of displaced rock out of the tunnel and into the cavern.

"I think that got their attention," said Lieutenant Konya from where he crouched near an outcropping of rock that formed a natural parapet offering all of them concealment from anyone on the cavern's main floor.

Tom Riker grunted. "Them and everyone else." From where he knelt along another section of rock, he gestured toward the cavern, and Crusher shifted her own position next to Ilona Daret to peer over the barrier. Below her and her companions, she saw movement among the rocks, discarded equipment and other flotsam littering the chamber floor. The intruder who had emerged from the tunnel was scrambling for cover, brandishing a weapon.

"Where are the others?" Cruzen asked. "I only saw the one." Counting the two Tom had just stunned and the pair the away team had dispatched earlier in the day, that still left at least four agents to deal with, counting the one who was already running around down below them.

Looking toward the other tunnels leading into the cavern, Crusher thought she detected movement at those entrances, as well. Tom's decision to use his phaser to incapacitate the first two agents to reveal themselves had provided his desired result, flushing other members of the group into the open. The motion sensors Cruzen and Konya had attached to the small explosive devices planted at the tunnel mouths had alerted him to the intruders' approach, and he had offered what he considered to be a thoughtful interval before arming and detonating the first device. Now the agent who had been closest to that explosion was reeling from the sudden surprise attack, but Crusher guessed it would not take him long to regain his composure.

"Fire in the hole," Tom said, tapping a control on his old-style Starfleet communicator. He had programmed the unit to transmit burst signals to the various improvised explosives he had positioned throughout the cavern and the tunnels leading into it. The device he contacted was close to the intruder—about twenty meters to his right and hidden within a pile of excavated rock. Its charge was smaller even than the ones Tom had used in the tunnel, but the resulting detonation still was enough to propel rock and dirt in an expanding sphere. Some of it rained down on the intruder, causing him to drop to the ground while throwing up his arms to protect his head.

"Incoming!" Konya shouted, and everyone ducked as a pair of phaser beams lanced across the cavern, striking the rock wall above them. Crusher covered her head with her free arm, flinching as chunks and bits of stone rained down on them.

Shifting her position, Cruzen said, "I think they know where we are." She rose up on one knee and rested her arm on the parapet, aiming her phaser at something on the cavern floor. Crusher peered over the edge to see two figures moving along the far wall as Cruzen opened fire, but her aim was off at this distance, and the shot went wide. Shards of rock erupted from where the weapon's beam chewed into the ground, giving the two new intruders a chance to seek cover.

"Damn it!" Cruzen fired again toward the pile of rock behind which the new arrivals had sought cover, but her second shot also had no effect.

Another small explosion rumbled through the cavern, and Crusher looked up to see two more figures emerging from yet another tunnel. These two seemed to have been better prepared than their companions, as they were well clear of the blast and were moving across the cavern floor by the time the charge detonated. They fired toward the away team's perch as they ran, the phaser beams hitting all around the outcropping and forcing Crusher and the others to drop to the ground.

"They're talking to each other," Konya said, rising up from his place of concealment to fire his phaser at one of the darting figures. Like Cruzen, the lieutenant was unable to hit his target, and Crusher looked up to see the intruder scampering to cover near one of the guard towers. Then she felt a hand on her arm before she was jerked back to the ground as another salvo of phaser fire slammed into the wall near their position.

Moving to a new vantage point, Tom once more brought up the outdated Starfleet communicator and pressed a control, only this time Crusher saw him tap the button multiple times. With each push came another explosion, each of the remaining charges detonating one after another in rapid succession until the echoes from the continuous blasts muddled into a single rolling cacophony.

"Get them!" he shouted, raising up and again aiming over the parapet. Crusher and the others followed suit, each tracking one of the intruders who now were running in all directions, shaken by the string of explosive charges placed at random points around the cavern. One of the humans, who had taken up position behind a dilapidated pull cart half filled with rock and dirt, stood up from his place of concealment and aimed his phaser at the away team, but he ducked once more out of sight when Konya and Cruzen fired at him.

Then Crusher was startled as first Cruzen's and then Konya's body jerked in reaction to being struck by phaser beams, not from the cavern floor but from somewhere *behind* her.

What . . . ?

"Hey!" Tom shouted, whirling toward the new threat but not moving fast enough before another phaser beam washed over him. His body went slack and he slumped against the parapet, and Crusher scrambled toward him.

"Don't move!" a voice shouted, but she ignored it, moving to Tom and placing her fingers along the side of his neck. She had time to feel his pulse, but before she even could breathe a sigh of relief, a furious cry startled her. Spinning around, she saw that Daret had lunged for the human standing at the mouth of the escape-route tunnel. The intruder obviously was caught off guard by the elder Cardassian's unexpected aggressiveness, freezing just for the moment Daret needed to close the distance and swing at him. Despite his age, his physical strength still outmatched the human's, and his single punch to the man's chest was enough to force him to his knees. He dropped his phaser, coughing and grimacing as Daret pressed his attack, lashing out with his other hand and catching the side of the human's head. The human, reeling from the assault, tried to roll away, and Daret followed, but then Crusher saw something metallic in the man's hand.

"Ilona!"

Before Daret could react to the warning or the new threat, the knife sank to its hilt in his midsection, and the Cardassian gasped in surprise and pain, stumbling backward before falling to the ground. His hands grasped his abdomen, and Crusher could see dark blood already staining his tunic and skin.

"Stay where you are!" a new voice shouted, and Crusher looked up from Daret to see a second man standing at the mouth of the tunnel, his phaser leveled at her. His companion, still wincing from the fight Daret had given him, stepped forward and reached for her jacket, and Crusher felt his fingers close around her communicator badge as he yanked it free. Dropping it to the ground at his feet, he stomped it with his boot.

"Let me help him!" Crusher snapped, pointing to where Daret still lay on the ground, clutching his blood-soaked midsection. "Isn't he the whole reason you're here? Are you going to let him die *now*?"

"Go," said the agent with the phaser still trained on her, gesturing with the weapon's muzzle toward Daret. "Just don't try anything stupid." He held up a small package, which Crusher recognized as one of the motion sensors placed by Konya and Cruzen. "Nice try with this, by the way." Dropping the sensor, he crushed it as he had the communicator.

Moving to Daret, Crusher pulled her tricorder from her jacket pocket, fumbling with the device as she set to work treating her friend, whose skin already seemed to have taken on an ominous pallor. She did her best to ignore her captors and the weapons they pointed at her, but her hands still shook as she activated the tricorder. On the ground, Daret looked up at her with eyes that looked glazed and heavy, and his breathing had grown rapid and shallow. Crusher did not need the tricorder to know he did not have much time.

Hold on, Ilona.

*   *   *

U.S.S. Enterprise

"Standard orbit, sir."

Rising from his command chair at Glinn Ravel Dygan's report, Picard stepped forward until he stood just behind the Cardassian officer and T'Ryssa Chen, though he kept his gaze focused on the image of the *U.S.S. Tonawanda* centered on the bridge's main viewscreen. The *Nebula*-class vessel was oriented so that the upper portion of its saucer-shaped primary hull faced toward Jevalan, and from this distance the seams of individual hull plates were visible, as were external markings such as the starship's registry number, NCC-71201. Picard suspected that the other ship's captain likely was studying the *Enterprise* in much the same way, though so far she had not deigned to respond to his attempts at communication.

"Their shields are up and their weapons are on standby," reported Lieutenant Šmrhová from her tactical station.

"Raise shields," Picard ordered, not wanting to take such action while facing off against another Starfleet vessel, but Captain Verauk was leaving him little choice. "Are they still in contact with someone on the surface?"

"Not at the moment, sir," Šmrhová said.

"Scan for the away team," Worf said as he moved from his own seat to stand next to Picard.

It took the security chief several seconds to carry out the task, after which she reported, "I've got them. Three of our comm badges, located in a large cavern almost three hundred meters beneath the surface. There are several life signs—human, Bajoran, and Cardassian—emanating from that immediate vicinity. My readings are indistinct, owing to interference from the mineral ore in that area playing havoc with our sensors."

"How many life signs?"

"Hard to say, sir. A dozen, at least."

"Notify the transporter room to lock onto the away team," Picard said.

"Sorry, sir, but we have the same problem as with the sensors. We won't be able to get a transporter lock so long as they're down there."

"What about upping the power?" suggested Chen from where she sat at the flight controller's station. "We may have to recalibrate to account for the interference and the power increase, but it should be possible. Even if we can't get a lock on the away team, we should still be able to beam someone down."

"Apprise Commander La Forge of the situation and have him begin making the necessary adjustments." Turning to Worf, he added, "Number One, prepare a security team. If we can't beam up our people, then you'll retrieve them."

"Aye, sir," replied the Klingon without hesitation. He already was moving for the turbolift when Šmrhová once more called out.

"I'm now picking up new activity. They're broadcasting a jamming field!"

"What?" Worf asked.

"Confirmed, sir," said Chen. "They're definitely emitting a powerful jamming signal. They really don't want us talking to anybody."

"Can we hail them?" Picard asked.

Šmrhová said, "No, sir. They're blocking all frequencies."

"How do we disable or defeat the jamming?" Picard knew that the options for such actions were few, but he was not about to accept this bizarre assault. "We need to make contact with the away team." He drew a calming breath, forcing back the irritation he could feel beginning to assert itself.

"Maybe with the navigational deflector," Chen said, turning in her seat to face Picard, "but engineering might need time to make the necessary adjustments."

"Update engineering, but transporters are still top priority." The captain let his gaze linger on the image of the *Tonawanda* for an additional moment before adding, "Arm quantum torpedoes and target their communications and sensor arrays. Stand by to fire at my command." There was a noticeable pause between his issuing the order and Šmrhová's acknowledgment; it was only an extra second, but there, nonetheless.

"Aye, sir. Torpedoes armed and ready."

An alert indicator sounded from the tactical station, and he turned to see Šmrhová hunching over her console. "They just armed their weapons, Captain, but they're not targeting us. Not yet, at least."

The situation was threatening to get out of hand. Picard knew that from a firepower standpoint, and despite its formidable arsenal, the *Tonawanda* stood no real chance against the *Enterprise,* but a fight still could be costly, and it was not what he wanted, anyway. Beyond the risk to lives on both vessels, such a senseless engagement would serve only to keep him from helping Beverly and the others.

Behind him, Šmrhová called out, "Captain! I've lost the away team's comm badges!" When Picard turned to look at her, she was shaking her head. "I had them, but then their signals started cutting out. All three of them are offline, sir."

Enough of this!

"Lieutenant, reacquire your targeting of their communications array. In fact, do it twice. I want Captain Verauk to have no doubts about what I'm doing."

At the ops station, Glinn Dygan said, "Captain, the *Tonawanda* is shifting its orbit."

A low rumble escaped Worf's lips. "They are aligning themselves to target us."

"Arm all weapons," Picard said without hesitation. "Stand by to route emergency power to the forward shield generators." Were they really going to do this? What in the name of hell was Verauk thinking?

"La Forge to bridge," said the voice of the *Enterprise*'s chief engineer, booming through the intercom system. *"We've found a way to punch through the interference. You should be able to hail the* Tonawanda.*"*

"Open a channel," Picard ordered, watching the other ship on the viewscreen as it altered its flight path so that it now appeared to be facing the *Enterprise* head-on. When Šmrhová reported that the frequency was established, he said, "*Tonawanda,* this is Captain Picard. I don't want to fight you, but I've lost contact with my away team on the surface. Let's discuss this, calmly and rationally." He looked over his shoulder at Šmrhová.

"No response, sir."

"Damn it, Captain Verauk!" Picard snapped, stepping toward the viewscreen. "You need to think about what you're doing. Does anything about your mission make the least bit of sense? Do your orders authorize you to fire on another Starfleet vessel and to put other Starfleet personnel at risk? Are you prepared to do that? My only concern here is for my people, and I won't allow you to simply make off with them; not without an explanation." When no response was forthcoming, he turned to the ops console. "Glinn Dygan, stand by for evasive."

"They're firing!" Šmrhová shouted, and on the screen Picard saw the first torpedo leave its launcher just below the primary hull. Alarms wailed across the bridge, and even before he could give the order, Dygan was altering the *Enterprise*'s course in an attempt to elude the incoming fire. Picard felt the deck shudder beneath his feet as the torpedo slammed into the ship's deflector shields, and he reached back to place a hand on the ops console and steady himself, keeping his attention focused on the viewscreen as the *Tonawanda* adjusted its own course in response to the *Enterprise*'s maneuvers.

"Target their weapons!" he shouted above the alert sirens,

gritting his teeth at the lunacy of it all. Starfleet vessels battling each other? Had it really come to this? "Fire!" He heard the steady, rhythmic pulse of power as four quantum torpedoes were launched, moving to converge on the *Tonawanda*. The weapons struck in rapid succession, energy flaring as they slammed into the other vessel's shields.

"Their shields are down thirty-six percent," Šmrhová reported. "They're trying to maneuver to a new firing position."

"Maintain evasive course," Worf ordered. "Prepare to fire."

"Wait!" Šmrhová almost shouted, and when Picard turned to her, he saw the disbelief in her eyes. "They're . . . they're powering down their weapons. They're *dropping their shields*!"

Picard frowned. "Are you certain?"

"Yes, sir, and the jamming field is gone, too." A moment later Picard heard another alert tone from her console, and the security chief said, "We're being hailed."

"On screen." Picard turned back to the viewscreen, steeling himself for a tense verbal confrontation with Captain Verauk, but instead of an Acamarian female, the image on the screen shifted from the *Tonawanda* to depict a large Rigellian Chelon male. The greenish tinge of his skin and the pale brown of his oversized proboscis contrasted with the maroon and black of his Starfleet tunic, which was stretched across his broad frame.

"*Captain Picard, I am Commander Latanun, first officer of the* Tonawanda. *Captain Verauk has been relieved of duty, and I have taken command of this vessel. Our weapons and defenses are deactivated, and I would appreciate it if you would show us the same courtesy.*"

Wary of deception, Picard said, "Forgive me, Commander, but can you at least explain to me what this is all about and what you're doing here?"

Latanun replied, *"I am not yet informed as to the details of our mission, sir. Captain Verauk claimed to be operating under top-secret orders issued to her from the highest echelons of Starfleet Command. I have not yet had the opportunity to review those orders, but rest assured I will do so at my earliest opportunity. For now, you have my word that no aggressive action will be taken against your vessel, and you are free to transport your personnel to or from the surface."*

After directing Šmrhová to place all weapons on standby, Picard returned his attention to the Rigellian officer. "Commander, are you saying your captain ordered your ship to this system without telling you why?"

"That is correct, sir. She claimed that her orders and accompanying security concerns prevented her from informing us about details of our mission. Only after our arrival were we notified about the instructions she received to take into custody a Cardassian physician, Ilona Daret, along with any Starfleet officers who may be aiding him."

Glancing to Worf, who seemed just as skeptical as he was, Picard asked, "What made you decide to defy your captain's orders?"

The commander did not hesitate. *"Because, in my judgment, nothing in those orders justifies firing on another Starfleet vessel."* He paused, nodding as though reassuring himself. *"Because those orders were wrong, sir."*

Thirty-six

Jevalan, Doltiri System

Crusher winced as the agent landed another blow to the side of Tom Riker's face. Tom already had been struck once, but the second strike was harder, almost knocking Tom off his feet.

"That's for killing one of my men," Barrows hissed before rearing back and swinging his other fist, this one connecting with Tom's jaw. "And that's for killing another of my men." Tom's knees buckled, but he was held up by another of Barrows's agents.

The agent had made the assumption that Tom, who was older than Konya and Cruzen, must be the group's leader and had ignored Konya's protests to the contrary. The two security officers were being held at phaser-point by another agent, while a third stood near Crusher as she knelt over Daret, who had been moved by Konya and Cruzen from the perch to the cavern floor. The remaining member of Barrows's team was moving around the cavern, waving a tricorder. While all of that was going on, Crusher had managed to stop his bleeding and seal the stab wound, but Daret had suffered tremendous blood loss and had slipped into shock. Stabilizing his condition was proving to be a challenge beyond the limited abilities of her medical kit, though she had managed to sedate him with a synthetic general tranquilizer that was compatible with a variety of humanoid species, but she was running out of time and options. Daret needed to be transported to the camp's medical clinic if he was to have any real chance at survival.

Stepping closer, Barrows gripped Tom by his hair and jerked his head so that their eyes met. "I'll ask you again. Where are the Cardie's files?" The agents already had searched the away team and found nothing, owing to Tom and Konya's decision to hide Daret's evidence and data in a secure location elsewhere in the mine. The copies of the data he and Crusher had made also had been stashed, but the remains of the real Ishan Anjar and other forensic evidence was—for the moment, at least—safe.

When Tom did not answer, Barrows slapped him across the face, grunting in irritation. "I don't have time for this, and I'm tired of being stuck like rats down here. Tell me what I want to know, *now*."

"I don't know what you're talking about," Tom replied, spitting blood on the ground between their feet.

"You're really going to make me go through with this?" Barrows drew from a scabbard beneath his jacket what Crusher recognized as a field knife, with a serrated edge and a blackened blade. "Why not save us all some trouble?"

"You can kill me," Tom replied, "but I still won't know what you want."

"I'm not going to kill *you*," Barrows said. He gestured toward Crusher and the others. "I'm not even going to kill them. Not yet, at least. You *know* that's not how this works. Maybe you don't care what I do to you, but I'm betting you'll feel different once I start in on one of *them*. Which one first?"

"Over here!"

Everyone turned at the sound of the other agent's voice to see the man standing near a piece of discarded mining equipment Crusher did not recognize. It was wheeled, most of its paneling had rusted or corroded, and like everything else here, it was covered with a thick layer of dust. The man was pointing to a metal box mounted to the vehicle's rear panel. "I think I found something. They tried to hide it by filling the thing with rocks. I almost missed it even with my tricorder."

Crusher and Tom exchanged glances. The mineral ore had almost succeeded in concealing what Konya had hidden there.

Almost.

The man began fumbling with the box's lid, at which point Barrows threw up his free hand and shouted, "Wait!"

He was too late, as the instant the lid lifted just the slightest bit, a loud pop echoed across the cavern. The box lid flew open, propelled by rocks and whatever else Konya and Tom had stuffed into the container. Pummeled by the blast of debris, the other man was thrown backward, his body twisting as it arced through the air before dropping to the ground several meters from the vehicle. He did not move.

Tom was reacting even as the blast's echo rolled across the chamber, thrusting an elbow up and into the chin of the agent guarding him. The man staggered back, his free hand reaching for his face, but Tom ignored him and instead lunged forward to tackle Barrows. Both men went tumbling to the ground, each twisting and scrambling to roll atop the other.

The man Tom had first attacked moved forward, extending his arm and trying to aim his phaser, but Konya and Cruzen now were taking action as well. Konya turned and kicked at the man nearest them, knocking away the man's phaser. Leaving him to take care of that threat, Cruzen charged the man closing in on Tom and Barrows, lowering her shoulder and driving them both to the ground. The man rolled onto his side and was already trying to regain his feet, but Cruzen was faster, dropping him with a swinging kick to his face.

Crusher caught movement to her left and saw the man guarding her and Daret stepping forward, his attention torn between the impromptu melee and his own prisoners, and that delay was all Crusher needed to grab the hypo spray lying on the ground next to her knee and jam it against the man's thigh. She pressed the control to activate the device and injected the hypo's remaining doses of tranquilizer, and the effects were immediate. The agent staggered, his phaser falling from his hand as he reached out with both arms to steady himself, before falling unconscious to the ground.

Almost as good as a phaser.

Looking up, Crusher was in time to see Konya grappling with his opponent. The security officer dodged and weaved against a flurry of punches, finally maneuvering behind the agent and landing a blow to the back of the man's head. Reeling from the attack, the agent turned in an attempt to defend himself, but then Konya was on him, gripping his opponent's arm and levering him across his hip to slam him to the rocky floor. He delivered a final punch to the man's face, and the agent's body went limp.

"Tom!" Crusher shouted, turning to see Tom rolling away from Barrows and both men pulling themselves to their feet. Hampered by the beating he had endured moments earlier, Tom was slower than his rival, but he still managed to block the agent's knife arm as Barrows brought in the blade to strike. Tom twisted his body and lashed out another elbow, driving it into Barrows's face. The agent's knees buckled as Tom repeated the attack, wresting the knife from the other man's hand. A third strike was needed before Barrows stumbled and fell back to the ground, groaning and muttering in pain as he reached for his broken, bloody nose.

Konya and Cruzen, having retrieved weapons from each of the agents, now were covering them as Crusher moved to Tom.

"Are you all right?" she asked, noting the swelling in his face.

Nodding, Tom attempted a small smile, and Crusher saw

the blood staining his teeth. "I've been better." He gestured to where Daret stil! lay on the ground behind her. "How's he?"

"He's lost a lot of blood," Crusher said, turning and moving to kneel beside her friend. Daret remained unconscious thanks to the tranquilizer, but the larger problem remained. "We need to get him to the surface."

Before she could say anything else, she was interrupted by the sound of a familiar high-pitched whine, and she and Tom turned to see six columns of white, cascading light appear at the far end of the cavern. The transporter beams solidified into the forms of Commander Worf and five security officers, all of them brandishing phaser rifles.

"Doctor Crusher!" Worf waved as he caught sight of her, and the six new arrivals began making their way toward them across the chamber.

"Well, that's some fine timing, if you ask me," Cruzen said, unable to suppress a tired smile.

"Damned fine," Crusher said, kneeling once more beside Daret and placing her hand on her friend's chest. "Hang on a little longer, Ilona," she said, knowing he could not hear her. "You can't leave me. Not now, when there's still so much to do."

U.S.S. Enterprise

Entering the sickbay's patient recovery area, Picard was greeted first by the sight of Thomas Riker. The upper portion of his bed had been raised so that he could sit up, and he was engaged in something displayed on a padd he held. He looked up at Picard's approach and when he smiled, Picard of course saw Will Riker.

Damn, but I'll never get used to that.

"Captain," Tom said, extending his hand as Picard

approached. "Good to see you again. I haven't had a chance to thank you for getting us out of there."

Taking the proffered hand and shaking it, Picard replied, "It is I who owe you my thanks, Mister Riker, for protecting my people. I'm in your debt."

"Not a chance, sir. There's nothing Will wouldn't do for you, and there's not a damned thing I wouldn't do for him." Tom reached up to gingerly touch his jaw, which Picard knew had been bruised and bloodied as a consequence of his ordeal on the planet's surface. "That said, I'm happy to accept any kind of alcoholic beverage that's not out of a replicator."

Chuckling, Picard nodded. "Consider it done, assuming your doctor agrees." He turned as Beverly Crusher entered the room and made her way to the bed where Ilona Daret lay. The Cardassian was unconscious, his head elevated, and he did not react as Beverly moved to stand beside his bed.

"What's his prognosis, Doctor?" Picard asked.

Beverly tapped a control on the monitor positioned behind Daret's head. "He'll recover, but I'm keeping him sedated for now. He suffered such traumatic blood loss that I'm surprised he didn't have a stroke. Considering his age, he's very lucky."

"It's that Cardassian constitution, Doctor," Tom said, swinging his feet from his own bed and standing up. "One thing I know about them is that they're tough." He nodded to Daret. "Your friend especially so, in more ways than one."

Turning from the bed, Beverly asked, "Have you had a chance to review the materials we brought back?"

"Indeed I have," Picard replied. He had been stunned by the revelations contained in the data and other forensic evidence collected by Ilona Daret and Raal Mosara. "It's astounding that the president was able to perpetrate such a hoax for so long."

"It's not as though he set out to become the president," Tom countered. "Remember, his concerns at the time were just staying alive and later fading into the background once the Occupation ended and the Bajorans started working to put their world back together. Everything else probably just spiraled out of control from there."

"You'd think he'd just want to live the rest of his life as quietly as possible," Beverly said.

"It was not his nature," Picard said. "Despite his penchant for placing his own self-interest above those of others, he still wanted to affect change. His tenure with the Bajoran provisional government is proof enough of that, even though one could argue that even that decision ultimately was self-serving, as it aided him to further conceal his true identity. He collaborated with the Cardassians on Jevalan, yes, but he also carried out attacks for the resistance and helped put into motion the actions that eventually caused the Cardassians to withdraw from that planet. That does not forgive his crimes, of course, but it does offer insight into his character, and his ego."

"It's the same now," Beverly said. "When you get to the heart of it, Ishan wants what's best for the Federation, though his outlook and approach are flawed. He's after safety and security, but he's willing to sacrifice principles for results now as well."

Picard sighed. "Safety, security, *and* strength. Peace *and* power."

And a kingdom to rule?

"So, what happens next?" Tom asked. "The trouble you're about to cause is pretty serious, Captain. Bringing forth evidence to remove a sitting president? You're going to make history of one sort or another, sir."

"And I've had rather enough of that," Picard said. This business with President Ishan—or Baras Rodirya, as he should be called—had brought into focus everything he had come to detest about where duty and obligation had seen fit to take him. None of this, no matter how necessary it might be, was why he had joined Starfleet, and all of it had done nothing but poison his soul. Something had to change.

It will, he promised himself, *and damned soon.*

"The evidence Daret and Raal collected," Beverly said. "Is it enough for the Federation attorney general to make a case?"

"Their evidence, along with our two guests down in the brig and other information Admiral Riker and his people have managed to obtain, should prove more than sufficient," Picard said. "Still, it won't be an easy fight, but if I know the attorney general as well as I think I do, then she's more than up for it."

Thirty-seven

Paris, Earth

Enjoying a precious few moments of privacy in the well-appointed anteroom that was adjacent to the Federation Council chambers and set aside for his private use, Ishan Anjar stood at the large window overlooking the bustling city below him. In the weeks since he had taken office, he had found the small, personal ritual to be quite therapeutic. Like meditation, looking out at the vista—itself a mixture of modern and antiquated buildings and other structures bearing testimony to the ageless city's distinguished history—helped Ishan to focus his mind and his emotions.

Speaking before the council, as he was scheduled to do in just a few minutes, always was a taxing experience. He did not fear speaking before an audience, but he already had grown weary of the constant debates and endless discussion required by any interaction with the council. Charged with acting on behalf of trillions of citizens scattered across hundreds of worlds, it seemed to Ishan that obtaining consensus for any but the most banal of issues was difficult if not impossible. He understood and appreciated the need to ensure that every world received equal attention and representation, but there were times when he would prefer to cast aside all of the trappings and pomp and circumstance and just get on with doing the things that needed to be done.

Democracy, he mused. *Perhaps the Cardassians were right all along.*

He also was concerned with the status of the mission to Jevalan. Ishan had heard nothing from his team on the planet's surface or from Captain Verauk of the *Tonawanda.* The matter should have been concluded, by Ishan's estimate. Could something have gone wrong? Had some other issue presented itself? Or, were Verauk and Barrows simply maintaining their communications blackout until all of the details had been addressed? They both were seasoned professionals, after all.

On the desk behind him, Ishan heard the tone of the intercom, followed by the voice of his assistant, Syliri Alvora.

"Mister President? It's time, sir."

Accompanied by members of his personal protection detail, the walk from his private room to the council chambers was the same dull, uninspired affair Ishan already loathed. The time wasted on such frivolous distractions would be better utilized on actual work, but he had come to accept that "showing the flag," as the humans called it, was necessary and even desirable on occasion. The tall, wide doors—wood, and both emblazoned with an etching of the Federation seal— parted at his approach, and he entered the chamber as every member of the council rose to his or her feet.

A wide, open expanse of dark polished tile ran the length of the room to a dais, upon which was placed a podium and six chairs. Illumination was provided by recessed lighting along the walls as well as from panels set into the room's curved ceiling. The far wall was dominated by a large viewscreen that currently displayed the UFP seal. To either side of the open floor were five rows of tiered seating. The lower three rows on either side were reserved for council members, with the remaining rows allocated for visiting dignitaries and other distinguished guests. At the moment, those seats were empty. Doors to either side of the dais led from the chamber to council member offices, and at present, they were guarded by members of the Federation Security Agency.

On the dais, Ziy Cradiix, a female Bolian serving as Speaker of the Council, moved from the podium to one of the chairs, nodding in greeting at his approach. Traversing the room and stepping onto the raised platform, Ishan returned the greeting as he took his place behind the podium. He gestured for everyone to take their seats, and once the council members had settled, he smiled.

"Madam Speaker and members of the council," he said, his voice amplified by microphones set into the podium and the dais as well as the room's exceptional acoustical properties, "as always it is my honor and pleasure to meet with you today, for it is here in this most hallowed chamber that the voice and will of the people are heard, acknowledged, and served." The opening remark elicited applause from the assembly, though to Ishan's ear the reaction seemed subdued, even reserved. Undeterred, he continued, "Before we turn to the formal agenda, I would like to . . ."

"Mister President," said Speaker Cradiix from behind him, and when she turned, he saw the Bolian had risen from her seat and had moved toward the front of the dais. "With all due respect, there is a matter that requires our immediate attention."

At first irritated by the interruption, Ishan maintained his bearing as he studied her. "And what might that be?"

Rather than answer him, Cradiix turned and nodded to one of the guards posted near the exit to Ishan's right, and he turned to see the man pressing a control to open the door. It slid aside, and a quartet of additional security officers entered the room, flanking a human woman Ishan recognized as the Federation's attorney general. Carrying a padd in her left hand, she was dressed in a conservative gray ensemble that flattered her lithe figure and complemented her reddish brown hair, which was cut in a short feminine style. Ishan said nothing as she and her entourage moved to stand before him, taking a position before the dais with her back to the assembled council.

"Good afternoon, Mister President," said Phillipa Louvois, her bright blue eyes fixed on him as she spoke. "By the power vested in me as the Federation's attorney general, I bring to the council the following charges: That you have knowingly and willfully violated the office to which you were appointed, as well as the full faith and confidence entrusted to you by the citizens of this Federation."

"You can't be serious," Ishan said, feeling his ire rising.

"Specifically," Louvois continued, "that you have purposely misrepresented yourself. I have in my possession evidence that you are not Ishan Anjar."

The words barely had left Louvois's mouth before a collective roar of shock and confusion swept the council chamber. Ishan could only stare at her, feeling his jaw slacken as he fought to retain his composure, as Speaker Cradiix spent nearly a full minute regaining order. That accomplished, she leveled her own stern gaze at Louvois.

"These are serious charges, Madam Attorney General. I assume you are prepared to offer evidence to support your allegations?"

"Indeed I am, Madam Speaker," Louvois replied. "The evidence I hold identifies this individual as a Bajoran national named Baras Rodirya. He assumed Ishan's identity as a means of concealing his complicity in the mistreatment and murder of interred Bajoran citizens during Bajor's Occupation by the Cardassian Union. Additionally, I also have in my possession evidence implicating the president pro tempore as having knowledge aforethought of the conspiracy to assassinate President Nanietta Bacco."

"*That is a lie!*" Ishan screamed over the renewed pandemonium erupting in the council chamber. "How dare you speak to me this way?"

Waiting until Cradiix once more had restored order, Louvois regarded him with a raised eyebrow. "I assure you, *Mister President,* that it only gets worse." Holding up her padd, she tapped its screen several times, and in response, the viewscreen behind Ishan and Cradiix activated, and when he turned to see what now was displayed upon it, he felt himself gripped by a sudden, ominous chill.

Four Cardassians stared out from the viewscreen, one of whom Ishan instantly recognized as Elim Garak, Castellan of the Cardassian Union. His companion, accompanied by two Cardassian soldiers, also was familiar. *Very* familiar.

No. It can't be!

"*Members of the Federation Council,*" said Garak, his expression unreadable as the obviously recorded message played, "*I bring you greetings from the people of the Cardassian Union. I understand that this communication is unusual and perhaps even unprecedented, but I assure you that I hold the best interests of all our people close to my heart.*

"*It was with great sorrow that I learned of the death of President Nanietta Bacco, as I believed her to be an inspiring leader possessed of great will and compassion, and a firm, unwavering desire to serve the Federation with distinction. Her death is a loss for all of us, but I am confident that you will find a way to move forward and to honor her legacy. Unfortunately, the person you have chosen to guide you on this journey is undeserving of the task.*"

"Turn this off!" Ishan shouted. "I demand that you cease this transmission!"

On the screen, Garak continued, "*Also troubling to me was learning that fellow Cardassians were responsible for President Bacco's murder. No matter what your current president has told you, her assassins were not Tzenkethi or any other member of the Typhon Pact. Her murder was perpetrated by members of the True Way, an anti-Federation extremist group whose sole purpose is to undermine any attempts at peace and cooperation between the Federation and Cardassia. It was members of this sect who carried out this horrible crime, with the help of this individual."* He gestured to the Cardassian standing with him. *"Rakan Urkar, a member of the True Way, has confessed to his involvement in the conspiracy, and he also has provided incontrovertible proof confirming your president's identity as Baras Rodirya."*

As close as he was to the viewscreen, even Ishan was having trouble hearing the playback over the sounds of the council members expressing their unfettered disbelief. The recorded message was paused while Speaker Cradiix once more sought to regain control of the proceedings, admonishing everyone in the chamber to remain silent.

"This evidence corroborates a great deal more forensic data collected by two brave individuals, Doctor Ilona Daret and the late Raal Mosara, proving beyond doubt that your president is an impostor and a war criminal sought by the Bajoran government. Further, there is additional evidence in the form of communications transcripts linking the True Way to the assassins, to your president, and to the president's former chief of staff. Indeed, it was Galif jav Velk who planned the entire affair, though he did so with your president's blessing."

"Lies!" Ishan snarled, pointing an accusatory finger at Louvois. "I had nothing to do with this, and neither did Velk. Even if he did, he's dead!"

"I'm afraid not, Mister President."

Hearing the door open on the room's opposite side, Ishan felt his knees weaken, and he had to grip the podium for support as he beheld the sight of Galif jav Velk, escorted by a trio of Federation Security officers as well as the Starfleet Commander himself, Admiral Leonard James Akaar.

"No!" Ishan shouted. "That's impossible!"

"Despite your best efforts, Mister President," Louvois said, "Mister Velk is very much alive and healthy. He's also been very forthcoming with details describing his and your

usurping of Starfleet Command's proper authority, the misuse of Starfleet personnel and resources, and the murder or
attempted murder of Starfleet officers and Federation citizens in order to cover up your complicity for President Bacco's assassination."

"I am the President of the United Federation of Planets!"
Ishan barked. "I will not be addressed in this manner!" How
was Velk still alive? And the evidence from Daret and Raal;
how was that a factor? What in the name of the Prophets had
happened on Jevalan?

No no no no . . .

Phillipa Louvois glared at him. "Baras Rodirya, you are
not the president. You are a liar and a murderer, and you
will be tried in a court of Federation law to answer for your
crimes." She paused, her eyebrow again rising in almost
Vulcan-like fashion. "Of course, you could choose to face
Bajoran justice?"

Though he considered attempting to resist, Ishan did
not fight as two Federation Security officers placed restraints
on his wrists. He would not give Louvois or the council any
further satisfaction. Let them parade him through the halls
and the streets. Yes, they would celebrate their victory here
today, but once that was done, the real issues would remain.
Should fate and the Prophets favor him, he would not survive
to see the Federation's inevitable end, brought about by its
own hubris and failure to learn from the harsh lessons of the
distant and recent past.

Fools, every last one of you.

Thirty-eight

"Tea, Earl Grey. Hot."

Watching as Admiral Riker placed the order and retrieved the cup and saucer from the replicator in his office's far corner, Picard could not help smiling. "I think I've become predictable in my advancing years."

"I prefer the term 'consistent,' myself," Riker replied, setting the tea in front of Picard before taking a seat next to Admiral Akaar on the opposite side of the circular conference table. From his own chair, Picard was afforded a spectacular view of the San Francisco skyline beyond the grounds of Starfleet Headquarters. At this point in the late morning, sunlight played across the polished metal and glass of the buildings towering into the radiant blue sky. It was a welcome break from the weather of the past few days, which had been dominated by clouds, fog, and rain. Picard could not help wondering if nature—or the planet's weather modification network—might be offering him some signal as to what changes the new day might bring.

"I've seen the updated status reports from McKinley Station," Akaar said. "The *Enterprise* repairs and upgrades should be completed by the end of next week, but I imagine you wouldn't object to extended shore leave for your crew before we send you out again."

"Not at all, sir." Picard already had authorized shore

leave for all off-duty and non-essential personnel, and his crew would welcome news that their stay at Earth was to be longer than expected.

"How's Doctor Crusher?" asked Akaar. Even as he reclined in his chair, the Capellan's large frame and hawkish features still looked imposing. "I trust she and the rest of your people are recovered from their ordeal on Jevalan?"

"Very much so, Admiral. Thank you for asking." Picard paused, smiling. "Her mood was greatly improved after she was reunited with René." He shrugged. "Of course, their time together was short-lived." Beverly already had departed for Deep Space 9. The orders assigning her the station's interim chief medical officer were real, and now that their primary purpose as a cover story for her mission to Jevalan had been served, she had agreed to complete the temporary duty until Julian Bashir or another permanent replacement was assigned. The separation, while necessary, had been the longest between mother and son since the boy's birth. Indeed, it was the first time since his and Beverly's marriage that Picard had endured such a lengthy parting from her.

Throughout his Starfleet career, he had observed the mixture of feelings displayed by uncounted friends and colleagues forced to deal with the realities of service life and the toll taken upon families and other personal relationships. It was one of the many reasons he had eschewed such troublesome entanglements for so many years, seeing it as unfair not only to himself but also those left behind as he carried out whatever assignment duty saw fit to give him. His marriage to Beverly and the birth of René had changed his outlook in so many ways, and never more so than during the past few days.

"What about Doctor Bashir?" he asked after taking a sip of his tea. "Captain Ro needs her chief medical officer back as much as I need mine, but something tells me he won't be heading back to Deep Space Nine anytime soon."

Akaar tapped the tabletop. "No. The charges against Bashir are very serious, Jean-Luc. While we understand the reasons he took the actions he did, the simple fact is that he accessed classified, highly sensitive information pertaining to Operation Vanguard and the Taurus Meta-Genome. Yes, using it helped the Andorians, but there's no telling who else may now have this data or what other long-term consequences we might face in the future."

"He may have saved the Andorian people from extinction," Picard said. "Surely that will be considered?"

"If I have my way, it will," Akaar replied. "The Parliament Andoria's already issued its own award to him. I think they're trying to offset some of the spectacle that will be coming from his court-martial." He sighed, reaching up to wipe his brow. "I sympathize with Doctor Bashir, Captain, I truly do, but Operation Vanguard was compartmentalized and buried for very good reasons, only a few of which you know, and I'm ordering you to forget those as of five minutes ago."

Without missing a beat, Picard asked, "Forget what, Admiral?"

Satisfied, Akaar nodded. "As for Captain Dax and the others, the new president pro tem has already authorized me to dismiss all charges against them. They will be reinstated to their former positions and issued commendations." He smiled. "We're also looking into another physician to fill Bashir's billet at Deep Space Nine. You'll have Doctor Crusher back in very short order; I promise you."

Nodding in approval, Picard regarded his tea. "Excellent. What about President Ishan . . . I mean . . . Baras Rodirya?"

"He's awaiting trial," Riker said. "Attorney General Louvois is champing at the bit to get on with it."

Akaar added, "The entire affair has been most distasteful."

"How in the world did you find Velk?" Picard asked.

Riker smiled. "Thank Tuvok and Torvig for that. They spent days tracking down communications between the president and his contacts inside Federation Security. Once we pinned down Velk's location, it was just a matter of being ready for when Baras made his move." He paused. "That was a hairy couple of days, waiting for the right moment to get him out of there without alerting Ishan, but now we have Velk, and Admiral Schlosser, and the covert action team sent against Beverly on Jevalan. That should keep Louvois busy for the foreseeable future."

"And this Cardassian from the Occupation?" Picard asked. "Urkar?"

"That was Velk," Akaar replied. "He's the one who made the initial contact with the True Way and used his knowledge of Baras's secret past to forge a 'relationship' with Urkar and other True Way members. Once we had Velk in our custody and convinced him of what we already knew, he eventually came around." The Capellan shrugged. "A life sentence at the Auckland Penal Facility is certainly preferable to being dead, or being sent to one of the penal colony planetoids."

"Extraordinary," Picard said, studying his tea. "It's hard to imagine the lengths they were willing to go. The lives ruined, the damage to our political standing. All of that, and for what?" He sighed. "I'm just glad it's over."

"I know that look," Riker said after a moment. "Just like I know you wouldn't ask for a meeting with us if you didn't have something important to discuss." He shrugged. "So, what's on your mind?"

Setting his cup on its saucer, Picard leaned back in his chair, resting his hands in his lap. "The future."

"Certainly a loaded topic," replied Akaar. "Particularly these days. The council is scrambling to salvage whatever might remain of the election. The other candidates are working around the clock, campaigning for support to whoever they think will listen."

"I can only imagine what the current president pro tem must be dealing with right now." Picard's knowledge of Sipak, the Vulcan who had served for several turns as a member of the Federation Council, was limited. Based on what he had read, Picard believed the elder politician possessed the ideal temperament to confront the challenges he would endure as he shouldered a very short, intense term until the election was complete. Sipak already had given a speech to the Council and the Federation at large, acknowledging the limited nature of his tenure and his desire to maintain stability until a properly elected president took office. Given recent and current events, Picard knew it was a tall order.

"I see little else for us to do," he said. "We've done our part for truth and justice, and now it resides upon the will of the people for democracy to take its course."

Akaar grunted. "You and your crew are the very reason the will—and the *voice*—of the people will be heard. You've done a great service to the Federation, Jean-Luc, and it's a debt that likely can never be repaid."

"You can repay me by keeping me away from political issues and their associated crises, Admiral," Picard said. "I dare say I've had my fill of them."

Leaning forward in his seat, Riker rested his elbows on the table, clasping his hands before him. "There's plenty to go around, that's for sure. Bajor and Cardassia Prime are already trying to figure out how best to address Ishan and everything surrounding him. It's opened a lot of old wounds that never completely healed, but both sides seemed determined to put the past behind them and keep moving forward. Only time will tell if that's possible, of course. I guess we'll have to wait and see."

"We have our own problems with the Cardassians," Akaar added. "The True Way's involvement in President Bacco's assassination—even if it is just rogue operatives within that organization—has still damaged our alliance. It'll take time to sort through all of that. Diplomats are already hard at work, but they'll likely be at it for weeks." He fixed Picard with his customary piercing gaze. "A seasoned negotiator like you would be of enormous assistance, Captain."

"With respect, sir," Picard replied, "I would prefer another assignment; something more in keeping with my rank and position."

Riker smiled. "You're one of the most gifted diplomats we have, with or without a uniform. It's just one of the reasons you were given so much latitude after the Borg invasion and during the rebuilding."

"Those were extraordinary circumstances," Picard countered, "calling for uncommon measures." He always had preferred the defined separation between Starfleet and the Federation's elected government, with Starfleet acting as the instrument of political policy and security, rather than the author. "Things are different now. Starfleet and the Federation are far more stable than they were even a year ago. We've put the worst of the aftermath behind us, and I believe it's time to return to the customary divisions between Starfleet and the Federation it serves. Starship captains are more than capable of acting as diplomatic envoys in first-contact situations and other scenarios far from home, but within our borders? Such actions and decisions are best left to elected officials—*civilian* officials—while we in Starfleet carry out the duties for which we are more aptly suited."

Akaar said, "I admire your dedication not simply to the letter of regulations, Captain, but also to its spirit. Would that everyone who wore a Starfleet uniform held themselves to the same standards to which you subscribe."

It required effort for Picard to maintain his passive expression, and he willed himself not to shift in his seat as he met the admiral's gaze. Far too many haunted memories prevented him from accepting Akaar's praise. "I've not always met that standard, sir, and there are decisions I will regret to the end of my days, but my desire has always been to uphold the oath I've sworn. I'd like to believe that even those most . . . unfortunate . . . of acts were in service to the greater good." He paused, clearing his throat. "I suppose history will be the final judge in that regard."

Both Riker and Akaar said nothing for a moment, though Picard noted them exchanging glances as though each hoped the other might have some particular insight into any hidden or special meaning behind his words. It was Riker who broke the silence.

"There's no one I trust more, and for whatever my opinion's worth, I agree with you about Starfleet's role." He sighed. "As it happens, we've got plenty to keep us busy on that front as well. We already talked about the alliance between the Cardassians and Bajor, which might require some smoothing of ruffled feathers before all's said and done. The Klingons also are upset about the loss of their strike team while searching for President Bacco's assassins. However, as you say, both of those are more diplomatic problems than issues for Starfleet. At least, for now."

"And let's not forget the Typhon Pact," said Akaar. "They've been rather quiet since President Bacco's death, but I don't expect that to last. While the consensus seems to be that the Pact is not looking for a fight from the Federation, I think it's safe to say they're going to be a thorn in our side for a while yet. We have no insight as to their long-term plans and goals, so for now we can only remain vigilant."

Picard said, "That has always been the case, Admiral, but may I ask when, precisely, did we allow our need for vigilance to define our existence?" The question had its desired effect, eliciting matching looks of surprise and confusion from Riker and Akaar. Both men exchanged another glance, though Picard sensed there was something more at work here than simple astonishment at the question's blunt nature. Had they been expecting him to broach this topic today?

"Starfleet's mission has always been to see to the safety and security of the Federation," Akaar said, returning his stern gaze to Picard. "That has been the case for more than two hundred years."

"Agreed," Picard said. "That is *one* of its missions, but Starfleet's charter also sets out for us another mandate: one of exploration and the expansion of knowledge. For two centuries, we were able to balance the need for security against our desire to push outward, to see what unknowns await us. When did that change? When did we *allow* it to change?"

"Starfleet's exploration efforts continue, Jean-Luc," Riker said.

"To a degree," Picard countered, "only now the emphasis is on finding new allies. We examine star systems for their strategic importance or the resources they can provide. Those things are important, yes, but if we allow such priorities to define us, then are we really so different from other space-faring races we've challenged on those very points? Where does one draw the line that separates acquiring an ally and conquering a subject, and how do we prevent that line from being moved too far in either direction?"

Akaar's eyes narrowed. "That seems a bit far-fetched, Captain."

"As far-fetched as a community of worlds dedicated to the philosophy of individual freedom and mutual coopera-tion allowing its very moral fabric to be unwoven by the likes of Ishan and those who agreed with him?" Picard shook his head. "There are those who still believe in his ideas even now, after he's been exposed. How long before we were at war with the Typhon Pact, Admiral, if Ishan had been allowed to remain in office?"

"But Ishan's gone," Akaar said, his tone hardening, "thanks to you and others like you, who upheld the very principles you're espousing."

"Yes," Picard said, "and now it's time for all of us to champion those principles, not simply because it's required to deal with one crisis, but because it's *who we are*. I believe that our defenses must be strong to answer whatever threats we may one day face, but we cannot sacrifice that which has defined us from the beginning. When I travel to another world and meet for the first time the leader of another species, I want to present myself, and the Federation, as someone who wishes to be their friend, rather than someone who needs them to be our ally against some other foe."

"Some would argue there's little distinction between the two," Riker said.

"And we know what kind of people they are," Picard retorted. "They don't speak for me, and I refuse to believe we would allow them to speak for all of us."

Once again, Akaar tapped the table with his fingers. "Yours is exactly the mindset and conviction that's needed right now, Captain, but forgive me when I say what I hear from you comes across as some sort of ultimatum."

Now we're getting somewhere.

"It's not my intention to present demands, Admiral," Picard replied. "I've made plain my loyalty to Starfleet. I have no desire to retire and become a diplomat or an ambassador, and neither will I be pressured into accepting such a posting. Fighting wars, or acting to prevent them, is not what drew me to Starfleet. I understand that there will be times when such actions are necessary, and so long as I wear this uniform, I will obey the lawful orders of my superiors, but if Starfleet is to lose or push aside one of its core tenets, then it's no longer the organization I pledged to serve. If my superiors—*our* superiors—feel this is necessary, then so be it, but it will have to happen without me."

Riker's eyes widened. "You'd leave it all behind? Just like that?"

"Oh, I'm not saying there won't be adjustments," Picard said, offering a small smile, "but it's not as though I haven't given this the occasional thought in recent years."

"I would think less of you if you hadn't." For the first time, Akaar allowed his own expression to soften. "The demands of family can be as unforgiving as those of the service, though they also carry with them their own rewards."

"Something I'm finally learning, Admiral." Picard leaned forward, placing his hands on the table. "I have no wish to leave Starfleet, but Beverly and I do have an obligation to our son to show him everything it and the Federation have to offer. If we're not able to do that while still serving, then we'll simply have to look elsewhere for such opportunities."

"You're not going to quote Jim Kirk again, are you?" Akaar asked.

Despite himself, Picard smiled at the memory of his last lengthy discussion with the admiral regarding his career options. On that occasion, he had invoked the small yet invaluable bit of wisdom given to him by the late Captain James T. Kirk, during their rather odd meeting nearly fifteen years earlier.

Don't let them promote you. Don't let them transfer you. Don't let them do anything that takes you off the bridge of that ship, because while you're there, you can make a difference.

Since that day—which had seen the tragic loss of the Starfleet legend—Picard always had remembered and done his best to heed Kirk's advice. He had declined promotion offers and other opportunities that, while advantageous to his career, would have removed him from the bridge of the *Enterprise*. So far, Starfleet had seen fit to accommodate his wishes. Would it do so again?

As Riker and Akaar studied him, Picard said, "I simply think that I'd be of better use to you out there, instead of acting as some sort of errand boy or manning a desk here on Earth or at some starbase. If circumstances require it, you know I will always answer the call of duty."

"To be honest," Riker said, "we figured you'd be coming here to tell us something like this, sooner or later. Hell, I've been asking myself for weeks what took you so long. The truth is that we have a new president, and a new beginning for the Federation now that Andor is back in the fold, and we've been given a new mandate." Reaching into a pocket of his uniform, the admiral extracted an isolinear optical data chip and placed it on the table. With one finger, he pushed it across the table toward Picard. "If you want to go searching for something interesting, we're hoping you might consider looking here."

Eyeing the data chip, Picard asked, "What is it?"

"New orders," Akaar replied. "Starfleet has been planning this for some time now, but something always seemed to come along and derail us. Our new president has decided that has to stop." He chuckled. "You're not the only one who feels the way you do, Captain; you're just the first person to come in here and say it to my face."

Riker added, "Starfleet's launching a new exploration initiative—the most comprehensive program of its type in more than a decade. We're talking multi-year missions, pushing the boundaries of explored space, the works. Everything we were excited about, oh . . . say twenty years or so ago. You know, the good old days."

Feeling a small yet unmistakable rush of excitement, Picard nodded. "Indeed."

Akaar said, "Yours is also one of the first ships we're sending out. Captain Sisko and the *Robinson* will be heading for the Gamma Quadrant, and we'll be sending other ships out there. That's been overdue for a long time. As for the *Enterprise*? You're going to a whole new sector. Only unmanned probes have charted some of these areas. Where you're going, none have gone before."

"And I'm as envious as hell," Riker said.

Reaching across the table, Picard retrieved the isolinear chip. It was an inanimate object, possessing no power source of its own but instead only stored information, and yet he imagined he sensed the energy radiating from it. "Well, this certainly puts a different spin on things, doesn't it?" What would Beverly have to say about this? He rather looked forward to that conversation. Despite their earlier discussions regarding René's upbringing and whether that was better served by one or both of them leaving Starfleet, he and Beverly knew that they were not yet ready to "settle down" in the conventional sense. If the Borg invasion and its aftermath had shown them anything, it was that no place could ever be absolutely safe, and there was never anything to be gained by living in fear of what might happen.

So, we move forward.

"Thank you both," Picard said. He knew they would not be heading out just yet, of course. Undertaking a mission of such duration would require various system upgrades and refits for the *Enterprise,* as well as personnel transfers in the event members of his crew might not want to commit to such a lengthy assignment far from home. But, once all that was complete? Picard already sensed the anticipation building within him, rivaling the excitement he had felt upon being given command of the *Enterprise*-D more than two decades earlier. What awaited him and his crew in that vast unknown?

"Good luck, Captain," Akaar said, rising from his chair and extending his hand.

Picard stood and accepted the handshake. "Thank you, Admiral." He then turned his attention to the man who had become his most trusted friend. "Admiral Riker. I only wish you could be going with us."

"Don't tempt me," Riker replied. "In fact, you should probably get out of here before I change my mind." The men shook hands, and the admiral was unable to suppress a wide grin. Picard saw in his eyes that all-too-familiar twinkle he remembered from uncounted occasions where the younger man had stood at his side as the *Enterprise* set course for some new assignment or adventure.

"Go, Jean-Luc. Go see what's out there."

Epilogue

How am I expected to accomplish anything, sitting here with a view like this?

Standing before the large curved window forming the rear wall of the office she now called her own, President Kellessar zh'Tarash regarded the breathtaking vista that was the city of Paris. The morning sky was a brilliant blue, accented only by a few small clouds. Sunlight glinted off the glass of nearby buildings, further emphasizing the bright new day that had greeted her. With a smile, zh'Tarash decided this could be a message—a hint of what lay before her as she set about the journey she had been asked to take.

"I'm told that a variety of drapes and other decorative tapestries are available, should you find the view a distraction, Zha President."

Unable to suppress a small laugh, zh'Tarash turned from the window to regard her chief of staff, Rasanis th'Priil. He stood before the expansive desk, dressed in a conservative ensemble of pants and jacket that seemed to enhance his position as the president's closest advisor and trusted confidant. He held a padd in one hand, and his expression was one of mild amusement. Zh'Tarash had not even heard him enter the office. How long had he been standing there?

"I trust that you won't be employing such stealth on a regular basis?" she asked.

His expression unchanging, th'Priil replied, "Only when I'm attempting to avoid meetings I find unnecessary. For the record, I find almost all meetings unnecessary."

"You should have stayed out of politics," zh'Tarash countered, "or any form of government employment. Or private enterprise, for that matter." She paused, enjoying the light banter as she always did with th'Priil. In the days to come, she imagined relying on the momentary diversions as a way of mitigating the pressures of her elected office. "Indeed, the more I consider your present situation, I wonder if you might not have been better served by taking that retirement you once mentioned."

"It is a thought that will haunt me every day of your term, Zha President." Then, in an obvious attempt to regain some semblance of control over the conversation, th'Priil made a show of raising his padd and scrutinizing its display screen. "As you have a full schedule for the day, I would suggest we get started."

"Yes," zh'Tarash said, "it's time to 'hit the ground running,' as some of our human friends say."

She already had seen the agenda prepared by her executive assistant and left for her on her personal computer station. Whereas the previous day only had allowed limited time for precious few pro forma tasks in between the inauguration ceremonies and the celebratory ball that evening, the first actual working day of her term would give her little opportunity to settle into her new role. Her schedule for the rest of the week would be dominated by meetings with key advisors and members of her senior staff, candidates for appointment to other prominent positions within the administration, and ambassadors and other diplomatic envoys from various Federation worlds. There also would be security briefings from Starfleet in the form of Admiral Akaar and members of his staff. Indeed, she already had reviewed several memos and other documentation from Akaar that had piqued her interest.

"Move up the meetings with the security advisor and Admiral Akaar," she said, "and tell the admiral that I'll want to discuss the Typhon Pact in particular."

In most uncharacteristic fashion and aside from that entire abortive affair with them trying to forge a trade deal with the Ferengi Alliance, the Pact had remained quiet in the months since Nanietta Bacco's assassination. The rival coalition apparently had been content to sit silent and watch how the Federation reacted to the loss of its beloved leader. That in itself seemed odd to zh'Tarash, given the Pact's efforts—spearheaded by the Tholians—to unsettle Andor to the point that its government had voted to secede from the Federation. The Pact had taken great pleasure in that unprecedented event and its immediate repercussions, but there was very little known about their reactions to the news that her world and its people had returned to the fold. What Pact leaders might be thinking and planning had occupied her thoughts for weeks, with an even greater focus now that she found herself sitting in this office.

"Ask Akaar to bring Admiral Riker along with him," zh'Tarash said after a moment. "I'd like to hear his perspective on this and a few other issues as well."

Th'Priil eyed her with a quizzical expression. "Riker? He's a fairly new addition to the Starfleet command hierarchy."

Moving to stand behind her desk, zh'Tarash nodded. "I know. Given his recent transition from starship command to headquarters, I believe he'll offer a fresh view that might be lacking in his . . . How shall I say it? His *planet-bound* counterparts?" She held up a hand. "No disrespect to the admiralty, most if not all of whom have distinguished themselves, but I think Starfleet's upper command structure benefits from the regular infusion of new perspectives. Since Jean-Luc Picard has elected to remain on starship duty and I won't be benefiting from his counsel on a regular basis, William Riker is an able substitute."

"Rumors are that Admiral Riker may be requesting a transfer back to full-time starship duty aboard the *Titan*," th'Priil replied.

"I could not fault him for such a choice," zh'Tarash said, "but perhaps we might persuade him to at least give the matter careful consideration before reaching a decision." Settling herself into the chair at her desk, she gestured toward the door. "Am I correct in assuming the others are standing outside, waiting with anticipation and ears or other auditory organs pressed to the door?"

Th'Priil laughed. "Correct you are, Zha President." He reached up to press the decorative pendant above his jacket's right breast pocket, the accessory also serving as the housing for a personal communicator. "Dimitri, the president is ready for us."

The doors leading from zh'Tarash's office parted to admit other members of her senior staff: Dimitri Velonov, th'Priil's deputy chief of staff; Leressi sh'Daran, the new administration's communications director; and Sovek, her press secretary. As they filed into the office and moved to stand before her desk, zh'Tarash could not help smiling. "If anyone wishes to reconsider their appointment—th'Priil is already having misgivings about postponing his own retirement—now would be a good time to flee for your lives." She paused for effect, while th'Priil made a show of turning to look at each of his companions. When no one moved or said anything, the chief of staff returned his attention to zh'Tarash.

"It appears as though we have nothing better to do, Zha President."

"That is welcome news," zh'Tarash replied, her smile widening, "as th'Priil keeps reminding me that there is much work ahead of us. However, there also is much to celebrate. With Andor's return and my election to this office, I sense we have a new opportunity to remind every citizen—and

anyone else who might be watching—about the importance
of a strong Federation. In weeks and months to come, I want
to demonstrate that the values and beliefs that drew every
member world to join us are at the very heart of the bond
that holds us together. Yes, we may disagree from time to
time, and we may even test the limits of that bond on occasion, but after all the sibling squabbling, we reunite and stand
together as we have since the Federation's founding. That is
what I want to emphasize. That is what I want to champion.
I want that ideal to complement and bolster any other issue
we might pursue during the next three years."

"Don't you mean the first three years?" Velonov asked,
offering a knowing grin. After a moment, he cleared his
throat. "That is, we hope it's only the first three years."

Shaking her head, zh'Tarash rose from her seat. "You
have been with me long enough to know that I don't make
assumptions, and neither do I take anything for granted.
What we know is that citizens of this Federation have seen fit
to place me in the position of leading them for what should
be the remainder of President Bacco's term. Whether we're
given another opportunity will depend entirely on what we
accomplish—and fail to accomplish—during this period.
I have no interest in discussing how I might convince the
citizenry into giving me another term; it's my intention to
demonstrate through word and action that I have earned that
privilege, and that is something I cannot do without each of
you."

She moved around her desk and stood before it, removing from between her and her trusted advisors and friends
not only the physical barrier it presented but also the position and power it symbolized. Reaching toward th'Priil, she
placed her hand on his left arm. "Because of fear and para-
noia engineered through lies and treacherous deeds, a very
tragic mistake was nearly visited upon all of us. We, as a
people, were prepared to sacrifice our principles in the quest

for . . . what? Security, whether actual safety or some illusion engineered for us?" She sighed. "We stumbled."

"Some would argue that we even crumbled under our own weight, Zha President," said Sovek. "At least, for a time."

"Perhaps we did. Now, however, we've regained our footing and, I believe, our balance. We're ready once more to resume moving forward." Gesturing to the press secretary and sh'Daran, zh'Tarash added, "That's going to be your primary mission in the weeks and months to come. We need to emphasize our new, total commitment to the core values and beliefs that are the Federation's very foundation, how they drew us all together, and how they continue to bolster us as we forge ahead. That attitude has to be present in everything we say, and everything we do."

Sh'Daran, her hands clasped behind her back, seemed to straighten her posture as zh'Tarash regarded her, and she offered a simple nod. "Understood, Zha President."

"Without question," added Sovek.

Once more, zh'Tarash smiled. "You all know I have a deep respect for President Bacco and much of what she worked to accomplish during her tenure in this office, in peace as well as during times of immense crisis. I know she was not perfect, and she made her share of mistakes, but it was her outlook and her genuine desire to serve with honor and integrity that I still admire."

She paused, regarding the people who had become almost as close and important to her as any member of her family. Each of them had chosen to forgo any semblance of a normal life, placing as secondary considerations their own families, to say nothing of their individual career aspirations, in order to commit themselves to a common, higher call to civic duty. It filled her with joy, gratitude, and confidence to know that people of such caliber and character would be supporting her in the months and years to come.

"Many challenges await us. There are wounds to heal,

promises to keep, and legacies to preserve. In the days ahead, I'll be making many, many demands of you, the first of which is this: Strive each day to meet the standard Nanietta Bacco established. This is not my presidency; these next three years belong to her. She left much good work unfinished, and it now falls to us to see her vision—her *dreams*—fulfilled. If we fail, I promise you it will not be due to lack of will or effort on our part."

A knowing, satisfied expression brightened th'Priil's features. "It most certainly will not, Zha President. We stand ready to serve."

"As do I, so I suppose we should begin. The Federation is waiting for us, as is the future." Zh'Tarash was buoyed by the energy and even eagerness radiating from the people she had asked to accompany her on this journey. A small group, possessed of purpose and determination; could they bring a new spirit of change and hope to the hundreds of billions of citizens who now would be looking to them—to *her*—for guidance and leadership?

There truly is only one way to find out.

Acknowledgments

Many thanks to my editors at Pocket Books for inviting me to contribute to *The Fall*. "Events" such as this are a challenge, requiring a great deal of coordination and cooperation between writer and editor as well as writer and other writer(s), and this was no exception. Thankfully, our editors were up to the formidable task of keeping all the trains on their respective tracks and just "being there" whenever I needed to hash out a bothersome plot point or three.

Tips of the hat and the glass go out to my fellow authors, David R. George III, Una McCormack, David Mack, and especially James Swallow. Each of them brought their A-game to this project, giving freely of their time and feedback as I strove (struggled?) to bring to a close everything they had established in their books. It's been quite the ride, lady and gents.

Finally, I offer my sincere thanks and continued appreciation to our readers. I mean, this really is all your fault, you know.

Until next time!

About the Author

Dayton Ward has been modified to fit this medium, to write in the space allotted, and has been edited for content. Reader discretion is advised.

Visit Dayton on the web at www.daytonward.com